between the sheets

BY ERICA SAKURAZAWA

ALSO AVAILABLE FROM TOKYOPOP®

MANGA

ANGELIC LAYER*
BABY BIRTH* (September 2003)
BATTLE ROYALE*
BRAIN POWERED* (June 2003)
BRIGADOON* (August 2003)
CARDCAPTOR SAKURA
CARDCAPTOR SAKURA: MASTER OF THE CLOW*
CLAMP SCHOOL DETECTIVES*
CHOBITS*
CHRONICLES OF THE CURSED SWORD (July 2003)
CLOVER
CONFIDENTIAL CONFESSIONS* (July 2003)
CORRECTOR YUI
COWBOY BEBOP*
COWBOY BEBOP: SHOOTING STAR* (June 2003)
DEMON DIARY (May 2003)
DIGIMON
DRAGON HUNTER (June 2003)
DRAGON KNIGHTS*
DUKLYON: CLAMP SCHOOL DEFENDERS* (September 2003)
ERICA SAKURAZAWA* (May 2003)
ESCAFLOWNE* (July 2003)
FAKE*(May 2003)
FLCL* (September 2003)
FORBIDDEN DANCE* (August 2003)
GATE KEEPERS*
G-GUNDAM* (June 2003)
GRAVITATION* (June 2003)
GTO*
GUNDAM WING
GUNDAM WING: ENDLESS WALTZ*
GUNDAM: THE LAST OUTPOST*
HAPPY MANIA*
HARLEM BEAT
INITIAL D*
I.N.V.U.
ISLAND
JING: KING OF BANDITS* (June 2003)
JULINE
KARE KANO*
KINDAICHI CASE FILES* (June 2003)
KING OF HELL (June 2003)

KODOCHA*
LOVE HINA*
LUPIN III*
MAGIC KNIGHT RAYEARTH* (August 2003)
MAGIC KNIGHT RAYEARTH II* (COMING SOON)
MAN OF MANY FACES* (May 2003)
MARMALADE BOY*
MARS*
MIRACLE GIRLS
MIYUKI-CHAN IN WONDERLAND* (October 2003)
MONSTERS, INC.
NIEA_7* (August 2003)
PARADISE KISS*
PARASYTE
PEACH GIRL
PEACH GIRL: CHANGE OF HEART*
PET SHOP OF HORRORS* (June 2003)
PLANET LADDER
PLANETS* (October 2003)
PRIEST
RAGNAROK
RAVE MASTER*
REAL BOUT HIGH SCHOOL*
REALITY CHECK
REBIRTH
REBOUND*
SABER MARIONETTE J* (July 2003)
SAILOR MOON
SAINT TAIL
SAMURAI DEEPER KYO* (June 2003)
SCRYED*
SHAOLIN SISTERS*
SHIRAHIME-SYO* (December 2003)
THE SKULL MAN*
SORCERER HUNTERS
TOKYO MEW MEW*
UNDER THE GLASS MOON (June 2003)
VAMPIRE GAME* (June 2003)
WILD ACT* (July 2003)
WISH*
X-DAY* (August 2003)
ZODIAC P.I.* (July 2003)

CINE-MANGA™

AKIRA*
CARDCAPTORS
JIMMY NEUTRON (COMING SOON)
KIM POSSIBLE
LIZZIE McGUIRE
SPONGEBOB SQUAREPANTS (COMING SOON)
SPY KIDS 2

NOVELS

SAILOR MOON
KARMA CLUB (COMING SOON)

TOKYOPOP KIDS

STRAY SHEEP (September 2003)

ART BOOKS

CARDCAPTOR SAKURA*
MAGIC KNIGHT RAYEARTH*

ANIME GUIDES

GUNDAM TECHNICAL MANUALS
COWBOY BEBOP
SAILOR MOON SCOUT GUIDES

OTHER BOOKS BY ERICA SAKURAZAWA
COMING SOON FROM TOKYOPOP

ANGEL (JULY 2003)
ANGEL NEST (SEPTEMBER 2003)
NOTHING BUT LOVING YOU (NOVEMBER 2003)
THE AROMATIC BITTERS (2004)

Translator - Yukiko Nakamura
English Adaption - Marion Brown
Editor - Julie Taylor
Retouch & Lettering - Monalisa de Asis
Cover Artist - Martine Trélaün

Managing Editor - Jill Freshney
Production Coordinator - Antonio DePietro
Production Manager - Jennifer Miller
Art Director - Matthew Alford
Director of Editorial - Jeremy Ross
VP of Production & Manufacturing - Ron Klamert
President & C.O.O. - John Parker
Publisher & C.E.O. - Stuart Levy

Email: editor@TOKYOPOP.com
Come visit us online at www.TOKYOPOP.com

A **TOKYOPOP**® Manga

TOKYOPOP® is an imprint of Mixx Entertainment, Inc.
5900 Wilshire Blvd. Suite 2000, Los Angeles, CA 90036

ISBN: 1-59182-323-4

First TOKYOPOP® printing: May 2003

10 9 8 7 6 5 4 3 2 1
Printed in the USA

table of contents

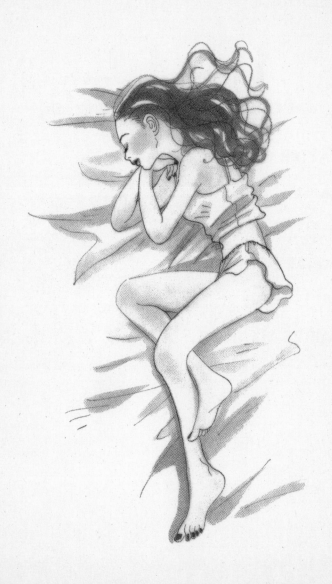

between the sheets

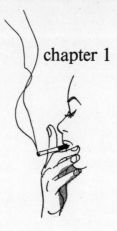

chapter 1

HERE I AM, PUTTING ON MY MAKEUP AT MIDNIGHT AND PRETENDING TO BE A MOVIE STAR. WHEN I'M DONE, I'LL PASS THE TIME BY PLAYING VIDEO GAMES AND MAKING PRANK CALLS.

OUR SECRET HONEYMOON...

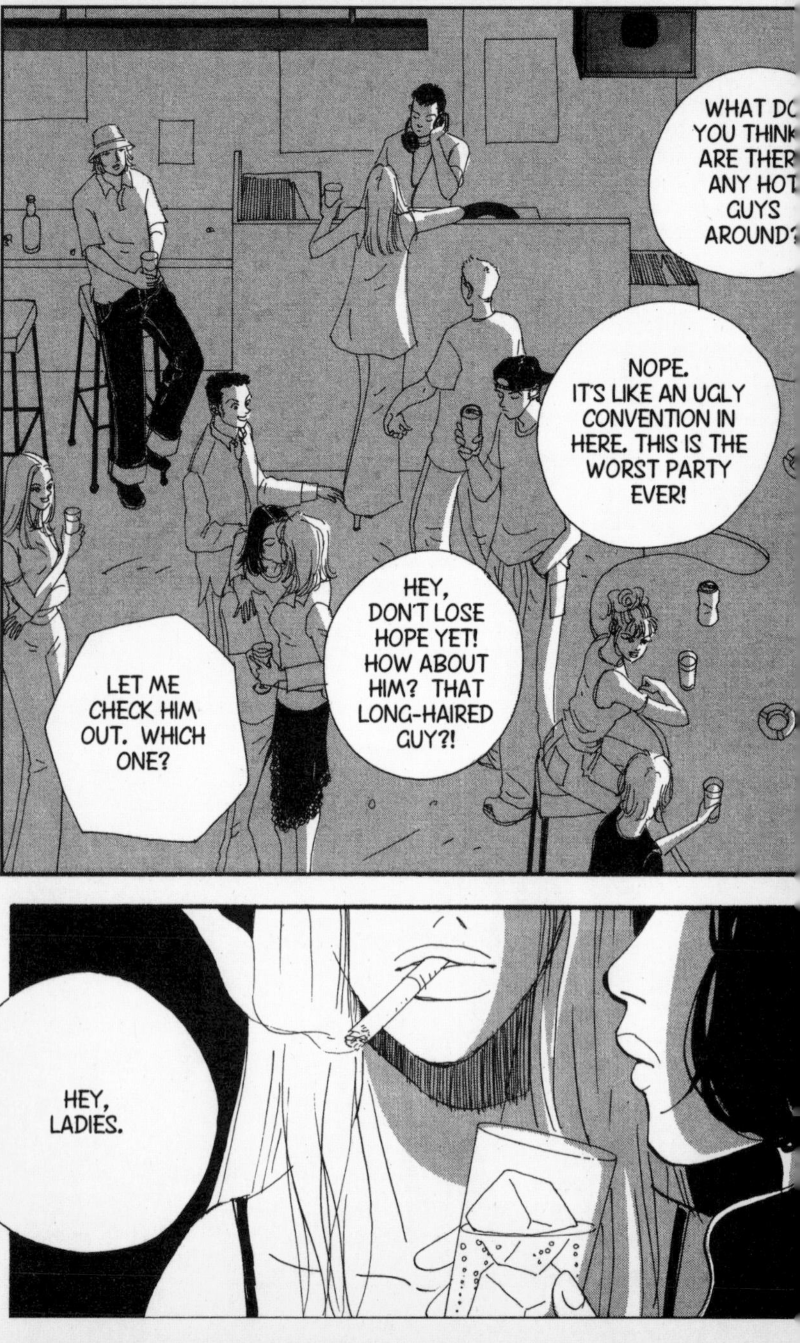
WHAT D YOU THIN ARE THER ANY HO GUYS AROUND
NOPE. IT'S LIKE AN UGLY CONVENTION IN HERE. THIS IS THE WORST PARTY EVER!
HEY, DON'T LOSE HOPE YET! HOW ABOUT HIM? THAT LONG-HAIRED GUY?!
LET ME CHECK HIM OUT. WHICH ONE?
HEY, LADIES.

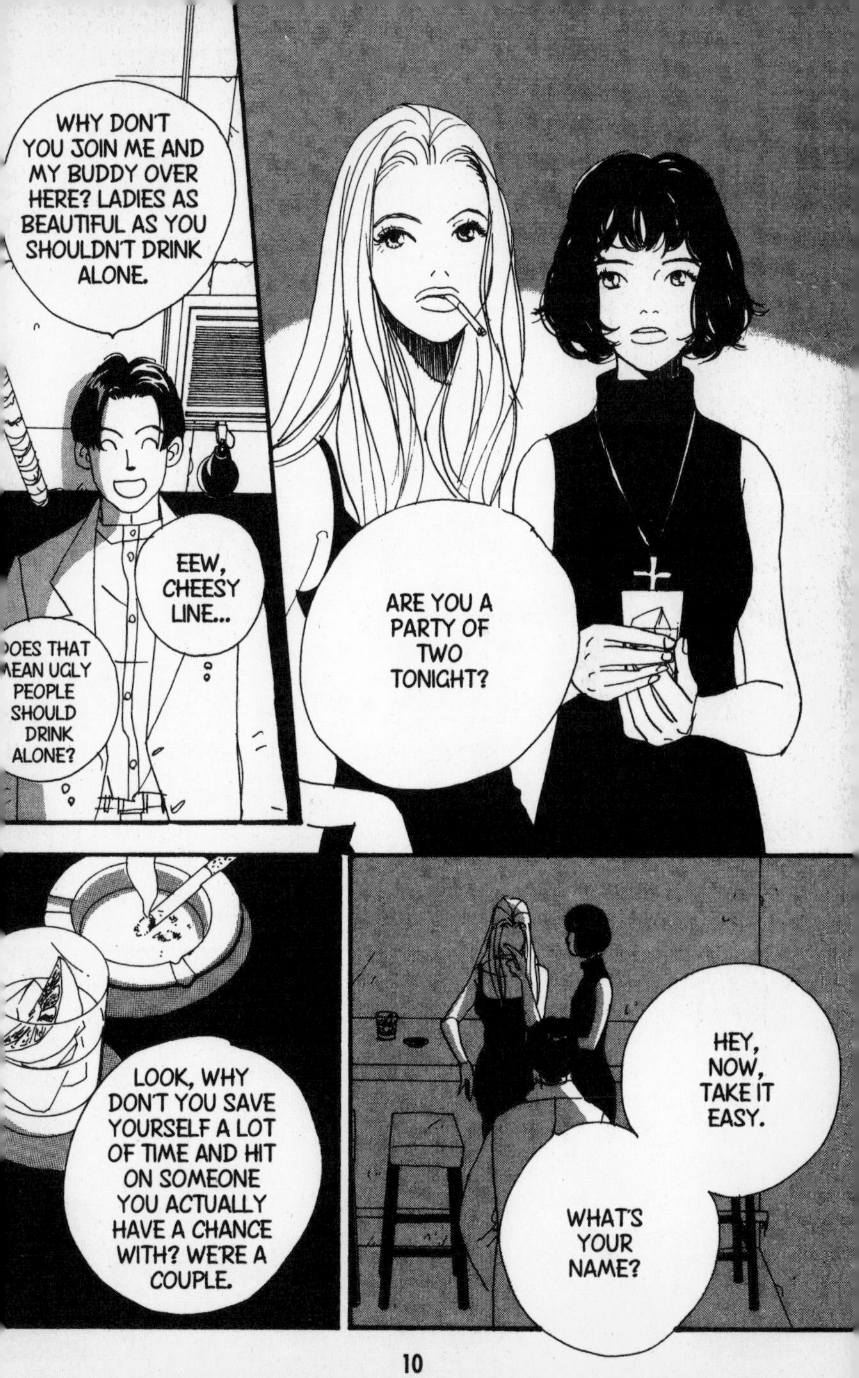
ARE YOU A PARTY OF TWO TONIGHT?
WHY DON'T YOU JOIN ME AND MY BUDDY OVER HERE? LADIES AS BEAUTIFUL AS YOU SHOULDN'T DRINK ALONE.
EEW, CHEESY LINE...
DOES THAT MEAN UGLY PEOPLE SHOULD DRINK ALONE?
HEY, NOW, TAKE IT EASY.
WHAT'S YOUR NAME?
LOOK, WHY DON'T YOU SAVE YOURSELF A LOT OF TIME AND HIT ON SOMEONE YOU ACTUALLY HAVE A CHANCE WITH? WE'RE A COUPLE.

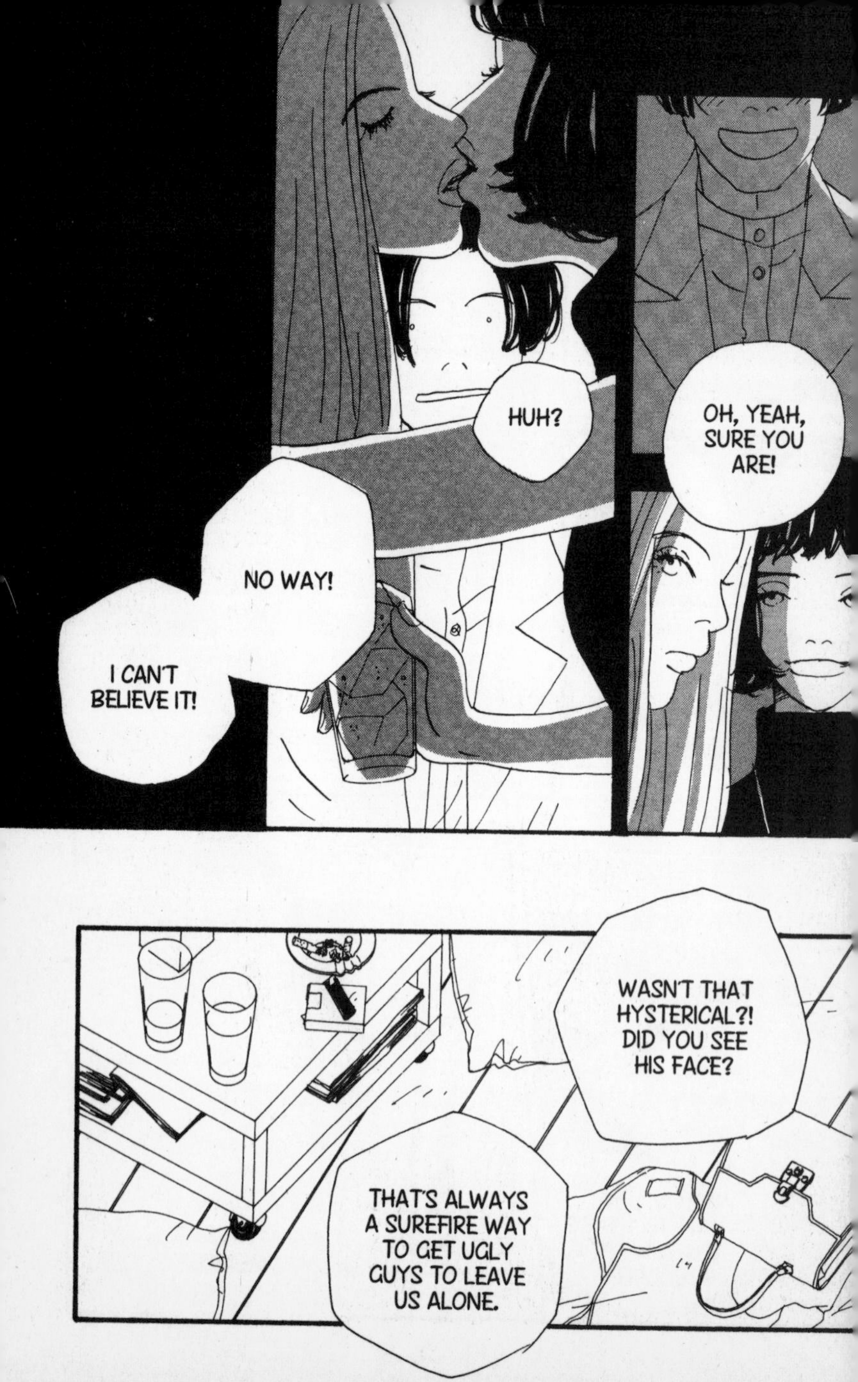
OH, YEAH, SURE YOU ARE!
HUH?
NO WAY!
I CAN'T BELIEVE IT!
WASN'T THAT HYSTERICAL?! DID YOU SEE HIS FACE?
THAT'S ALWAYS A SUREFIRE WAY TO GET UGLY GUYS TO LEAVE US ALONE.

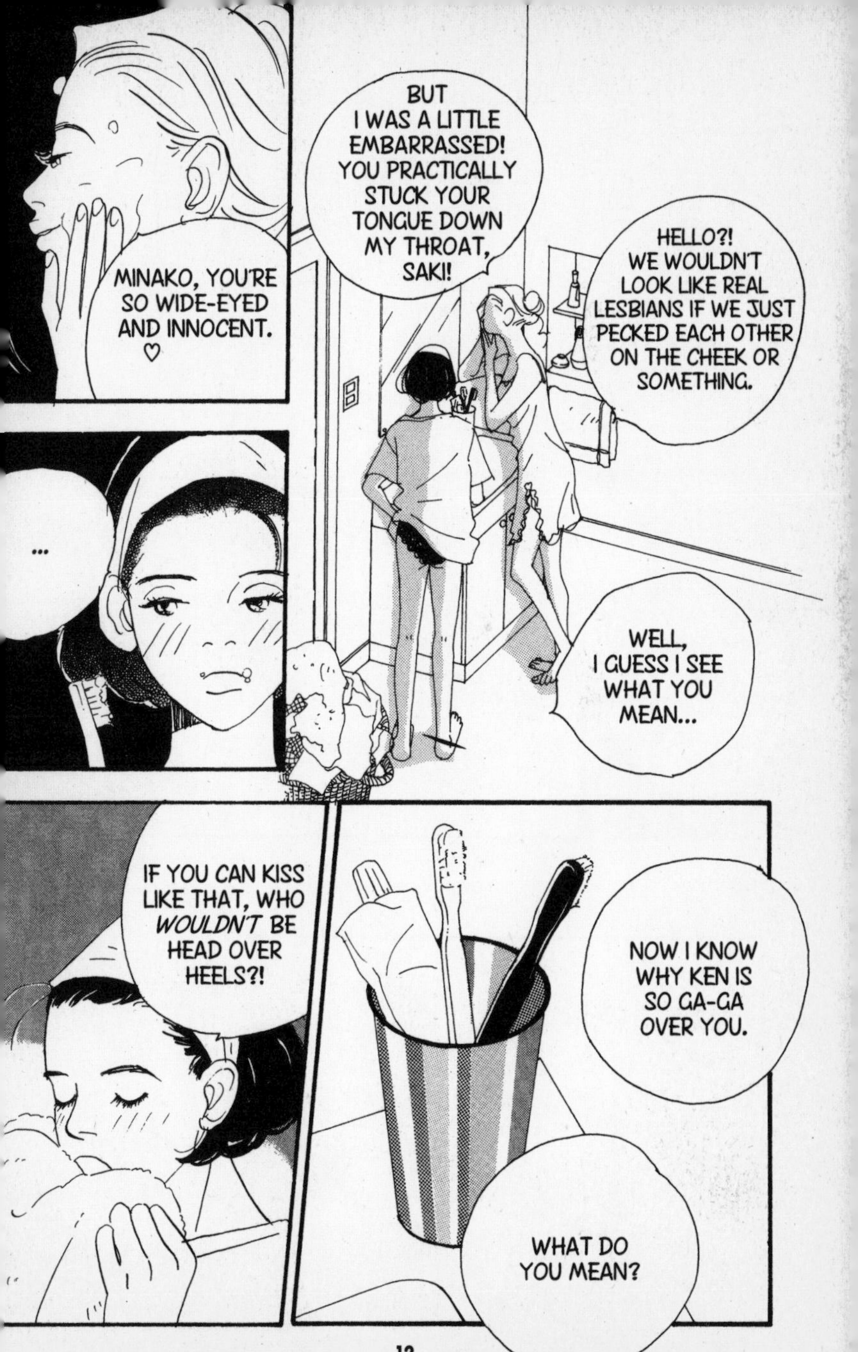
BUT I WAS A LITTLE EMBARRASSED! YOU PRACTICALLY STUCK YOUR TONGUE DOWN MY THROAT, SAKI!
HELLO?! WE WOULDN'T LOOK LIKE REAL LESBIANS IF WE JUST PECKED EACH OTHER ON THE CHEEK OR SOMETHING.
WELL, I GUESS I SEE WHAT YOU MEAN...
MINAKO, YOU'RE SO WIDE-EYED AND INNOCENT. ♡
...
NOW I KNOW WHY KEN IS SO GA-GA OVER YOU.
WHAT DO YOU MEAN?
IF YOU CAN KISS LIKE THAT, WHO *WOULDN'T* BE HEAD OVER HEELS?!

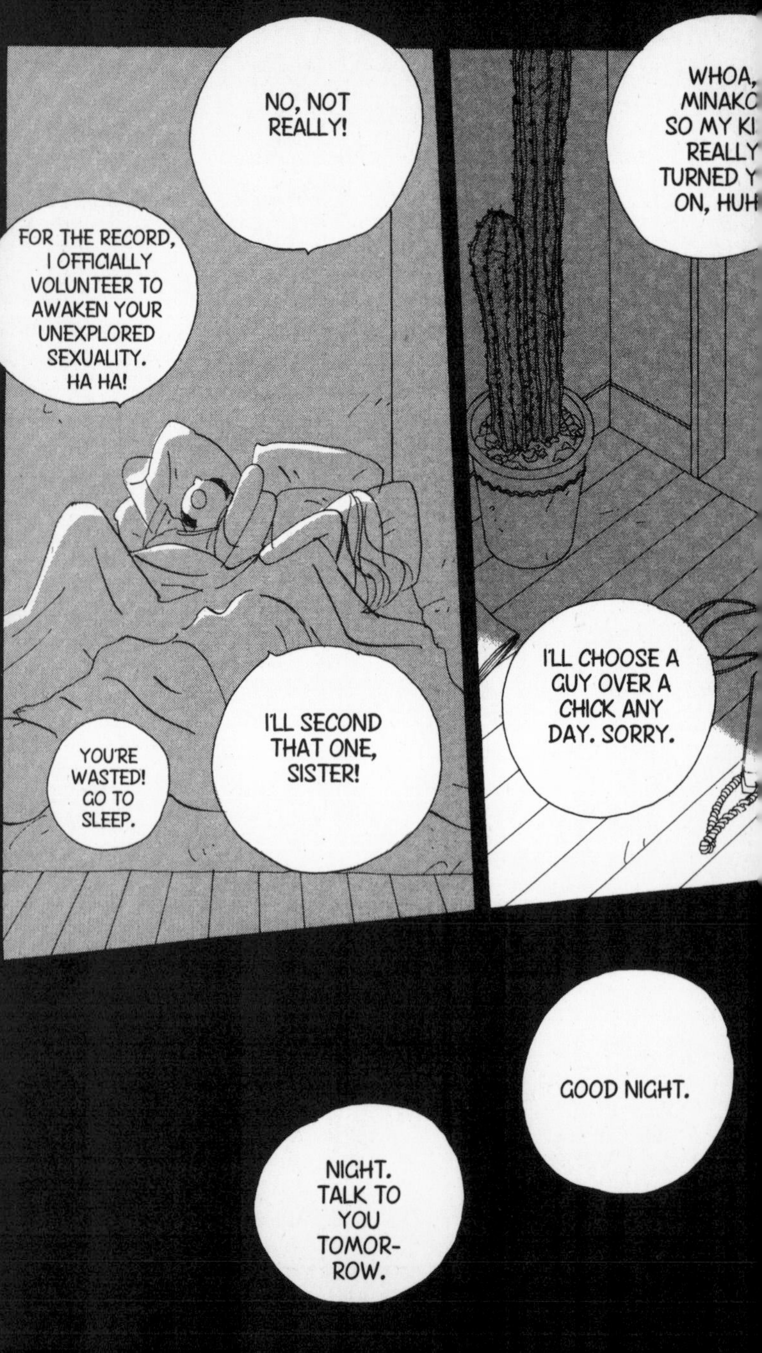
WHOA, MINAKC SO MY KI REALLY TURNED Y ON, HUH
I'LL CHOOSE A GUY OVER A CHICK ANY DAY. SORRY.
NO, NOT REALLY!
FOR THE RECORD, I OFFICIALLY VOLUNTEER TO AWAKEN YOUR UNEXPLORED SEXUALITY. HA HA!
I'LL SECOND THAT ONE, SISTER!
YOU'RE WASTED! GO TO SLEEP.
GOOD NIGHT.
NIGHT. TALK TO YOU TOMOR-ROW.

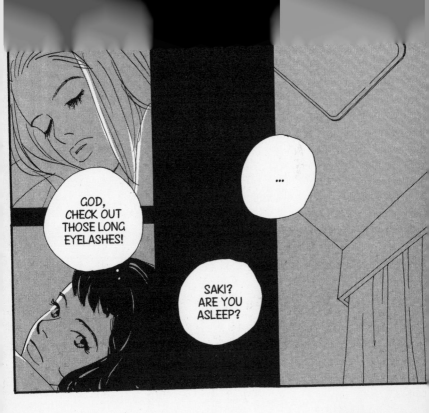

...
SAKI? ARE YOU ASLEEP?
GOD, CHECK OUT THOSE LONG EYELASHES!

SAKI'S SO ADORABLE.

AND SHE LOOKS SO SWEET, SLEEPING LIKE THAT.

IF I WAS A GUY, I WOULD DEFINITELY BE IN LOVE WITH HER!

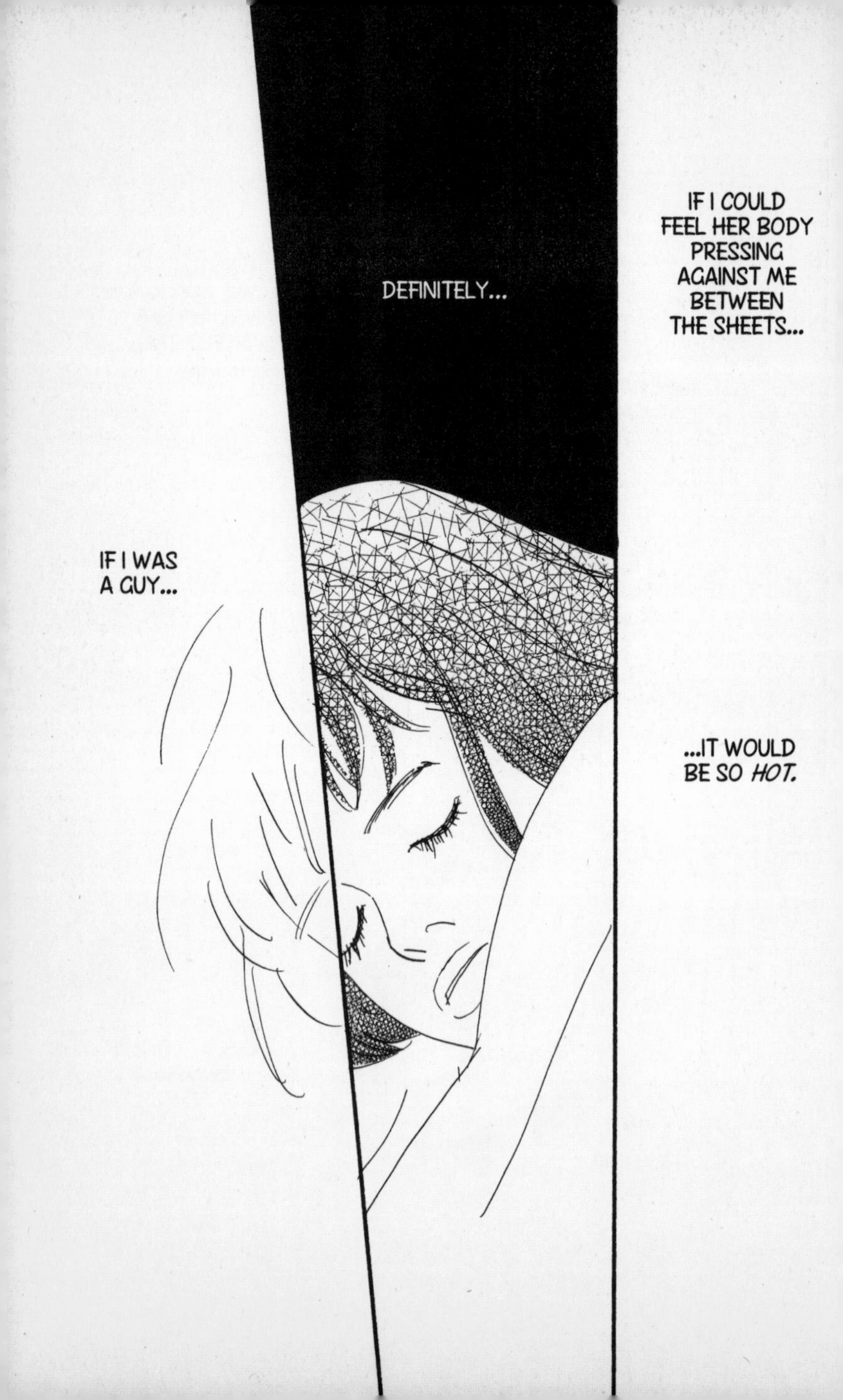
IF I COULD FEEL HER BODY PRESSING AGAINST ME BETWEEN THE SHEETS...
DEFINITELY...
IF I WAS A GUY...
...IT WOULD BE SO *HOT.*

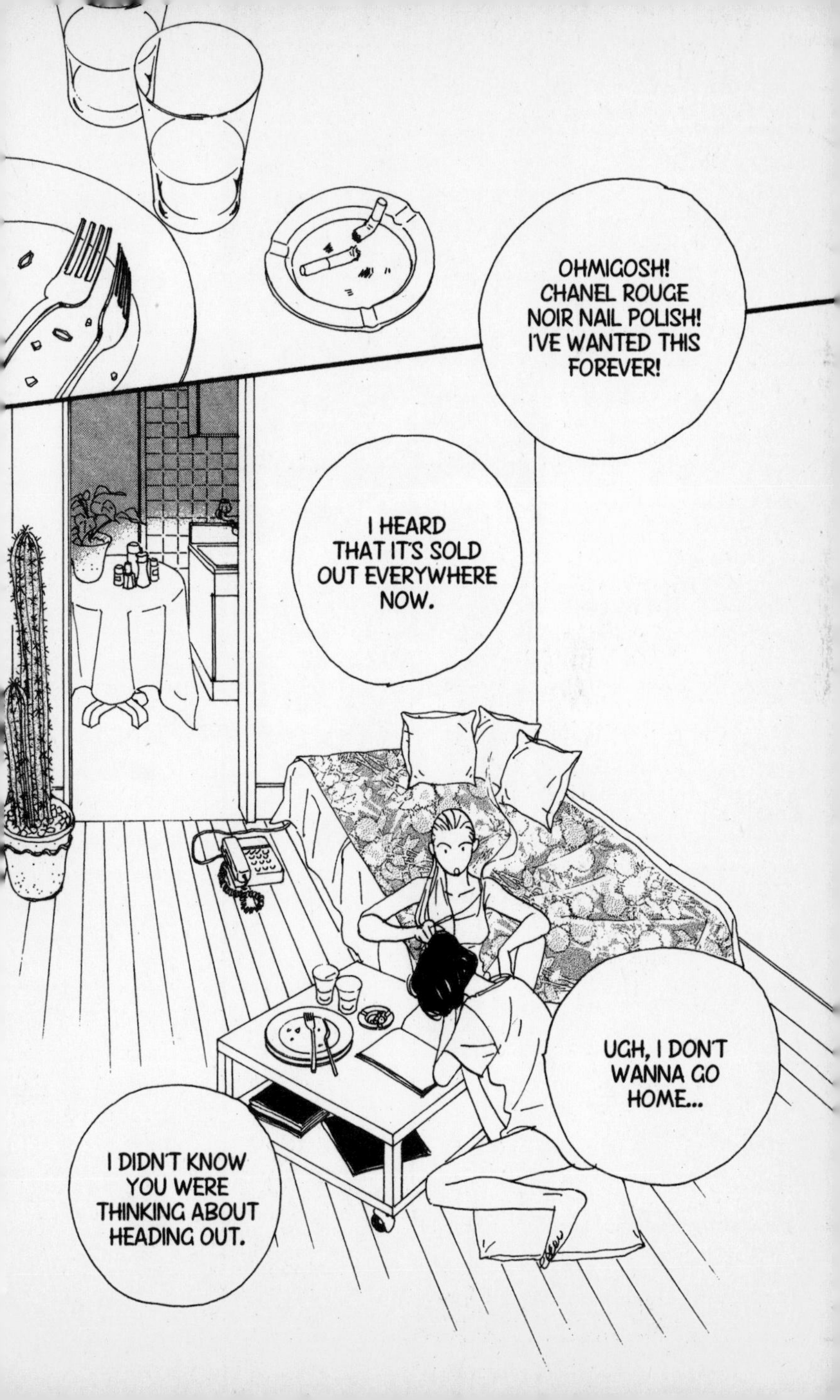
OHMIGOSH! CHANEL ROUGE NOIR NAIL POLISH! I'VE WANTED THIS FOREVER!
I HEARD THAT IT'S SOLD OUT EVERYWHERE NOW.
UGH, I DON'T WANNA GO HOME...
I DIDN'T KNOW YOU WERE THINKING ABOUT HEADING OUT.

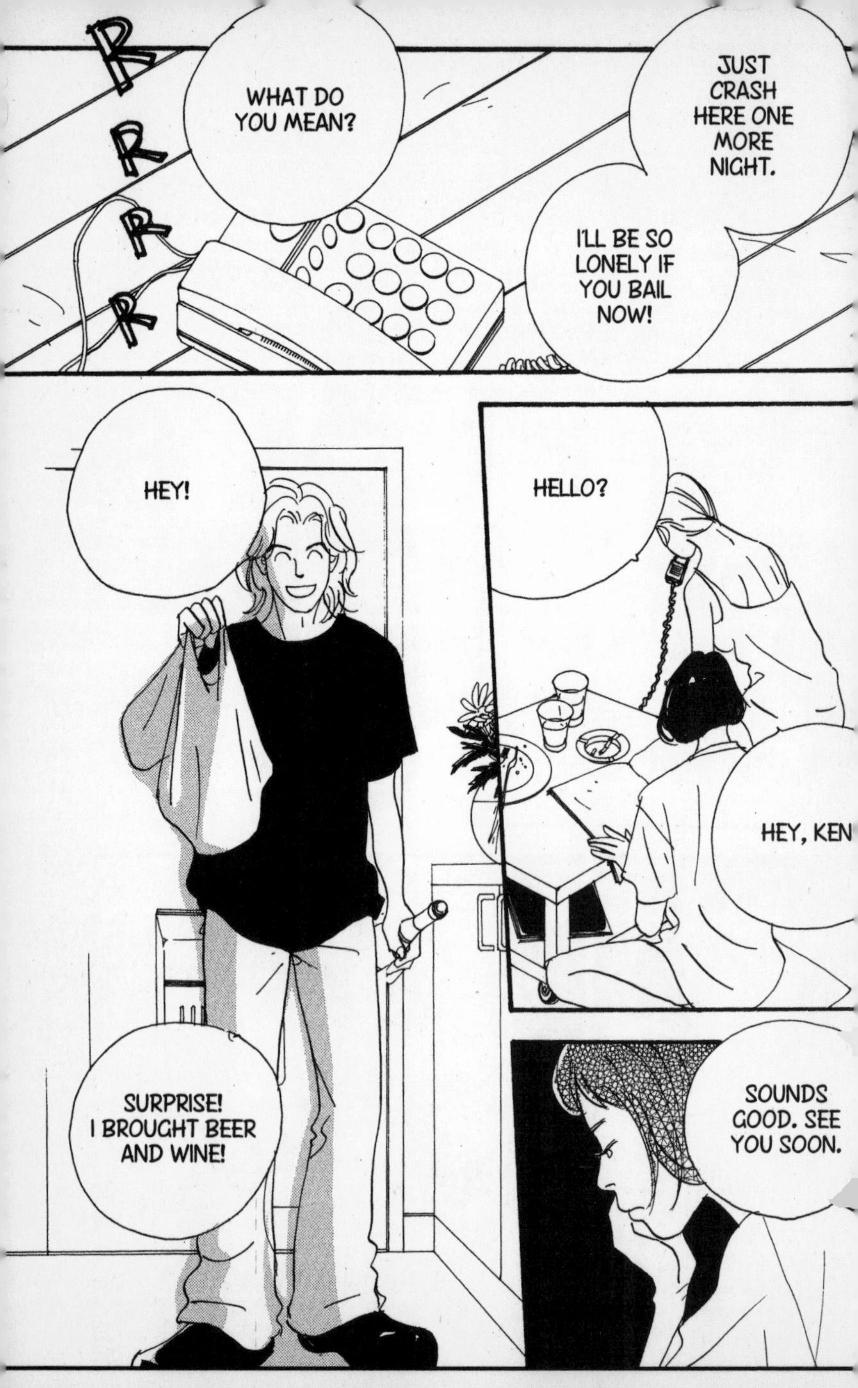
JUST CRASH HERE ONE MORE NIGHT.
WHAT DO YOU MEAN?
I'LL BE SO LONELY IF YOU BAIL NOW!
RRRR
HELLO?
HEY, KEN
SOUNDS GOOD. SEE YOU SOON.
HEY!
SURPRISE! I BROUGHT BEER AND WINE!

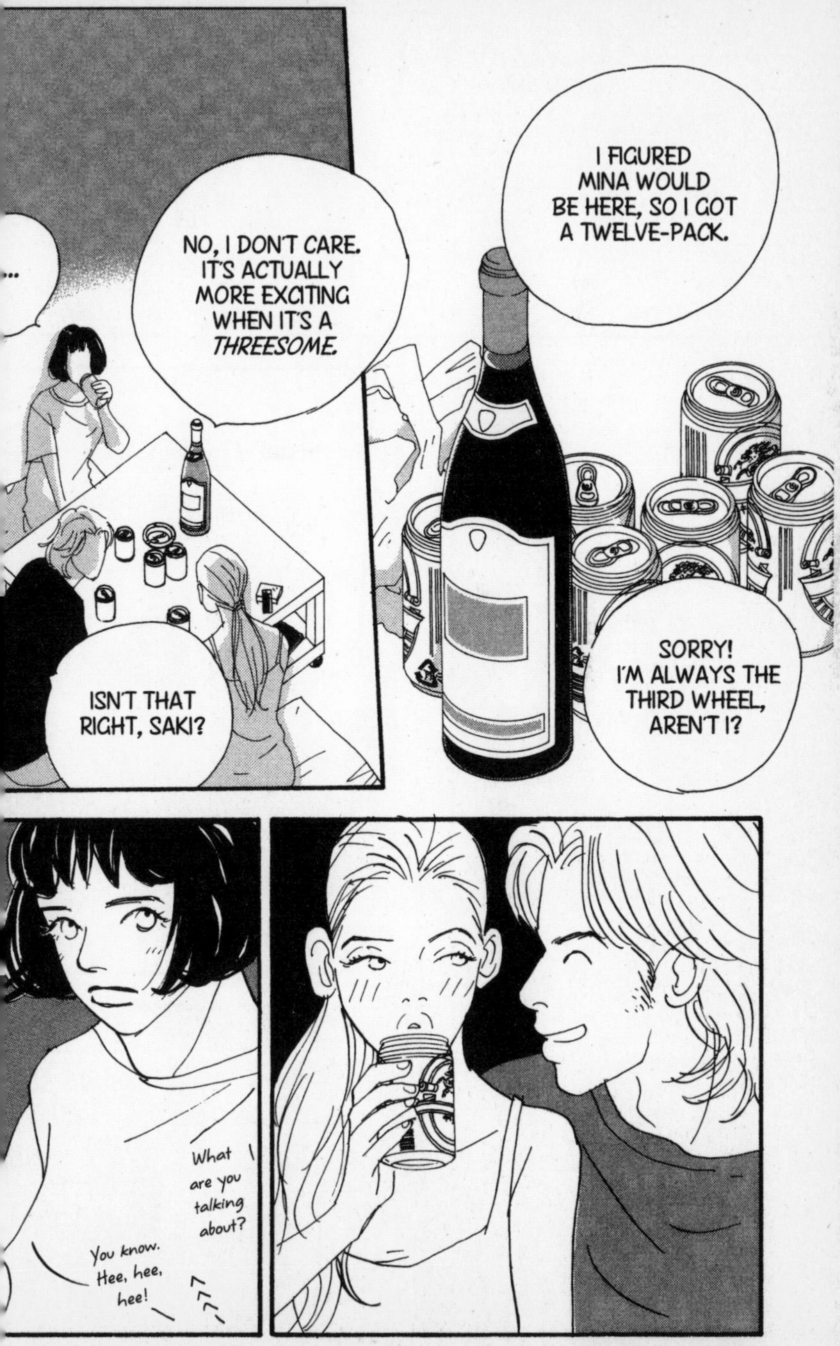
I FIGURED MINA WOULD BE HERE, SO I GOT A TWELVE-PACK.
SORRY! I'M ALWAYS THE THIRD WHEEL, AREN'T I?
NO, I DON'T CARE. IT'S ACTUALLY MORE EXCITING WHEN IT'S A *THREESOME.*
...
ISN'T THAT RIGHT, SAKI?
What are you talking about?
You know. Hee, hee, hee!

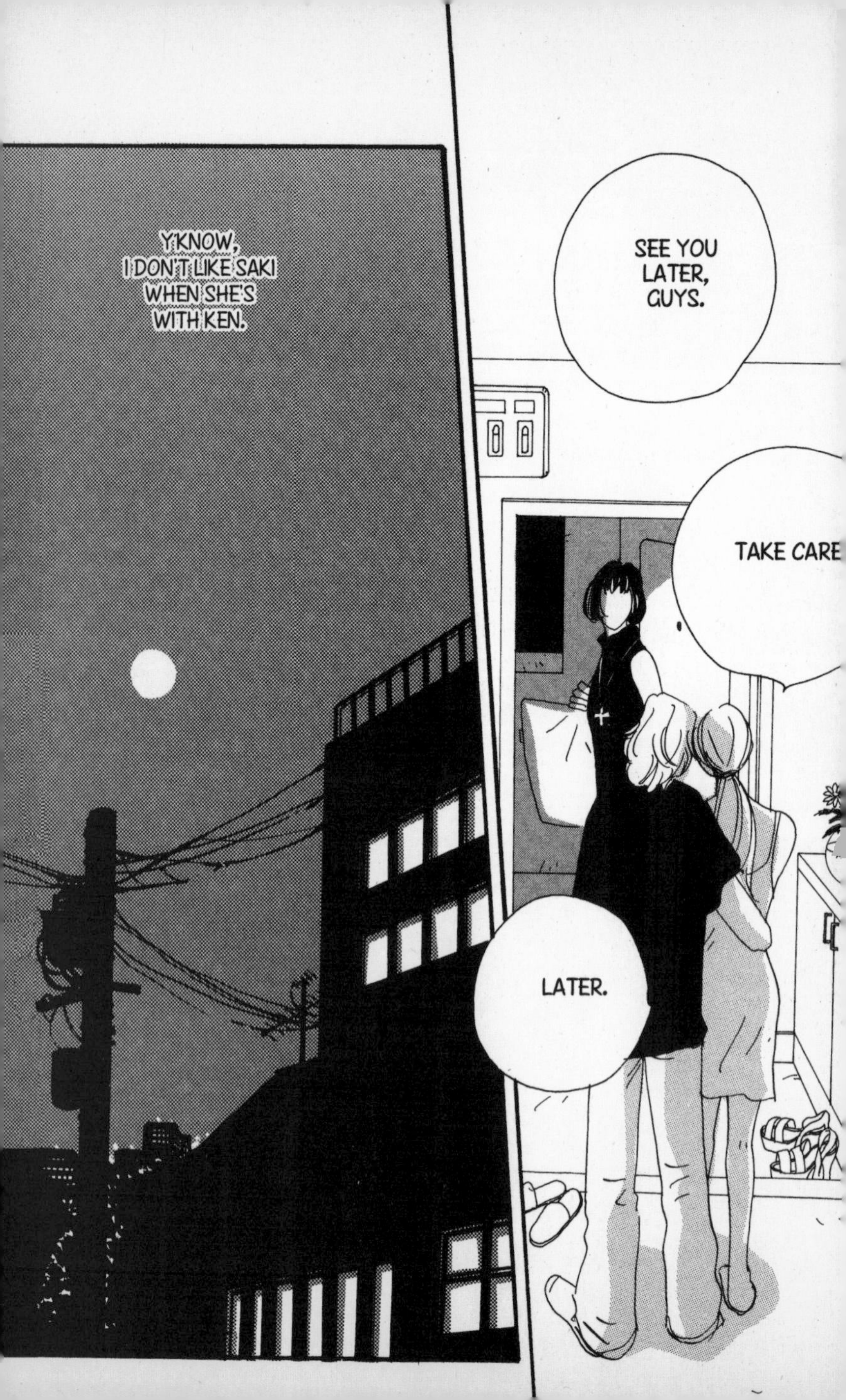
SEE YOU LATER, GUYS.
TAKE CARE
LATER.
Y'KNOW, I DON'T LIKE SAKI WHEN SHE'S WITH KEN.

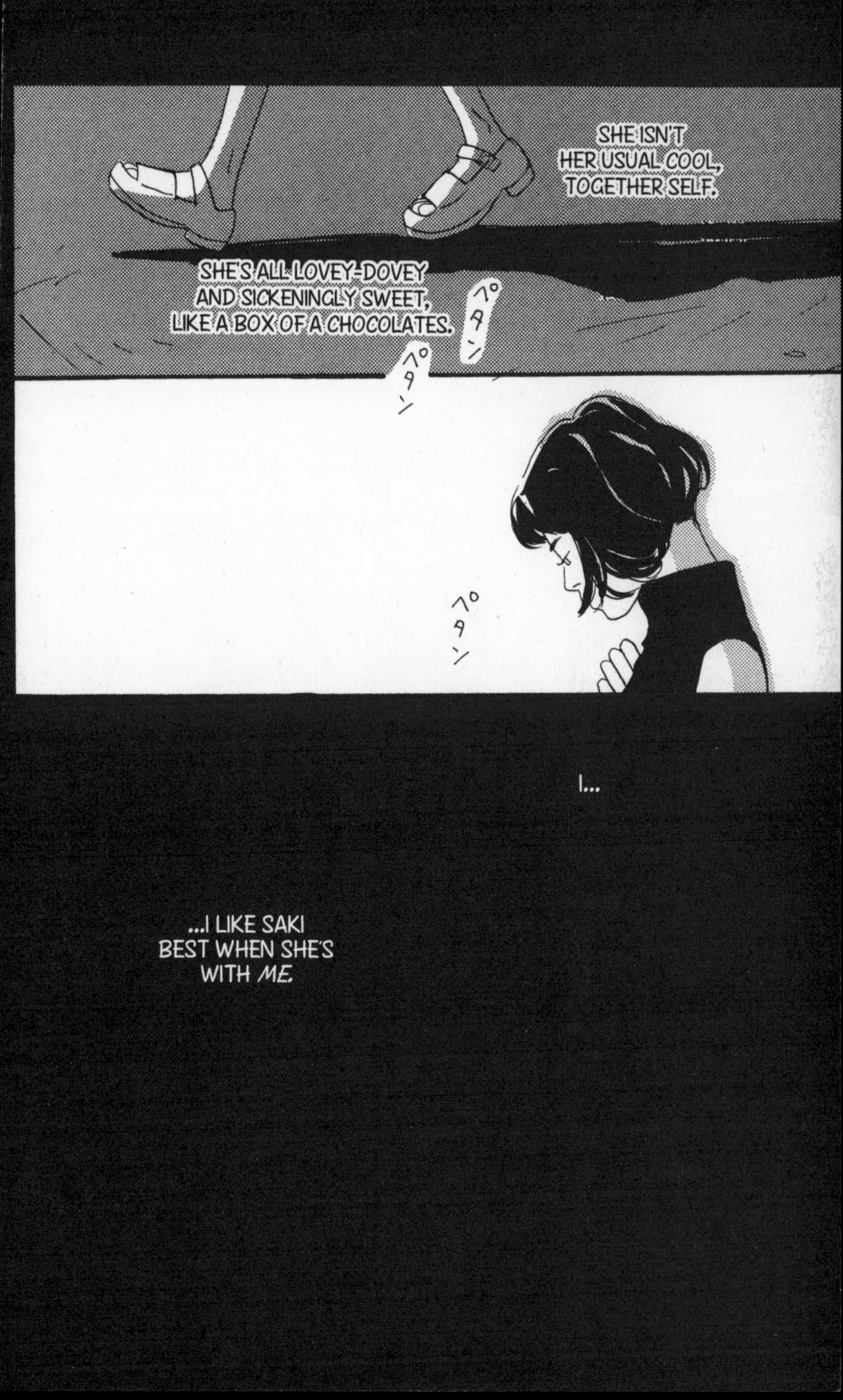
SHE ISN'T HER USUAL COOL, TOGETHER SELF.
SHE'S ALL LOVEY-DOVEY AND SICKENINGLY SWEET, LIKE A BOX OF A CHOCOLATES.
I...
...I LIKE SAKI BEST WHEN SHE'S WITH *ME.*

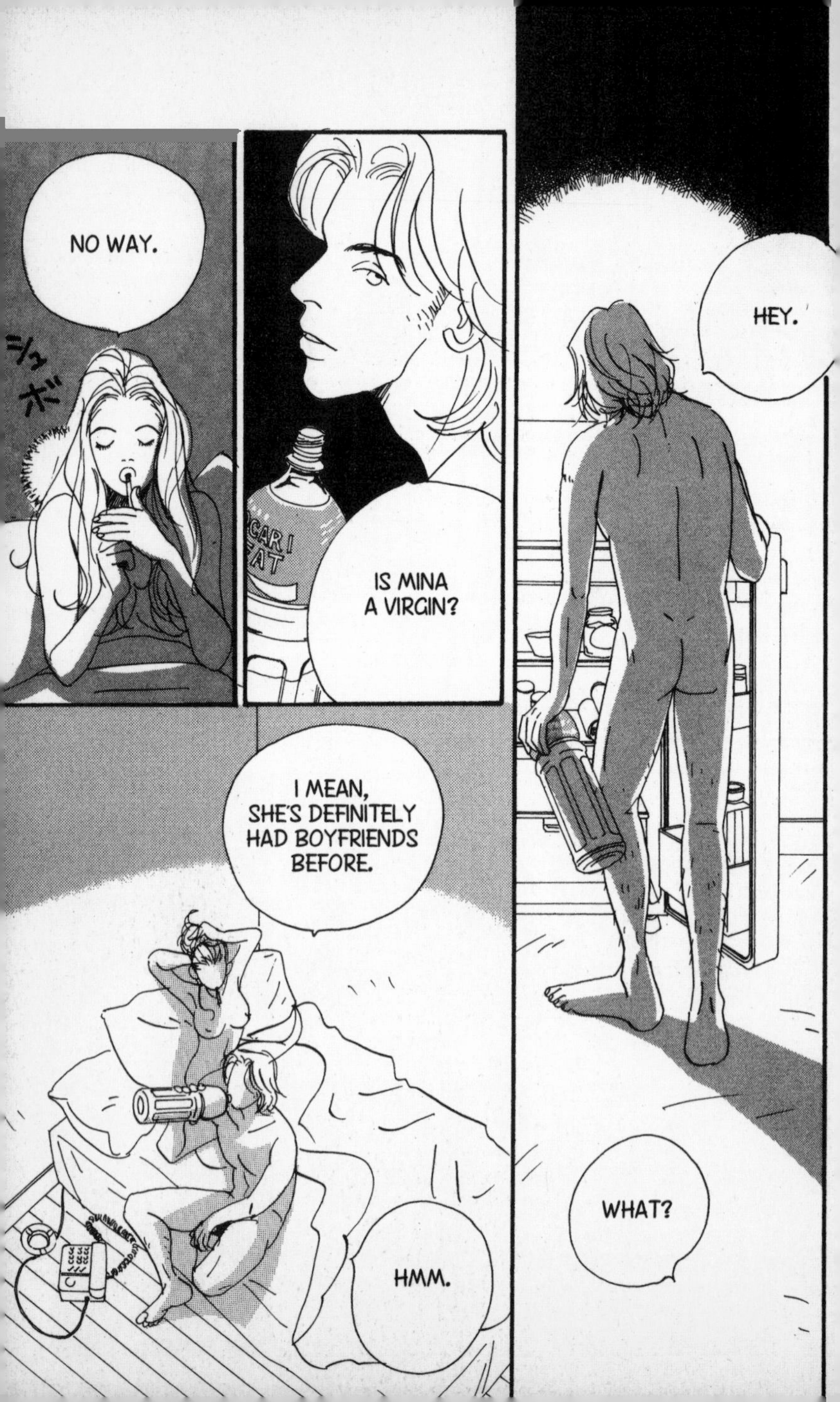
HEY.
WHAT?
IS MINA A VIRGIN?
NO WAY.
シュボ
I MEAN, SHE'S DEFINITELY HAD BOYFRIENDS BEFORE.
HMM.

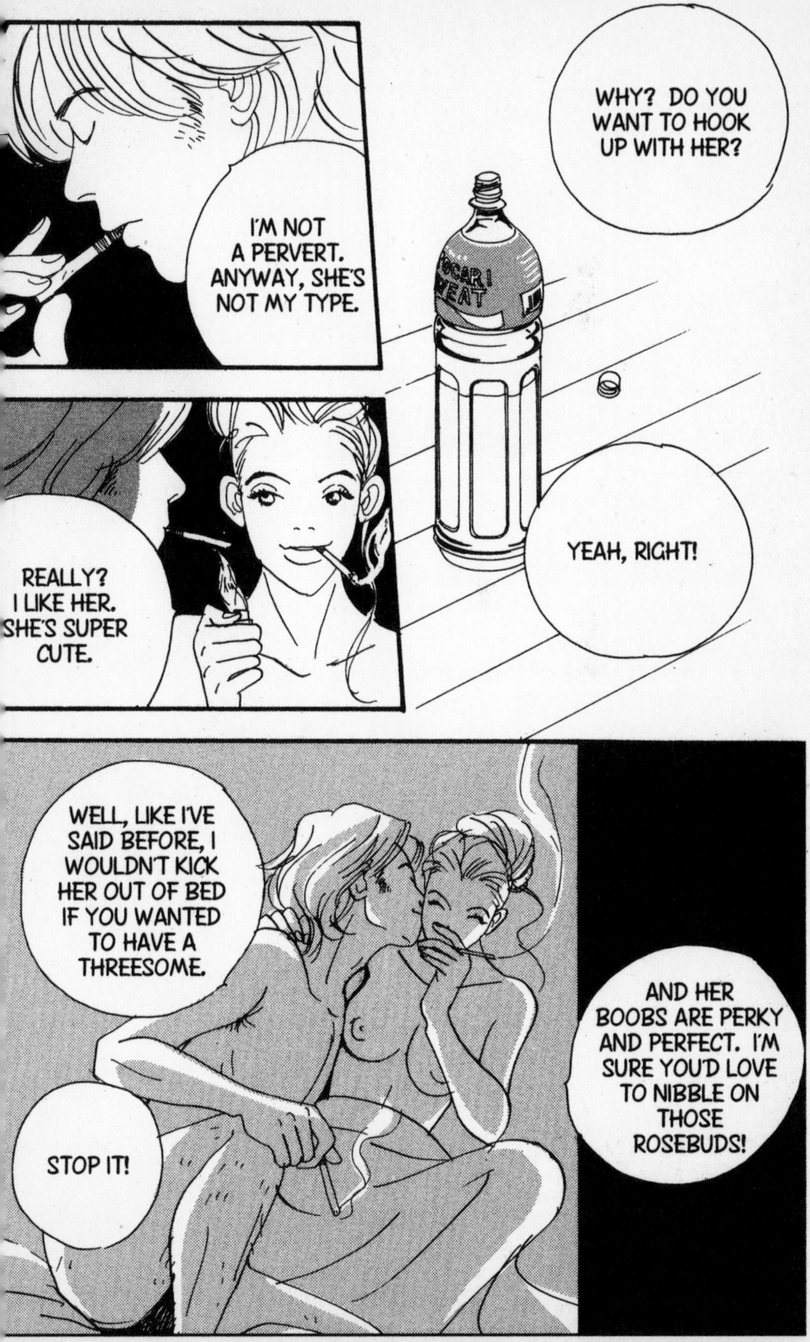
WHY? DO YOU WANT TO HOOK UP WITH HER?
YEAH, RIGHT!
I'M NOT A PERVERT. ANYWAY, SHE'S NOT MY TYPE.
REALLY? I LIKE HER. SHE'S SUPER CUTE.
WELL, LIKE I'VE SAID BEFORE, I WOULDN'T KICK HER OUT OF BED IF YOU WANTED TO HAVE A THREESOME.
AND HER BOOBS ARE PERKY AND PERFECT. I'M SURE YOU'D LOVE TO NIBBLE ON THOSE ROSEBUDS!
STOP IT!

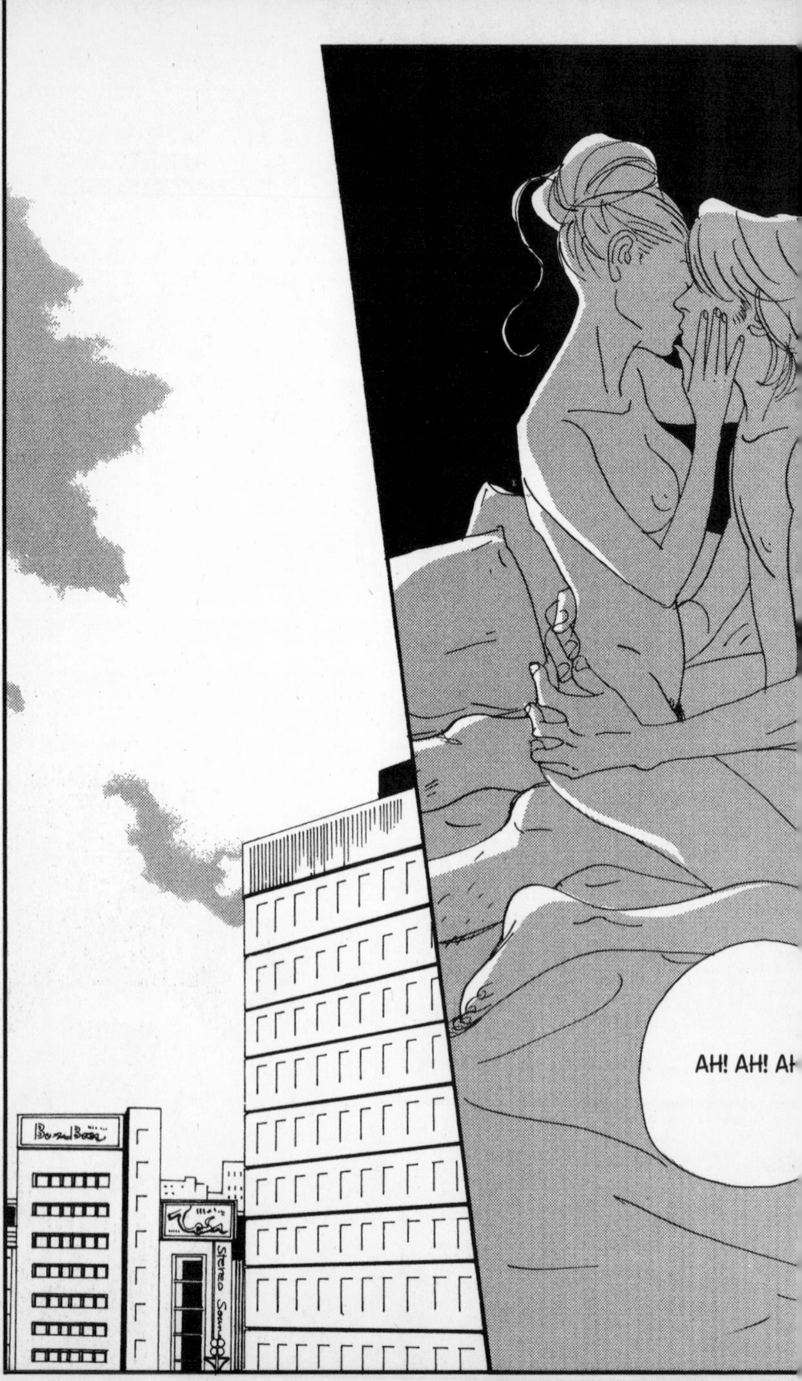
AH! AH!

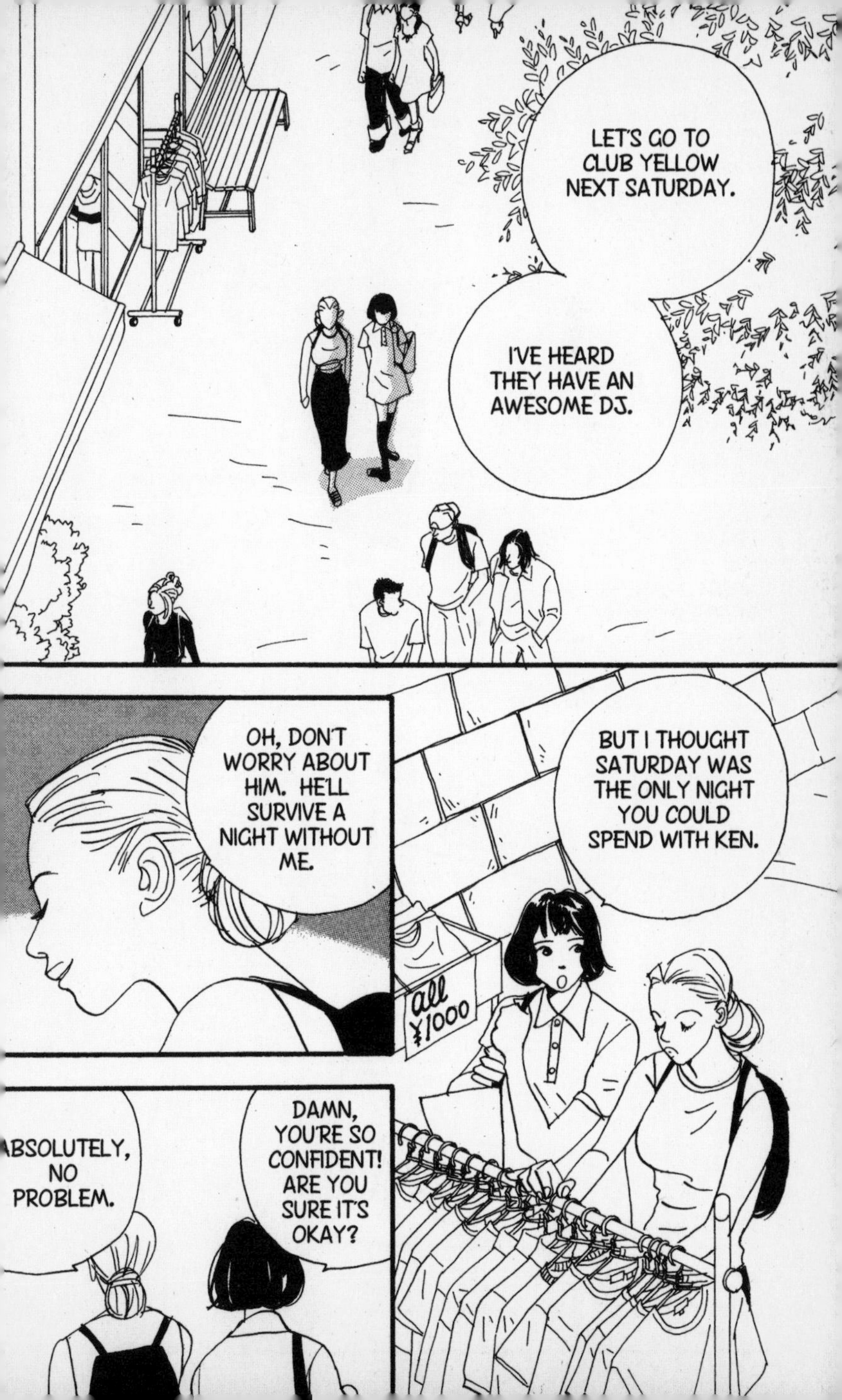
LET'S GO TO CLUB YELLOW NEXT SATURDAY.
I'VE HEARD THEY HAVE AN AWESOME DJ.
BUT I THOUGHT SATURDAY WAS THE ONLY NIGHT YOU COULD SPEND WITH KEN.
all ¥1000
OH, DON'T WORRY ABOUT HIM. HE'LL SURVIVE A NIGHT WITHOUT ME.
DAMN, YOU'RE SO CONFIDENT! ARE YOU SURE IT'S OKAY?
BSOLUTELY, NO PROBLEM.

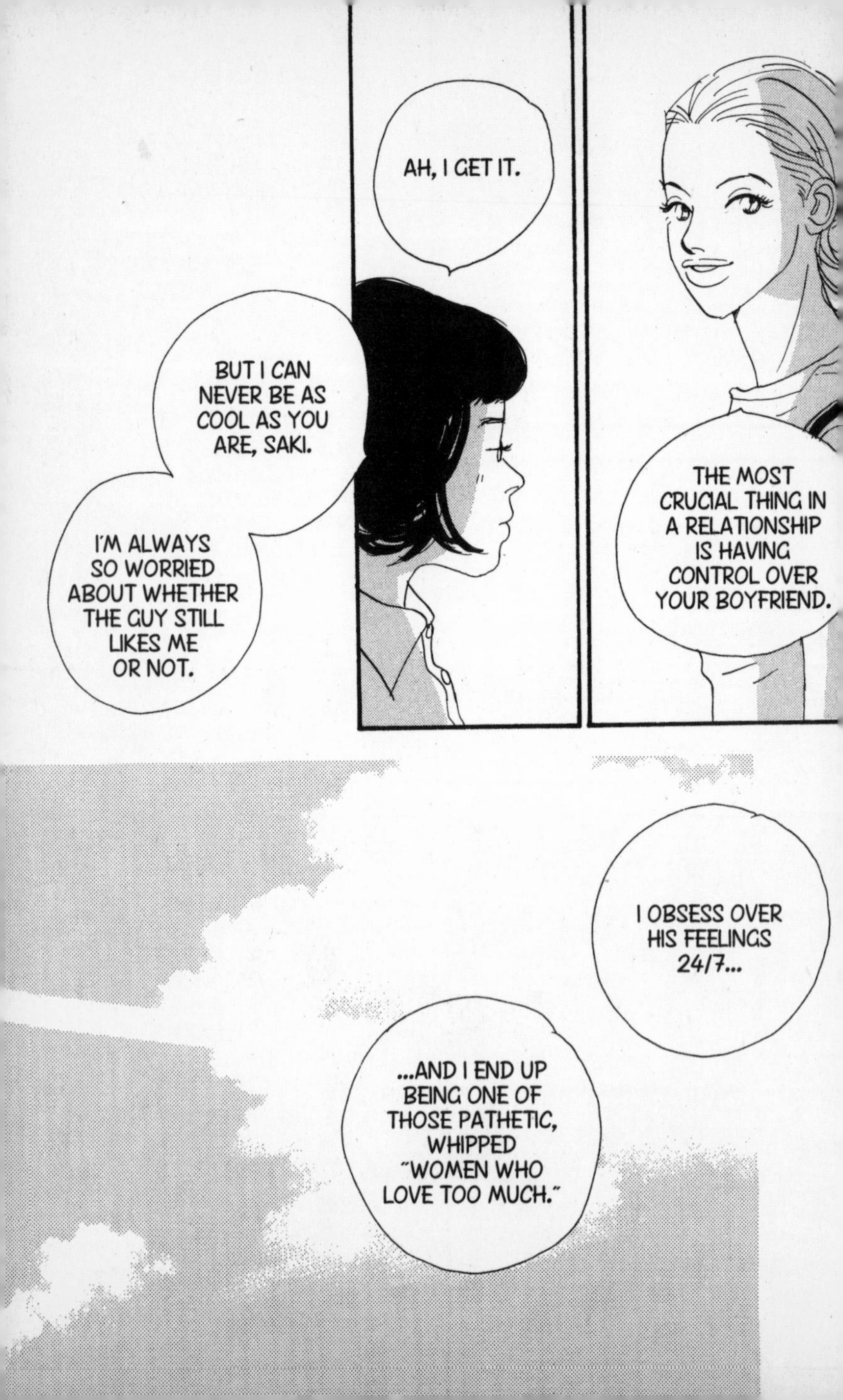
THE MOST CRUCIAL THING IN A RELATIONSHIP IS HAVING CONTROL OVER YOUR BOYFRIEND.
AH, I GET IT.
BUT I CAN NEVER BE AS COOL AS YOU ARE, SAKI.
I'M ALWAYS SO WORRIED ABOUT WHETHER THE GUY STILL LIKES ME OR NOT.
I OBSESS OVER HIS FEELINGS 24/7...
...AND I END UP BEING ONE OF THOSE PATHETIC, WHIPPED "WOMEN WHO LOVE TOO MUCH."

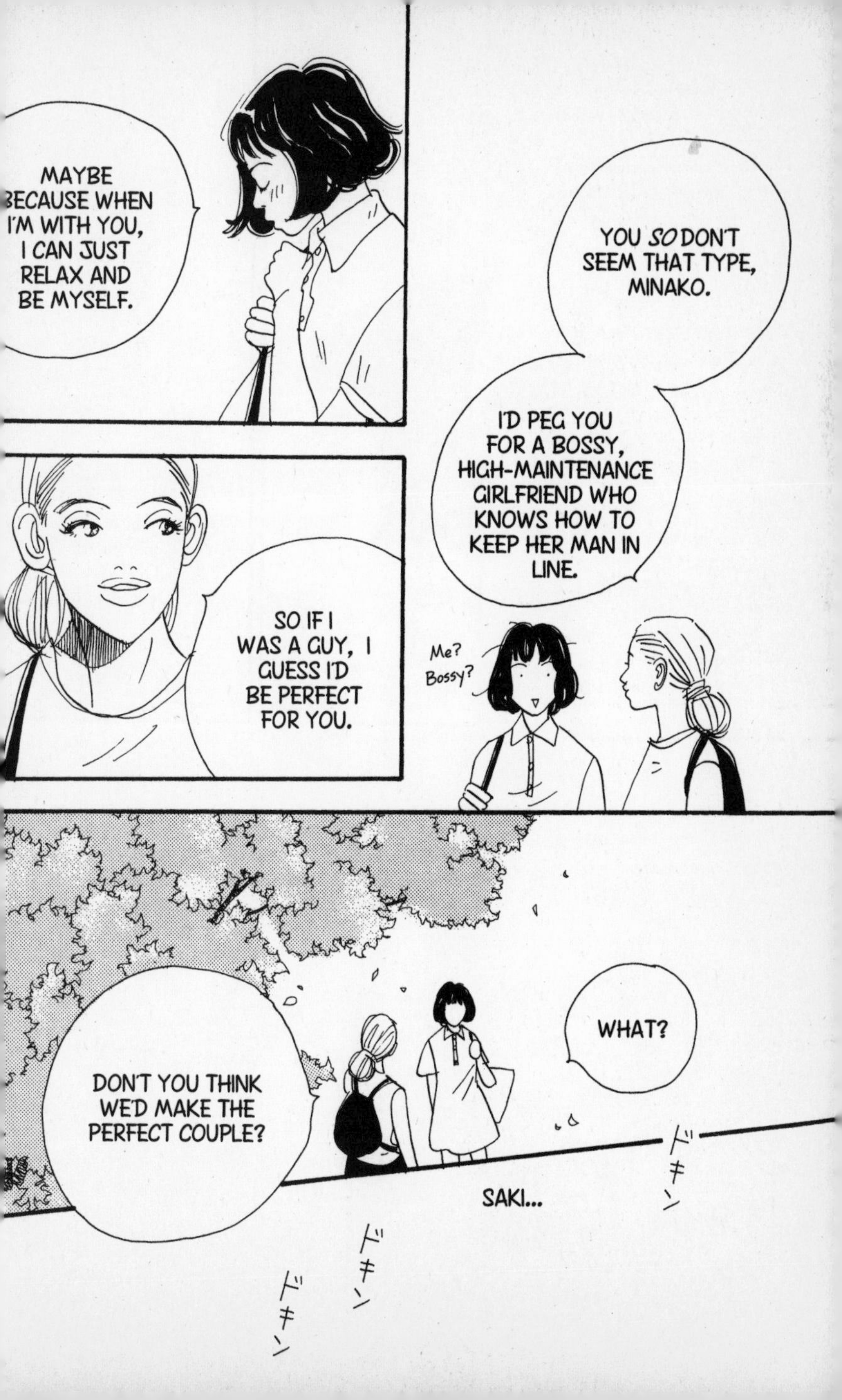

YOU *SO* DON'T SEEM THAT TYPE, MINAKO.
I'D PEG YOU FOR A BOSSY, HIGH-MAINTENANCE GIRLFRIEND WHO KNOWS HOW TO KEEP HER MAN IN LINE.
Me? Bossy?
MAYBE BECAUSE WHEN I'M WITH YOU, I CAN JUST RELAX AND BE MYSELF.
SO IF I WAS A GUY, I GUESS I'D BE PERFECT FOR YOU.
DON'T YOU THINK WE'D MAKE THE PERFECT COUPLE?
WHAT?
ドキン
SAKI...
ドキン
ドキン

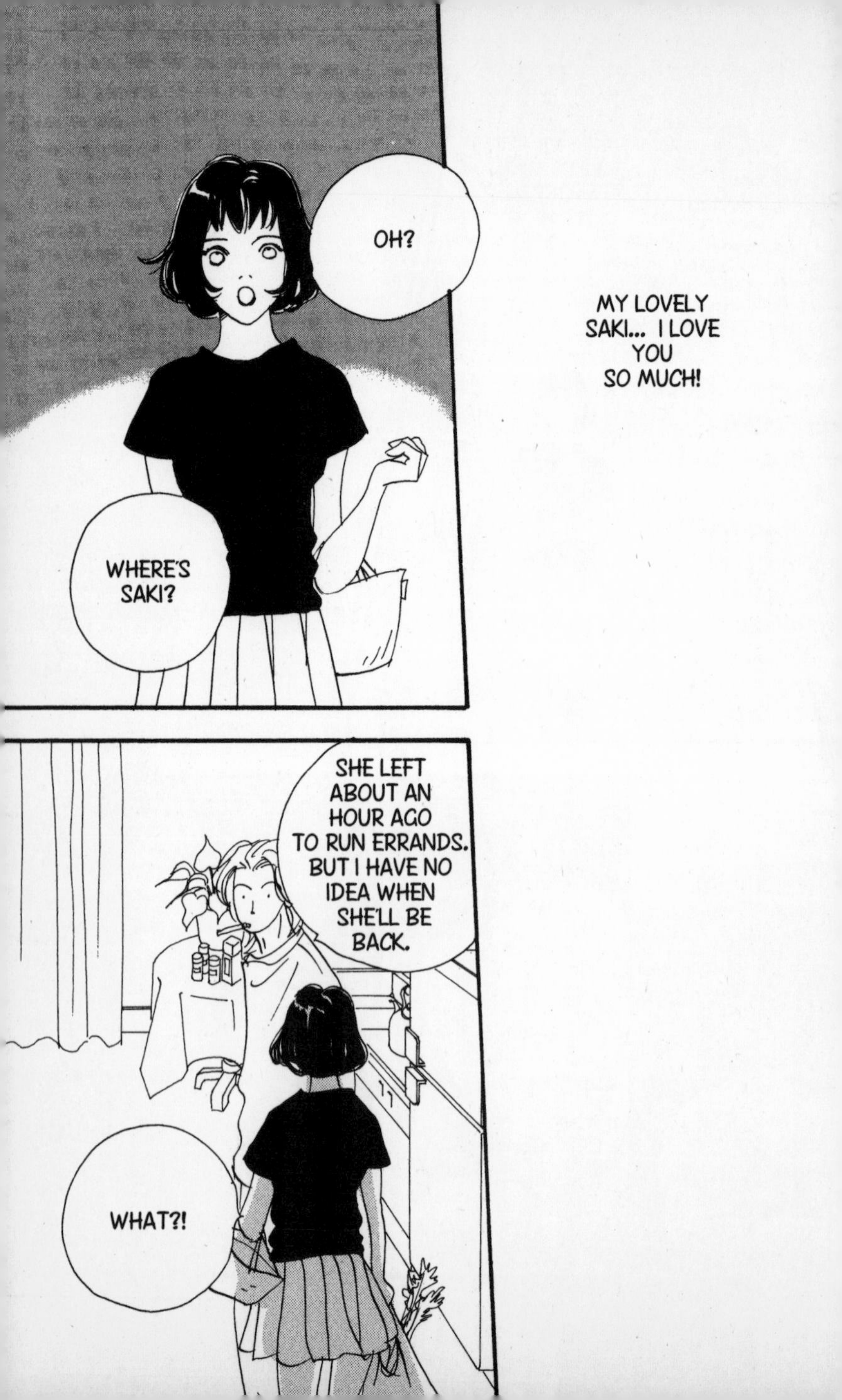
MY LOVELY SAKI... I LOVE YOU SO MUCH!
OH?
WHERE'S SAKI?
SHE LEFT ABOUT AN HOUR AGO TO RUN ERRANDS. BUT I HAVE NO IDEA WHEN SHE'LL BE BACK.
WHAT?!

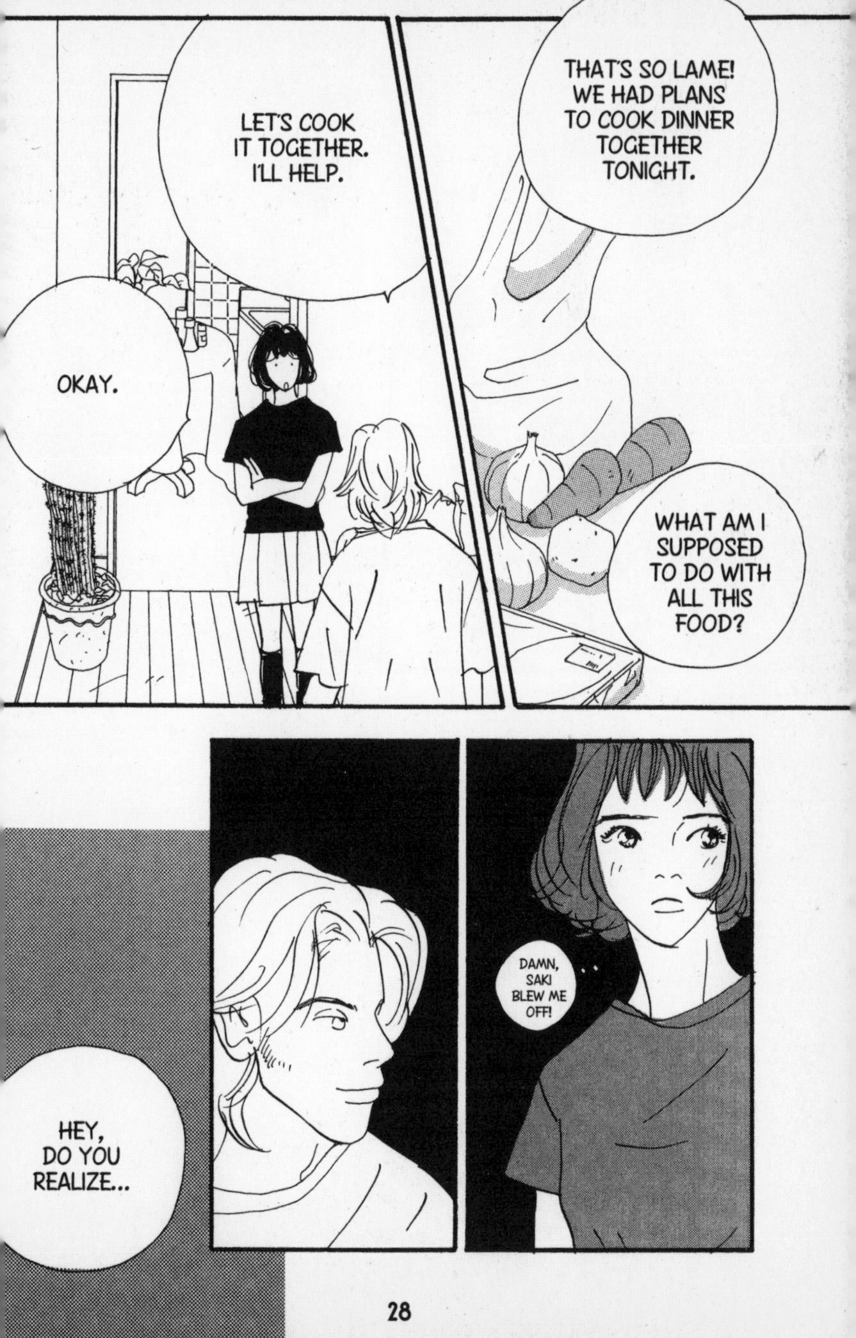
THAT'S SO LAME! WE HAD PLANS TO COOK DINNER TOGETHER TONIGHT.
WHAT AM I SUPPOSED TO DO WITH ALL THIS FOOD?
LET'S COOK IT TOGETHER. I'LL HELP.
OKAY.
DAMN, SAKI BLEW ME OFF!
HEY, DO YOU REALIZE...

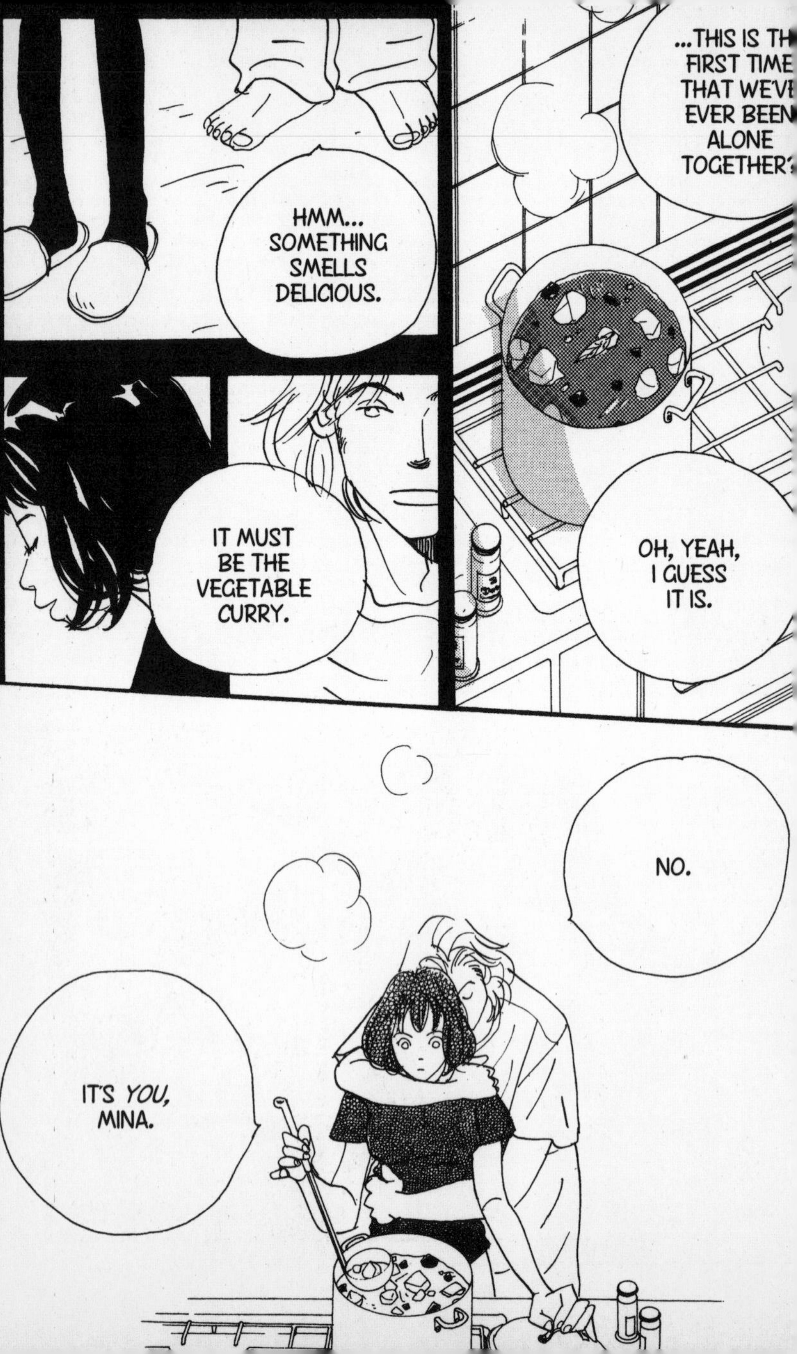
...THIS IS THE FIRST TIME THAT WE'VE EVER BEEN ALONE TOGETHER?
OH, YEAH, I GUESS IT IS.
HMM... SOMETHING SMELLS DELICIOUS.
IT MUST BE THE VEGETABLE CURRY.
NO.
IT'S *YOU*, MINA.

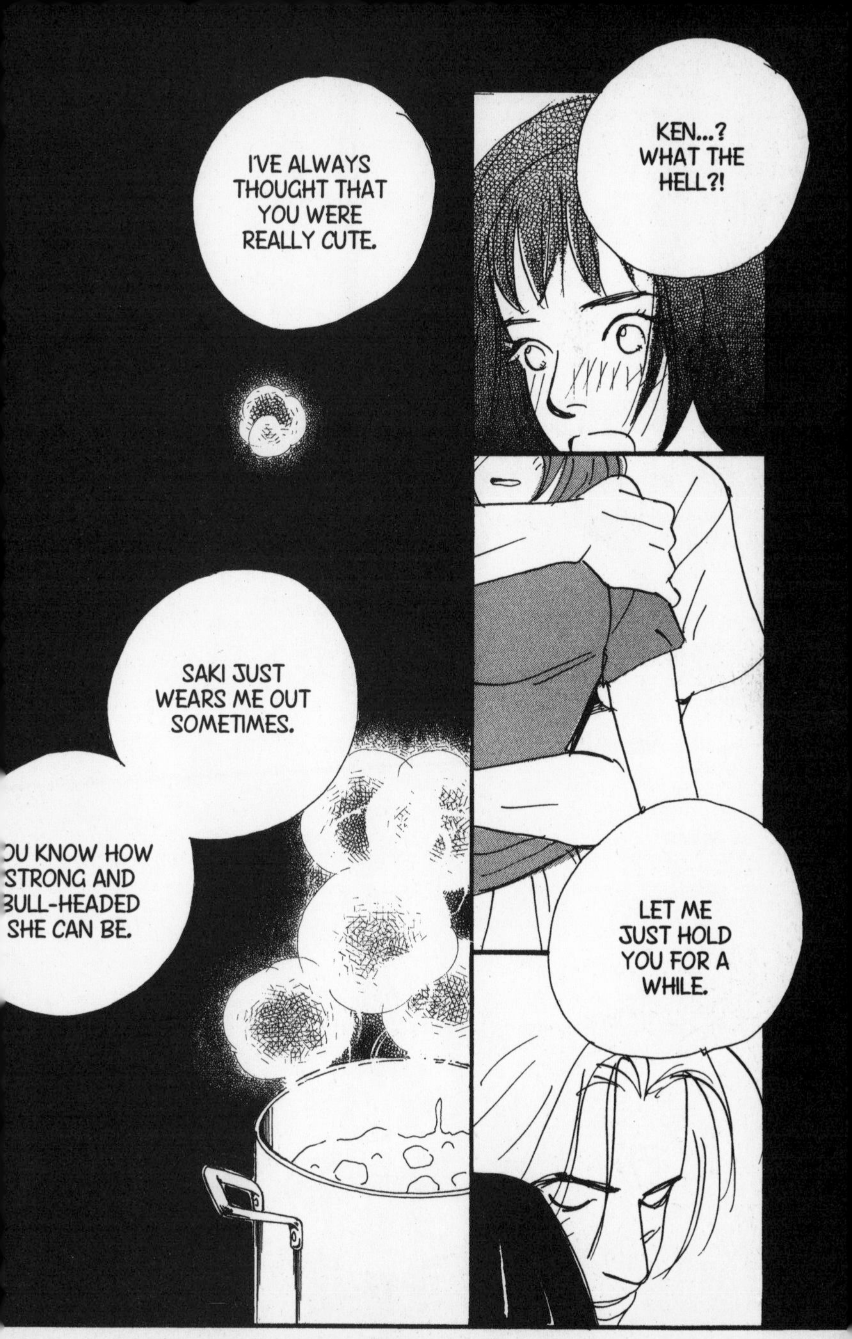
KEN...? WHAT THE HELL?!
LET ME JUST HOLD YOU FOR A WHILE.
I'VE ALWAYS THOUGHT THAT YOU WERE REALLY CUTE.
SAKI JUST WEARS ME OUT SOMETIMES.
OU KNOW HOW STRONG AND ULL-HEADED SHE CAN BE.

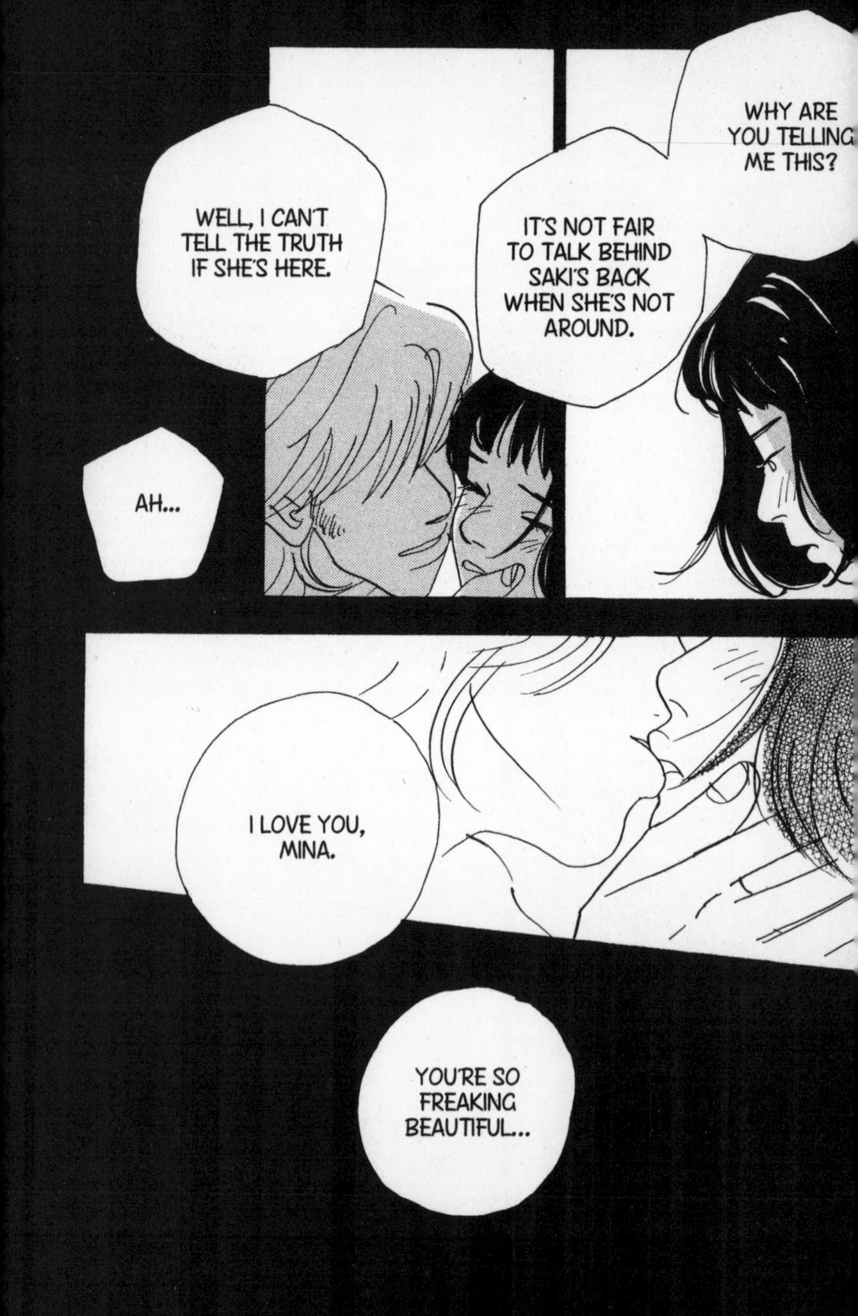
WHY ARE YOU TELLING ME THIS?
IT'S NOT FAIR TO TALK BEHIND SAKI'S BACK WHEN SHE'S NOT AROUND.
WELL, I CAN'T TELL THE TRUTH IF SHE'S HERE.
AH...
I LOVE YOU, MINA.
YOU'RE SO FREAKING BEAUTIFUL...

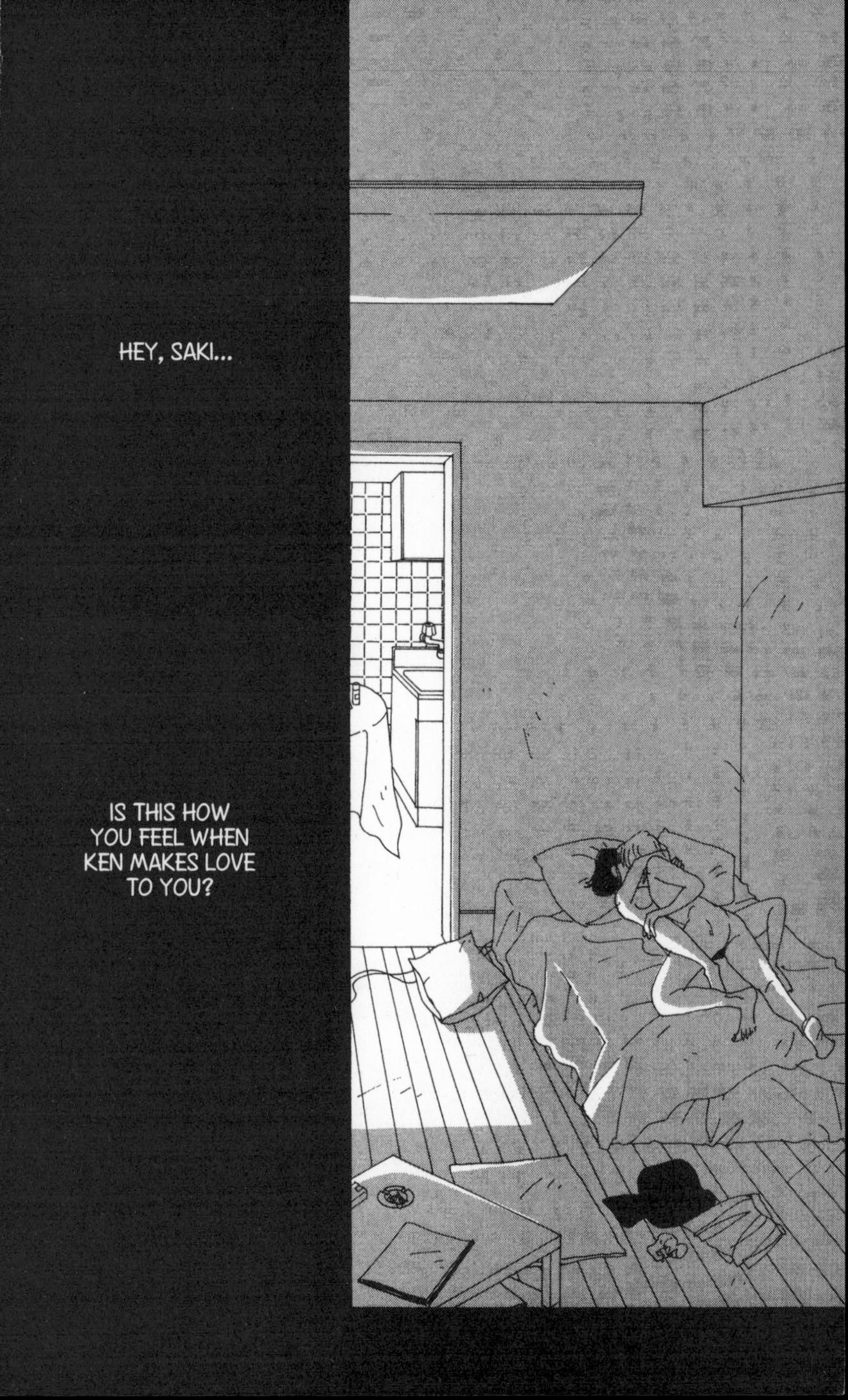
HEY, SAKI...
IS THIS HOW YOU FEEL WHEN KEN MAKES LOVE TO YOU?

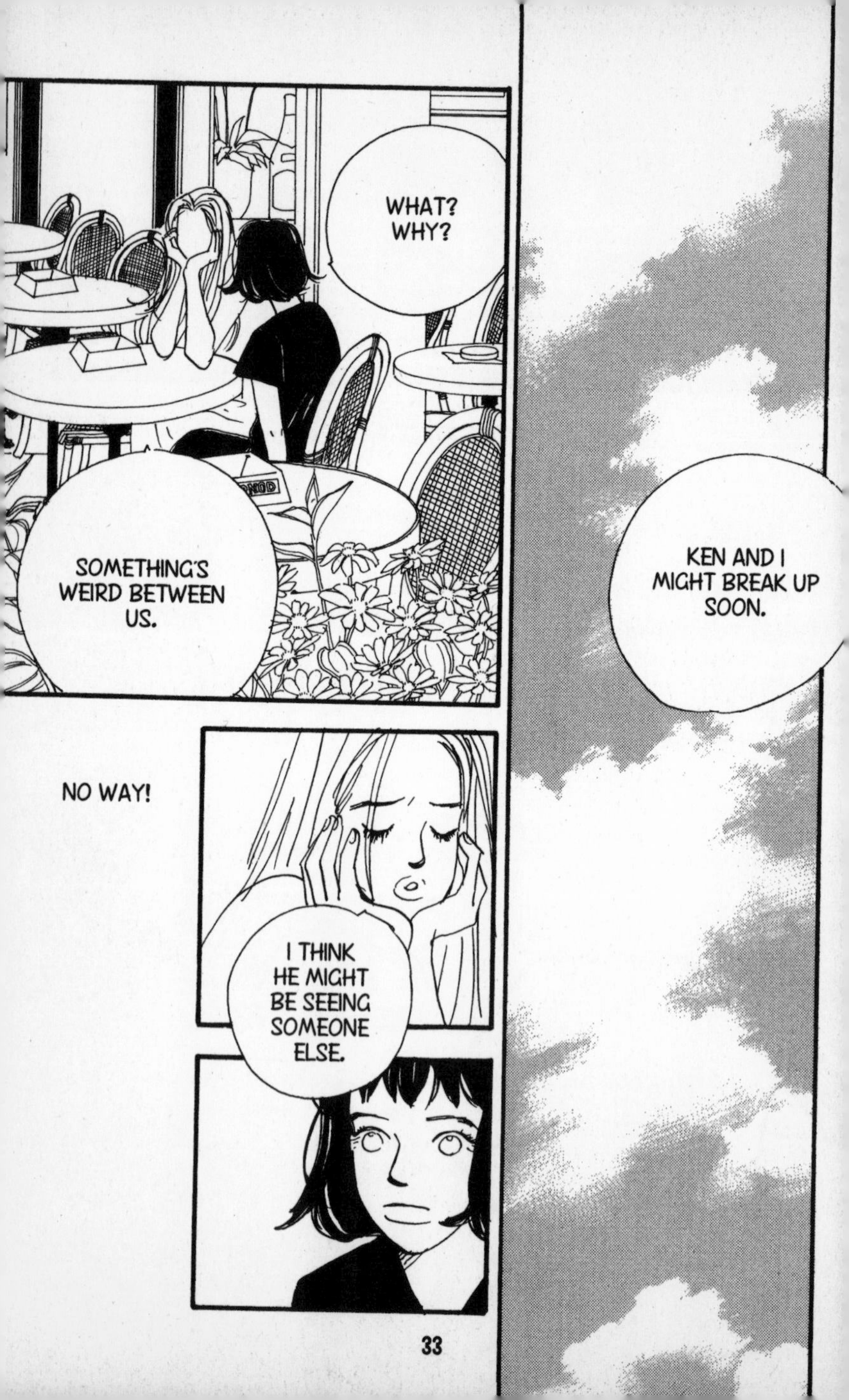
KEN AND I MIGHT BREAK UP SOON.
WHAT? WHY?
SOMETHING'S WEIRD BETWEEN US.
NO WAY!
I THINK HE MIGHT BE SEEING SOMEONE ELSE.

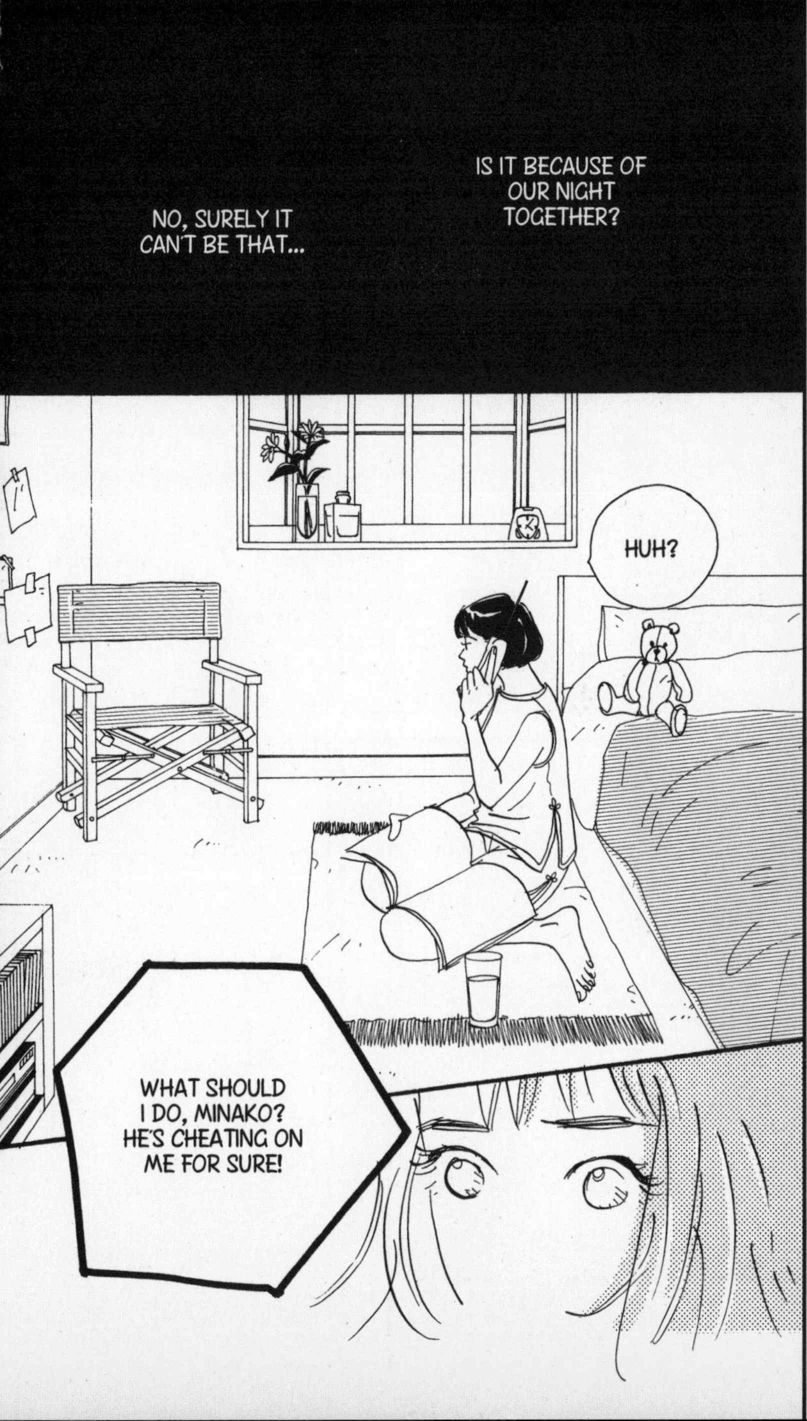
IS IT BECAUSE OF OUR NIGHT TOGETHER?
NO, SURELY IT CAN'T BE THAT...
HUH?
WHAT SHOULD I DO, MINAKO? HE'S CHEATING ON ME FOR SURE!

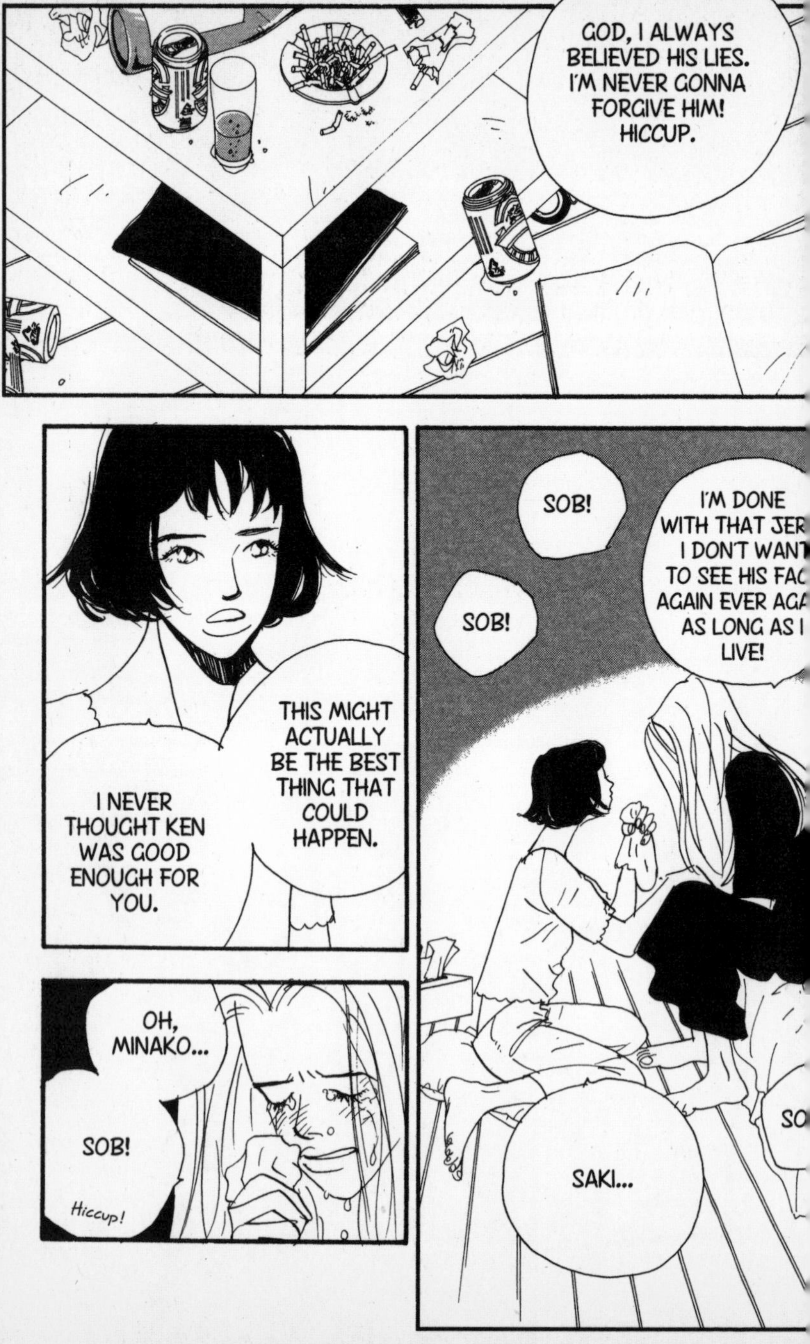
GOD, I ALWAYS BELIEVED HIS LIES. I'M NEVER GONNA FORGIVE HIM! HICCUP.
I'M DONE WITH THAT JER I DON'T WANT TO SEE HIS FAC AGAIN EVER AGA AS LONG AS I LIVE!
SOB!
SOB!
SO
SAKI...
THIS MIGHT ACTUALLY BE THE BEST THING THAT COULD HAPPEN.
I NEVER THOUGHT KEN WAS GOOD ENOUGH FOR YOU.
OH, MINAKO...
SOB!
Hiccup!

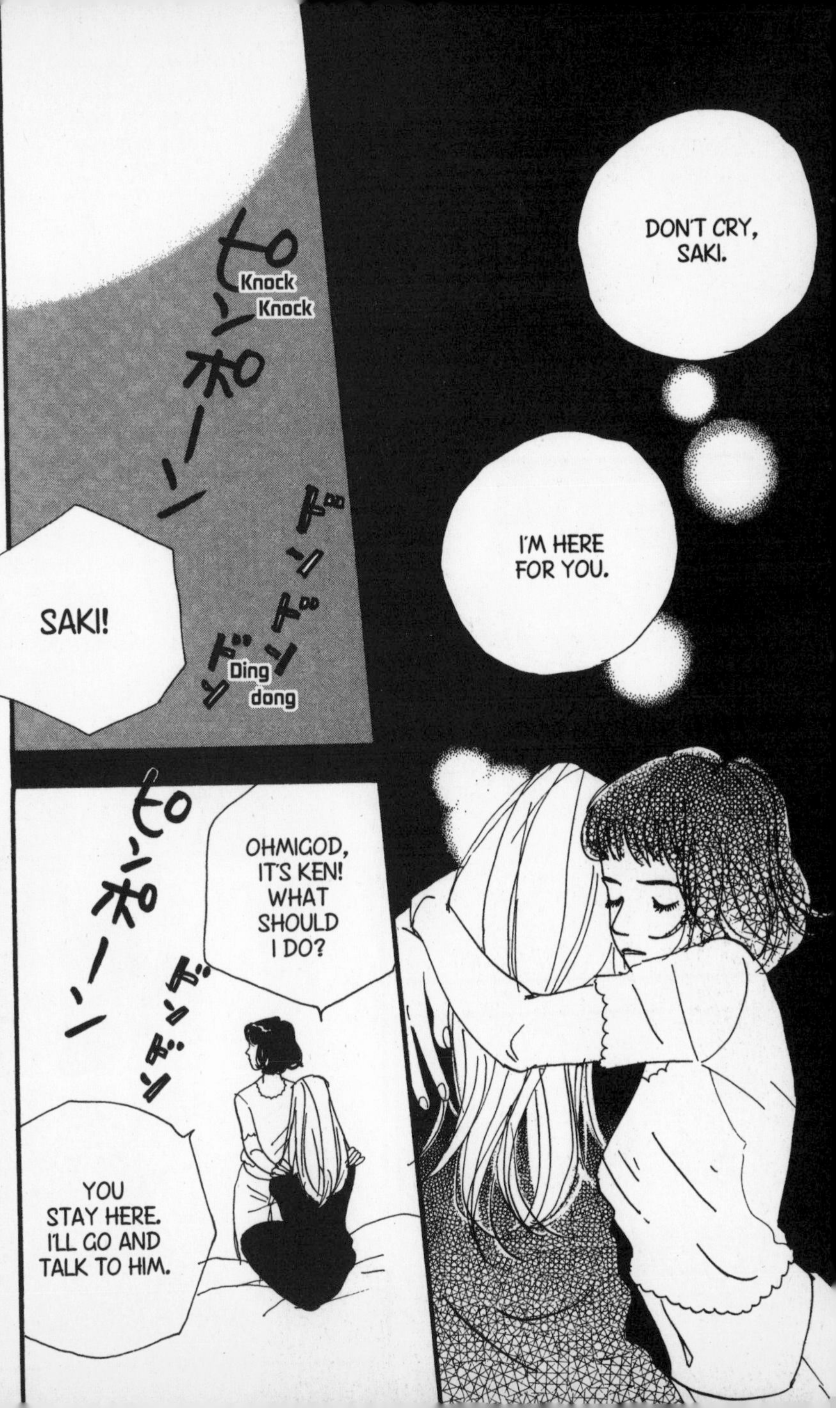
DON'T CRY, SAKI.
I'M HERE FOR YOU.
Knock Knock
Ding dong
SAKI!
OHMIGOD, IT'S KEN! WHAT SHOULD I DO?
YOU STAY HERE. I'LL GO AND TALK TO HIM.

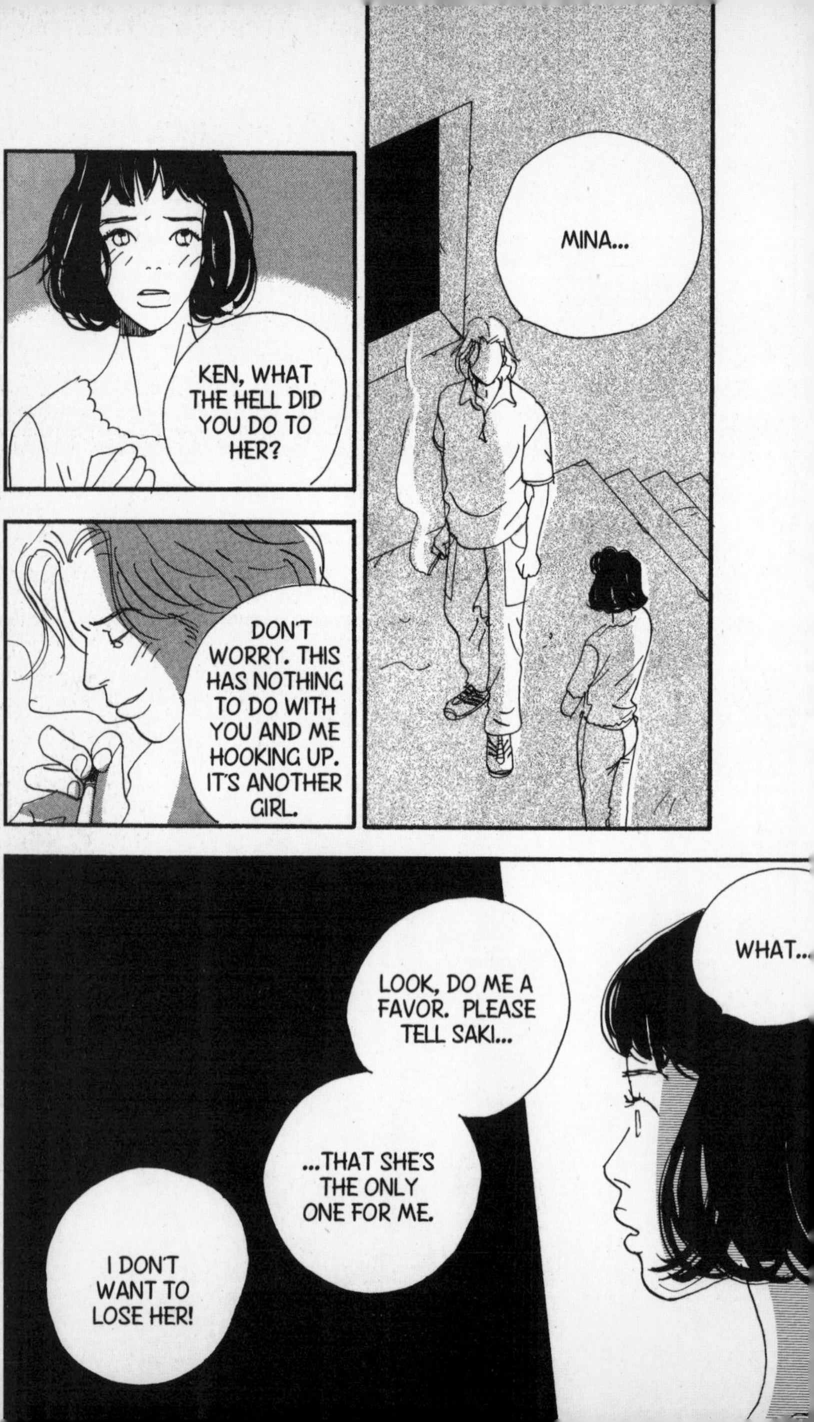
MINA...
KEN, WHAT THE HELL DID YOU DO TO HER?
DON'T WORRY. THIS HAS NOTHING TO DO WITH YOU AND ME HOOKING UP. IT'S ANOTHER GIRL.
WHAT...
LOOK, DO ME A FAVOR. PLEASE TELL SAKI...
...THAT SHE'S THE ONLY ONE FOR ME.
I DON'T WANT TO LOSE HER!

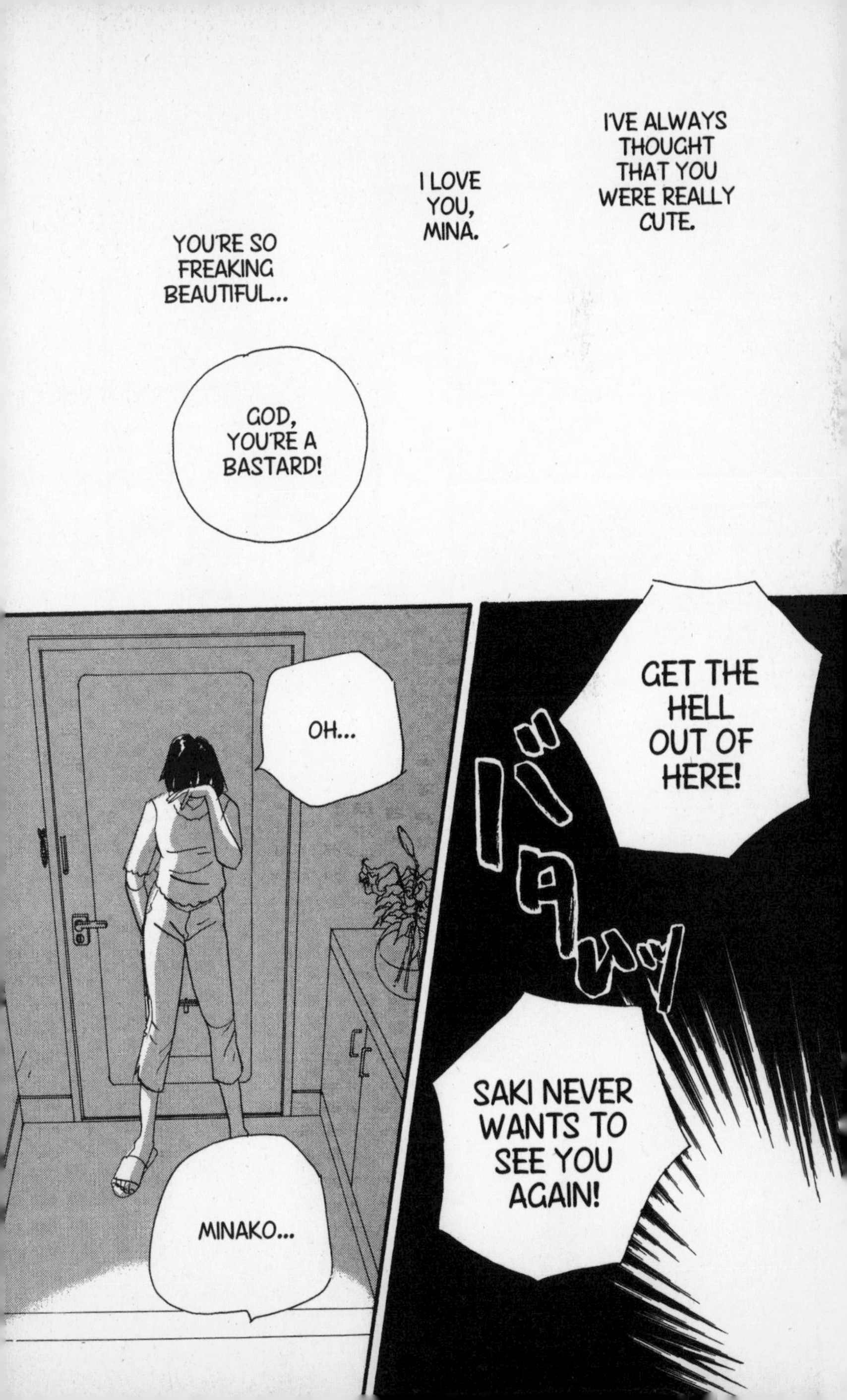
I'VE ALWAYS THOUGHT THAT YOU WERE REALLY CUTE.
I LOVE YOU, MINA.
YOU'RE SO FREAKING BEAUTIFUL...
GOD, YOU'RE A BASTARD!
GET THE HELL OUT OF HERE!
バタンッ
SAKI NEVER WANTS TO SEE YOU AGAIN!
OH...
MINAKO...

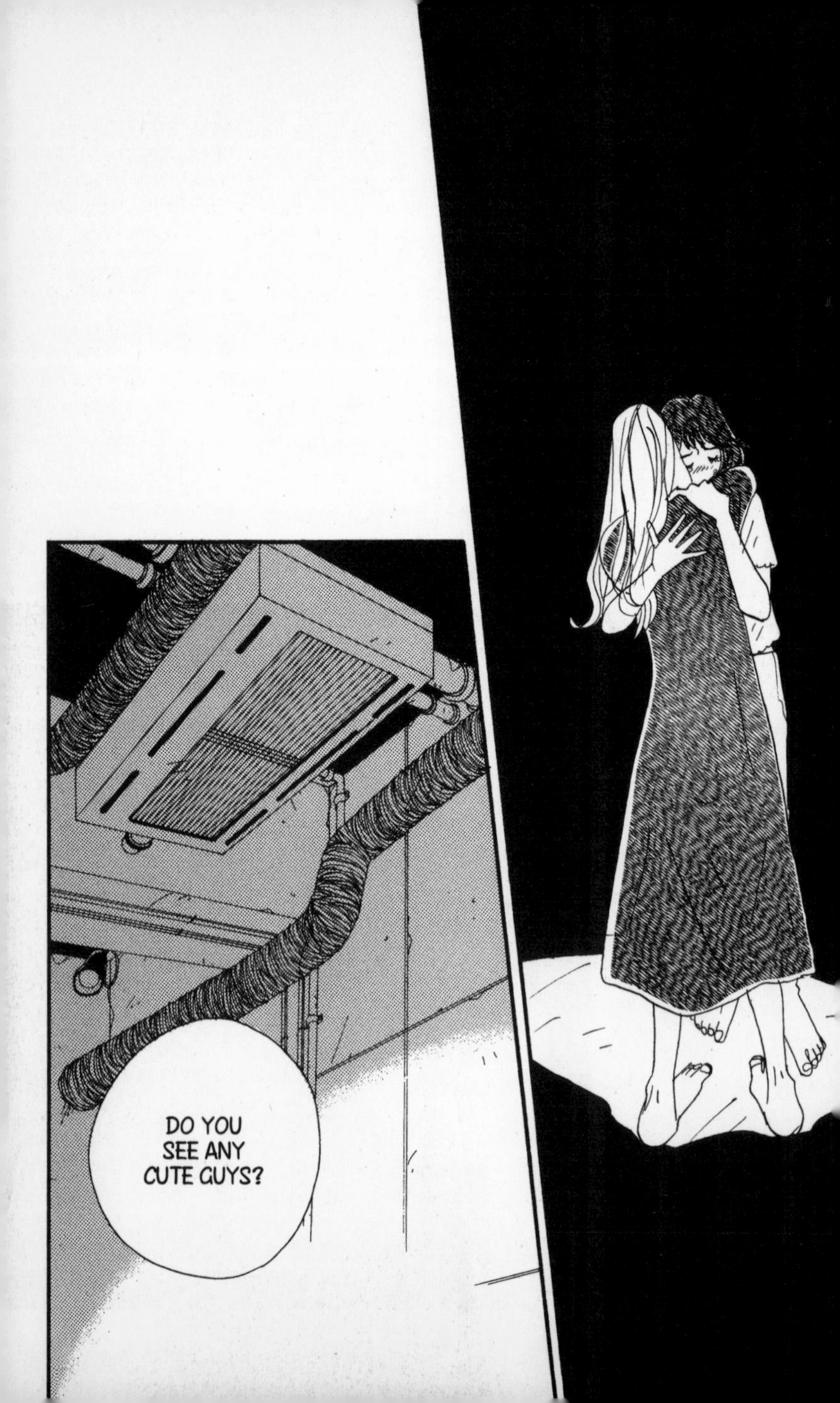
DO YOU
SEE ANY
CUTE GUYS?

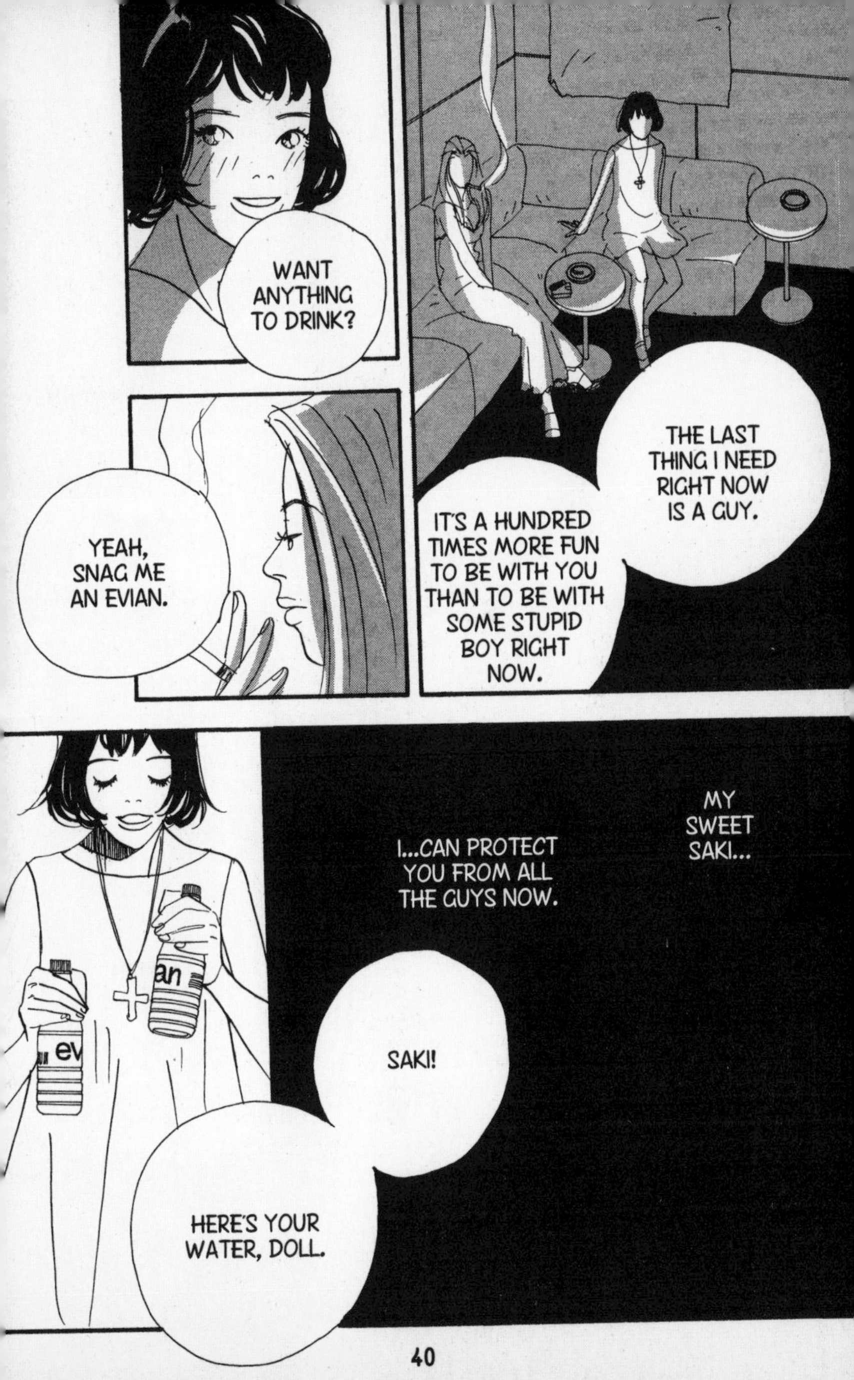
THE LAST THING I NEED RIGHT NOW IS A GUY.
IT'S A HUNDRED TIMES MORE FUN TO BE WITH YOU THAN TO BE WITH SOME STUPID BOY RIGHT NOW.
WANT ANYTHING TO DRINK?
YEAH, SNAG ME AN EVIAN.
MY SWEET SAKI...
I...CAN PROTECT YOU FROM ALL THE GUYS NOW.
SAKI!
HERE'S YOUR WATER, DOLL.

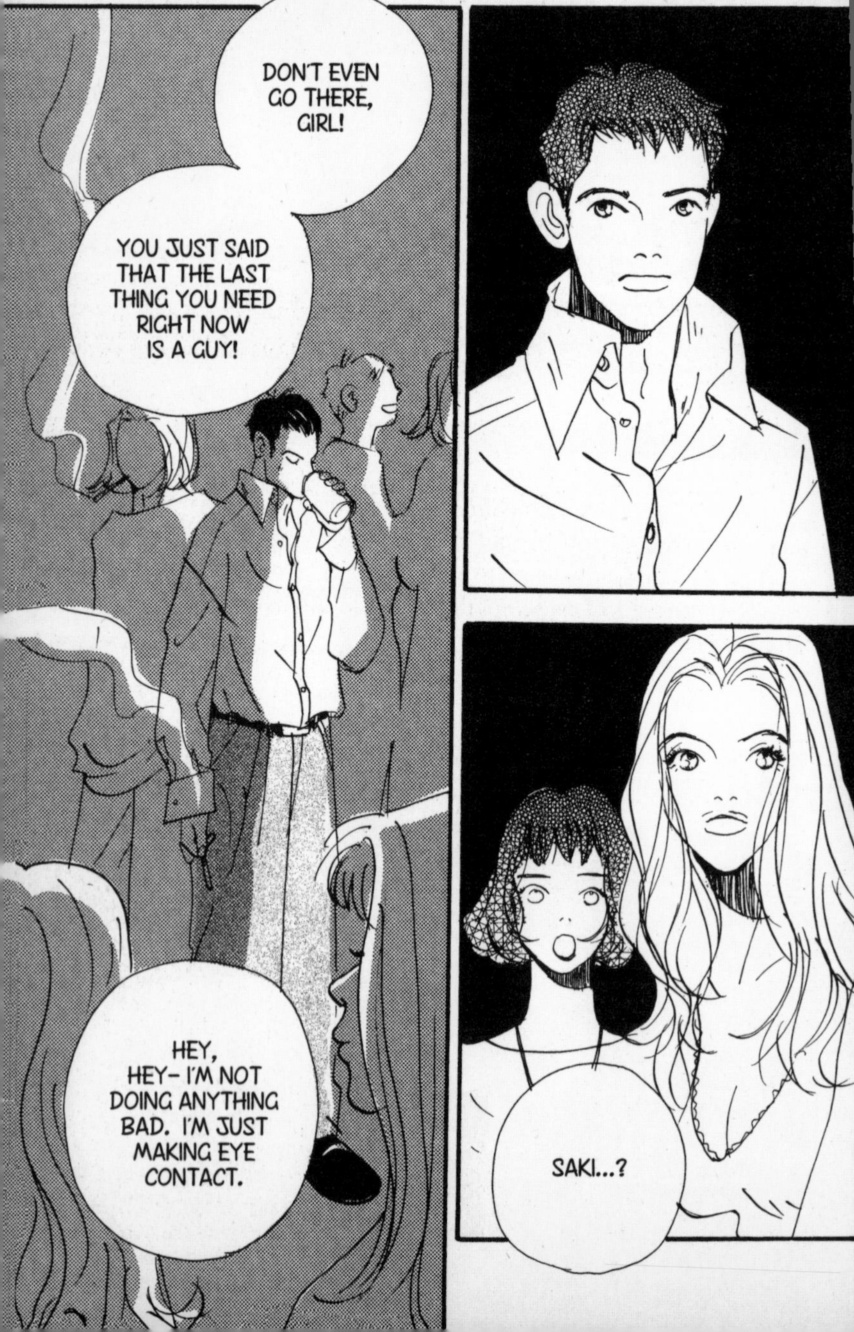
SAKI...?
DON'T EVEN GO THERE, GIRL!
YOU JUST SAID THAT THE LAST THING YOU NEED RIGHT NOW IS A GUY!
HEY, HEY– I'M NOT DOING ANYTHING BAD. I'M JUST MAKING EYE CONTACT.

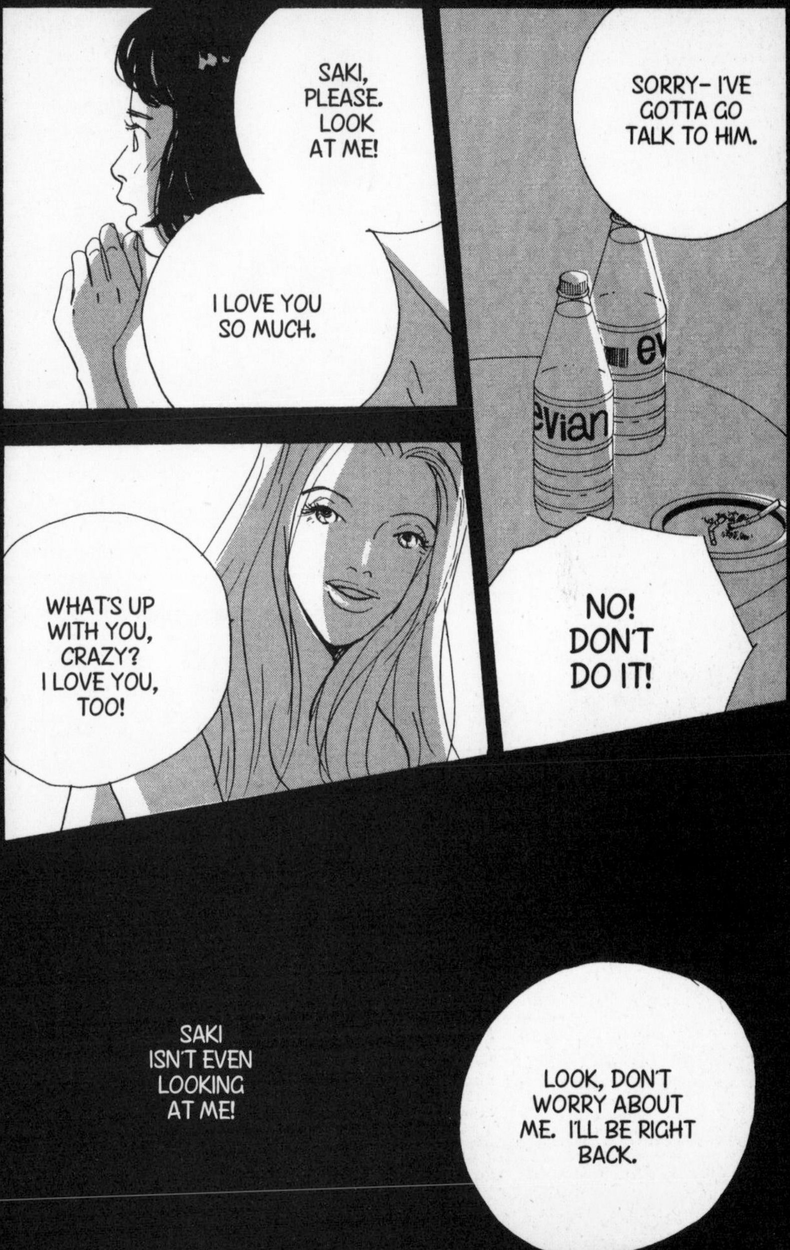
SORRY- I'VE GOTTA GO TALK TO HIM.
evian
NO! DON'T DO IT!
SAKI, PLEASE. LOOK AT ME!
I LOVE YOU SO MUCH.
WHAT'S UP WITH YOU, CRAZY? I LOVE YOU, TOO!
LOOK, DON'T WORRY ABOUT ME. I'LL BE RIGHT BACK.
SAKI ISN'T EVEN LOOKING AT ME!

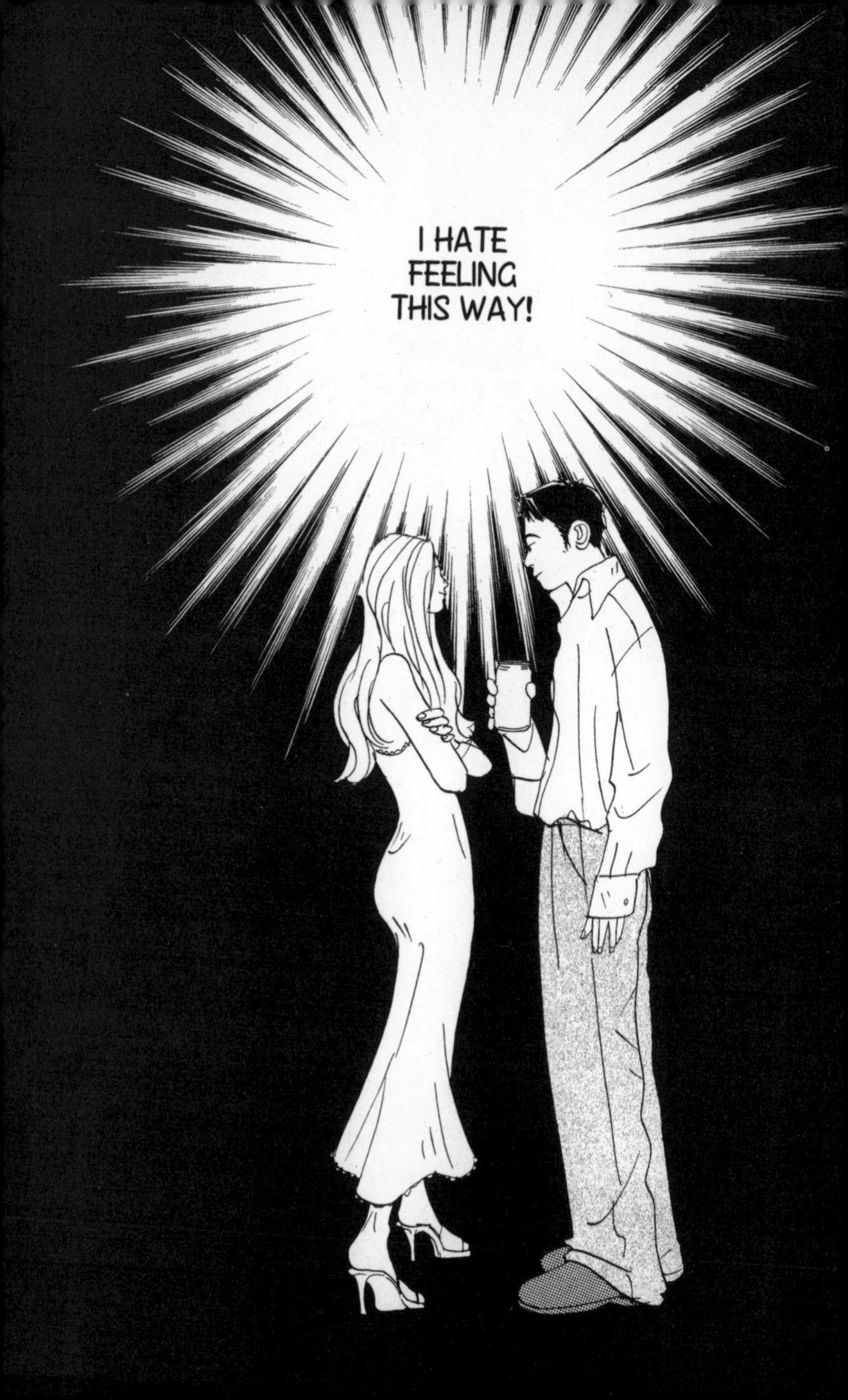
I HATE FEELING THIS WAY!

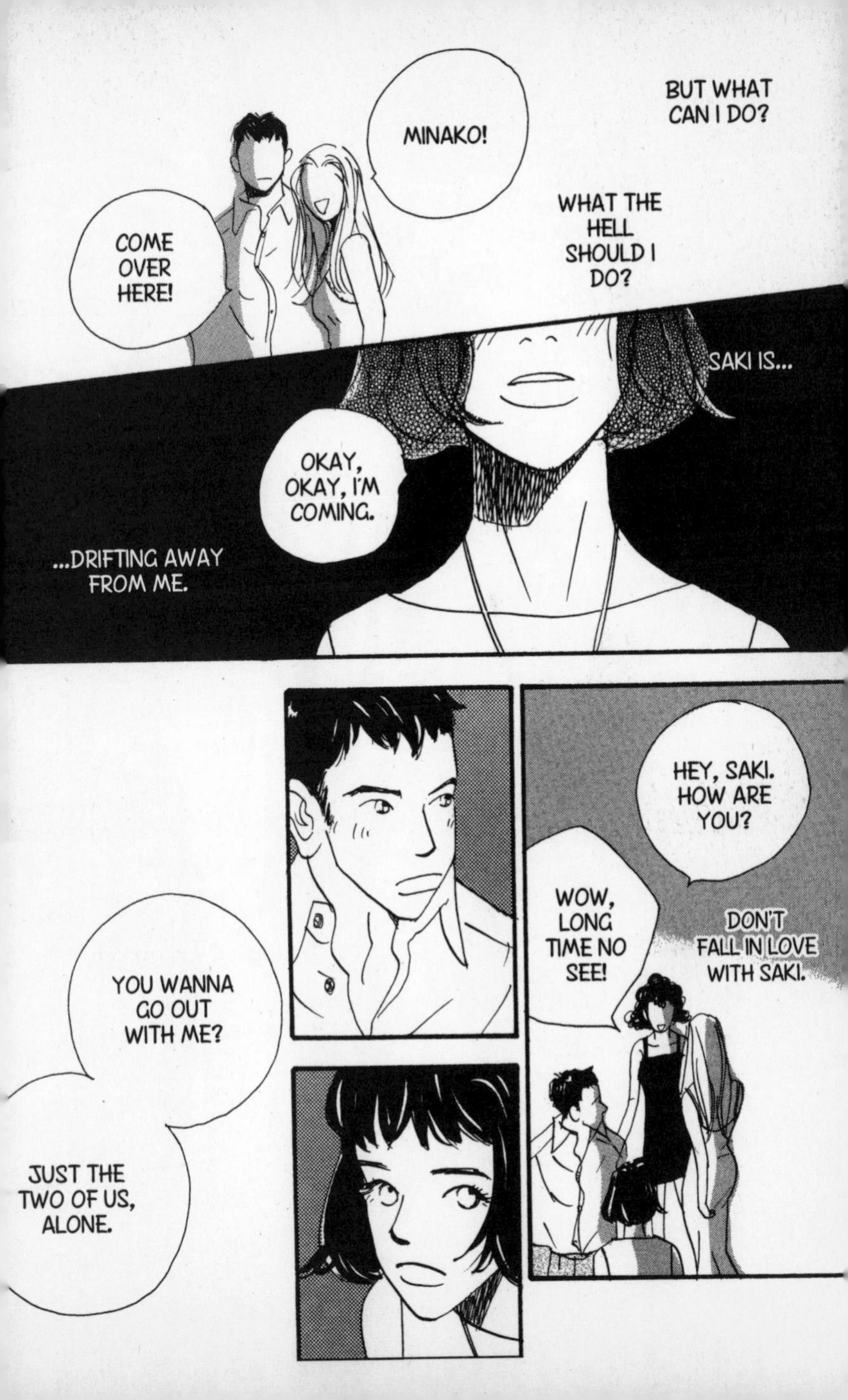
BUT WHAT CAN I DO?
MINAKO!
WHAT THE HELL SHOULD I DO?
COME OVER HERE!
SAKI IS...
OKAY, OKAY, I'M COMING.
...DRIFTING AWAY FROM ME.
HEY, SAKI. HOW ARE YOU?
WOW, LONG TIME NO SEE!
DON'T FALL IN LOVE WITH SAKI.
YOU WANNA GO OUT WITH ME?
JUST THE TWO OF US, ALONE.

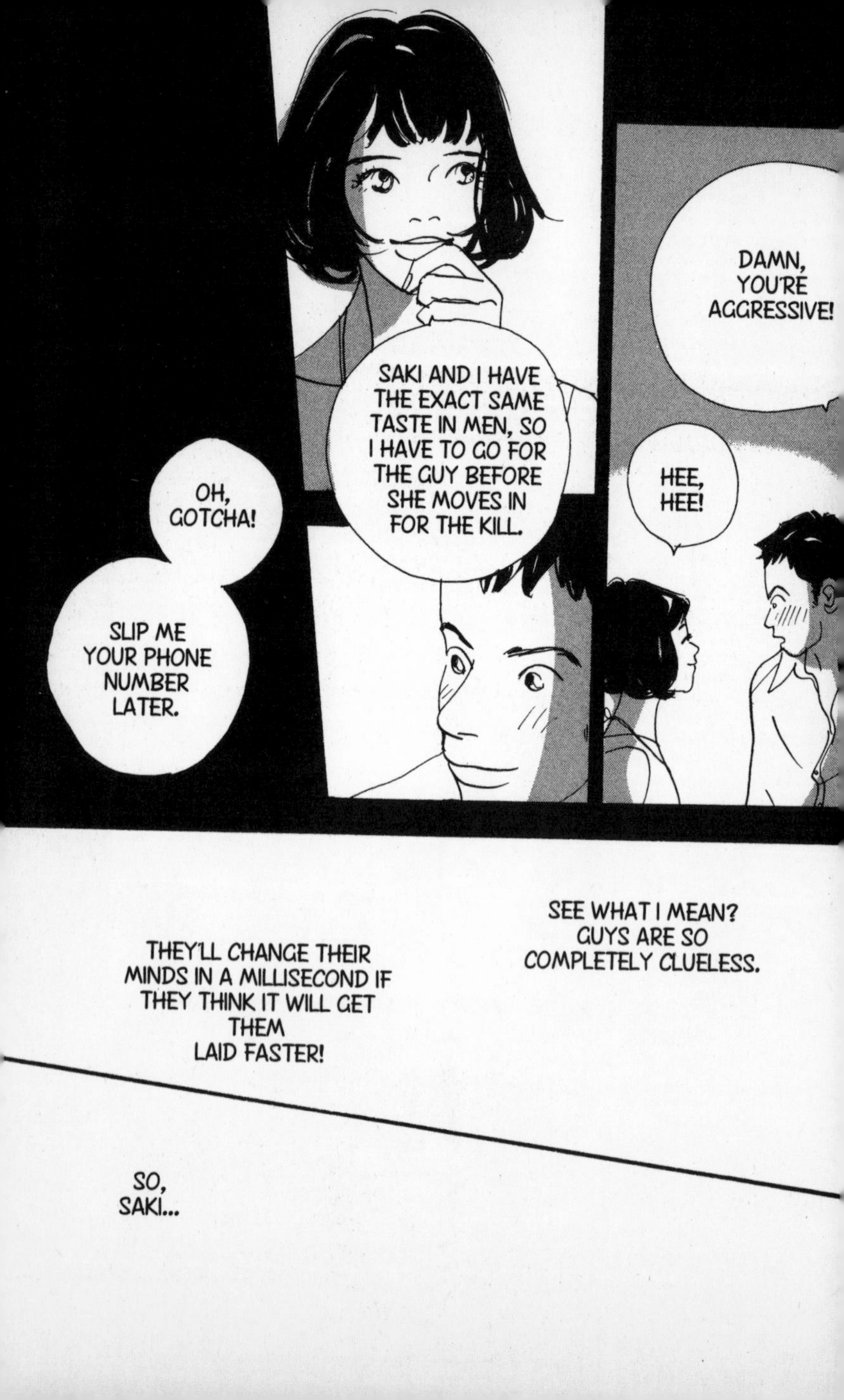
SAKI AND I HAVE THE EXACT SAME TASTE IN MEN, SO I HAVE TO GO FOR THE GUY BEFORE SHE MOVES IN FOR THE KILL.
DAMN, YOU'RE AGGRESSIVE!
HEE, HEE!
OH, GOTCHA!
SLIP ME YOUR PHONE NUMBER LATER.
SEE WHAT I MEAN? GUYS ARE SO COMPLETELY CLUELESS.
THEY'LL CHANGE THEIR MINDS IN A MILLISECOND IF THEY THINK IT WILL GET THEM LAID FASTER!
SO, SAKI...

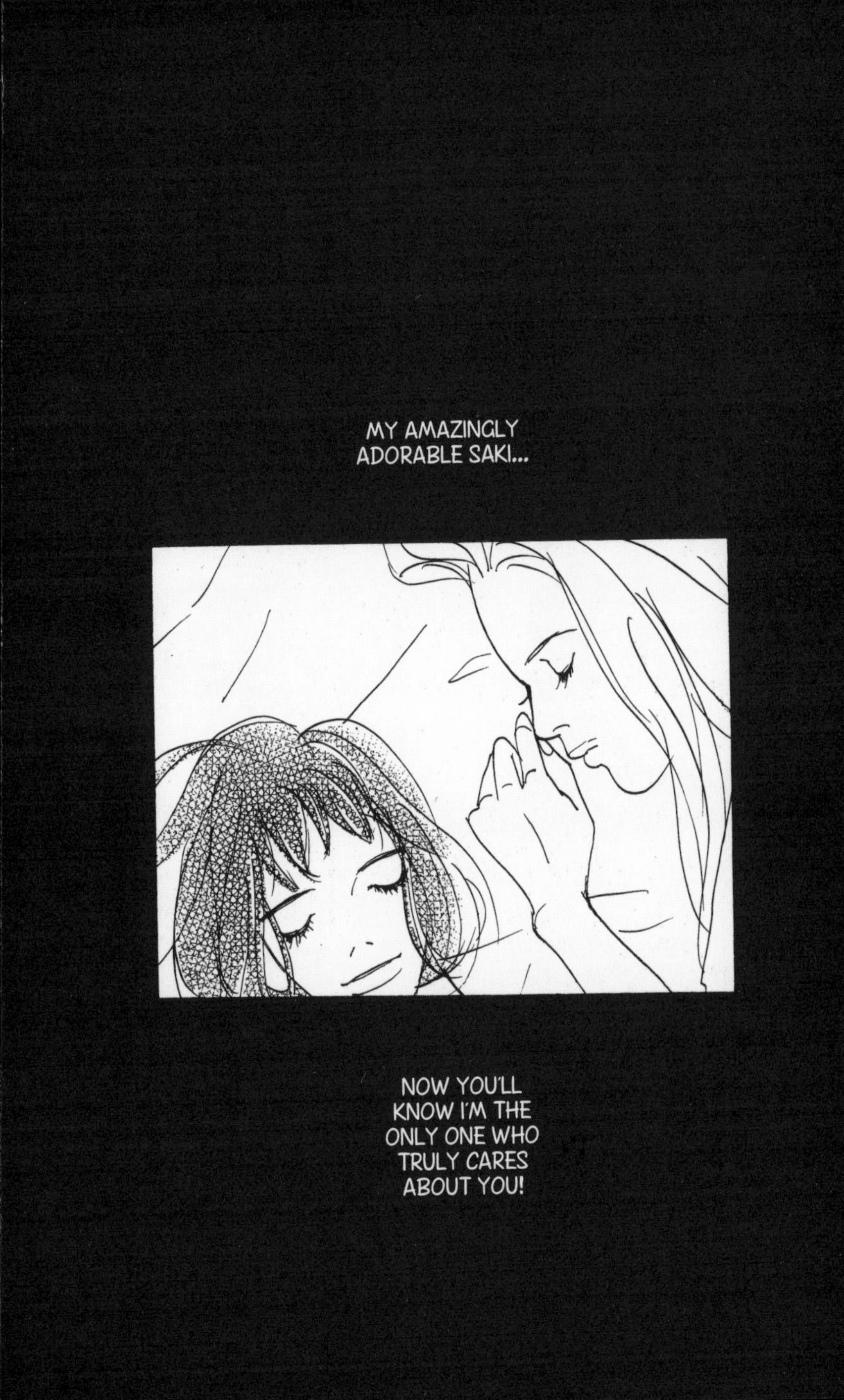
MY AMAZINGLY ADORABLE SAKI...
NOW YOU'LL KNOW I'M THE ONLY ONE WHO TRULY CARES ABOUT YOU!

between the sheets

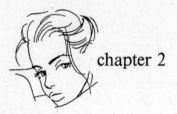

chapter 2

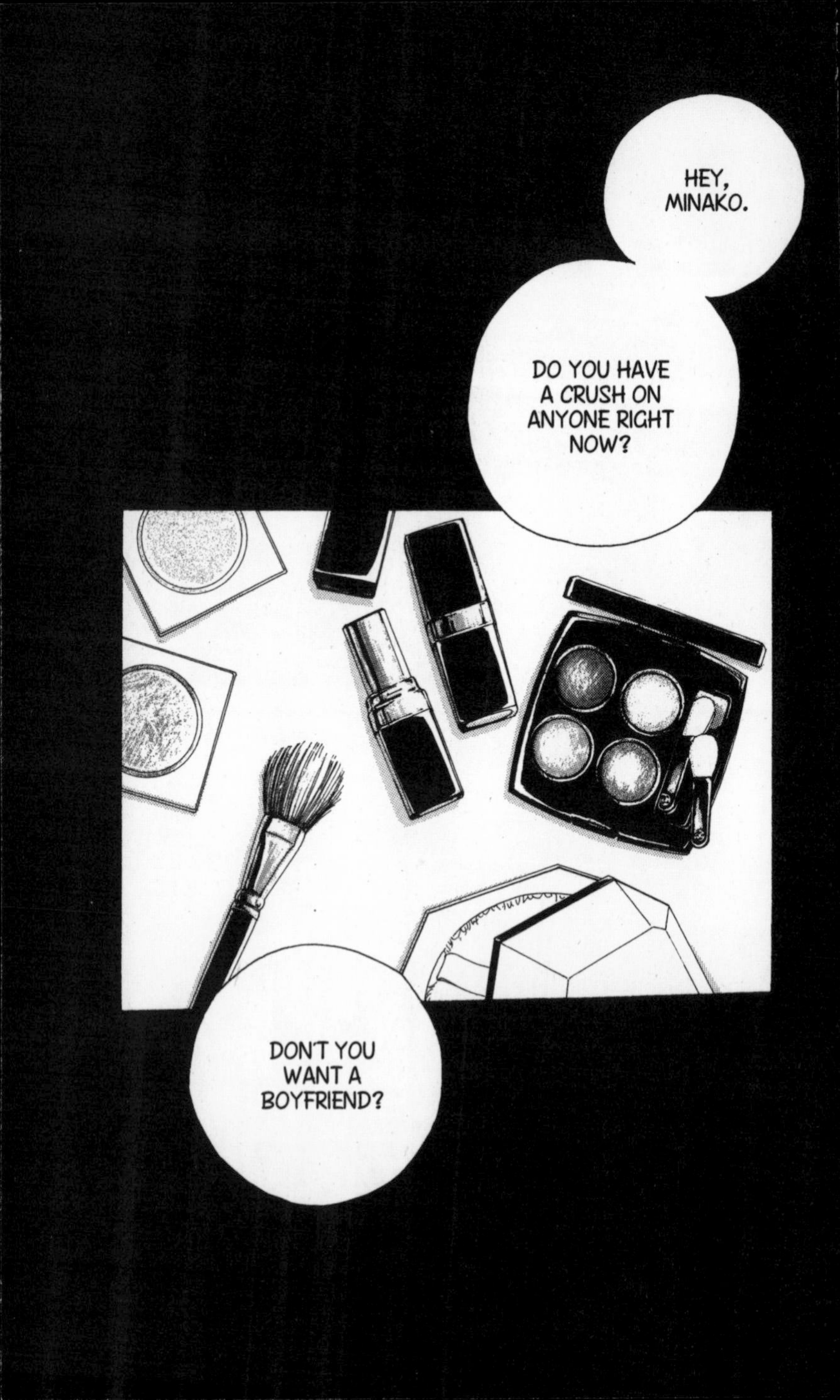
HEY, MINAKO.
DO YOU HAVE A CRUSH ON ANYONE RIGHT NOW?
DON'T YOU WANT A BOYFRIEND?

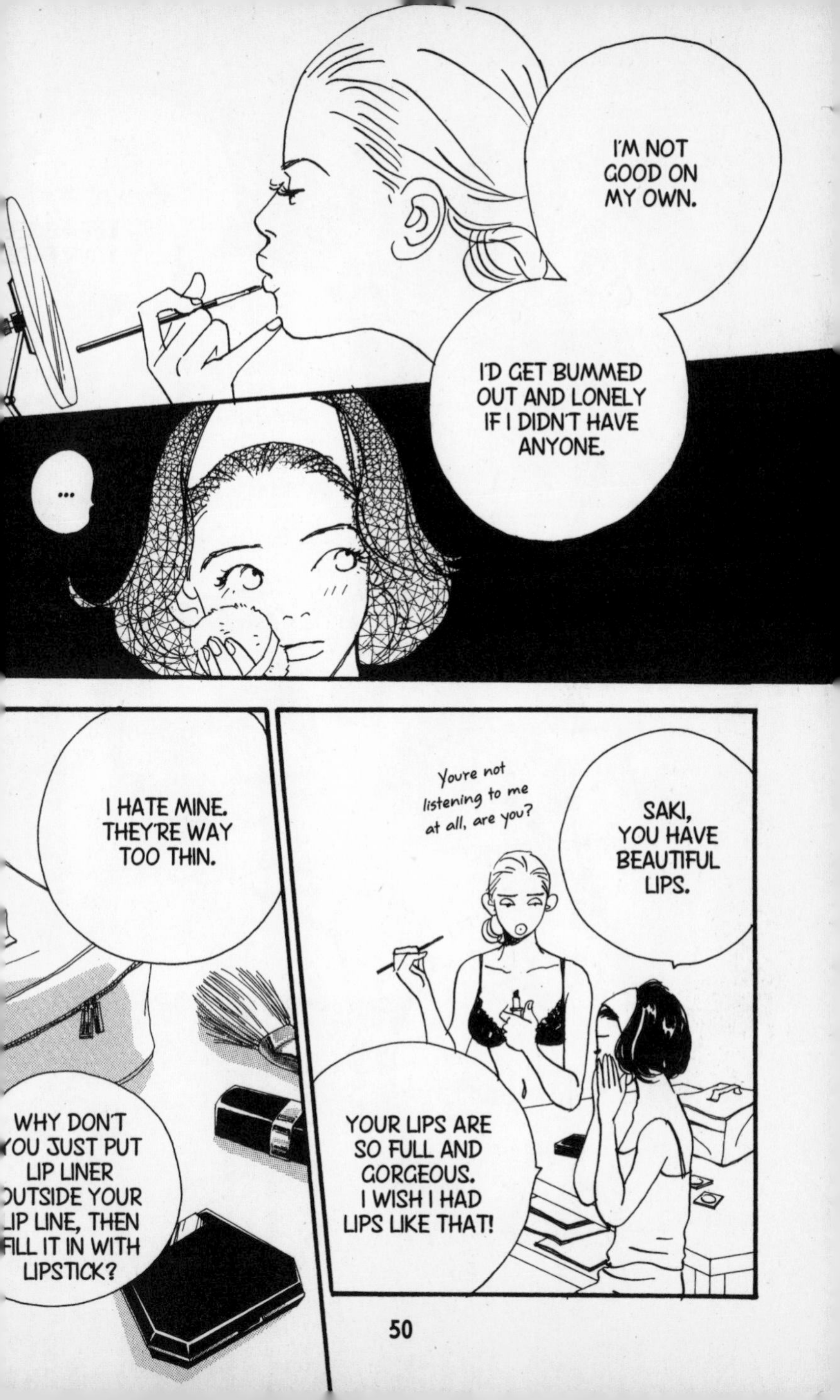
I'M NOT GOOD ON MY OWN.
I'D GET BUMMED OUT AND LONELY IF I DIDN'T HAVE ANYONE.
...
SAKI, YOU HAVE BEAUTIFUL LIPS.
You're not listening to me at all, are you?
YOUR LIPS ARE SO FULL AND GORGEOUS. I WISH I HAD LIPS LIKE THAT!
I HATE MINE. THEY'RE WAY TOO THIN.
WHY DON'T YOU JUST PUT LIP LINER OUTSIDE YOUR LIP LINE, THEN FILL IT IN WITH LIPSTICK?

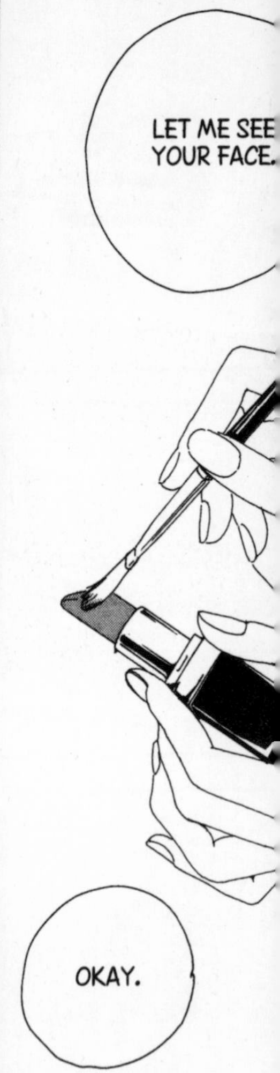
LET ME SEE YOUR FACE.
OKAY.

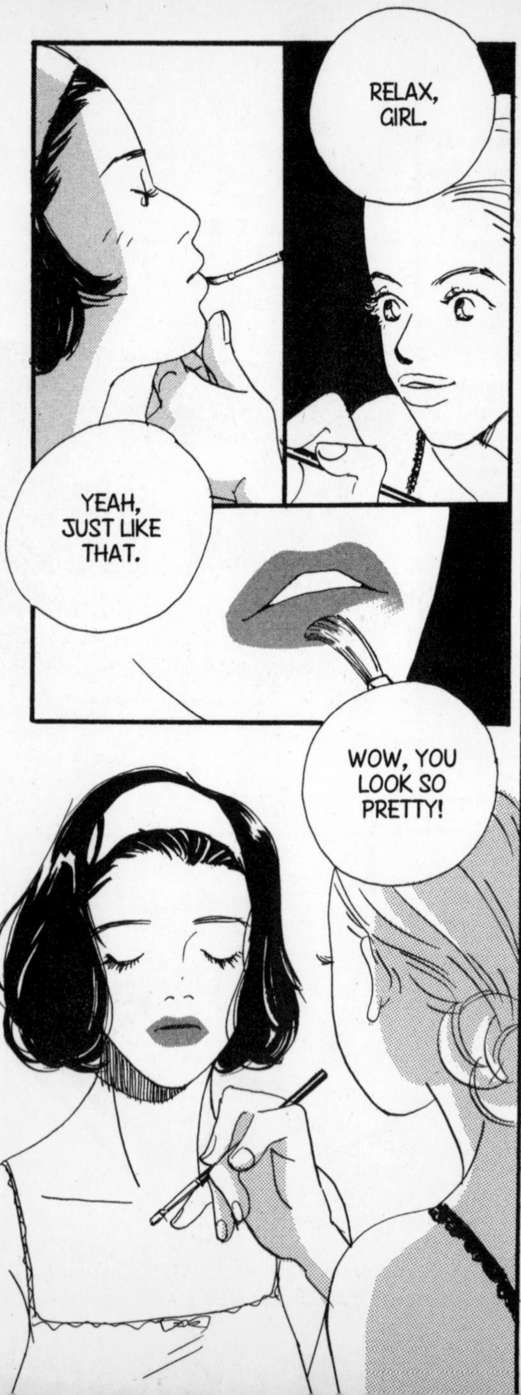
RELAX, GIRL.
YEAH, JUST LIKE THAT.
WOW, YOU LOOK SO PRETTY!

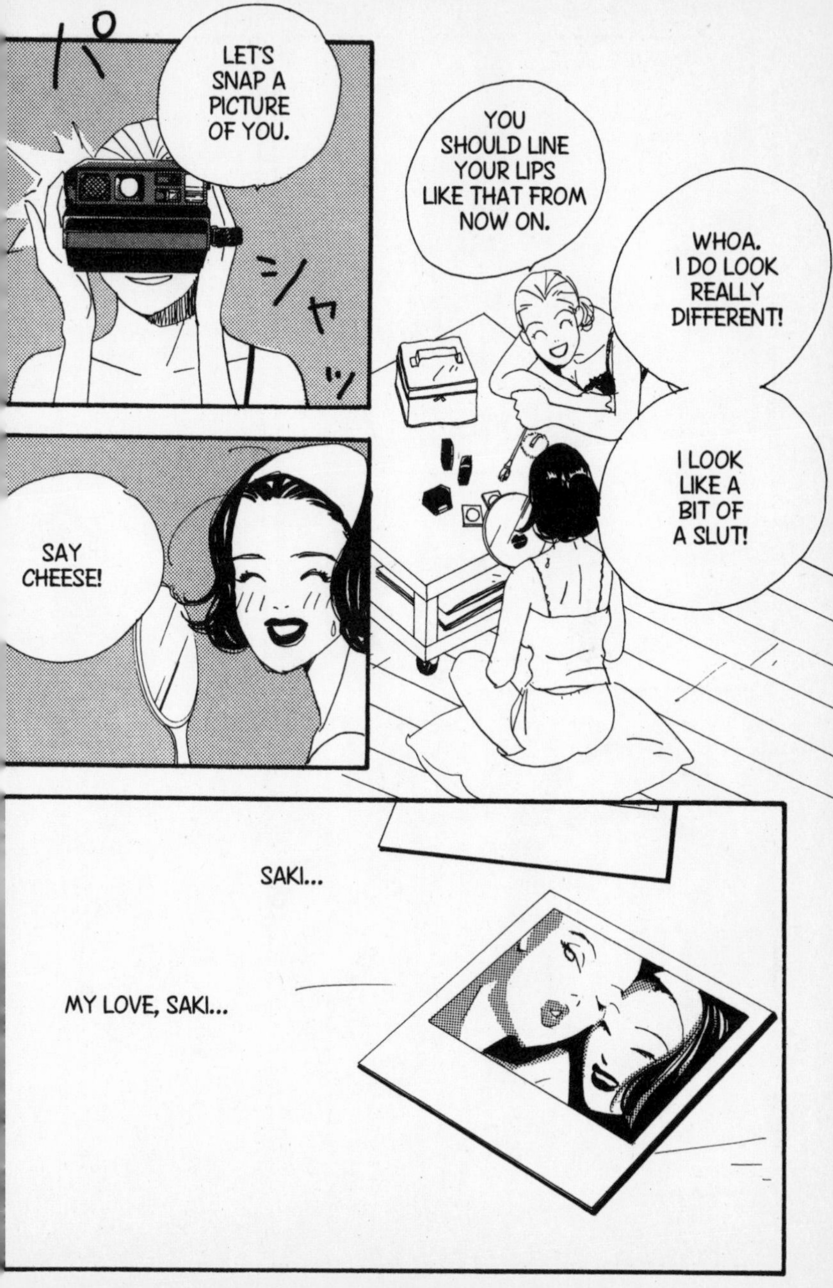
YOU SHOULD LINE YOUR LIPS LIKE THAT FROM NOW ON.
WHOA. I DO LOOK REALLY DIFFERENT!
I LOOK LIKE A BIT OF A SLUT!
LET'S SNAP A PICTURE OF YOU.
パ
シャッ
SAY CHEESE!
SAKI...
MY LOVE, SAKI...

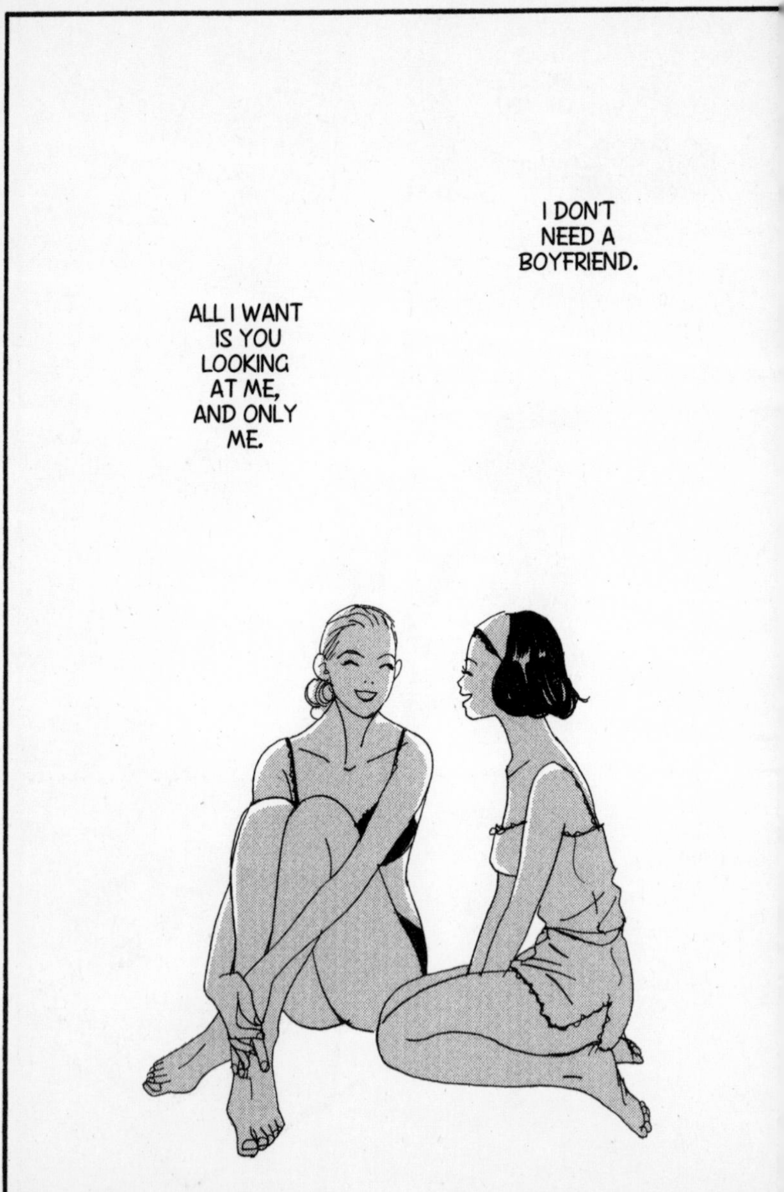
I DON'T NEED A BOYFRIEND.
ALL I WANT IS YOU LOOKING AT ME, AND ONLY ME.

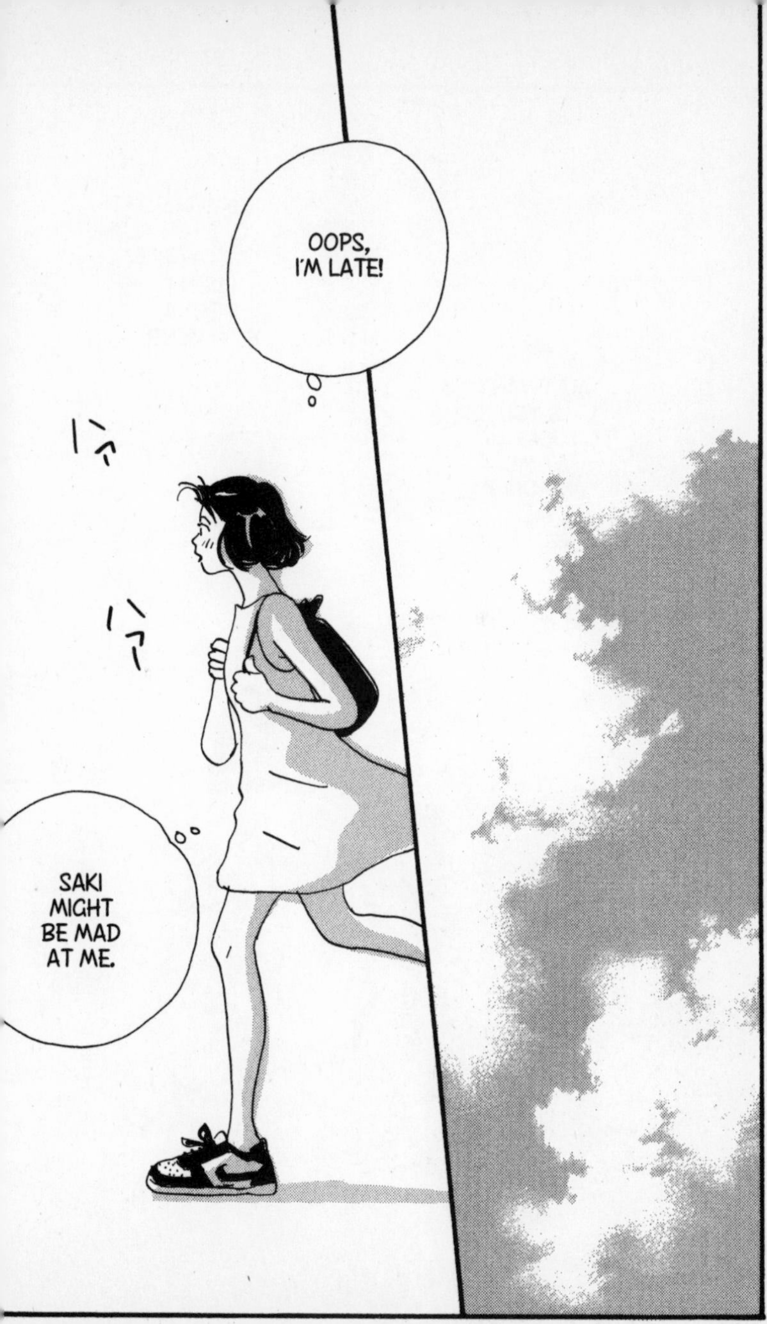
OOPS, I'M LATE!
ハァ
ハァ
SAKI MIGHT BE MAD AT ME.

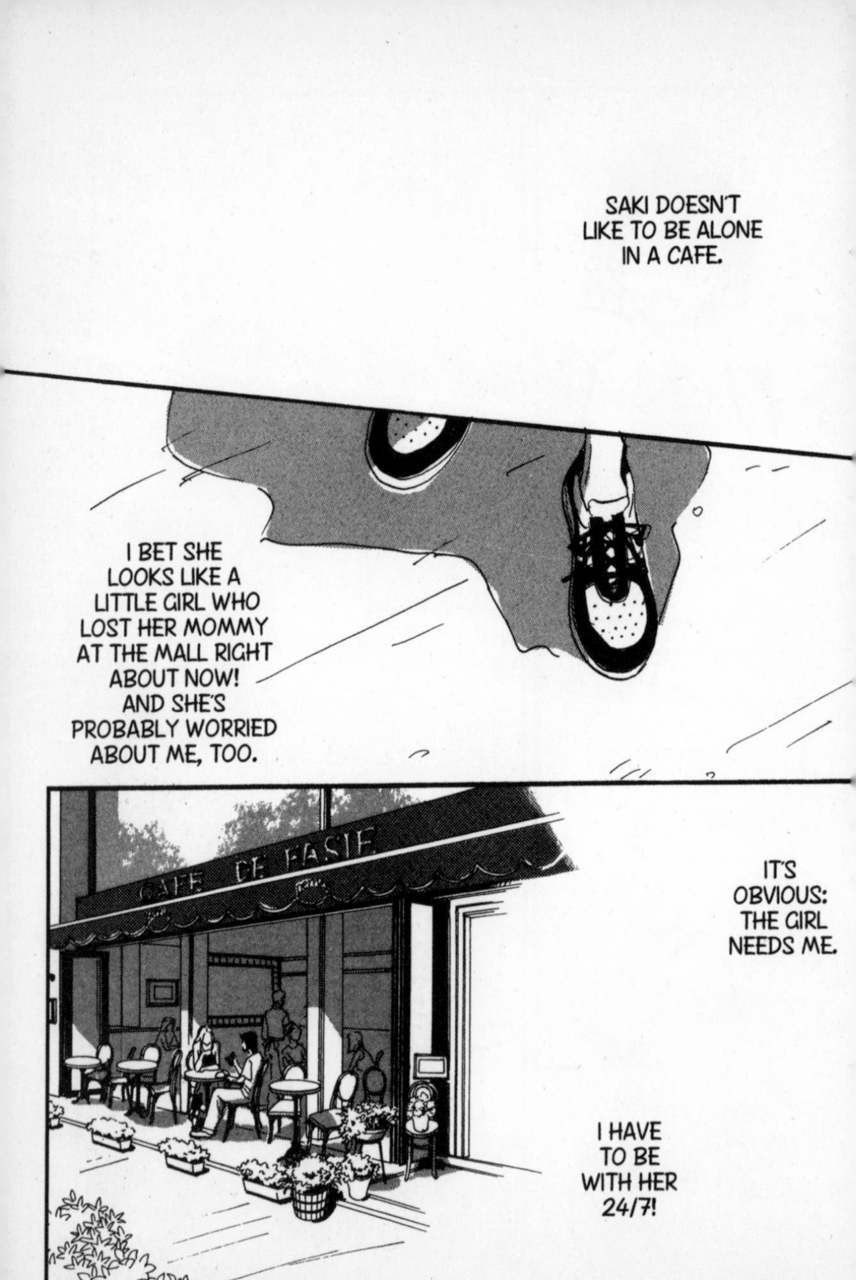
SAKI DOESN'T LIKE TO BE ALONE IN A CAFE.
I BET SHE LOOKS LIKE A LITTLE GIRL WHO LOST HER MOMMY AT THE MALL RIGHT ABOUT NOW! AND SHE'S PROBABLY WORRIED ABOUT ME, TOO.
IT'S OBVIOUS: THE GIRL NEEDS ME.
I HAVE TO BE WITH HER 24/7!

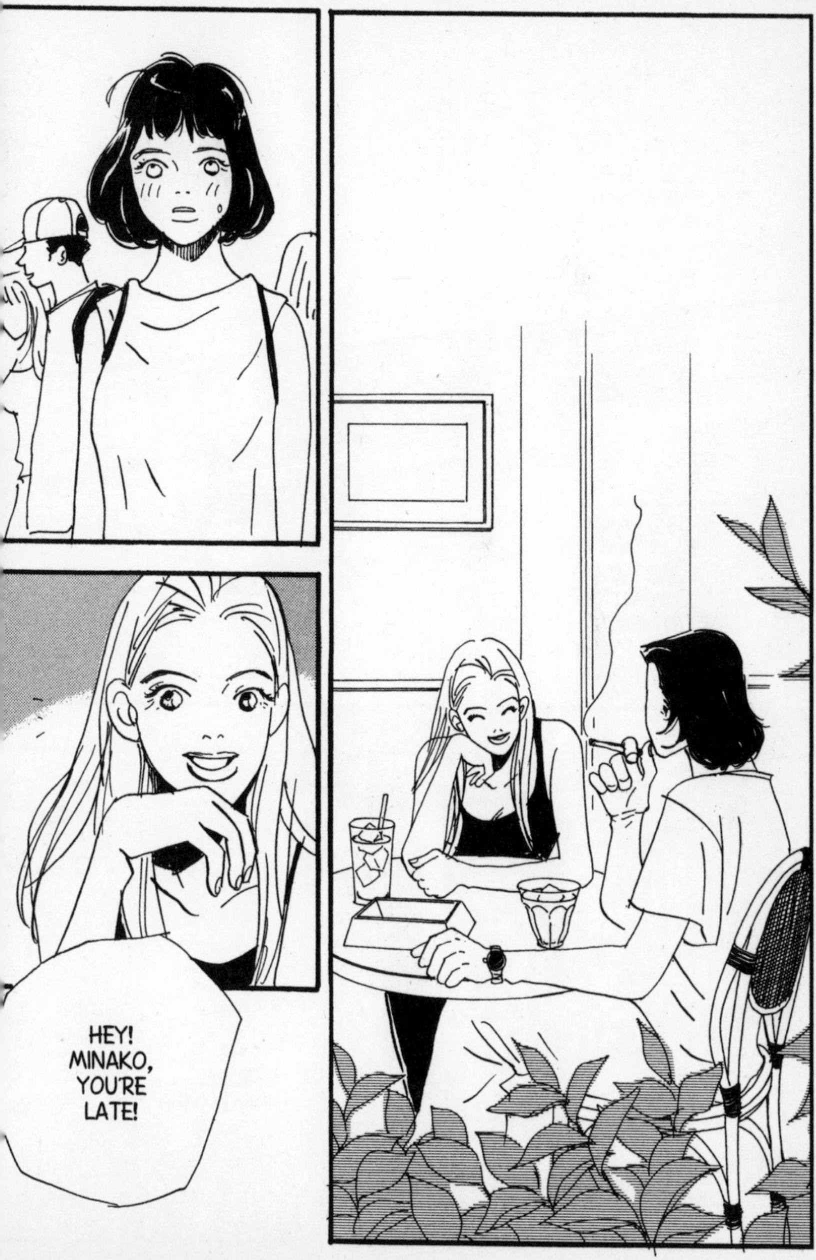
HEY! MINAKO, YOU'RE LATE!

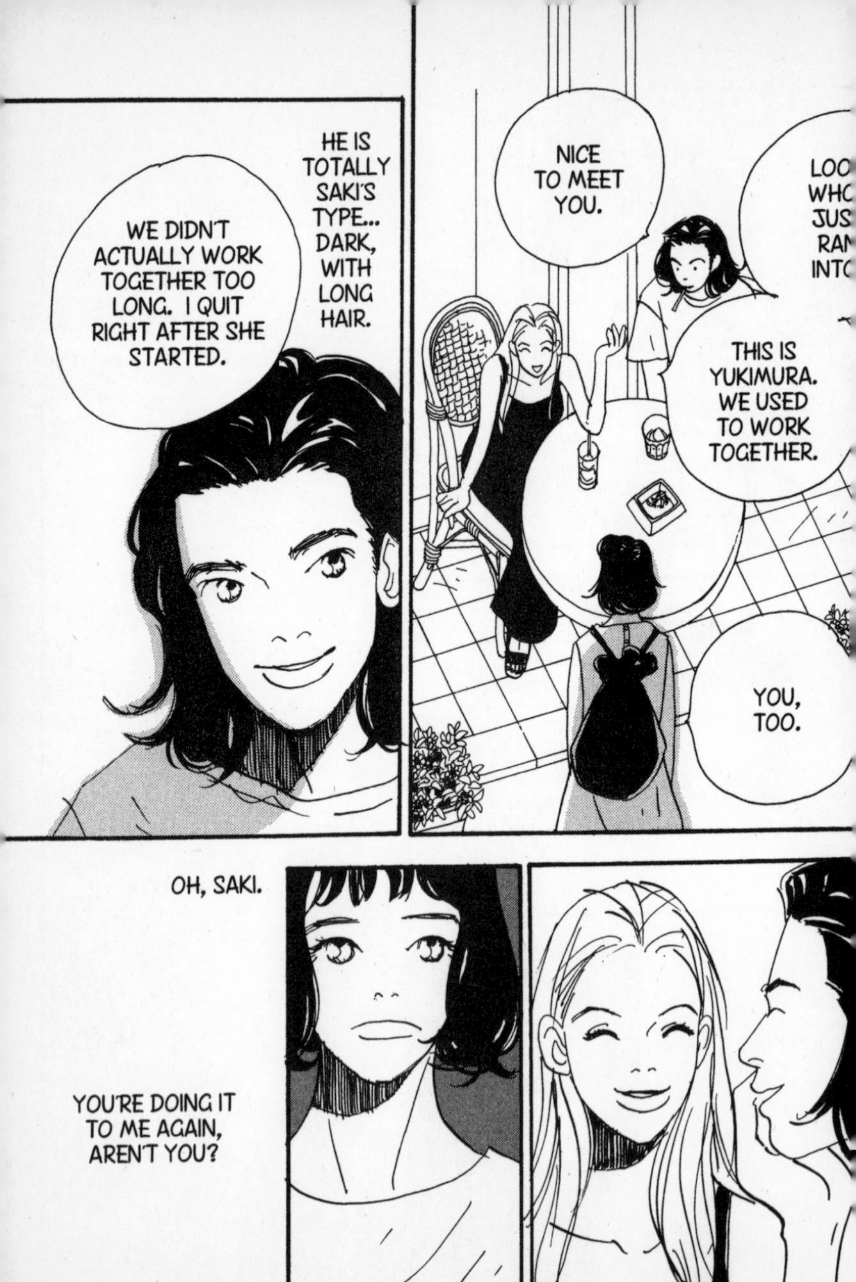
LOO WHO JUS RAN INT
THIS IS YUKIMURA. WE USED TO WORK TOGETHER.
NICE TO MEET YOU.
YOU, TOO.
HE IS TOTALLY SAKI'S TYPE... DARK, WITH LONG HAIR.
WE DIDN'T ACTUALLY WORK TOGETHER TOO LONG. I QUIT RIGHT AFTER SHE STARTED.
OH, SAKI.
YOU'RE DOING IT TO ME AGAIN, AREN'T YOU?

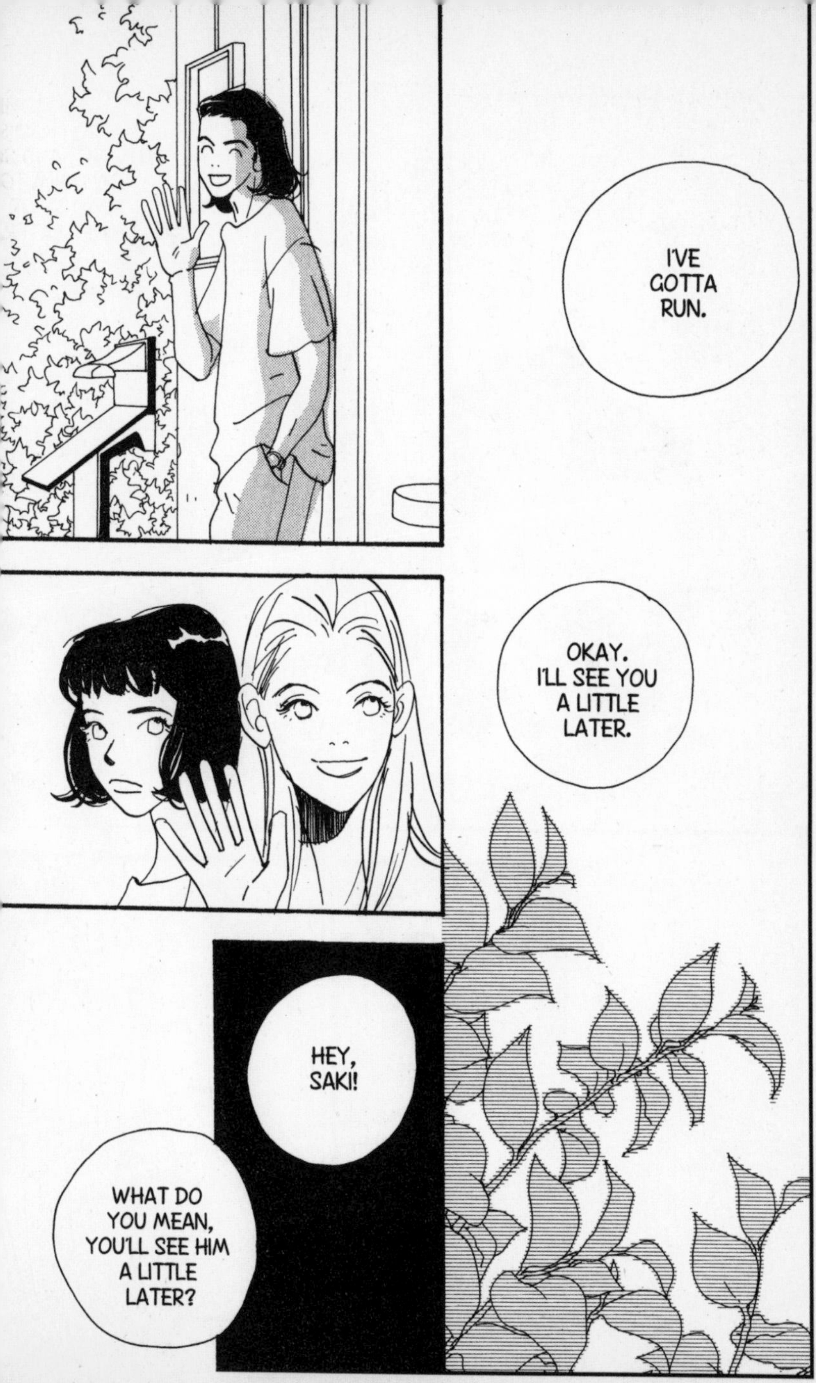
I'VE GOTTA RUN.
OKAY. I'LL SEE YOU A LITTLE LATER.
HEY, SAKI!
WHAT DO YOU MEAN, YOU'LL SEE HIM A LITTLE LATER?

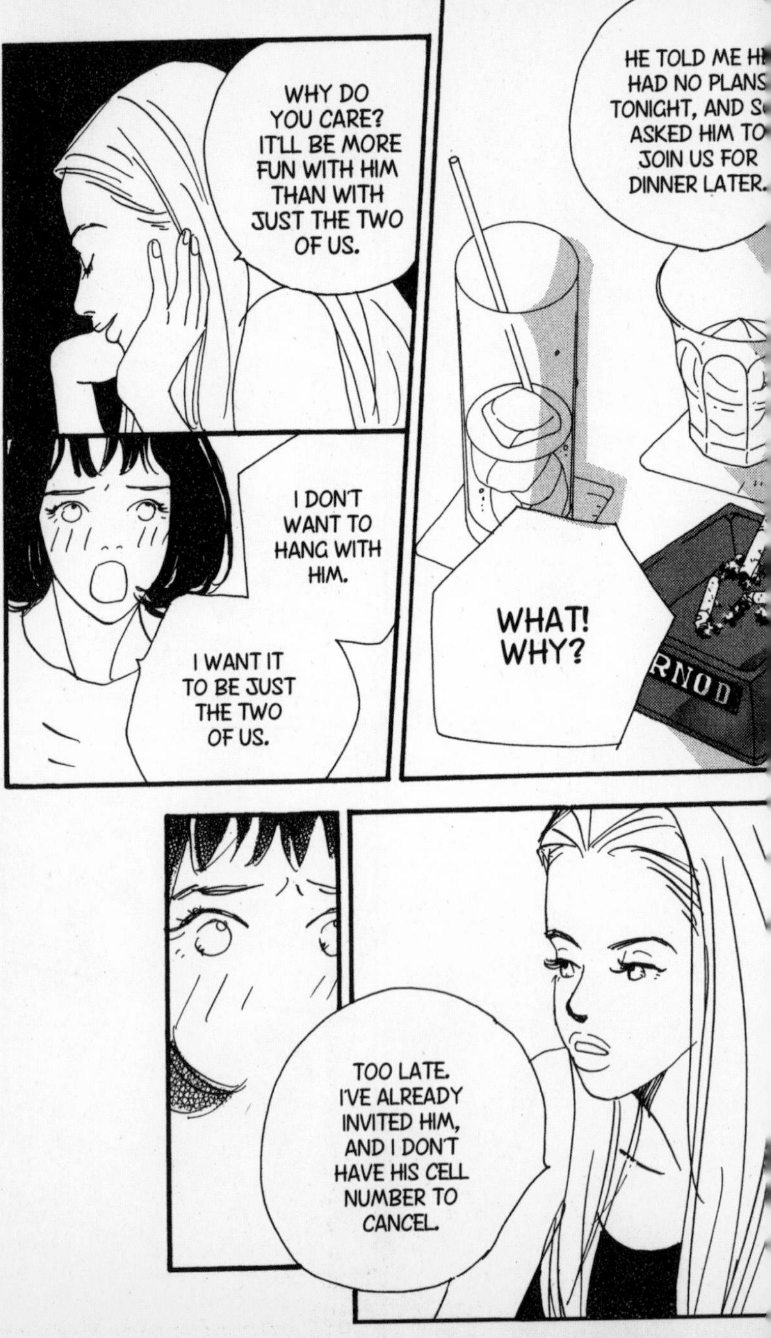
HE TOLD ME H HAD NO PLANS TONIGHT, AND S ASKED HIM TO JOIN US FOR DINNER LATER.
WHAT! WHY?
RNOD
WHY DO YOU CARE? IT'LL BE MORE FUN WITH HIM THAN WITH JUST THE TWO OF US.
I DON'T WANT TO HANG WITH HIM.
I WANT IT TO BE JUST THE TWO OF US.
TOO LATE. I'VE ALREADY INVITED HIM, AND I DON'T HAVE HIS CELL NUMBER TO CANCEL.

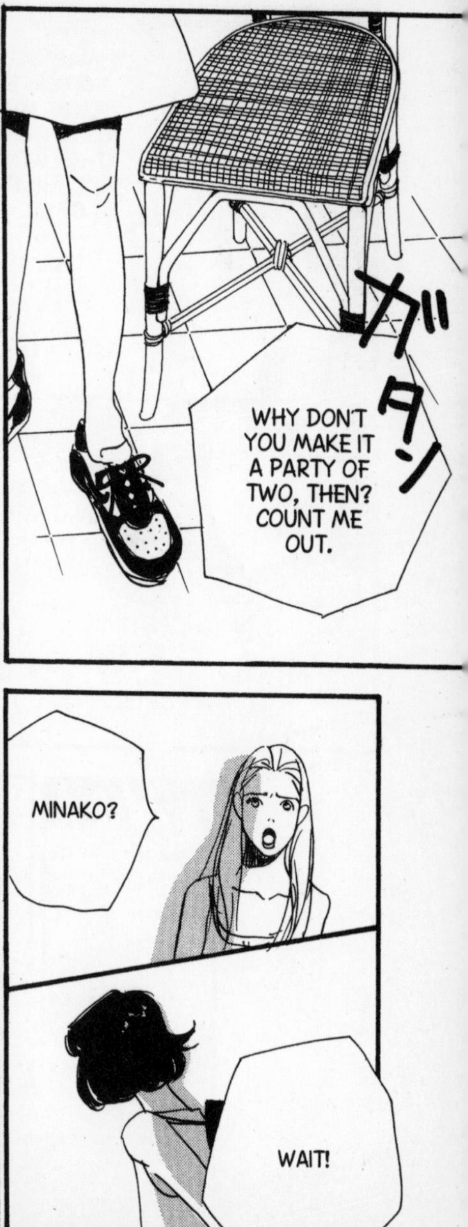
ガタン
WHY DON'T YOU MAKE IT A PARTY OF TWO, THEN? COUNT ME OUT.
MINAKO?
WAIT!

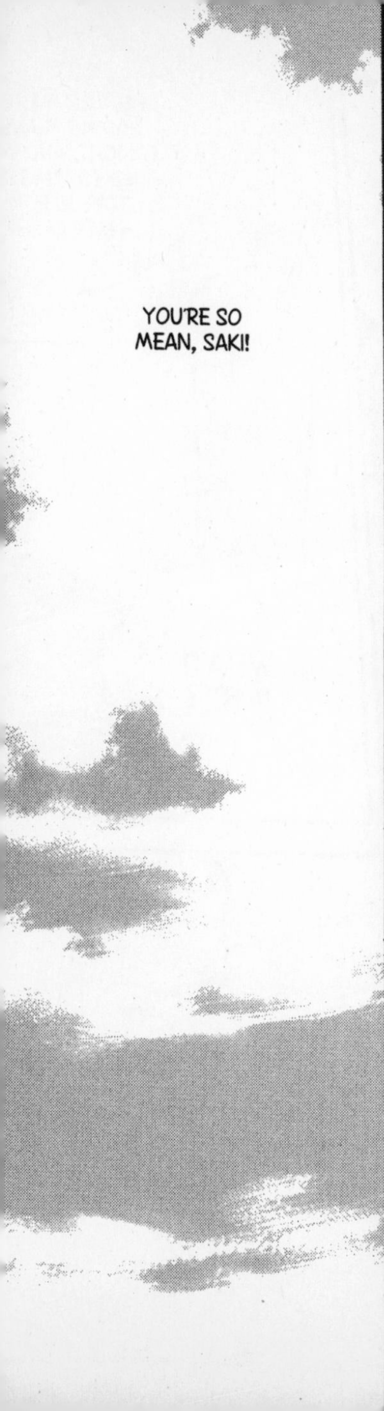
YOU'RE SO MEAN, SAKI!

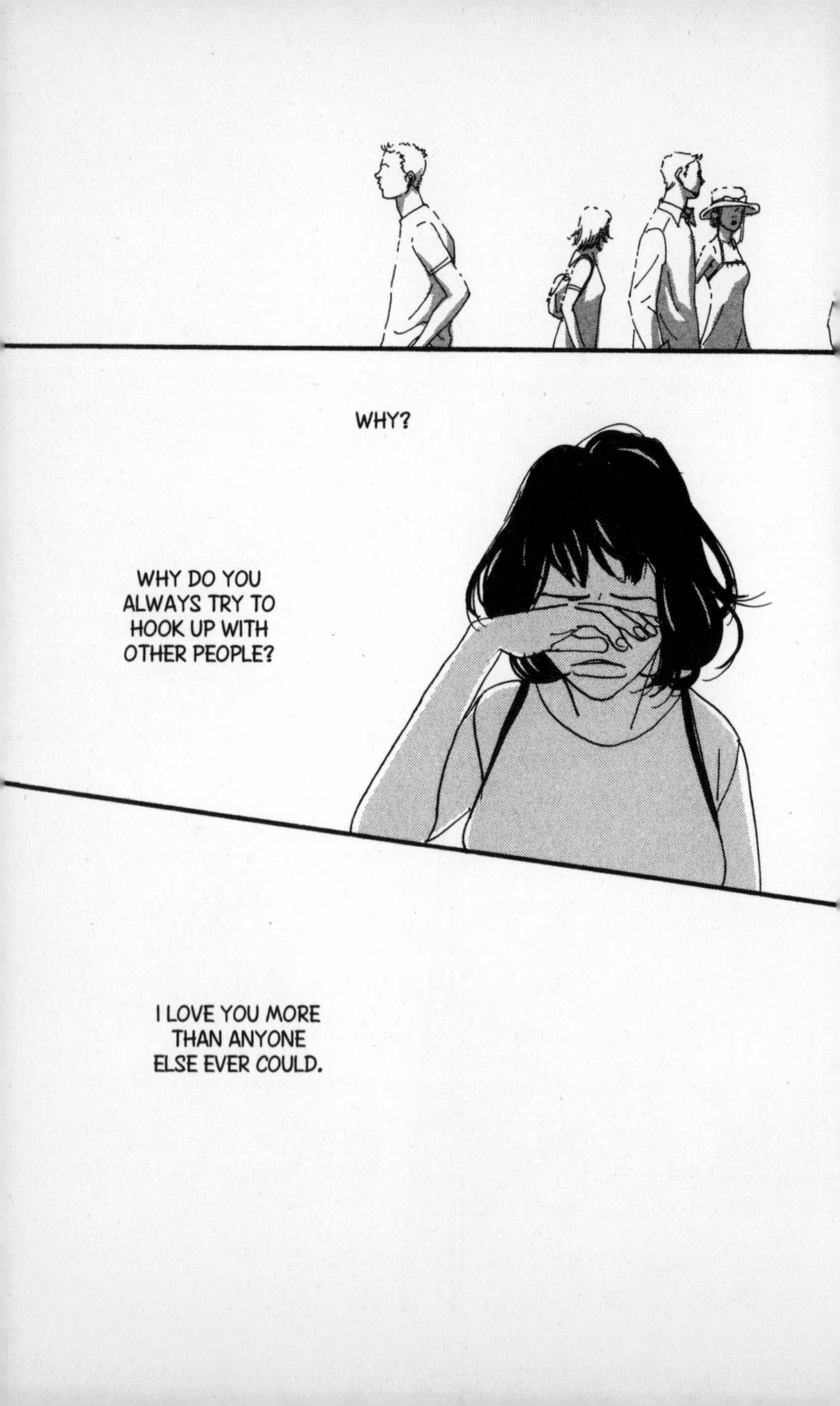
WHY?
WHY DO YOU ALWAYS TRY TO HOOK UP WITH OTHER PEOPLE?
I LOVE YOU MORE THAN ANYONE ELSE EVER COULD.

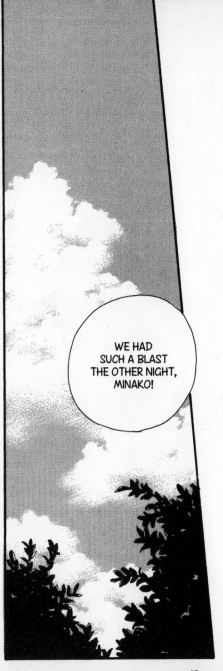

WHY NOT ME?

WE HAD
SUCH A BLAST
THE OTHER NIGHT,
MINAKO!

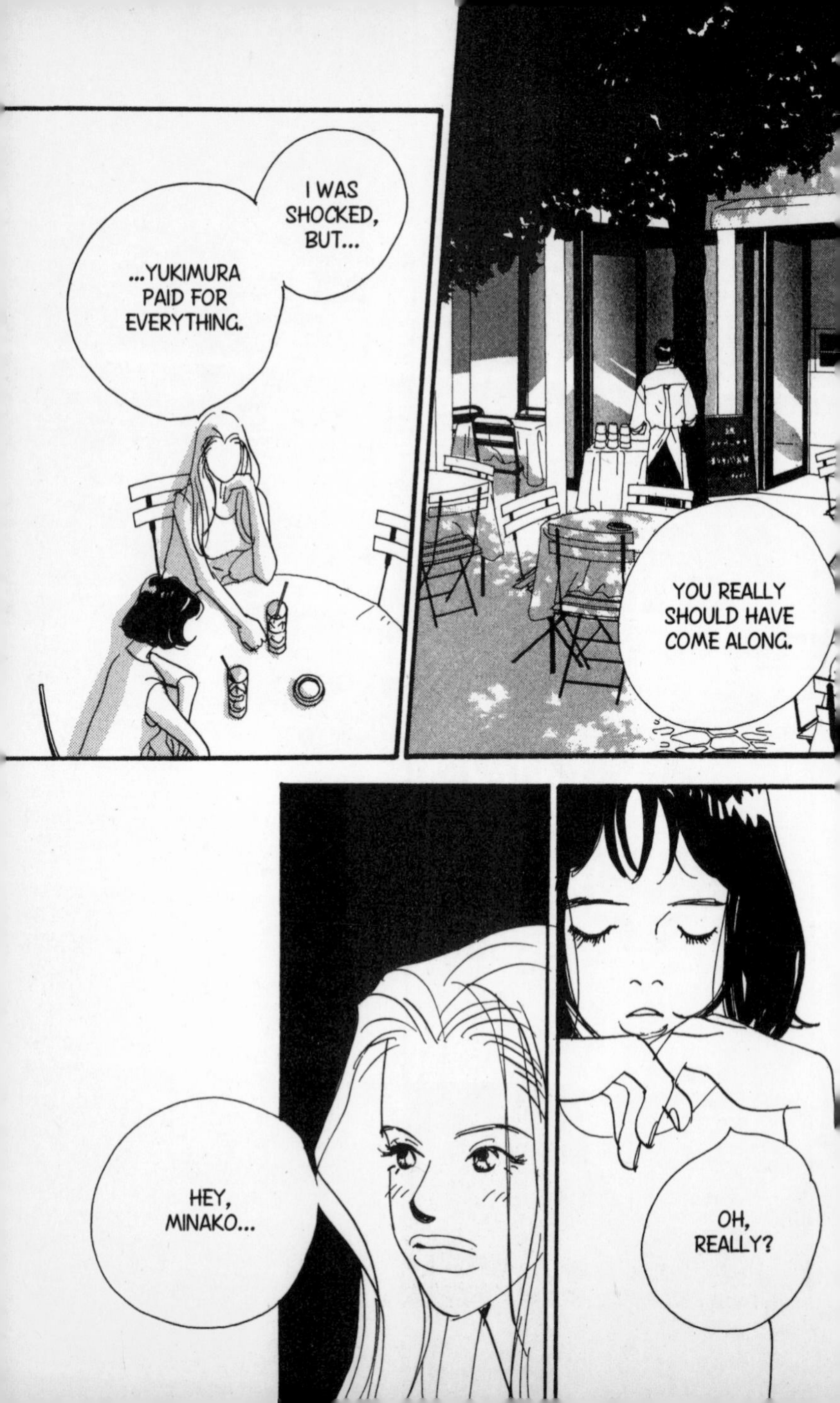
YOU REALLY SHOULD HAVE COME ALONG.
I WAS SHOCKED, BUT...
...YUKIMURA PAID FOR EVERYTHING.
OH, REALLY?
HEY, MINAKO...

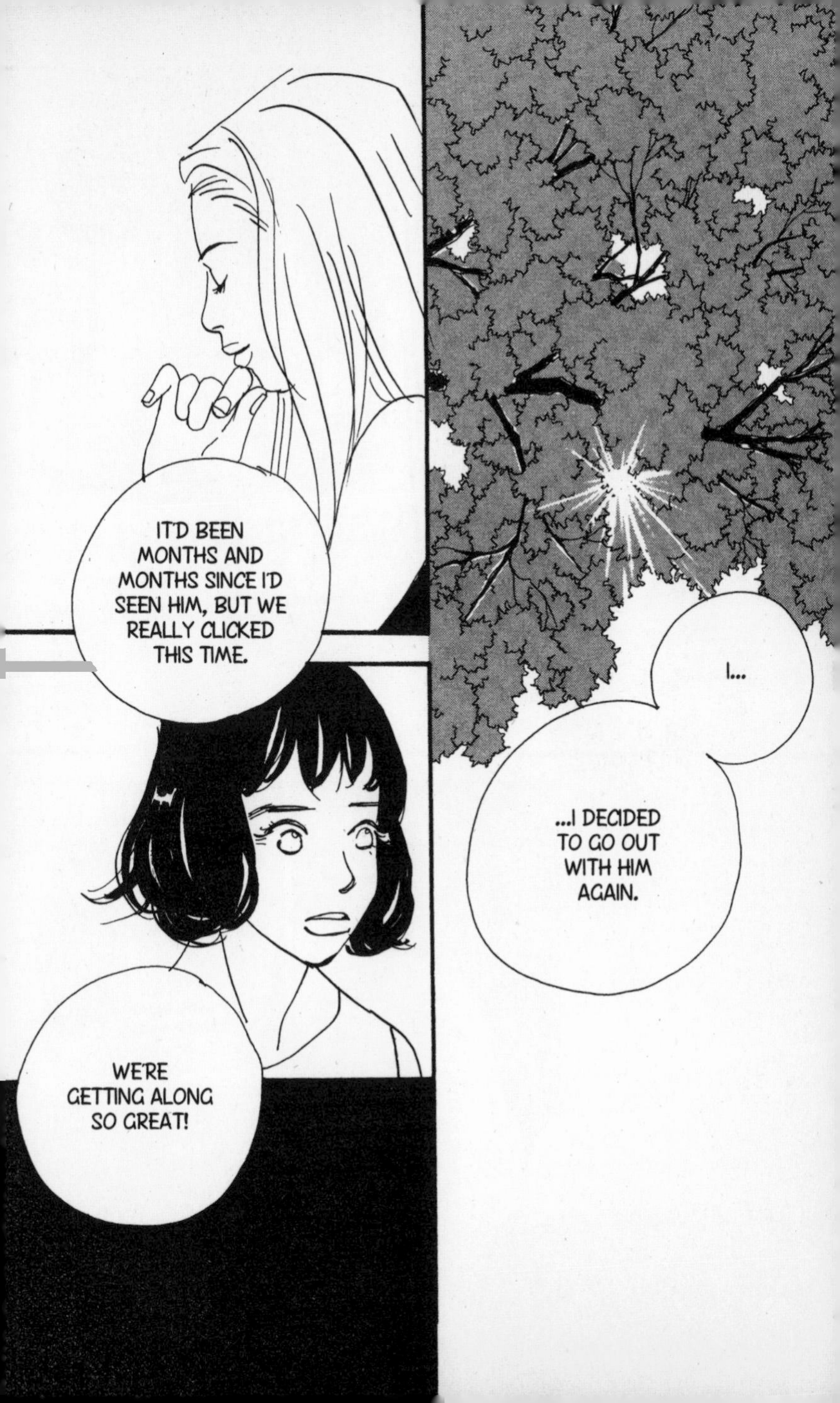
I...
...I DECIDED TO GO OUT WITH HIM AGAIN.
IT'D BEEN MONTHS AND MONTHS SINCE I'D SEEN HIM, BUT WE REALLY CLICKED THIS TIME.
WE'RE GETTING ALONG SO GREAT!

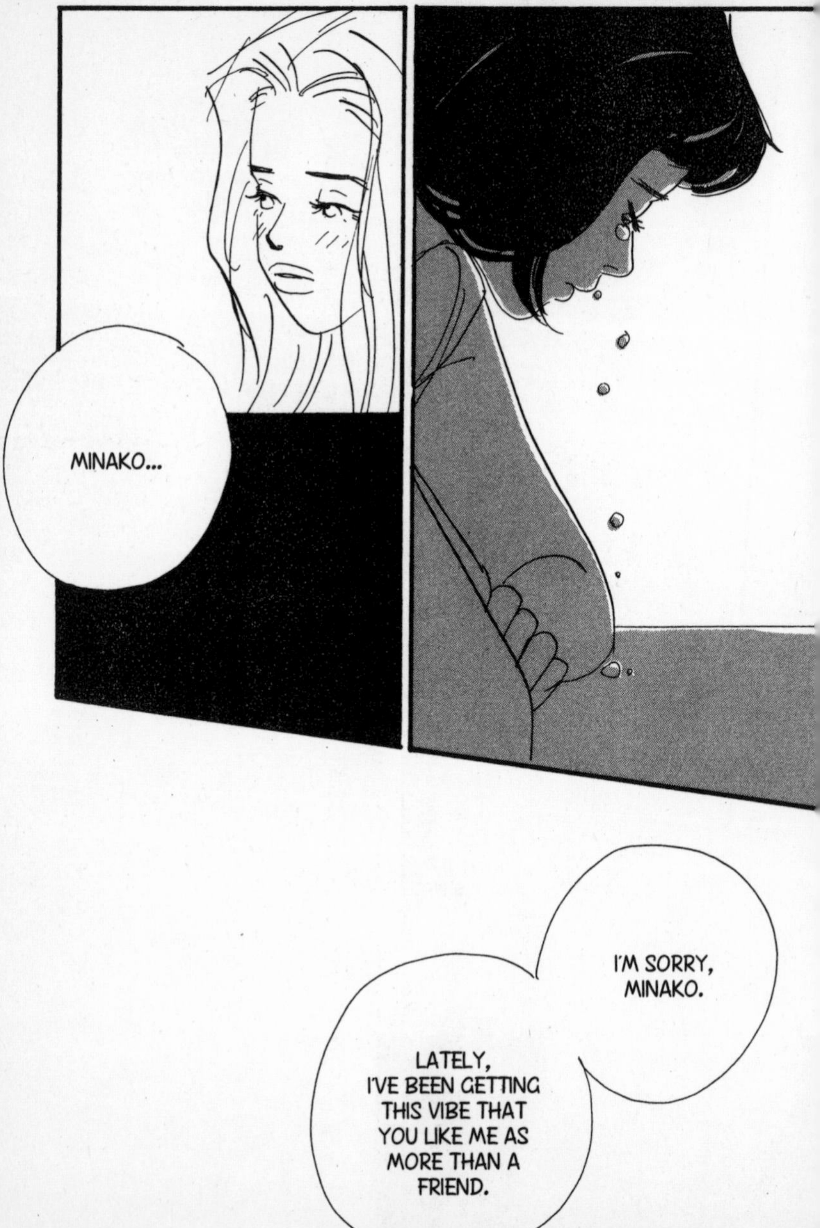
MINAKO...
I'M SORRY, MINAKO.
LATELY, I'VE BEEN GETTING THIS VIBE THAT YOU LIKE ME AS MORE THAN A FRIEND.

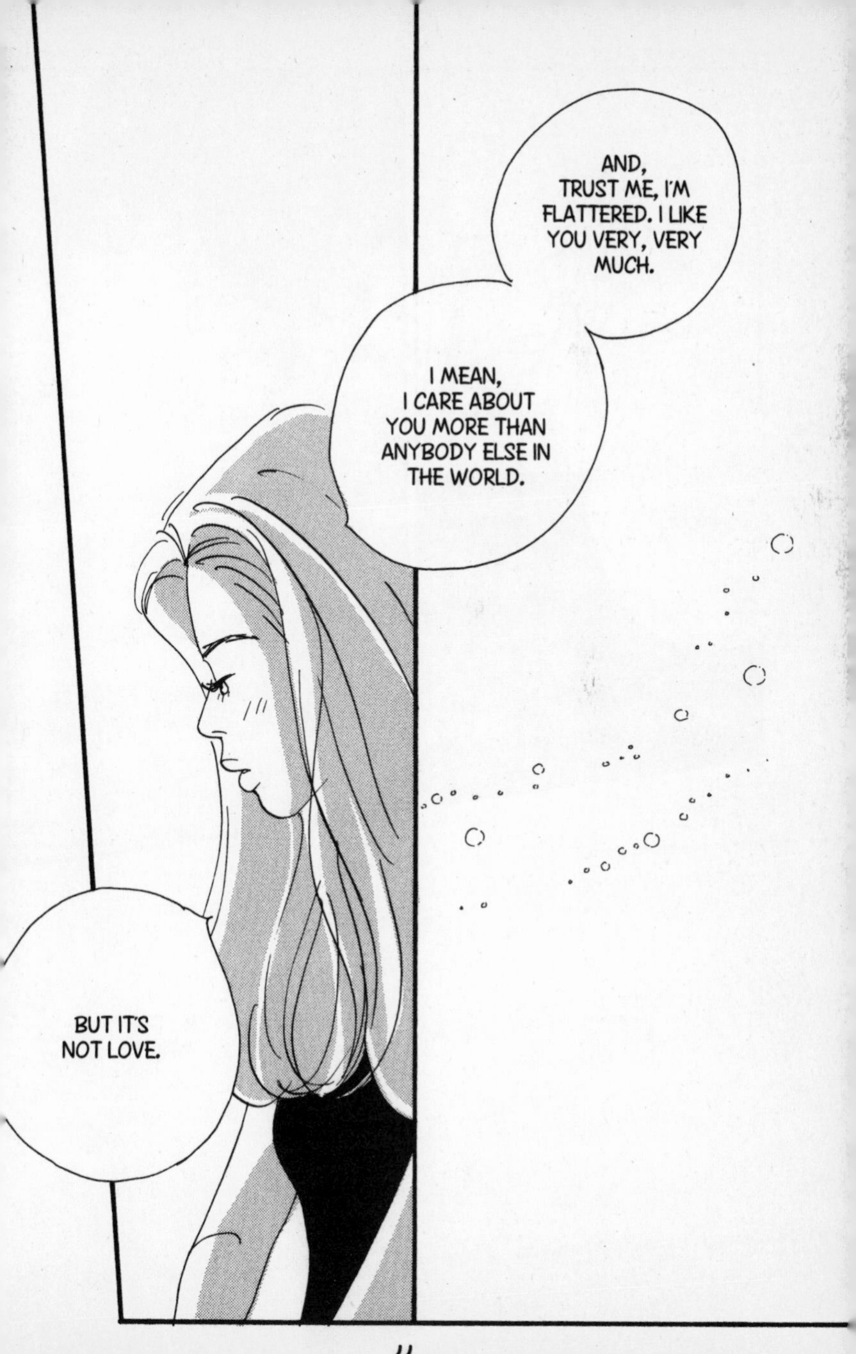
AND, TRUST ME, I'M FLATTERED. I LIKE YOU VERY, VERY MUCH.
I MEAN, I CARE ABOUT YOU MORE THAN ANYBODY ELSE IN THE WORLD.
BUT IT'S NOT LOVE.

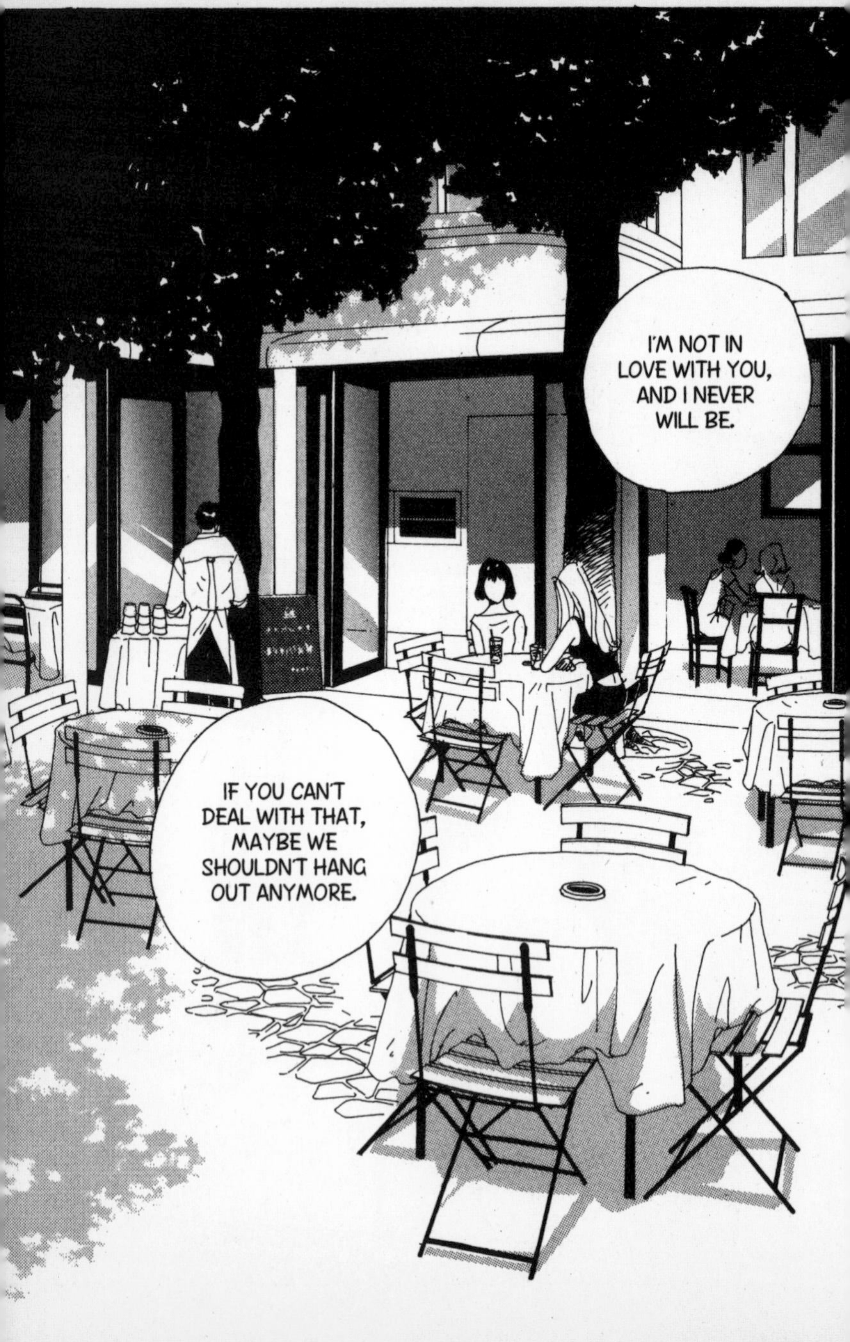
I'M NOT IN LOVE WITH YOU, AND I NEVER WILL BE.
IF YOU CAN'T DEAL WITH THAT, MAYBE WE SHOULDN'T HANG OUT ANYMORE.

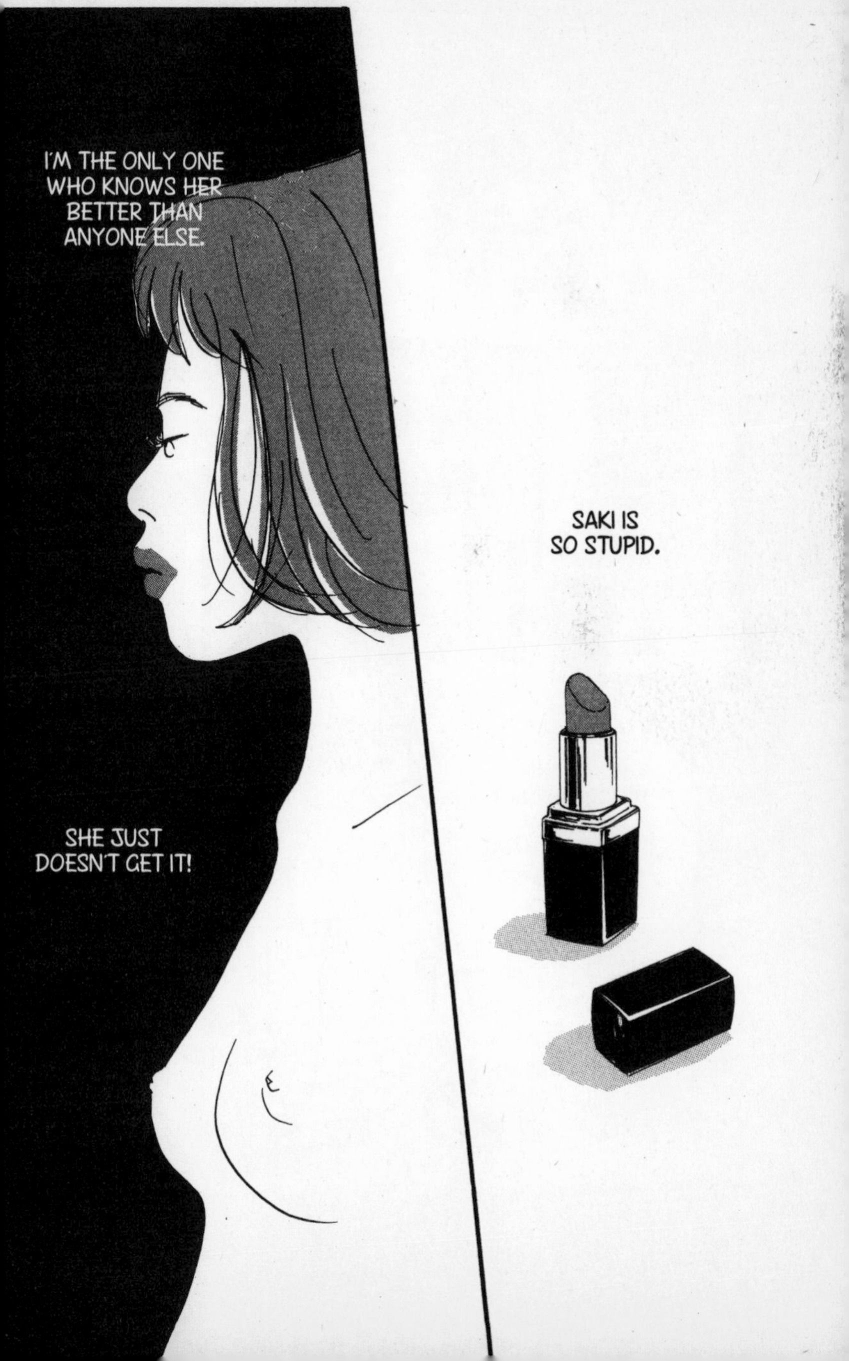
SAKI IS SO STUPID.
I'M THE ONLY ONE WHO KNOWS HER BETTER THAN ANYONE ELSE.
SHE JUST DOESN'T GET IT!

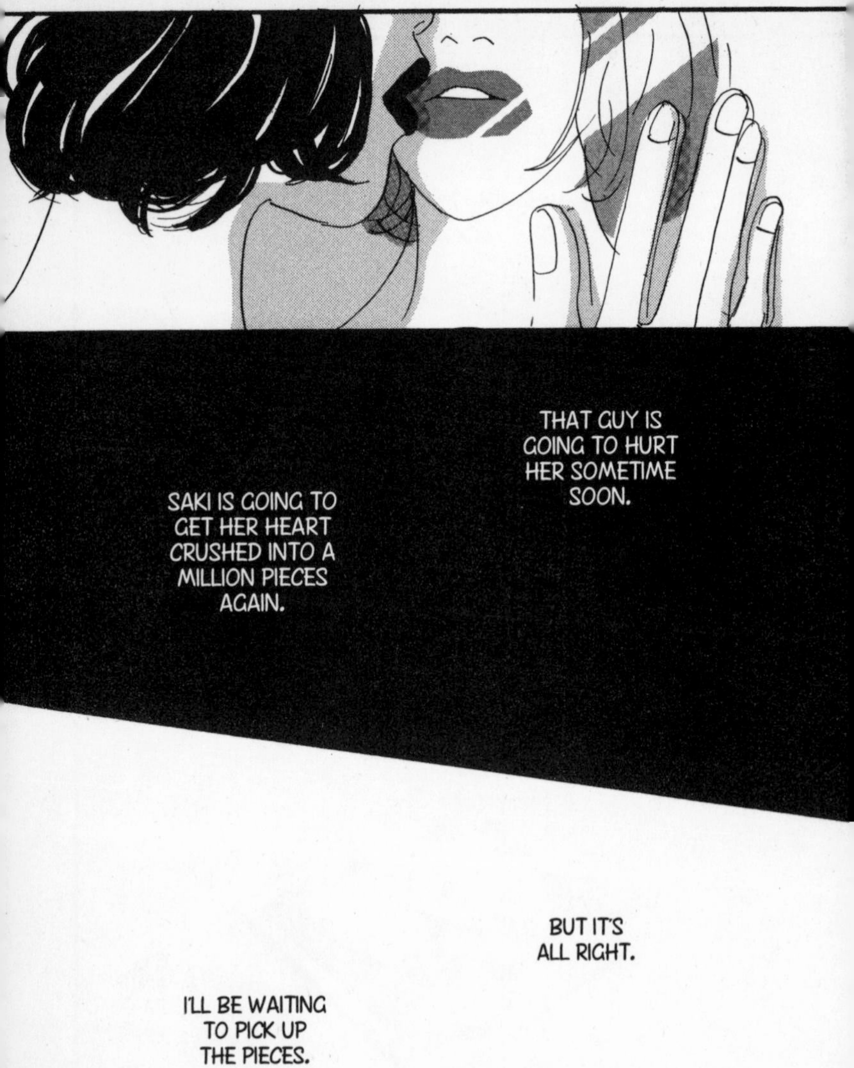
THAT GUY IS GOING TO HURT HER SOMETIME SOON.
SAKI IS GOING TO GET HER HEART CRUSHED INTO A MILLION PIECES AGAIN.
BUT IT'S ALL RIGHT.
I'LL BE WAITING TO PICK UP THE PIECES.

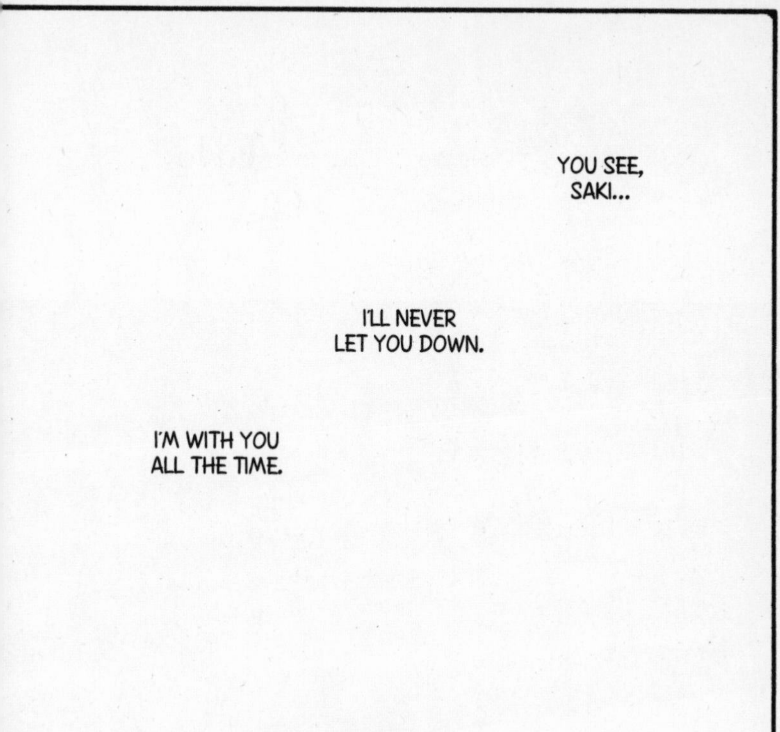

YOU SEE,
SAKI...

I'LL NEVER
LET YOU DOWN.

I'M WITH YOU
ALL THE TIME.

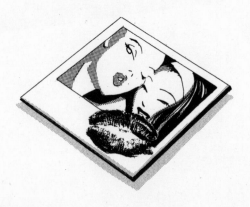

between the sheets

chapter 3

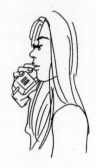

I WISH SAKI NEVER
DISCOVERED MY
TRUE FEELINGS.

IF SHE DIDN'T, I
COULD BE WITH
HER EVEN NOW...

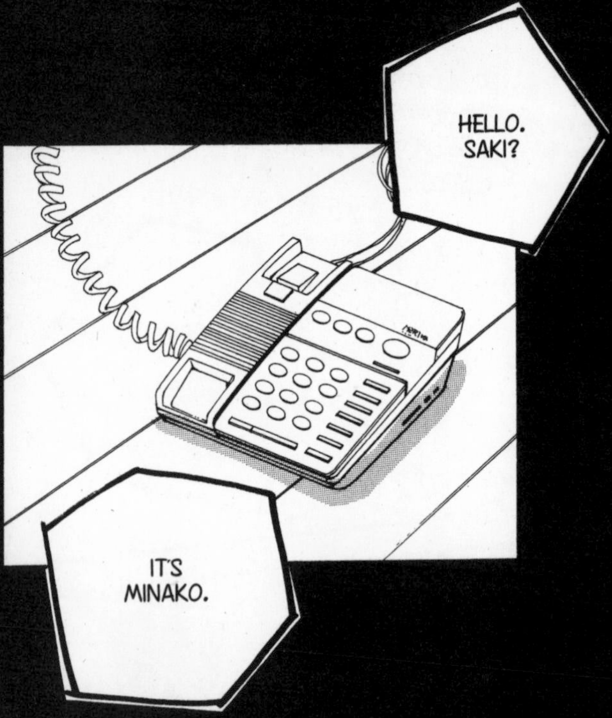
HELLO. SAKI?
IT'S MINAKO.

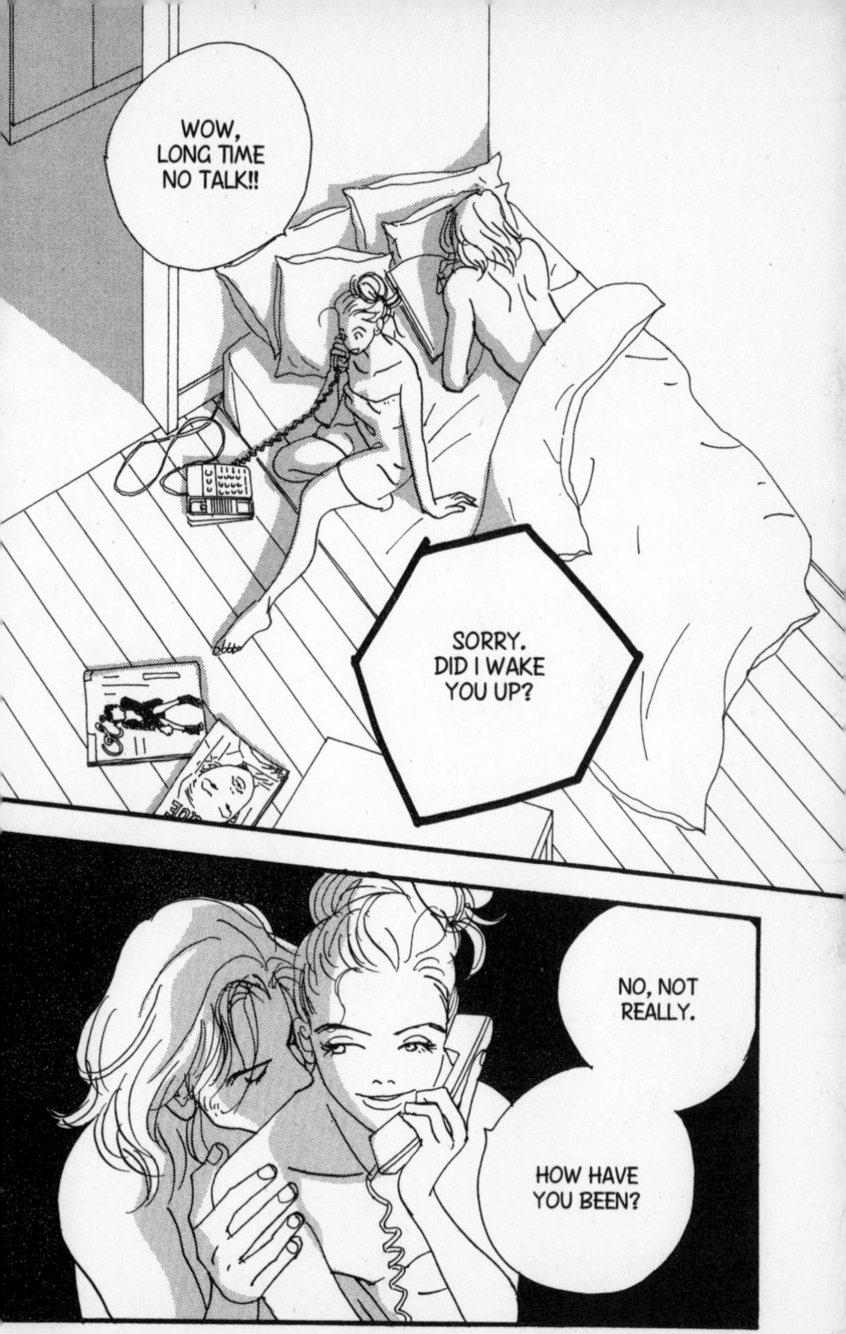
WOW, LONG TIME NO TALK!!
SORRY. DID I WAKE YOU UP?
NO, NOT REALLY.
HOW HAVE YOU BEEN?

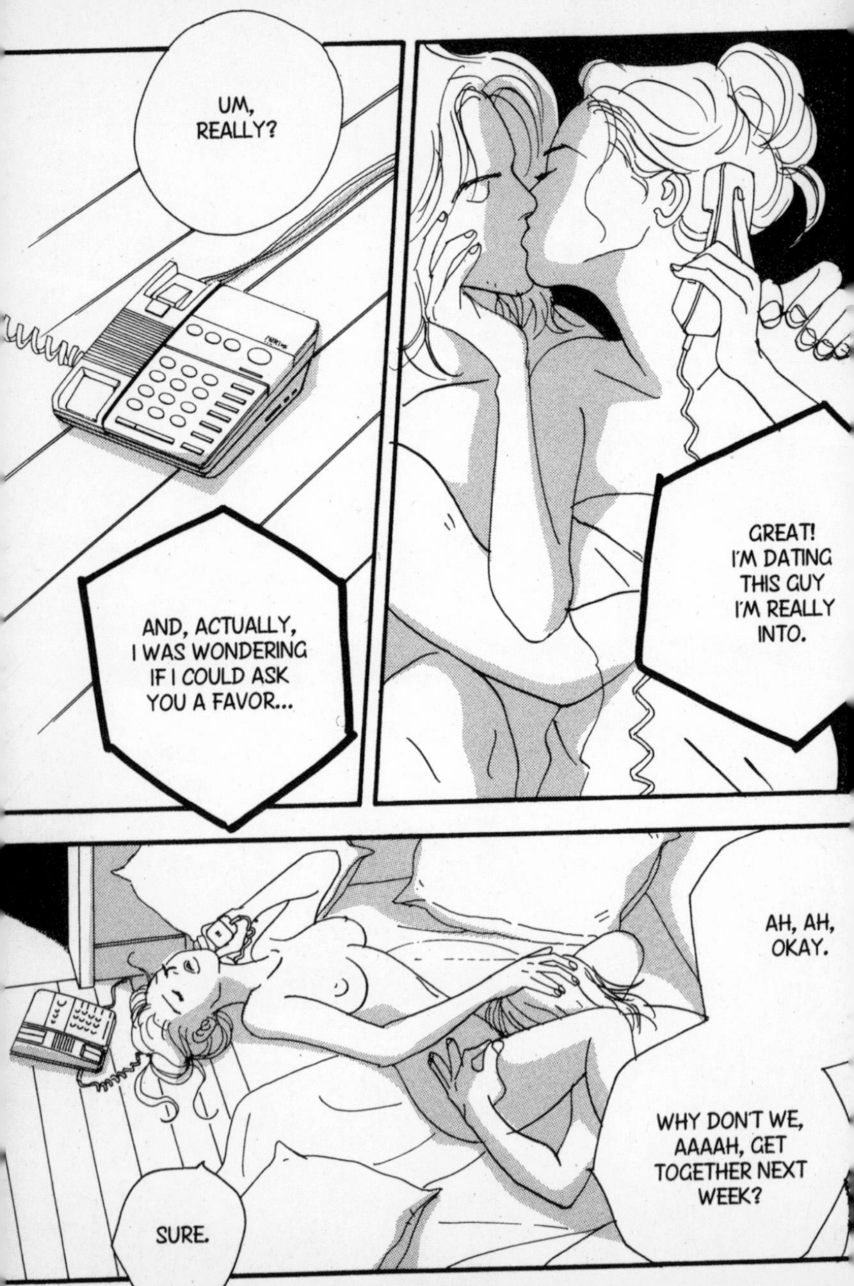
GREAT! I'M DATING THIS GUY I'M REALLY INTO.
UM, REALLY?
AND, ACTUALLY, I WAS WONDERING IF I COULD ASK YOU A FAVOR...
AH, AH, OKAY.
WHY DON'T WE, AAAAH, GET TOGETHER NEXT WEEK?
SURE.

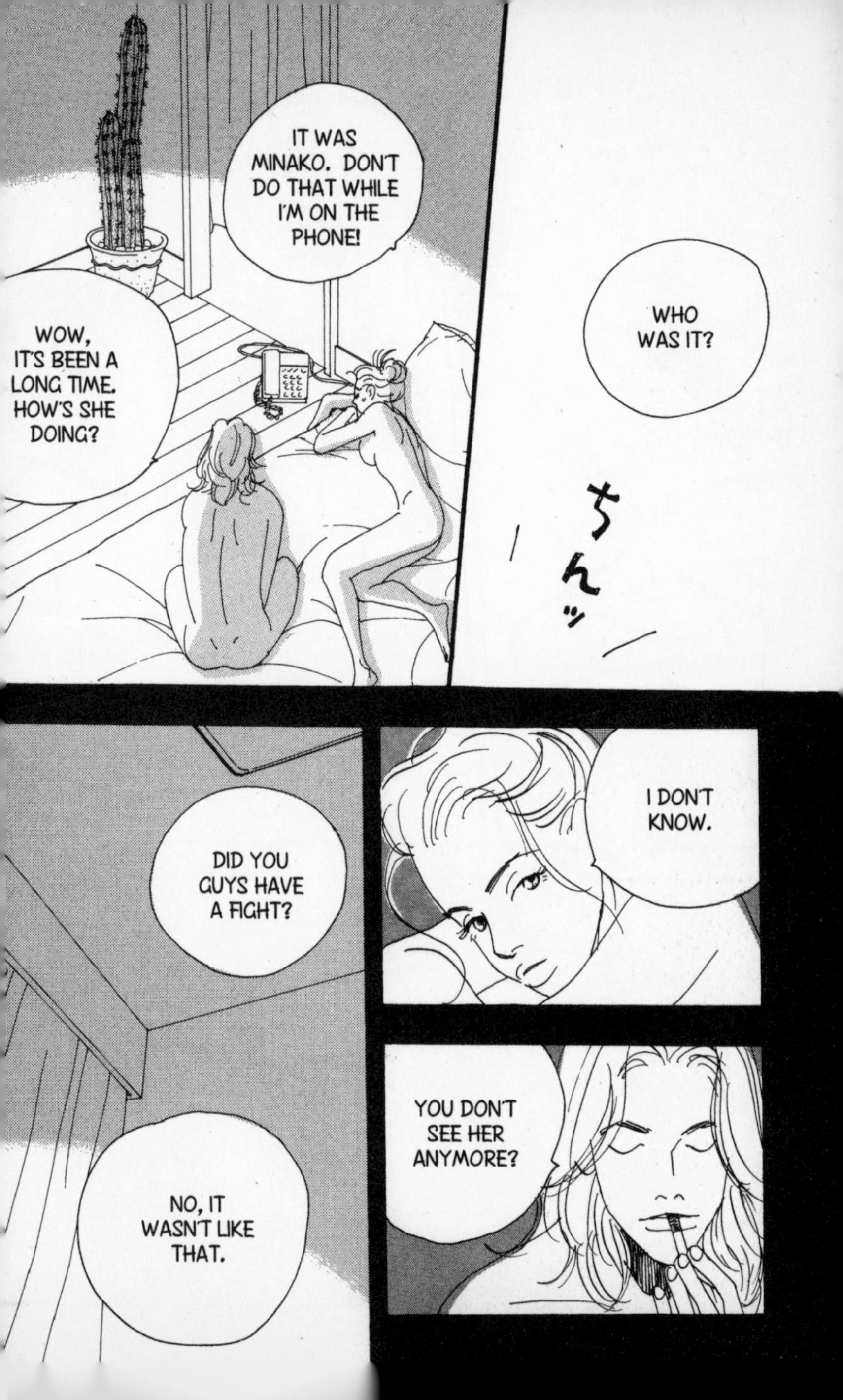

WHO WAS IT?
ちんッ
IT WAS MINAKO. DON'T DO THAT WHILE I'M ON THE PHONE!
WOW, IT'S BEEN A LONG TIME. HOW'S SHE DOING?
I DON'T KNOW.
YOU DON'T SEE HER ANYMORE?
DID YOU GUYS HAVE A FIGHT?
NO, IT WASN'T LIKE THAT.

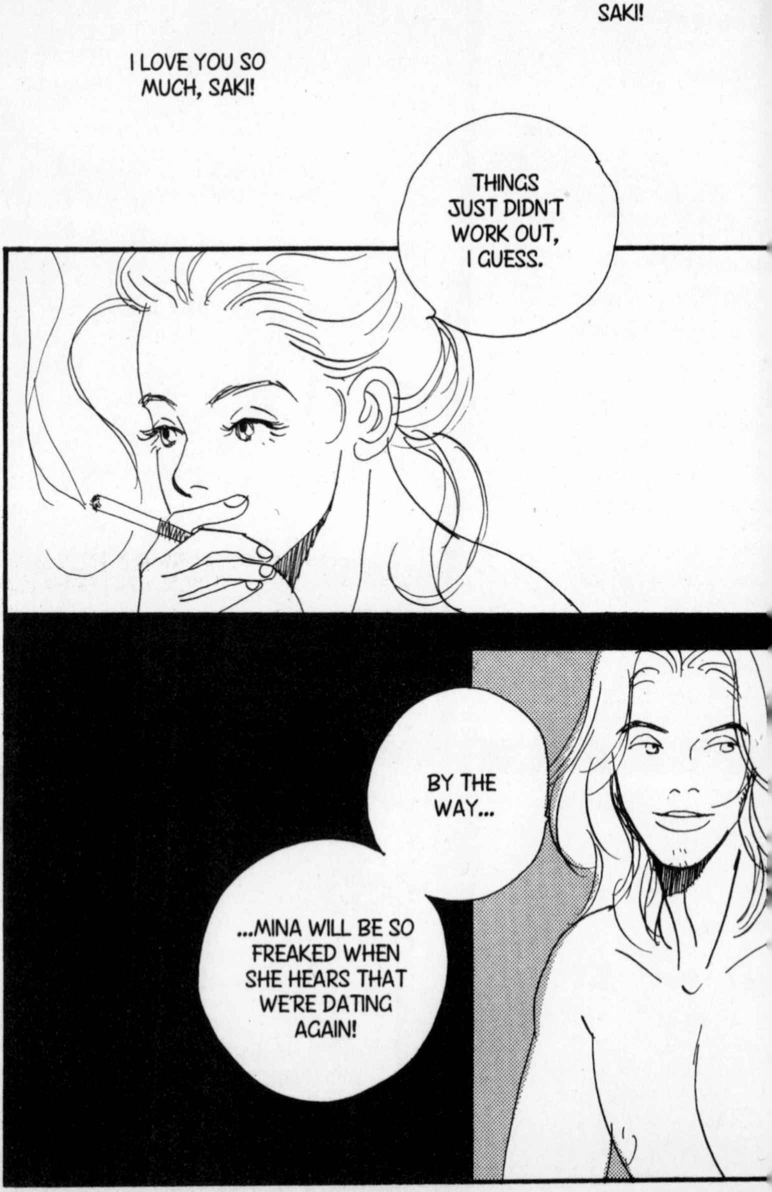
SAKI!
I LOVE YOU SO MUCH, SAKI!
THINGS JUST DIDN'T WORK OUT, I GUESS.
BY THE WAY...
...MINA WILL BE SO FREAKED WHEN SHE HEARS THAT WE'RE DATING AGAIN!

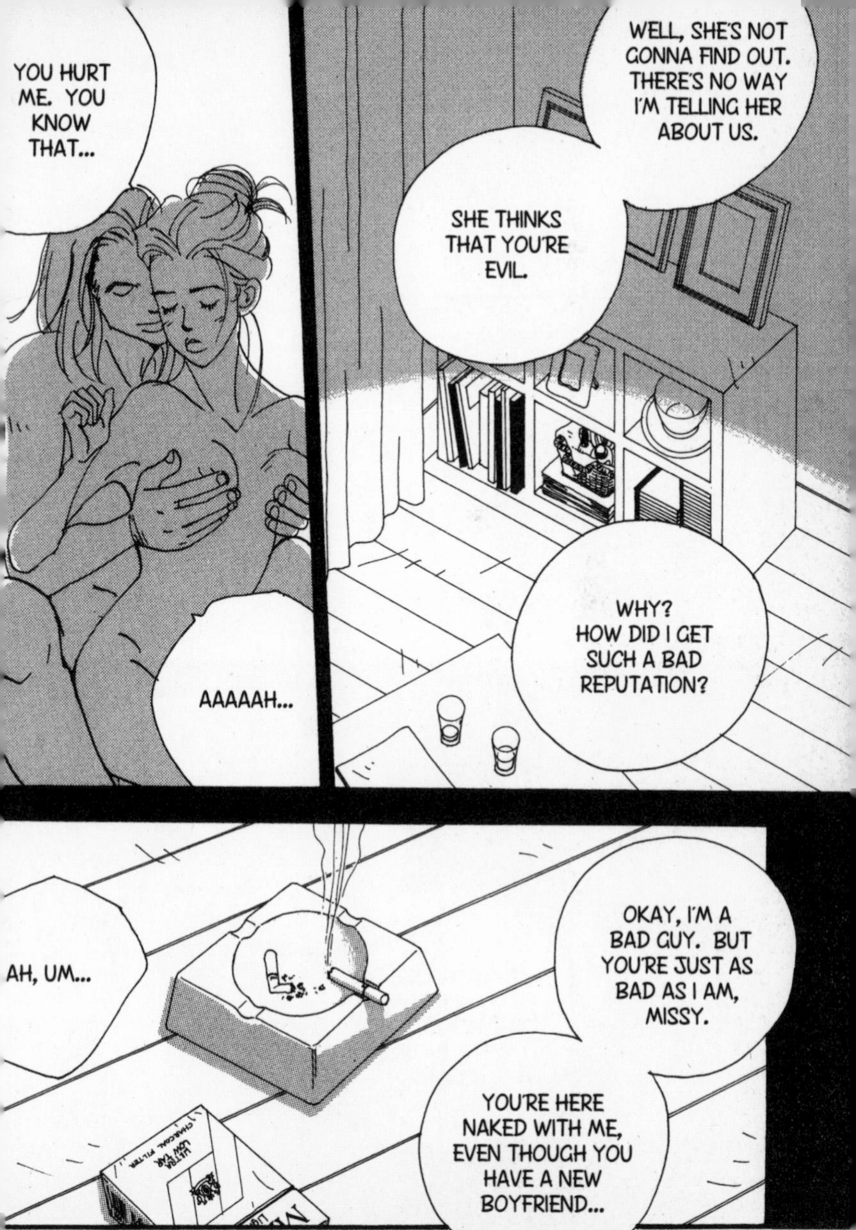
WELL, SHE'S NOT GONNA FIND OUT. THERE'S NO WAY I'M TELLING HER ABOUT US.
SHE THINKS THAT YOU'RE EVIL.
WHY? HOW DID I GET SUCH A BAD REPUTATION?
YOU HURT ME. YOU KNOW THAT...
AAAAAH...
OKAY, I'M A BAD GUY. BUT YOU'RE JUST AS BAD AS I AM, MISSY.
YOU'RE HERE NAKED WITH ME, EVEN THOUGH YOU HAVE A NEW BOYFRIEND...
AH, UM...

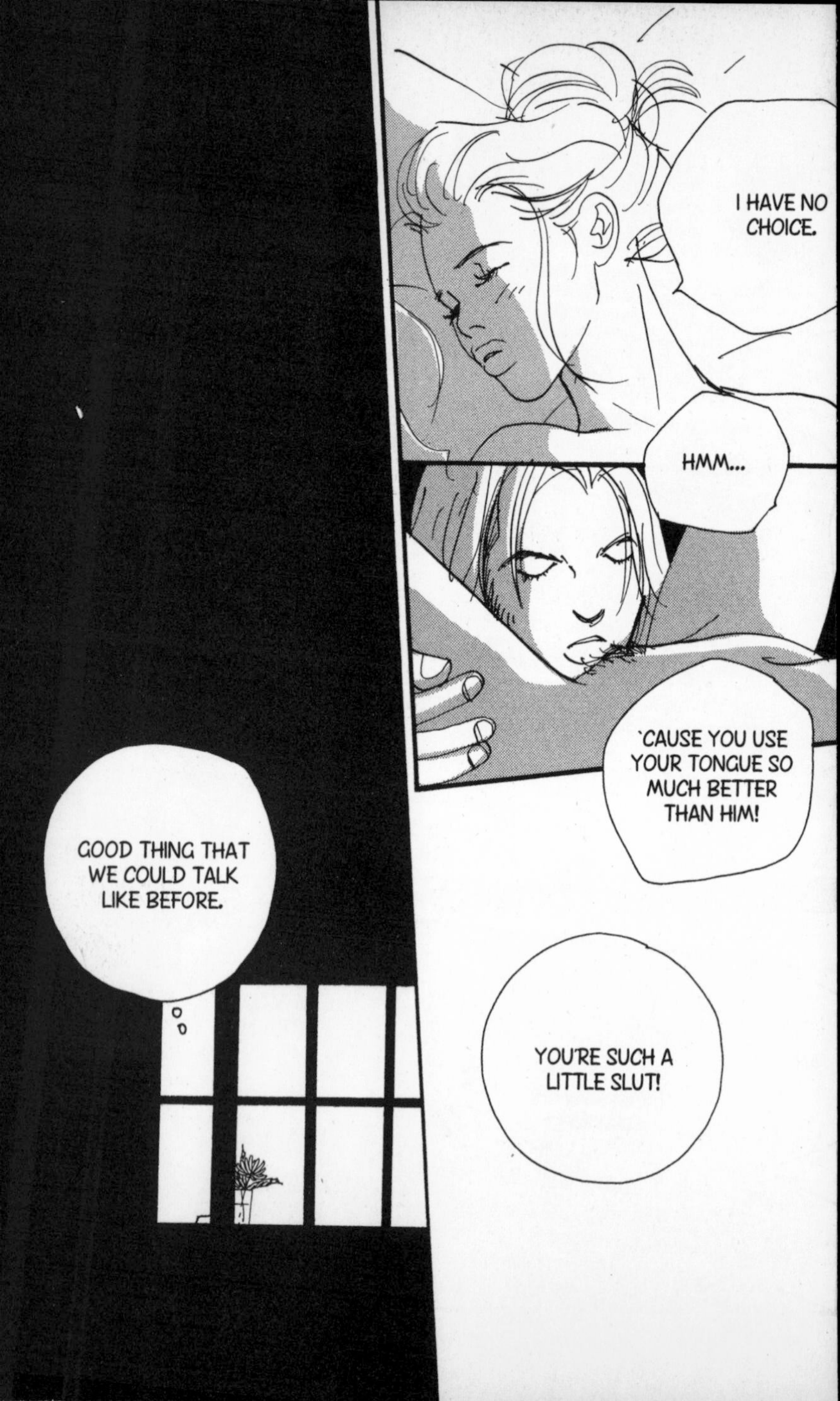
I HAVE NO CHOICE.
HMM...
`CAUSE YOU USE YOUR TONGUE SO MUCH BETTER THAN HIM!
YOU'RE SUCH A LITTLE SLUT!
GOOD THING THAT WE COULD TALK LIKE BEFORE.

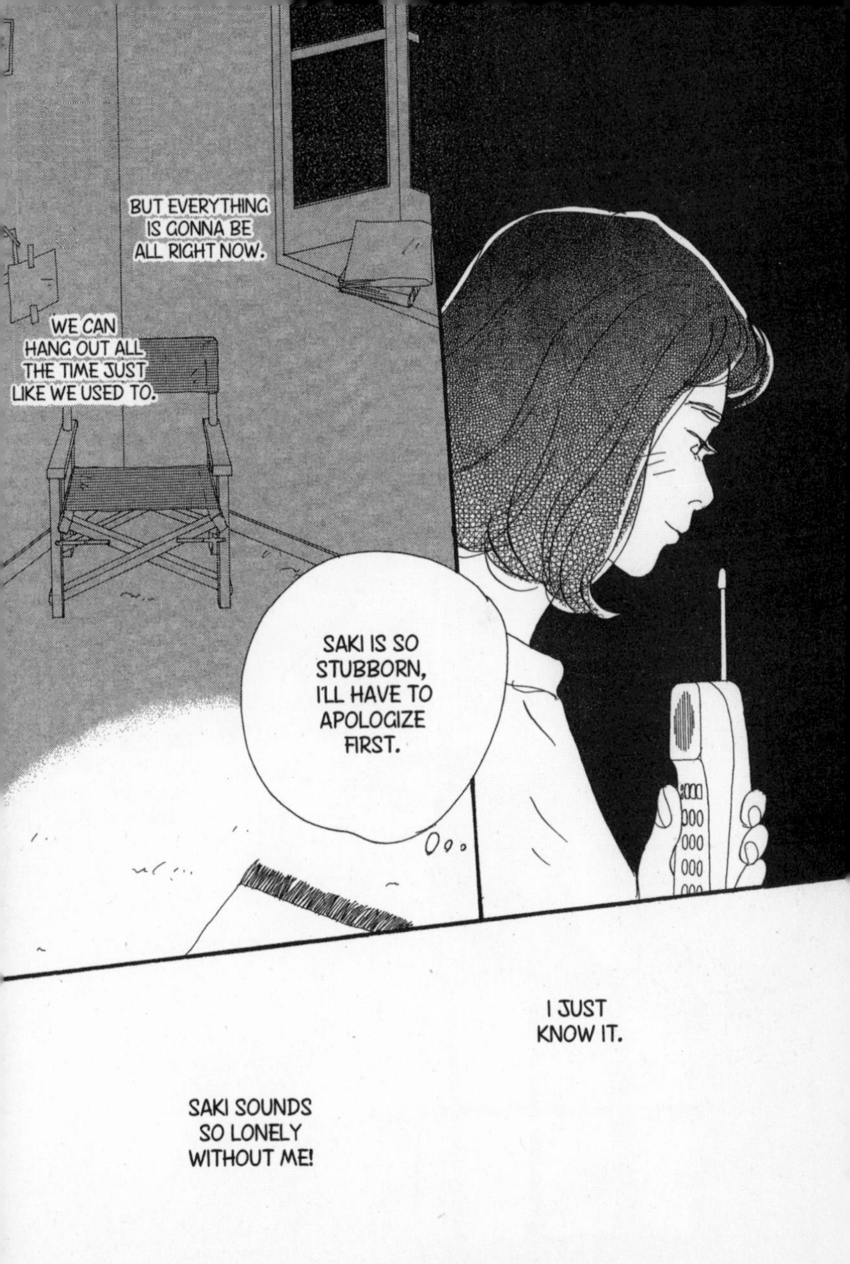
SAKI IS SO STUBBORN, I'LL HAVE TO APOLOGIZE FIRST.
BUT EVERYTHING IS GONNA BE ALL RIGHT NOW.
WE CAN HANG OUT ALL THE TIME JUST LIKE WE USED TO.
I JUST KNOW IT.
SAKI SOUNDS SO LONELY WITHOUT ME!

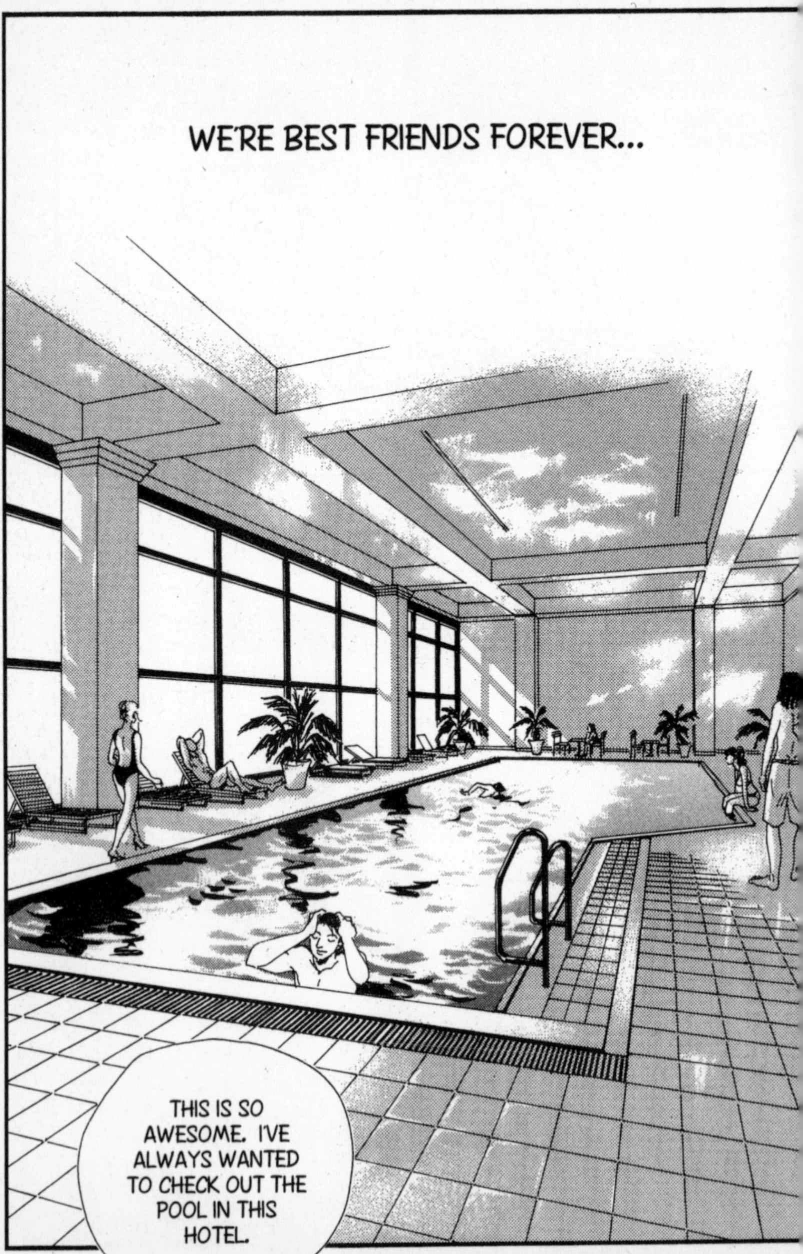
WE'RE BEST FRIENDS FOREVER...
THIS IS SO AWESOME. I'VE ALWAYS WANTED TO CHECK OUT THE POOL IN THIS HOTEL.

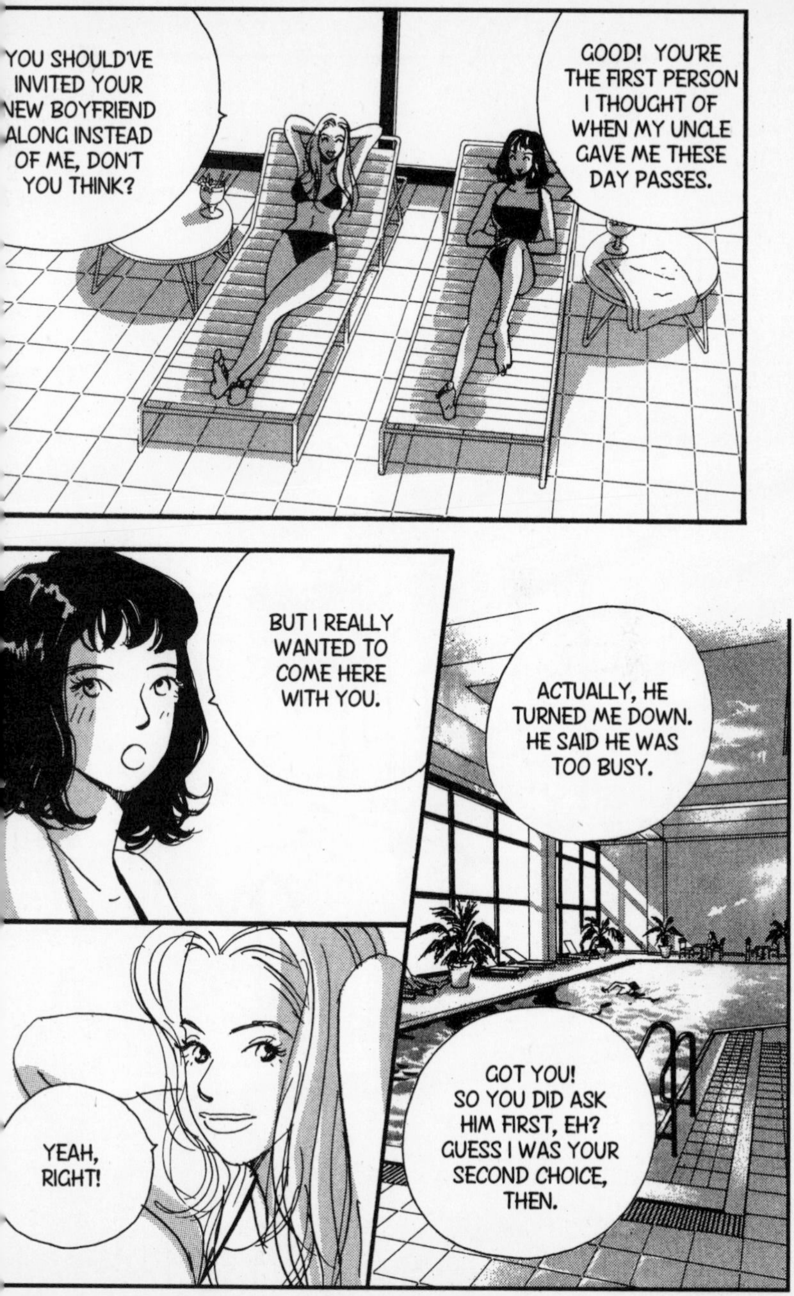
GOOD! YOU'RE THE FIRST PERSON I THOUGHT OF WHEN MY UNCLE GAVE ME THESE DAY PASSES.
YOU SHOULD'VE INVITED YOUR NEW BOYFRIEND ALONG INSTEAD OF ME, DON'T YOU THINK?
BUT I REALLY WANTED TO COME HERE WITH YOU.
YEAH, RIGHT!
ACTUALLY, HE TURNED ME DOWN. HE SAID HE WAS TOO BUSY.
GOT YOU! SO YOU DID ASK HIM FIRST, EH? GUESS I WAS YOUR SECOND CHOICE, THEN.

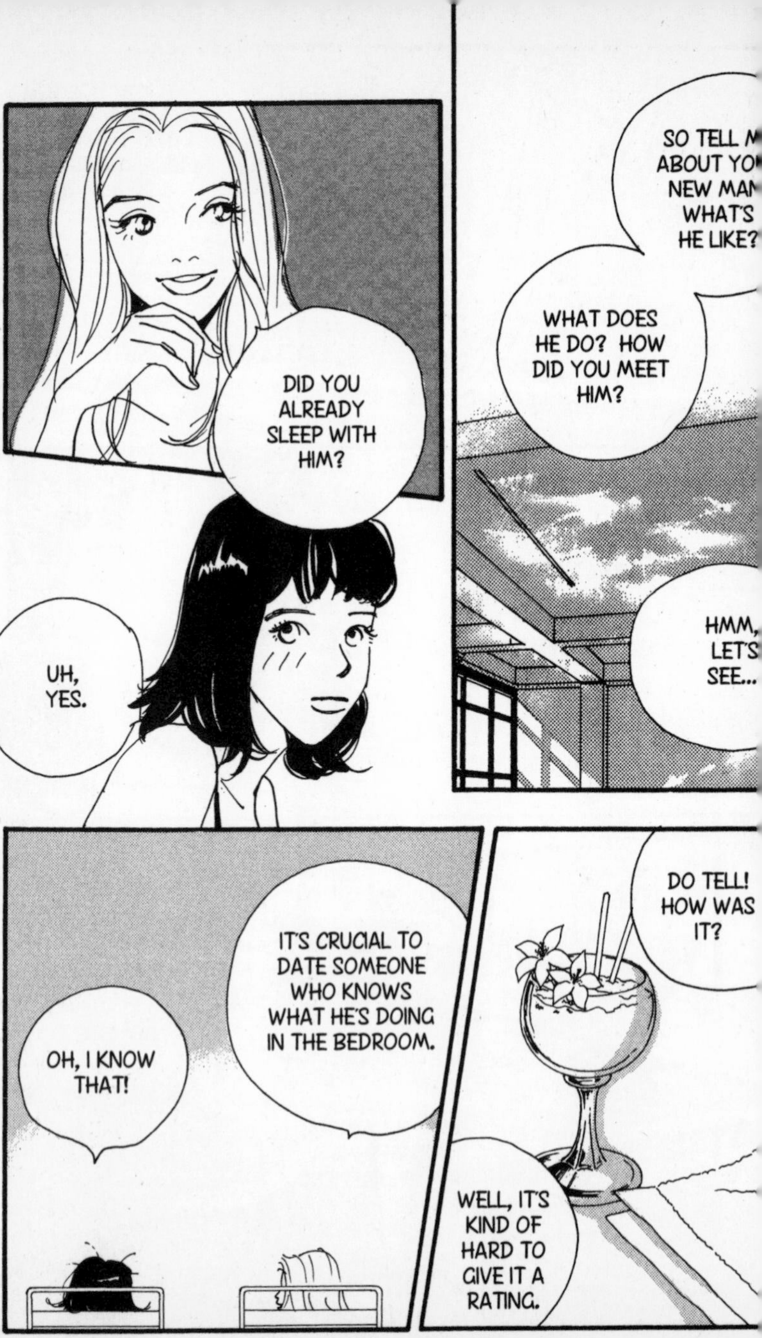

SO TELL M ABOUT YO NEW MA WHAT'S HE LIKE?
WHAT DOES HE DO? HOW DID YOU MEET HIM?
HMM, LET'S SEE...
DID YOU ALREADY SLEEP WITH HIM?
UH, YES.
DO TELL! HOW WAS IT?
WELL, IT'S KIND OF HARD TO GIVE IT A RATING.
IT'S CRUCIAL TO DATE SOMEONE WHO KNOWS WHAT HE'S DOING IN THE BEDROOM.
OH, I KNOW THAT!

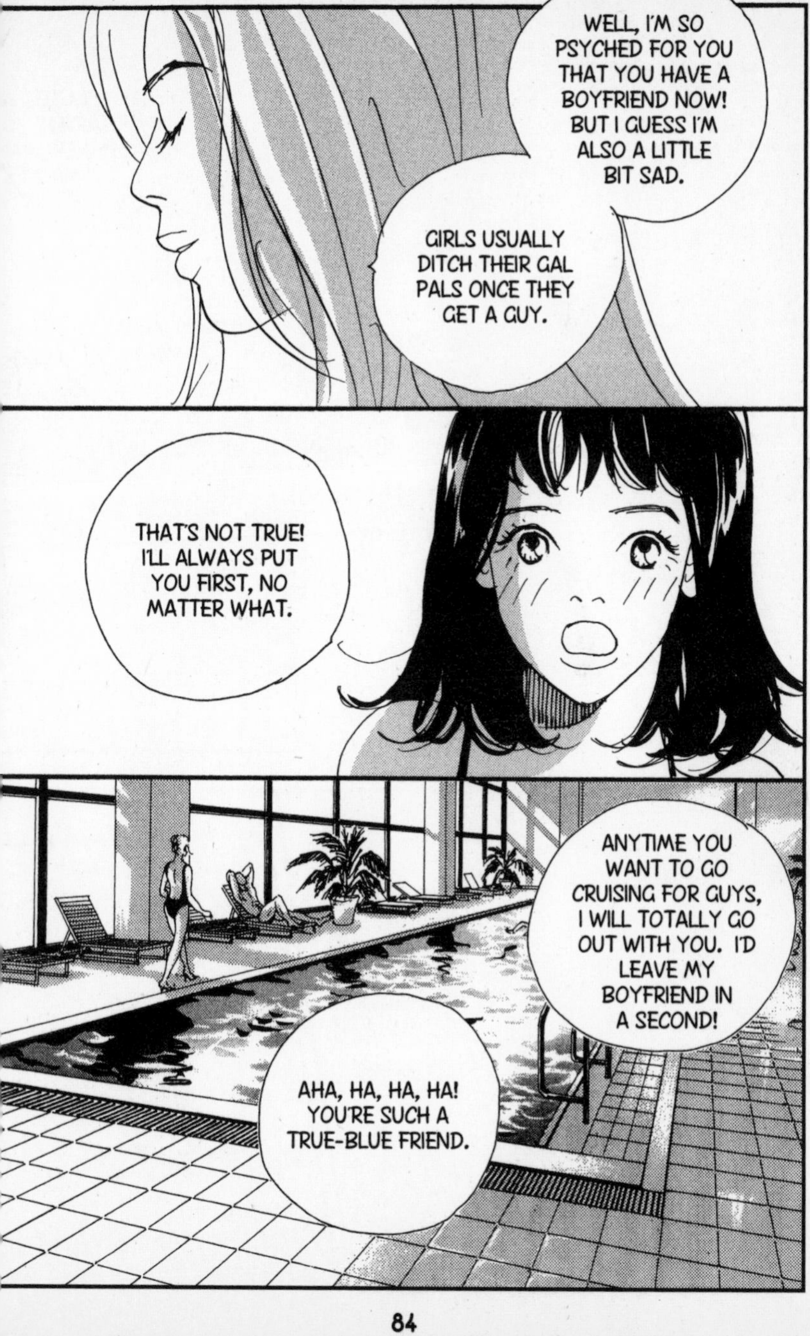
WELL, I'M SO PSYCHED FOR YOU THAT YOU HAVE A BOYFRIEND NOW! BUT I GUESS I'M ALSO A LITTLE BIT SAD.
GIRLS USUALLY DITCH THEIR GAL PALS ONCE THEY GET A GUY.
THAT'S NOT TRUE! I'LL ALWAYS PUT YOU FIRST, NO MATTER WHAT.
ANYTIME YOU WANT TO GO CRUISING FOR GUYS, I WILL TOTALLY GO OUT WITH YOU. I'D LEAVE MY BOYFRIEND IN A SECOND!
AHA, HA, HA, HA! YOU'RE SUCH A TRUE-BLUE FRIEND.

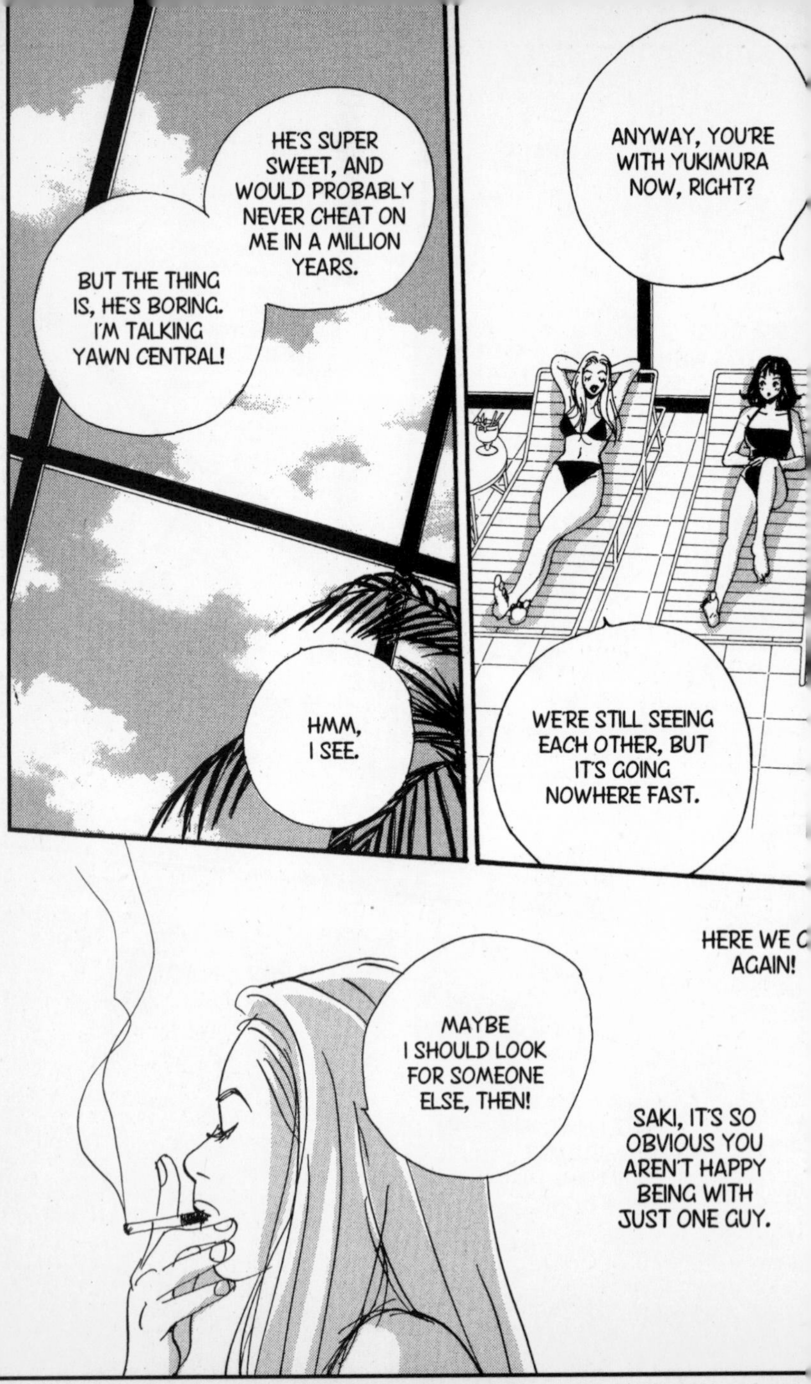
ANYWAY, YOU'RE WITH YUKIMURA NOW, RIGHT?
WE'RE STILL SEEING EACH OTHER, BUT IT'S GOING NOWHERE FAST.
HE'S SUPER SWEET, AND WOULD PROBABLY NEVER CHEAT ON ME IN A MILLION YEARS.
BUT THE THING IS, HE'S BORING. I'M TALKING YAWN CENTRAL!
HMM, I SEE.
HERE WE AGAIN!
SAKI, IT'S SO OBVIOUS YOU AREN'T HAPPY BEING WITH JUST ONE GUY.
MAYBE I SHOULD LOOK FOR SOMEONE ELSE, THEN!

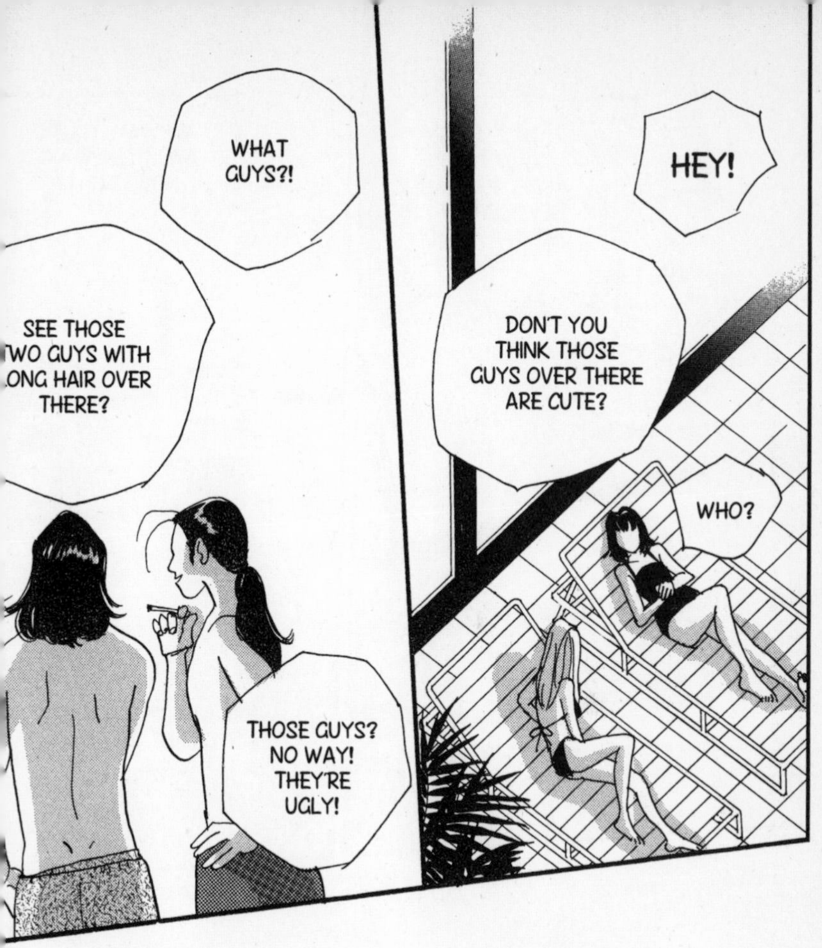
HEY!
DON'T YOU THINK THOSE GUYS OVER THERE ARE CUTE?
WHO?
WHAT GUYS?!
SEE THOSE TWO GUYS WITH LONG HAIR OVER THERE?
THOSE GUYS? NO WAY! THEY'RE UGLY!

YES, THIS IS HOW IT SHOULD BE!

SAKI IS SUCH A FREE SPIRIT. SHE SHOULDN'T BELONG TO ANYONE.

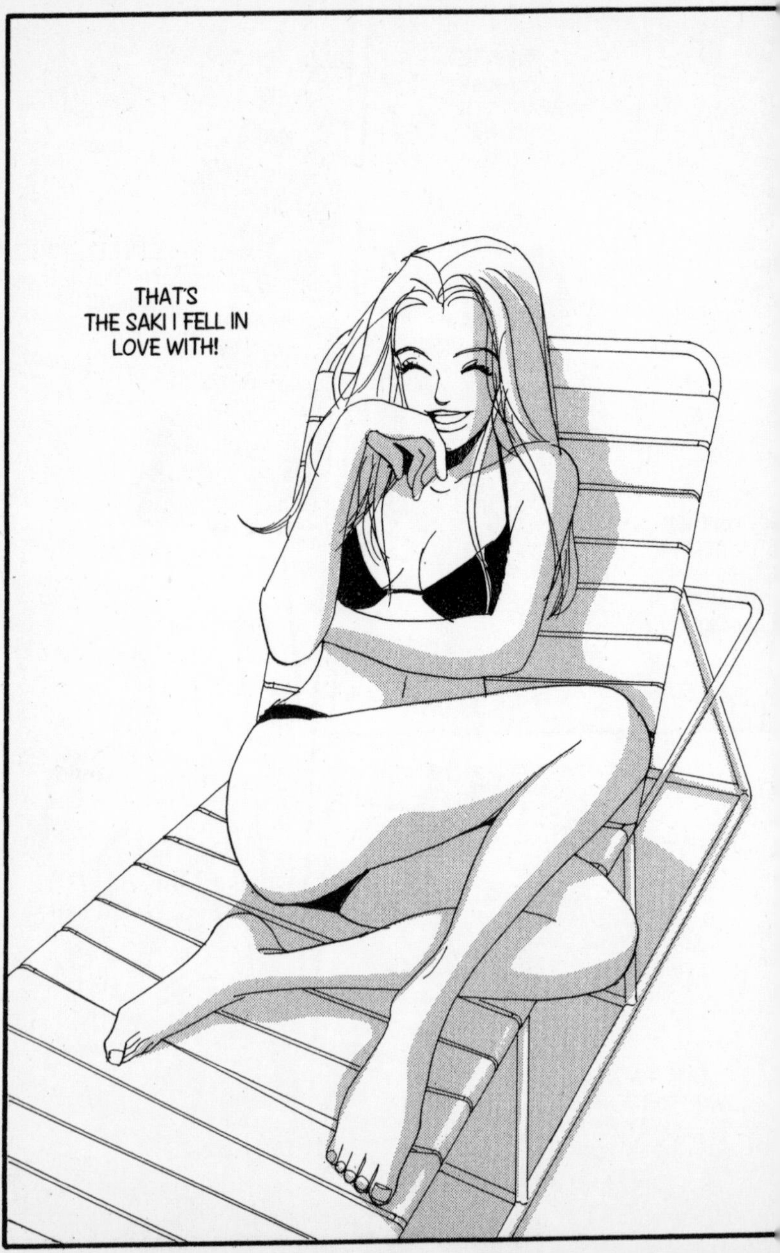
THAT'S THE SAKI I FELL IN LOVE WITH!

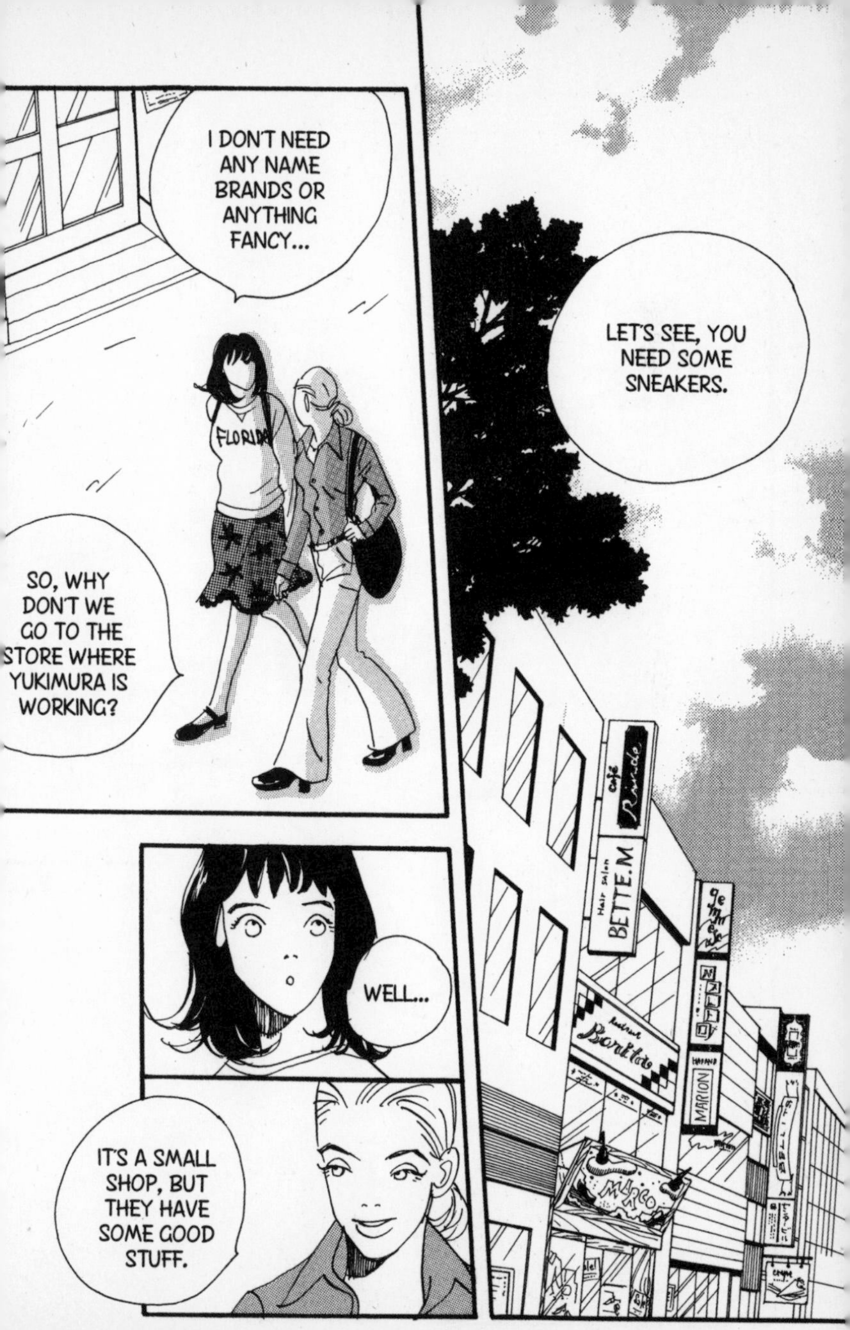
LET'S SEE, YOU NEED SOME SNEAKERS.
Hair salon
BETTE.M
MARION
I DON'T NEED ANY NAME BRANDS OR ANYTHING FANCY...
SO, WHY DON'T WE GO TO THE STORE WHERE YUKIMURA IS WORKING?
WELL...
IT'S A SMALL SHOP, BUT THEY HAVE SOME GOOD STUFF.

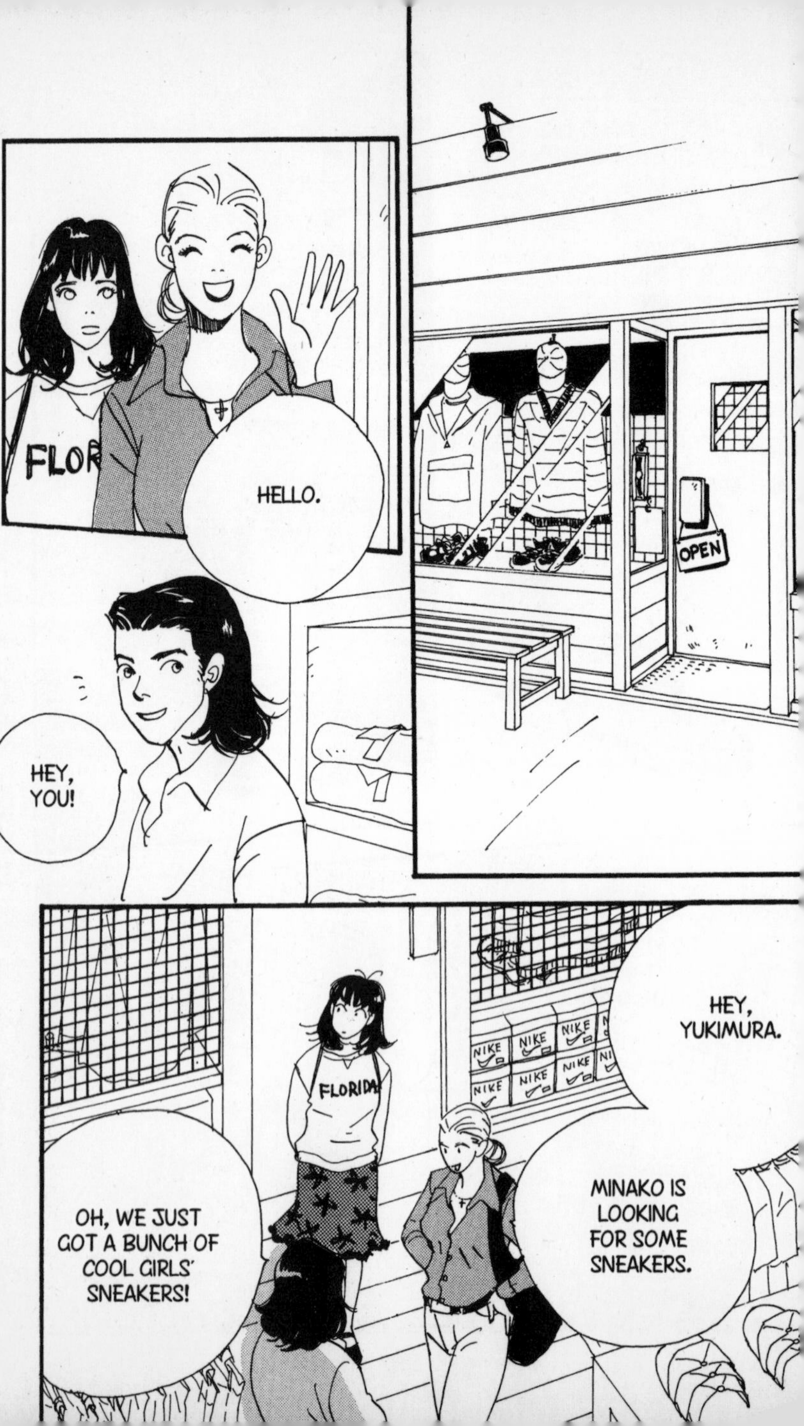
OPEN
HELLO.
FLOR
HEY, YOU!
HEY, YUKIMURA.
MINAKO IS LOOKING FOR SOME SNEAKERS.
FLORIDA
NIKE
OH, WE JUST GOT A BUNCH OF COOL GIRLS' SNEAKERS!

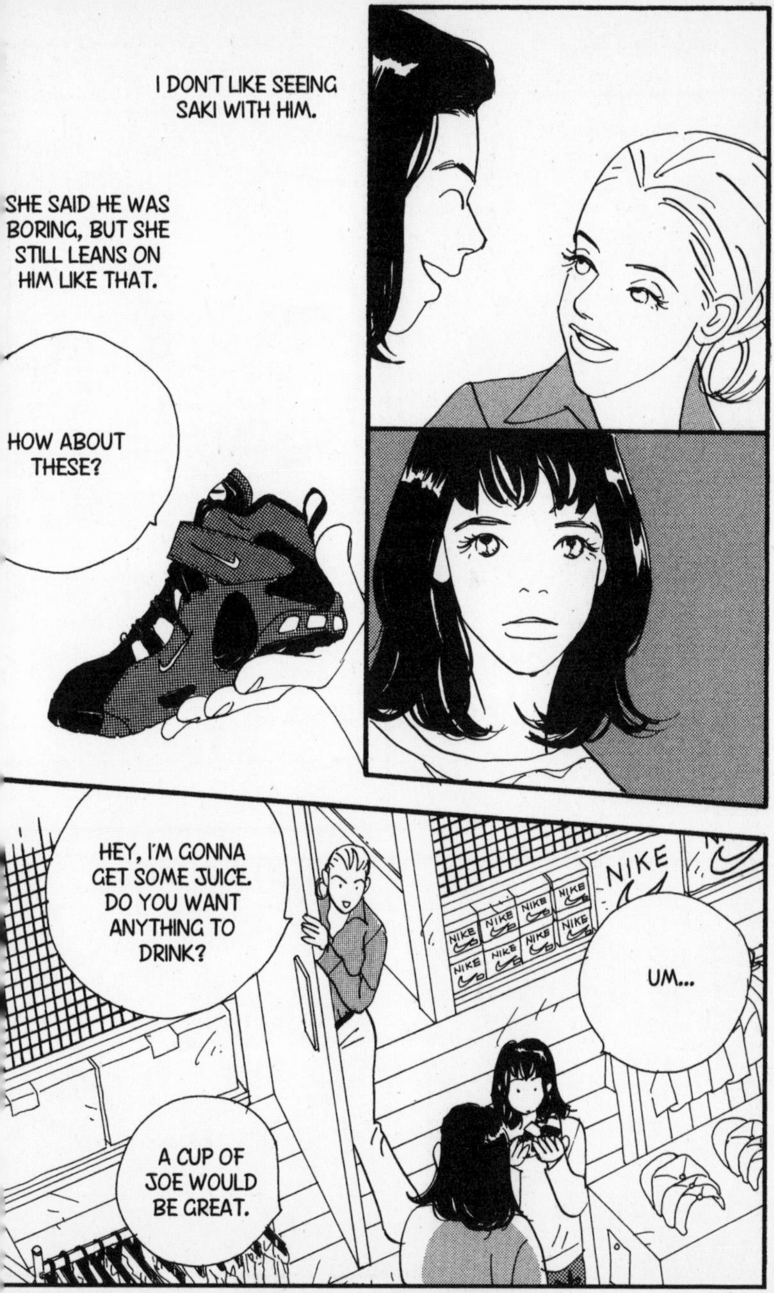
I DON'T LIKE SEEING SAKI WITH HIM.
SHE SAID HE WAS BORING, BUT SHE STILL LEANS ON HIM LIKE THAT.
HOW ABOUT THESE?
NIKE
HEY, I'M GONNA GET SOME JUICE. DO YOU WANT ANYTHING TO DRINK?
UM...
A CUP OF JOE WOULD BE GREAT.

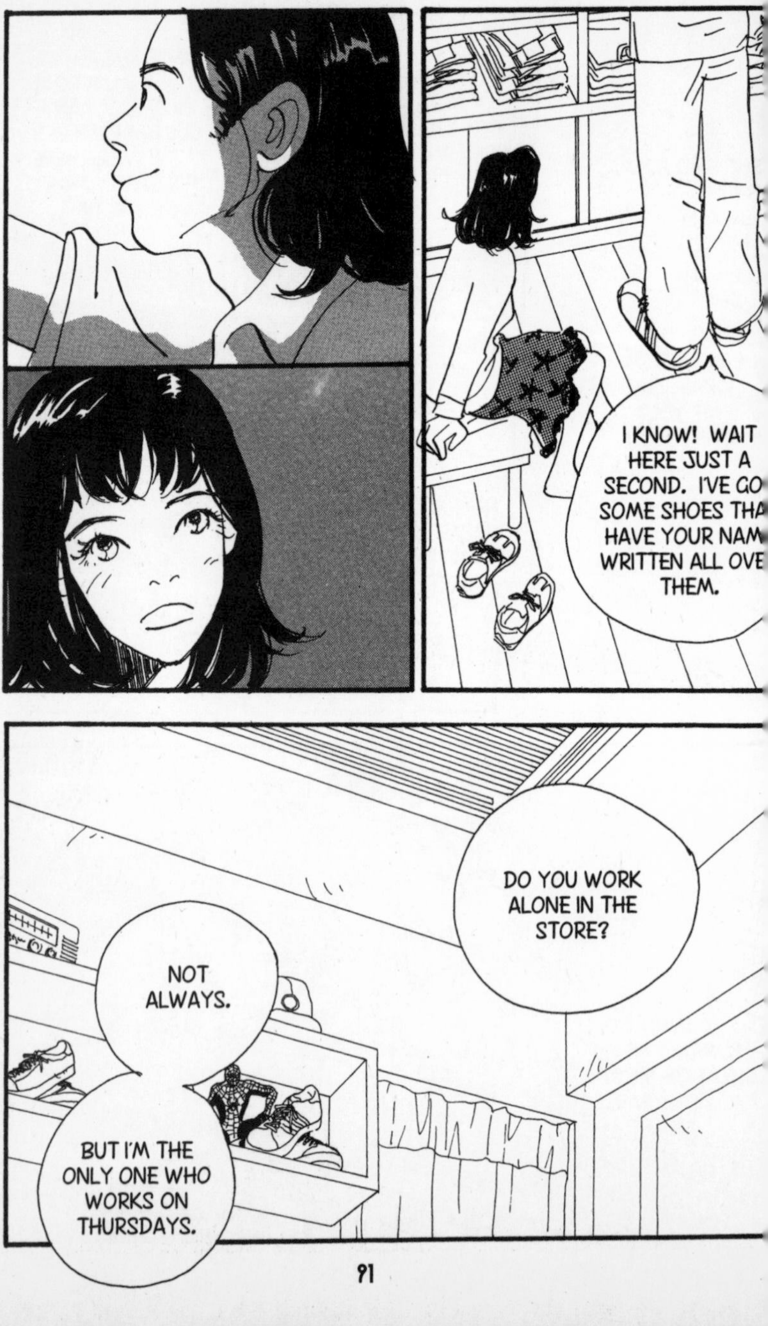
I KNOW! WAIT HERE JUST A SECOND. I'VE GO SOME SHOES THA HAVE YOUR NAM WRITTEN ALL OVE THEM.
DO YOU WORK ALONE IN THE STORE?
NOT ALWAYS.
BUT I'M THE ONLY ONE WHO WORKS ON THURSDAYS.

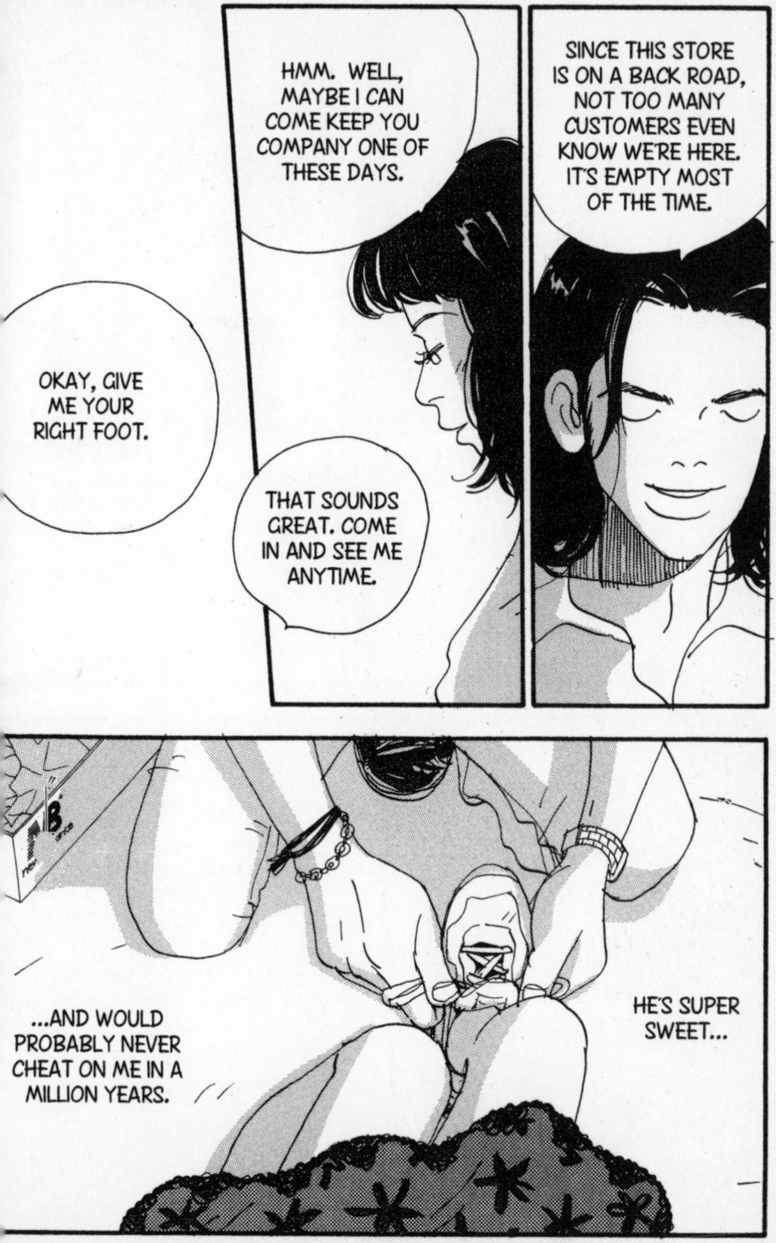
SINCE THIS STORE IS ON A BACK ROAD, NOT TOO MANY CUSTOMERS EVEN KNOW WE'RE HERE. IT'S EMPTY MOST OF THE TIME.
HMM. WELL, MAYBE I CAN COME KEEP YOU COMPANY ONE OF THESE DAYS.
THAT SOUNDS GREAT. COME IN AND SEE ME ANYTIME.
OKAY, GIVE ME YOUR RIGHT FOOT.
HE'S SUPER SWEET...
...AND WOULD PROBABLY NEVER CHEAT ON ME IN A MILLION YEARS.

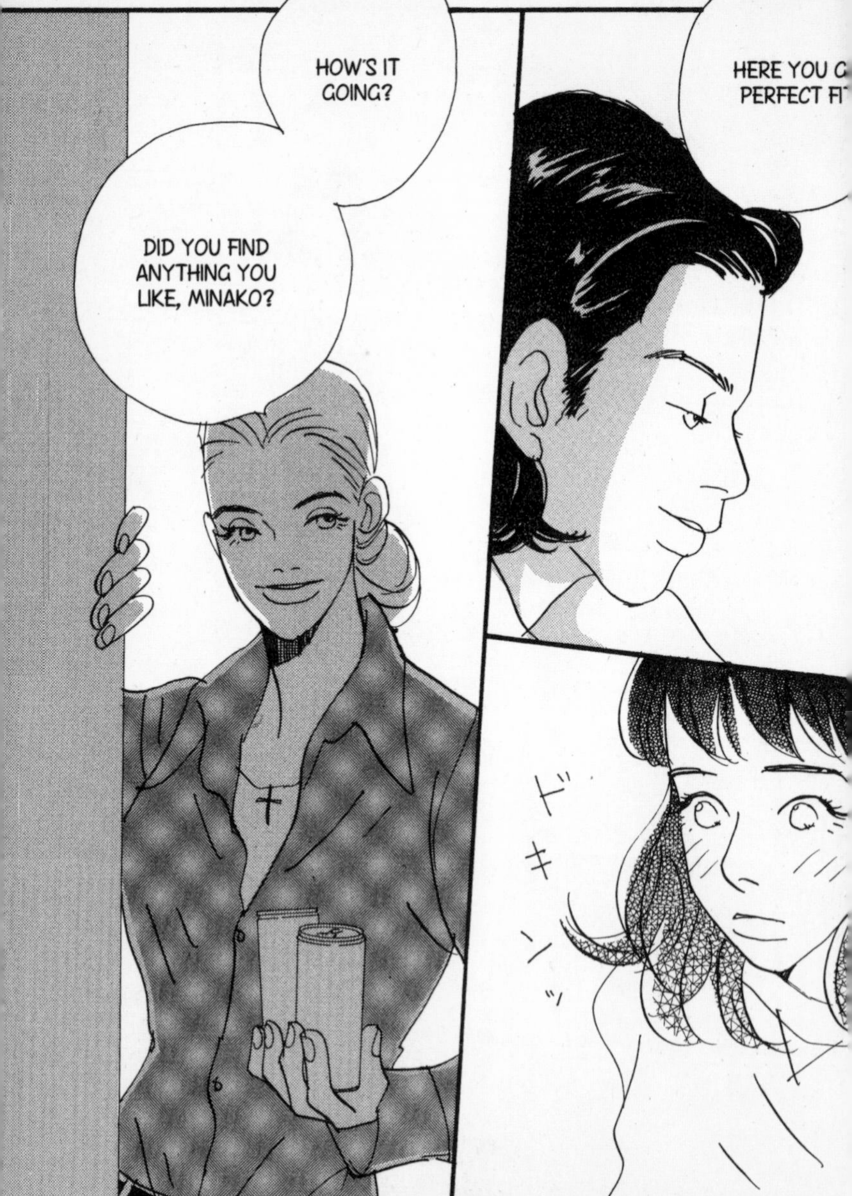
HERE YOU C PERFECT FI
ドキンッ
HOW'S IT GOING?
DID YOU FIND ANYTHING YOU LIKE, MINAKO?

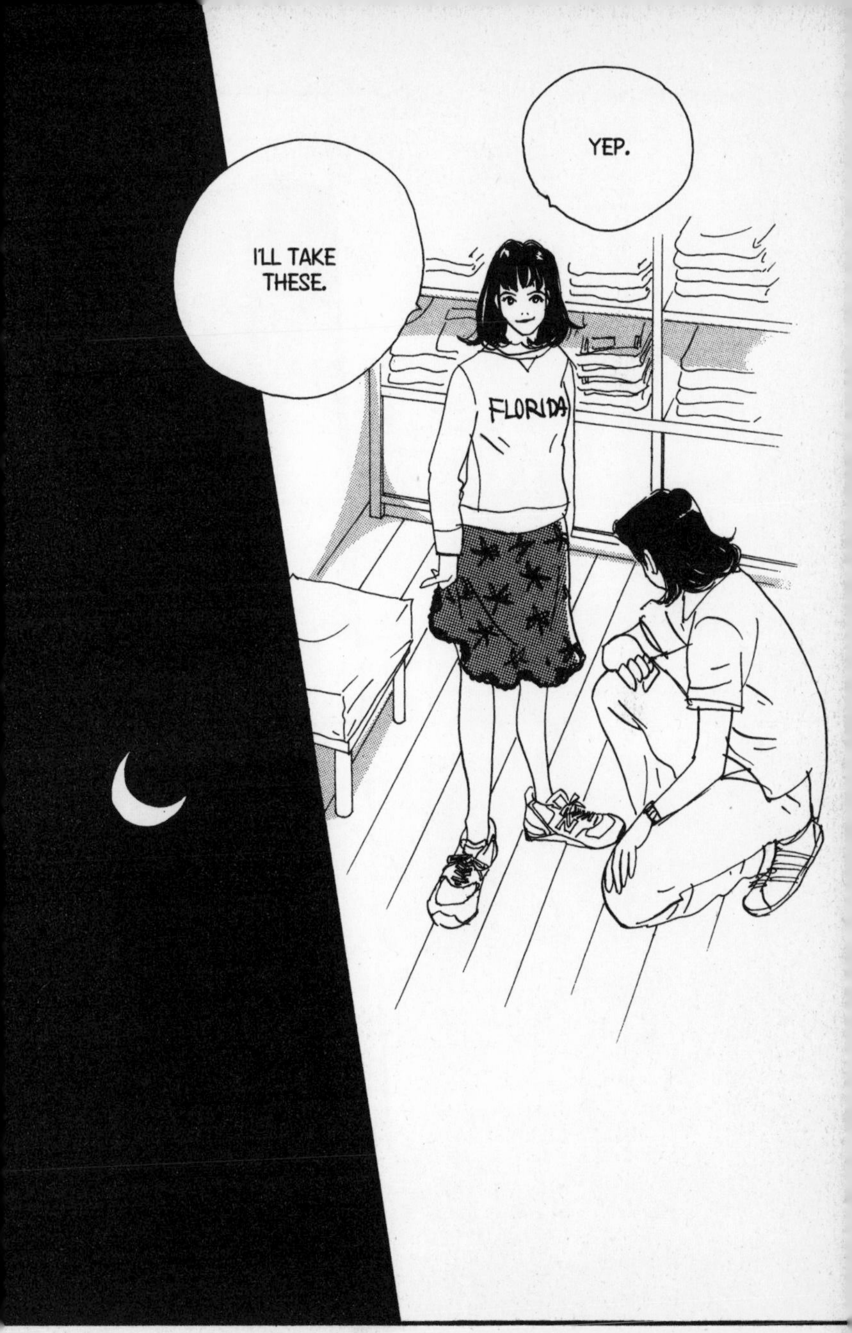
YEP.
I'LL TAKE THESE.
FLORIDA

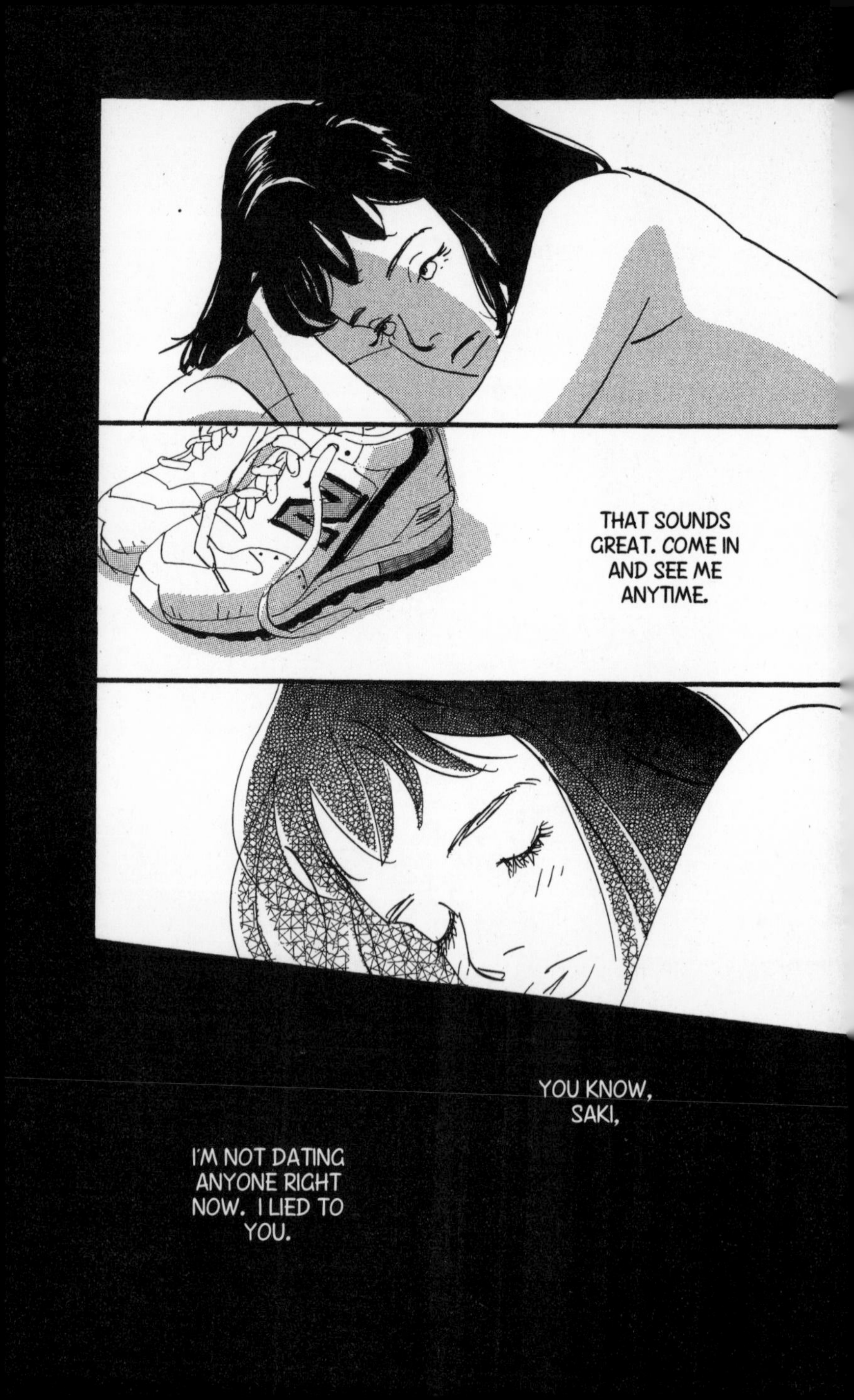
THAT SOUNDS GREAT. COME IN AND SEE ME ANYTIME.
YOU KNOW, SAKI,
I'M NOT DATING ANYONE RIGHT NOW. I LIED TO YOU.

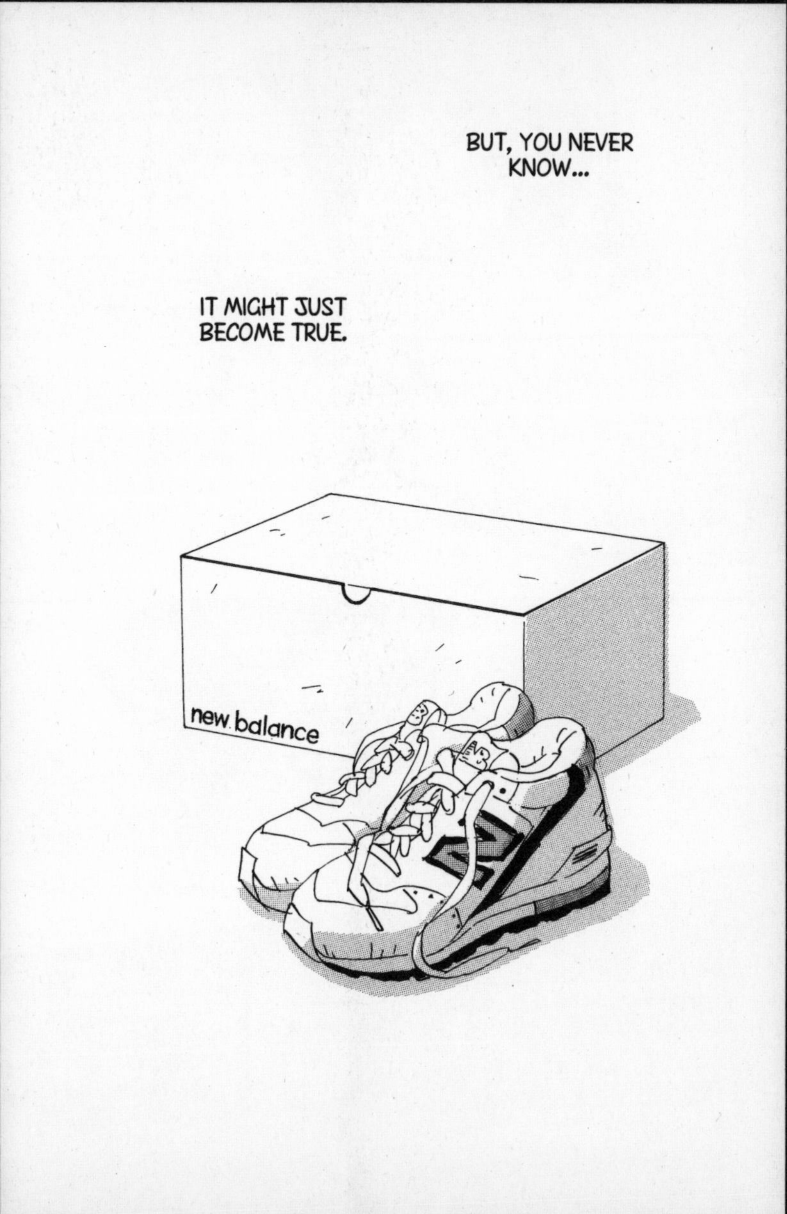
BUT, YOU NEVER KNOW...
IT MIGHT JUST BECOME TRUE.
new balance

between the sheets

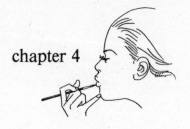

chapter 4

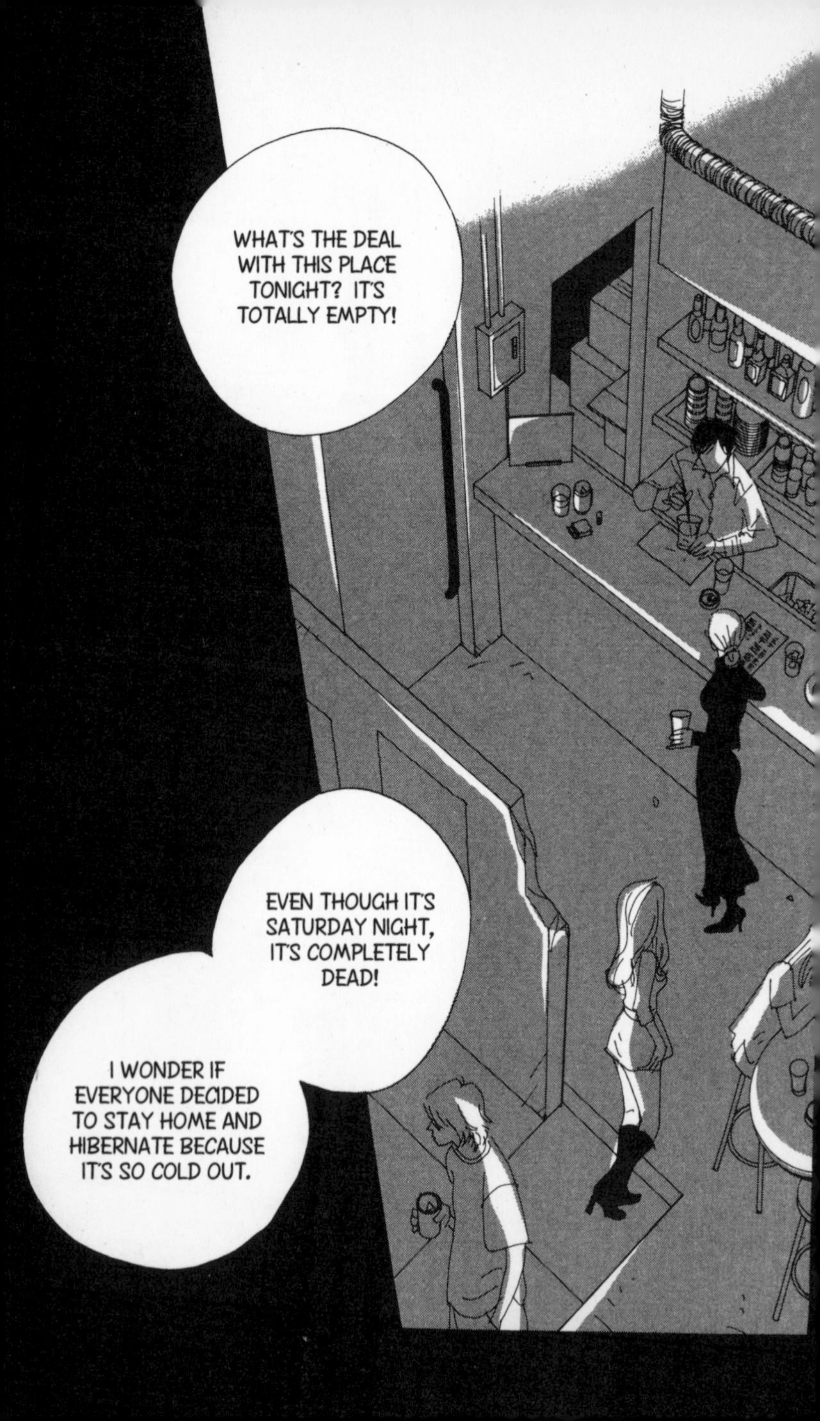
WHAT'S THE DEAL WITH THIS PLACE TONIGHT? IT'S TOTALLY EMPTY!
EVEN THOUGH IT'S SATURDAY NIGHT, IT'S COMPLETELY DEAD!
I WONDER IF EVERYONE DECIDED TO STAY HOME AND HIBERNATE BECAUSE IT'S SO COLD OUT.

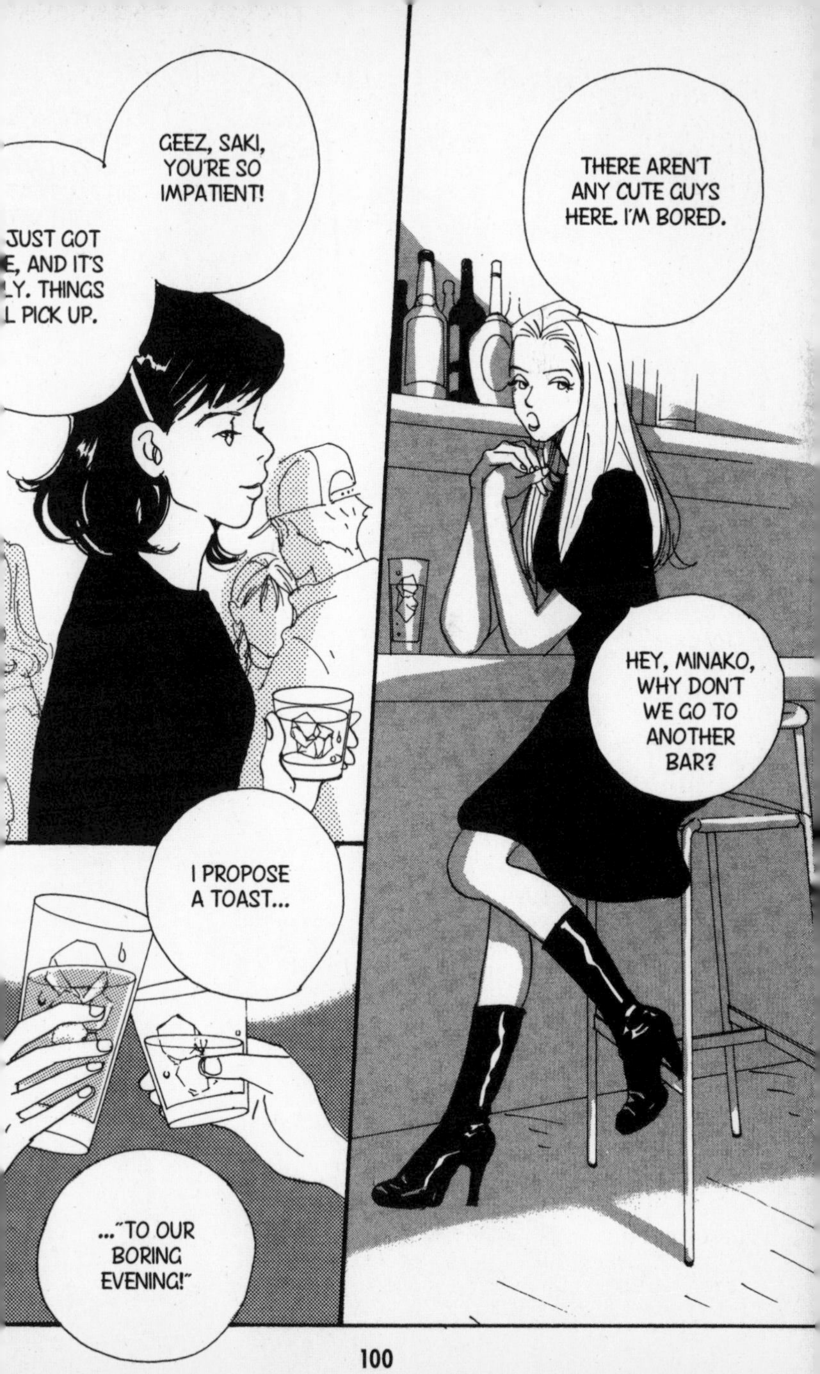
THERE AREN'T ANY CUTE GUYS HERE. I'M BORED.
HEY, MINAKO, WHY DON'T WE GO TO ANOTHER BAR?
GEEZ, SAKI, YOU'RE SO IMPATIENT!
JUST GOT E, AND IT'S LY. THINGS L PICK UP.
I PROPOSE A TOAST...
..."TO OUR BORING EVENING!"

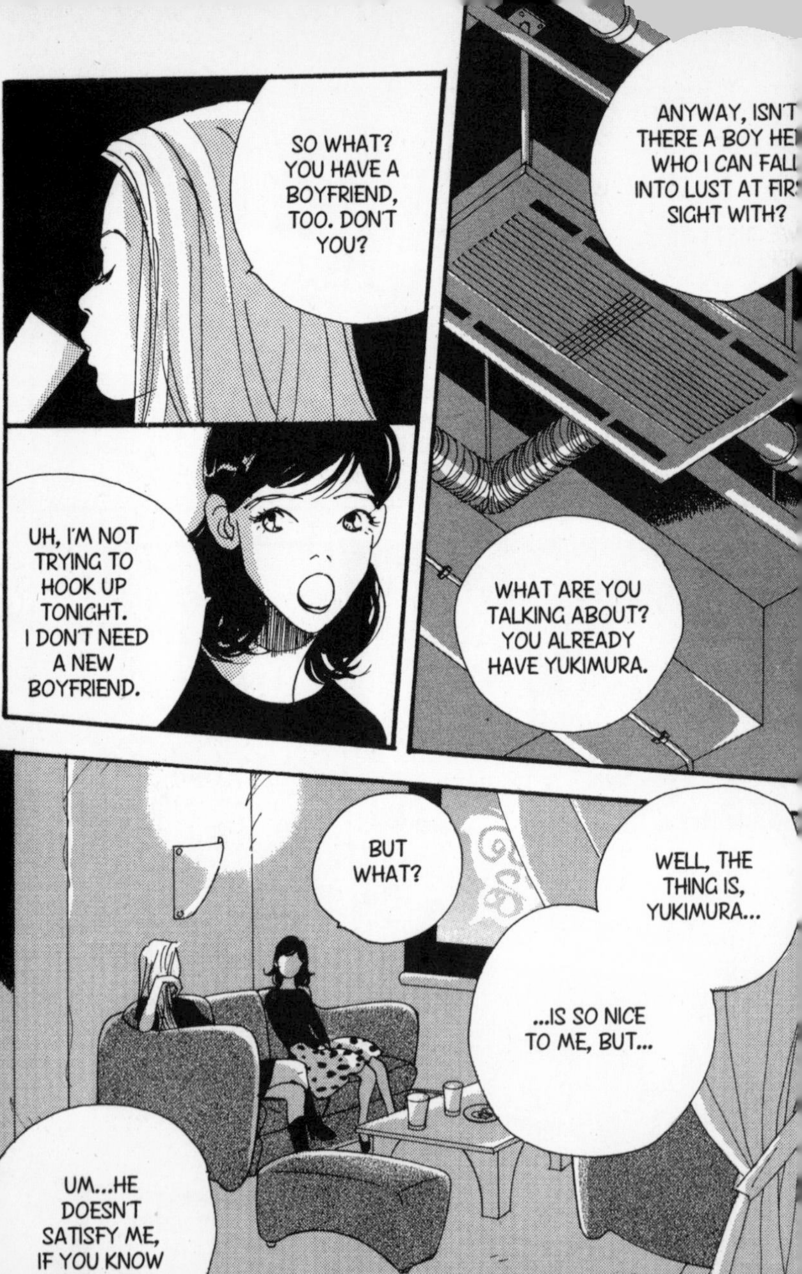
ANYWAY, ISN'T THERE A BOY HE WHO I CAN FALL INTO LUST AT FIR SIGHT WITH?
WHAT ARE YOU TALKING ABOUT? YOU ALREADY HAVE YUKIMURA.
SO WHAT? YOU HAVE A BOYFRIEND, TOO. DON'T YOU?
UH, I'M NOT TRYING TO HOOK UP TONIGHT. I DON'T NEED A NEW BOYFRIEND.
WELL, THE THING IS, YUKIMURA...
...IS SO NICE TO ME, BUT...
BUT WHAT?
UM...HE DOESN'T SATISFY ME, IF YOU KNOW WHAT I MEAN.

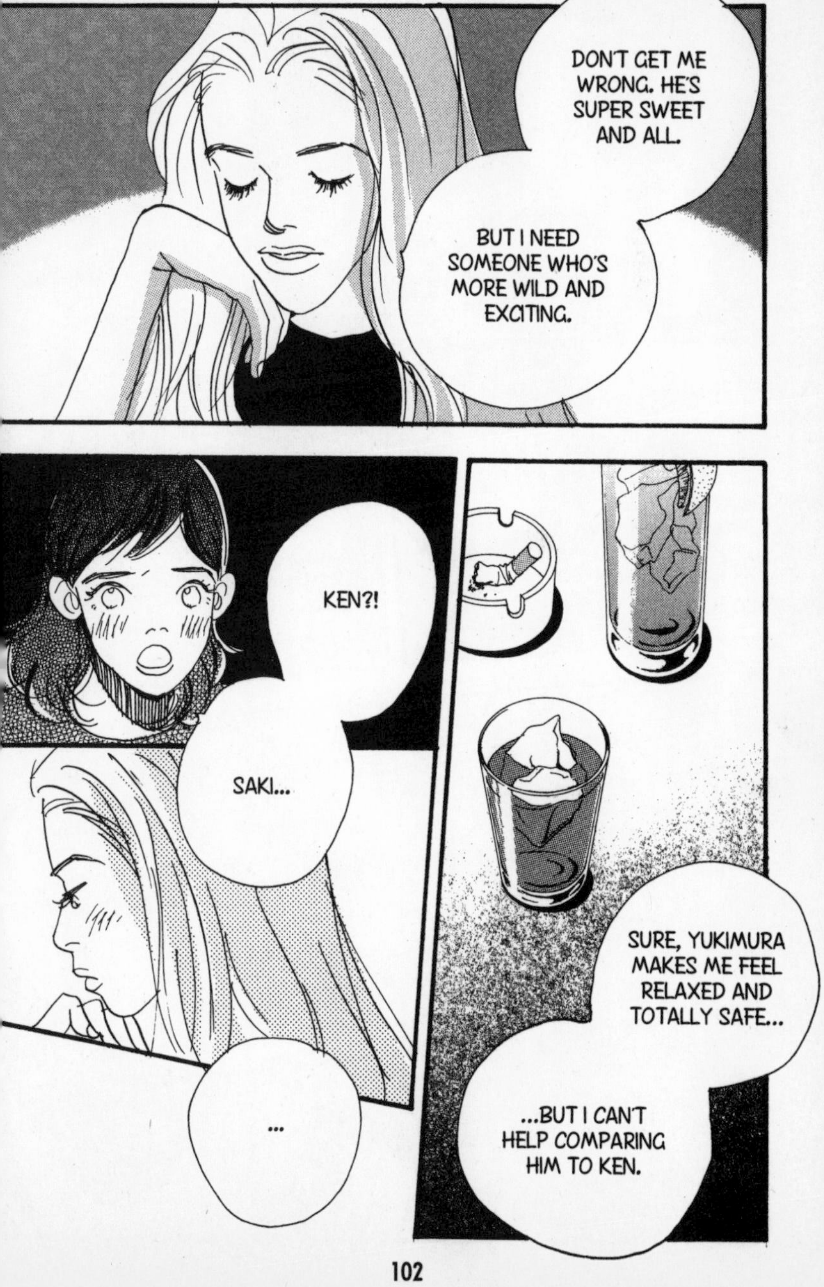
DON'T GET ME WRONG. HE'S SUPER SWEET AND ALL.
BUT I NEED SOMEONE WHO'S MORE WILD AND EXCITING.
SURE, YUKIMURA MAKES ME FEEL RELAXED AND TOTALLY SAFE...
...BUT I CAN'T HELP COMPARING HIM TO KEN.
KEN?!
SAKI...
...

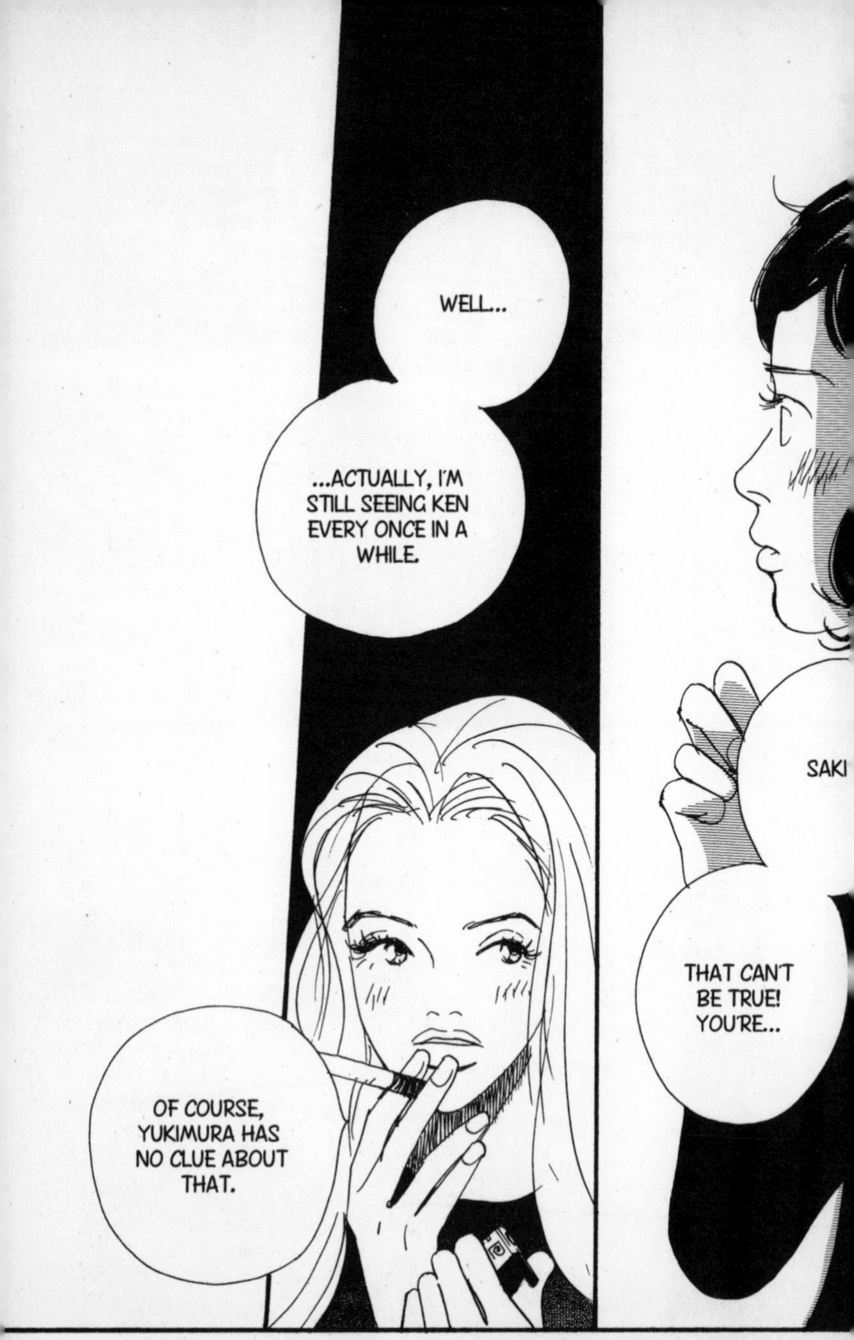
SAKI
THAT CAN'T BE TRUE! YOU'RE...
WELL...
...ACTUALLY, I'M STILL SEEING KEN EVERY ONCE IN A WHILE.
OF COURSE, YUKIMURA HAS NO CLUE ABOUT THAT.

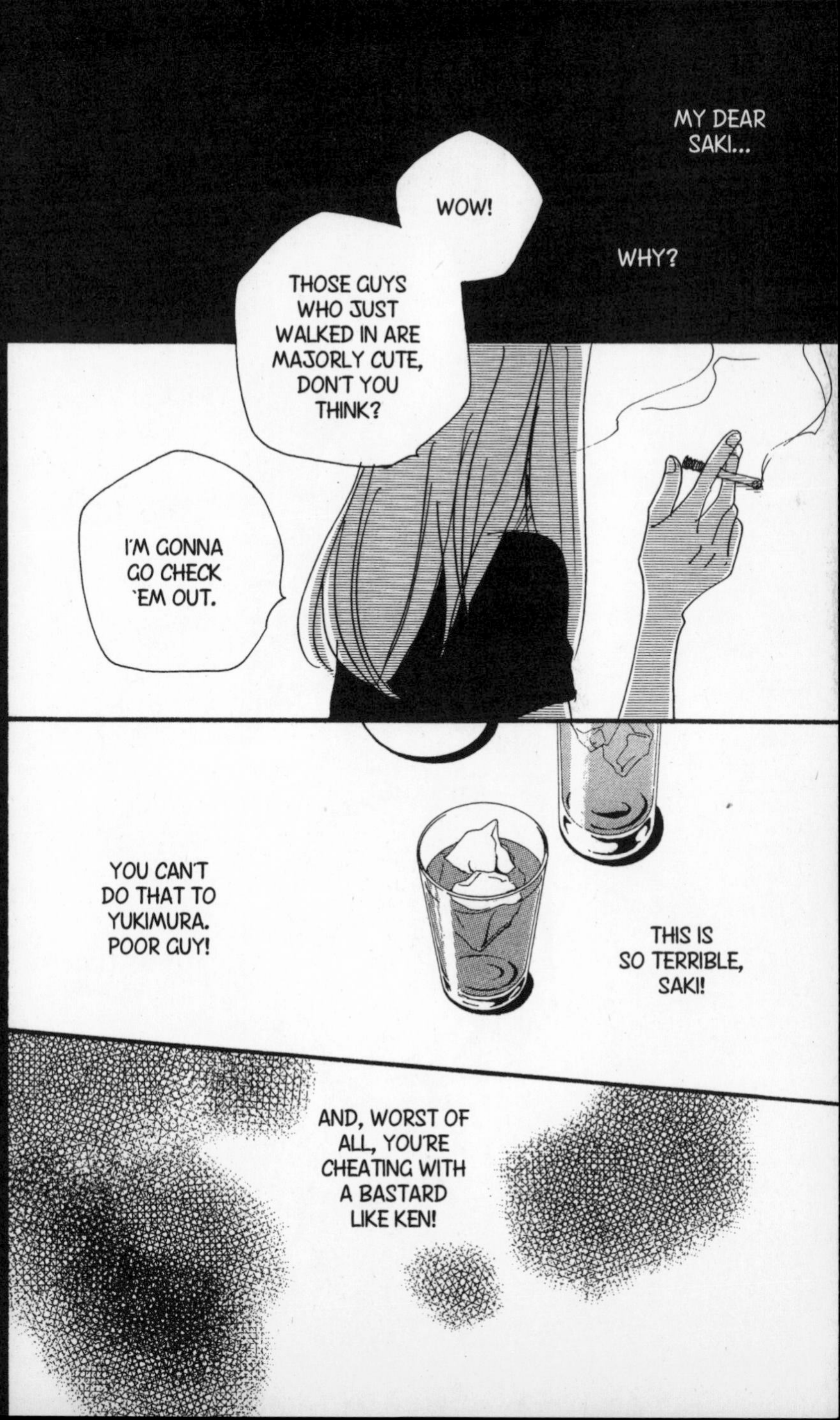
MY DEAR SAKI...
WHY?
WOW!
THOSE GUYS WHO JUST WALKED IN ARE MAJORLY CUTE, DON'T YOU THINK?
I'M GONNA GO CHECK 'EM OUT.
THIS IS SO TERRIBLE, SAKI!
YOU CAN'T DO THAT TO YUKIMURA. POOR GUY!
AND, WORST OF ALL, YOU'RE CHEATING WITH A BASTARD LIKE KEN!

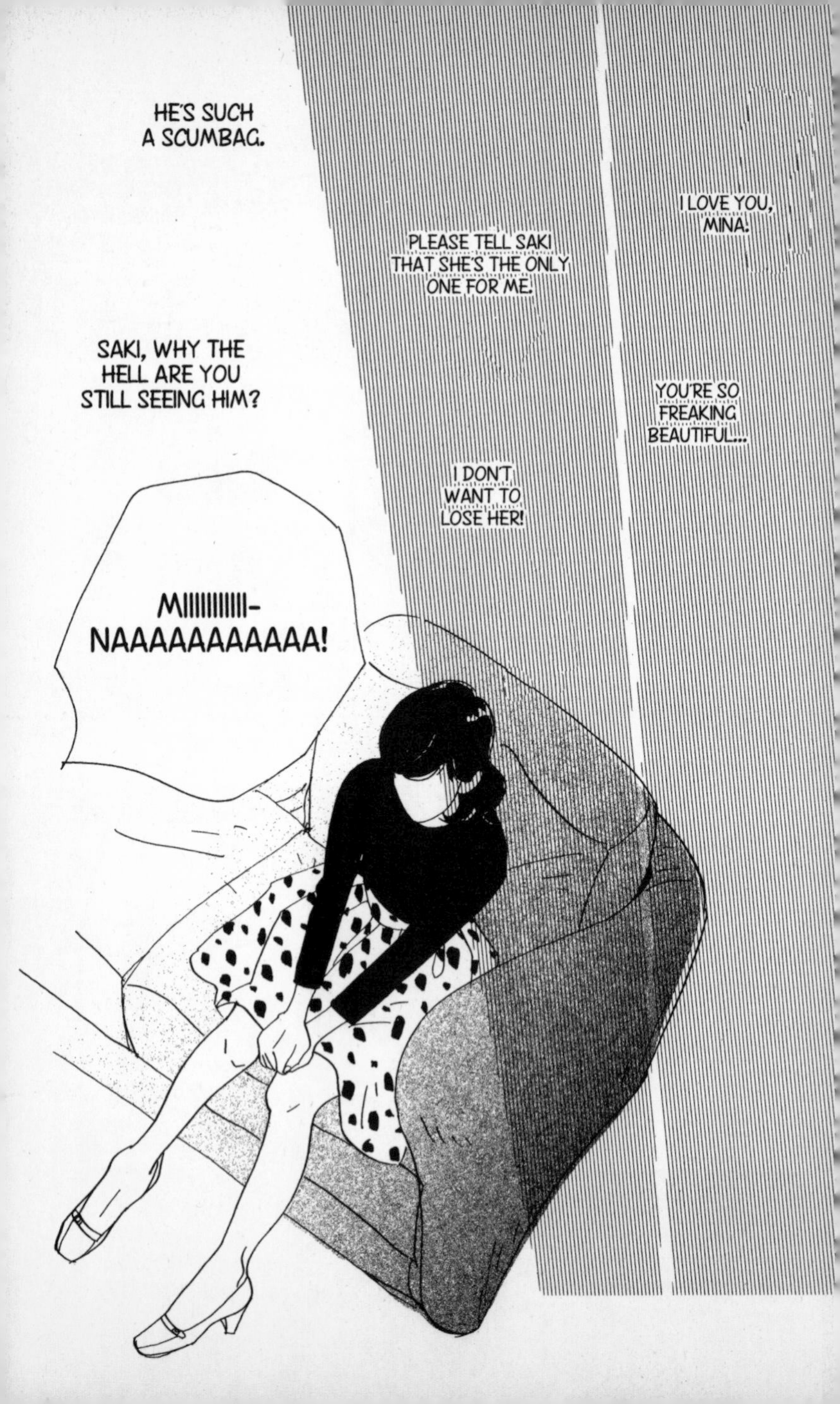
I LOVE YOU, MINA.
PLEASE TELL SAKI THAT SHE'S THE ONLY ONE FOR ME.
YOU'RE SO FREAKING BEAUTIFUL...
I DON'T WANT TO LOSE HER!
HE'S SUCH A SCUMBAG.
SAKI, WHY THE HELL ARE YOU STILL SEEING HIM?
MIIIIIIIIIII-NAAAAAAAAAAA!

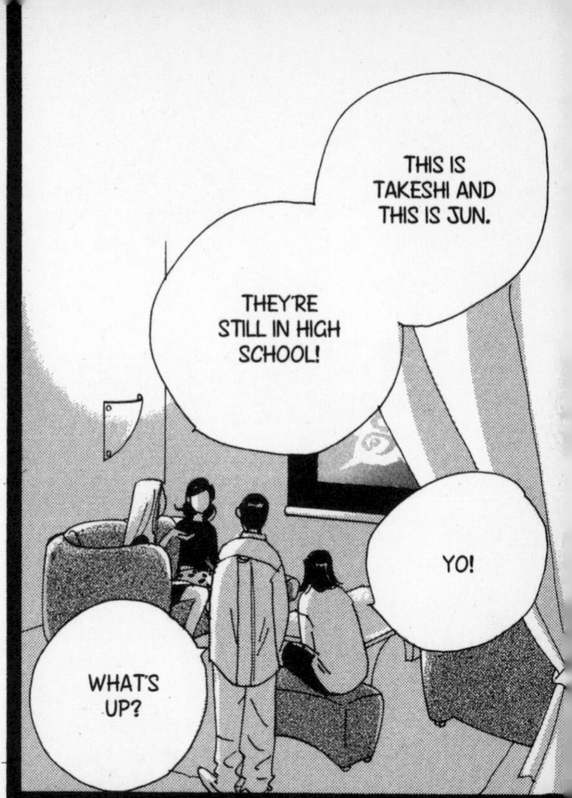
THIS IS TAKESHI AND THIS IS JUN.
THEY'RE STILL IN HIGH SCHOOL!
YO!
WHAT'S UP?

MY DARING SAKI...

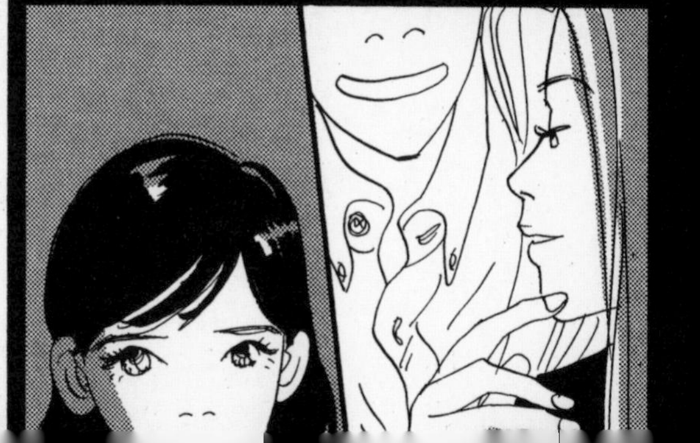

DO YOU MIND IF I STEAL YOUR BOYFRIEND?

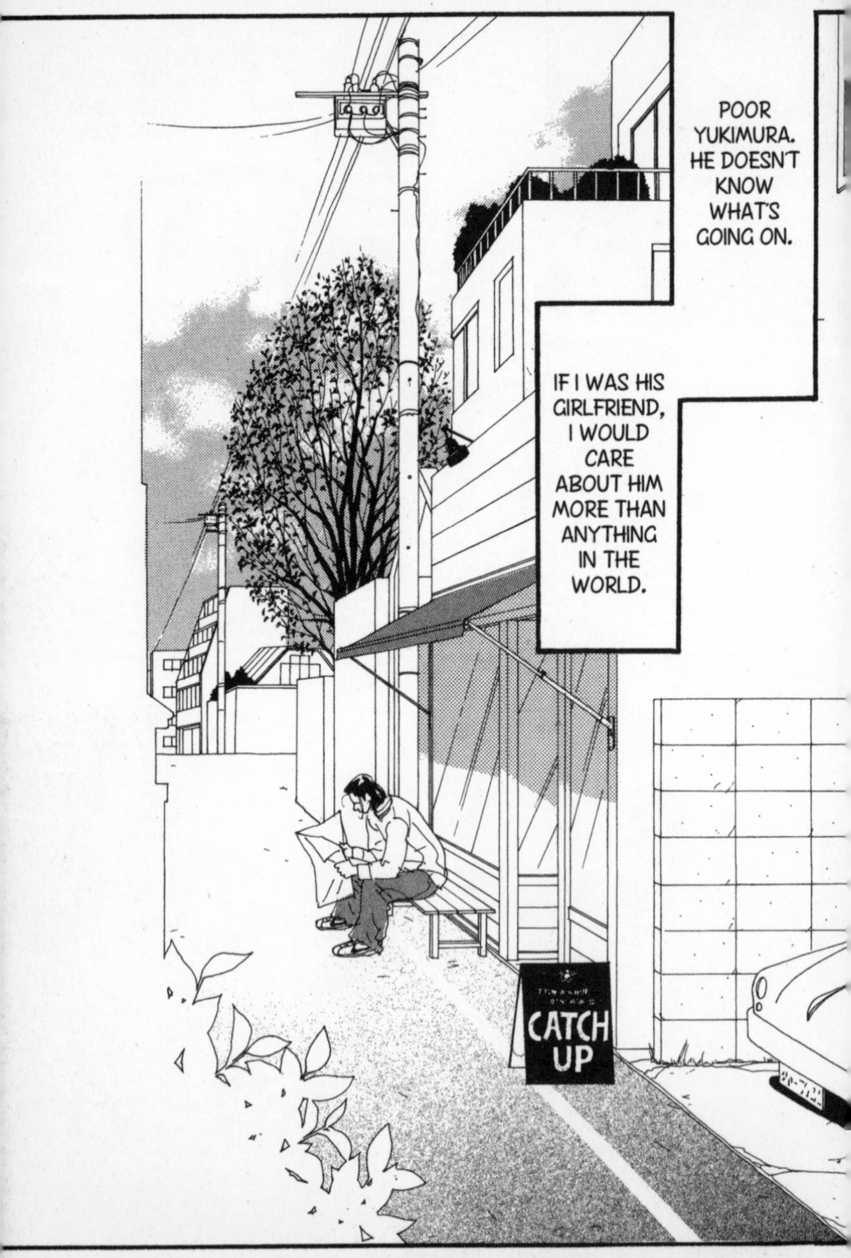
POOR YUKIMURA. HE DOESN'T KNOW WHAT'S GOING ON.
IF I WAS HIS GIRLFRIEND, I WOULD CARE ABOUT HIM MORE THAN ANYTHING IN THE WORLD.
CATCH UP

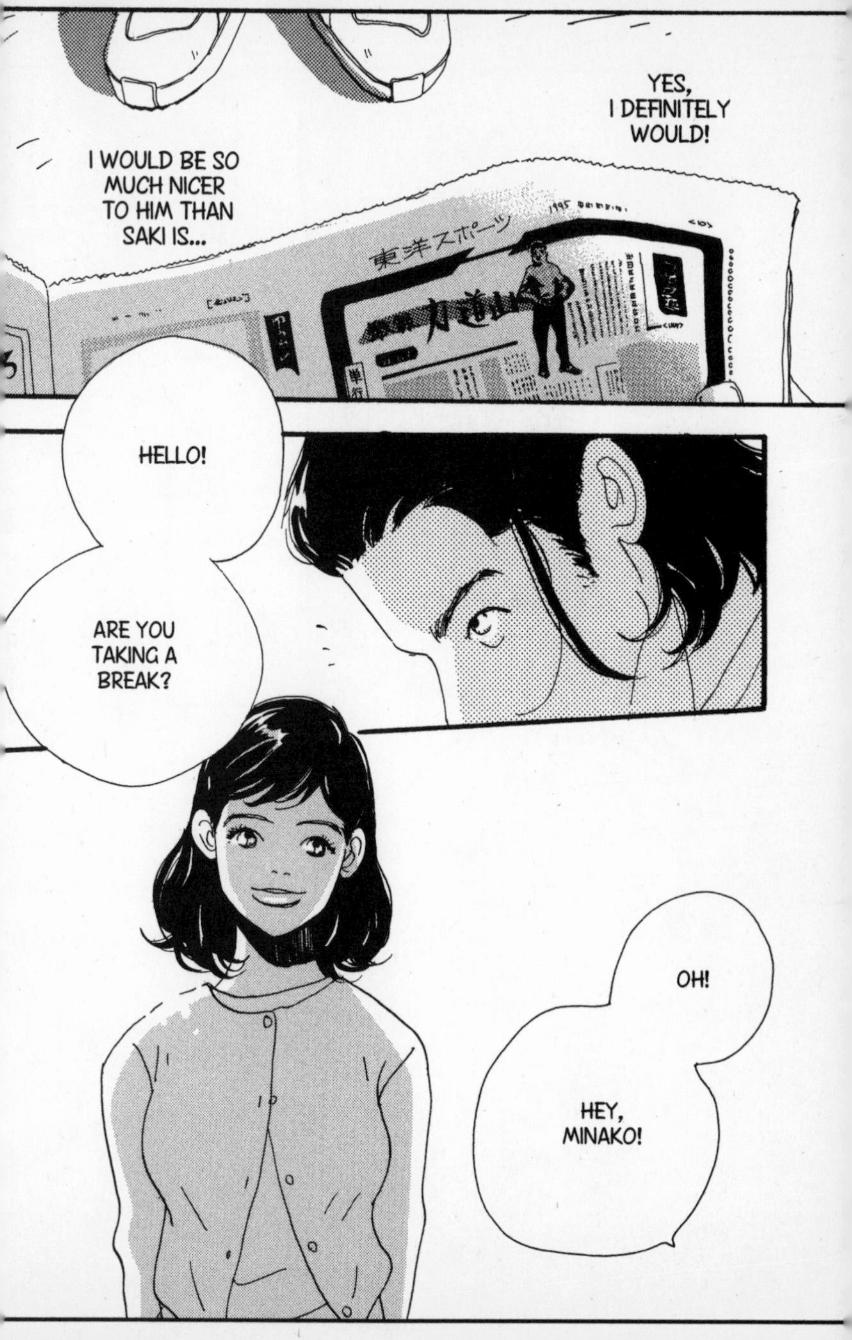
YES, I DEFINITELY WOULD!
I WOULD BE SO MUCH NICER TO HIM THAN SAKI IS...
東洋スポーツ
HELLO!
ARE YOU TAKING A BREAK?
OH!
HEY, MINAKO!

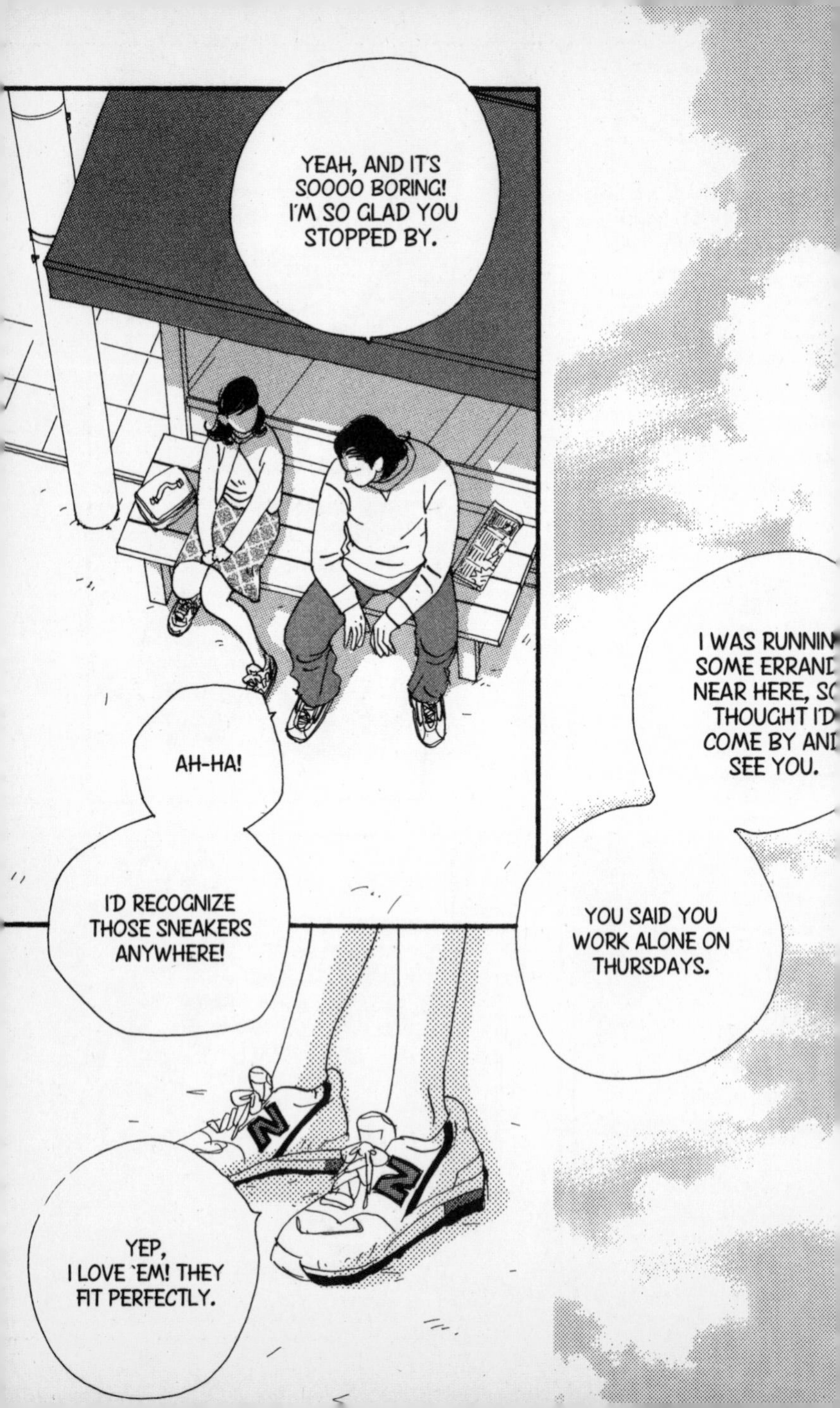
I WAS RUNNIN SOME ERRAND NEAR HERE, S THOUGHT I'D COME BY AN SEE YOU.
YOU SAID YOU WORK ALONE ON THURSDAYS.
YEAH, AND IT'S SOOOO BORING! I'M SO GLAD YOU STOPPED BY.
AH-HA!
I'D RECOGNIZE THOSE SNEAKERS ANYWHERE!
YEP, I LOVE 'EM! THEY FIT PERFECTLY.

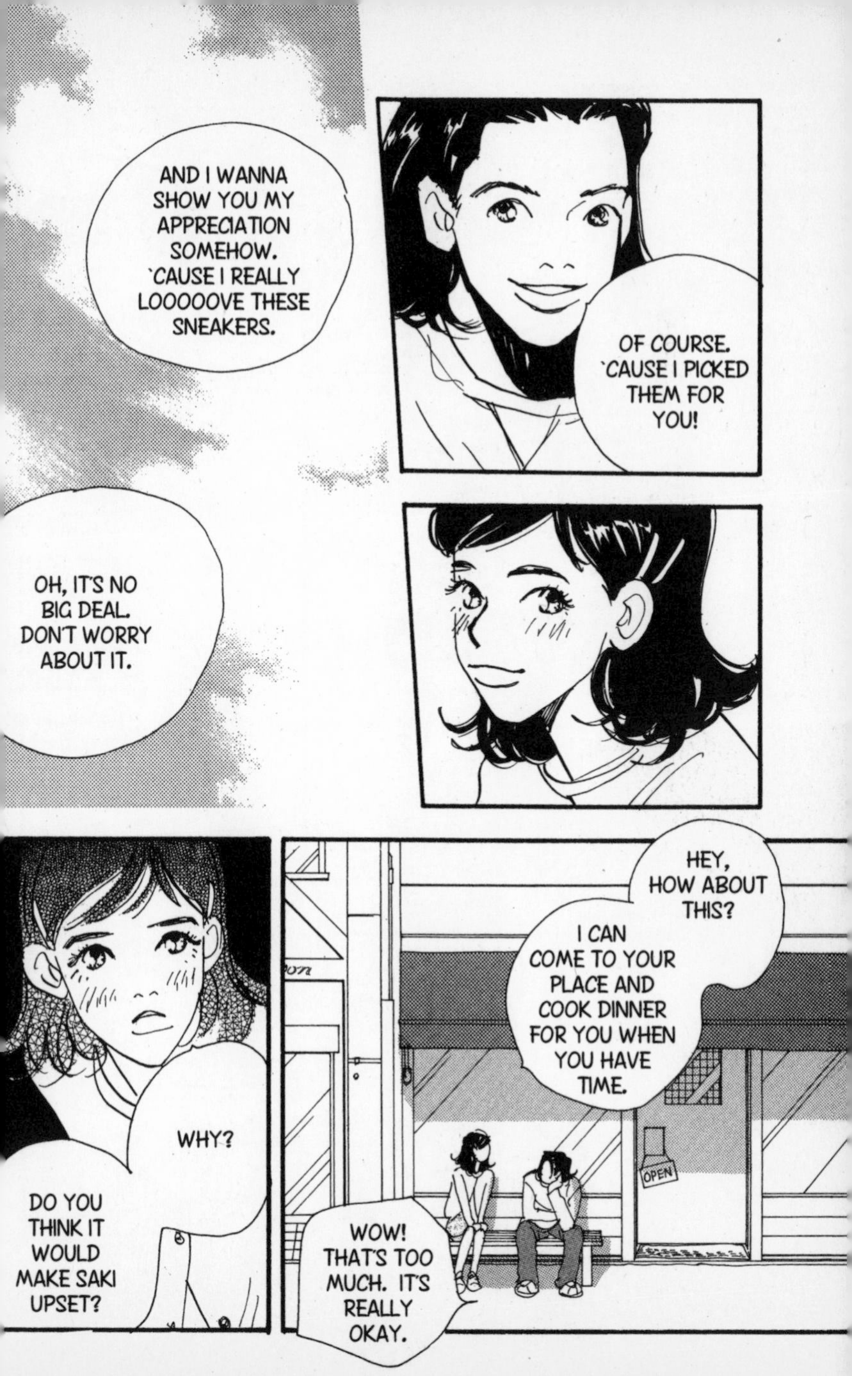
AND I WANNA SHOW YOU MY APPRECIATION SOMEHOW. `CAUSE I REALLY LOOOOOVE THESE SNEAKERS.
OF COURSE. `CAUSE I PICKED THEM FOR YOU!
OH, IT'S NO BIG DEAL. DON'T WORRY ABOUT IT.
HEY, HOW ABOUT THIS?
I CAN COME TO YOUR PLACE AND COOK DINNER FOR YOU WHEN YOU HAVE TIME.
OPEN
WOW! THAT'S TOO MUCH. IT'S REALLY OKAY.
WHY?
DO YOU THINK IT WOULD MAKE SAKI UPSET?

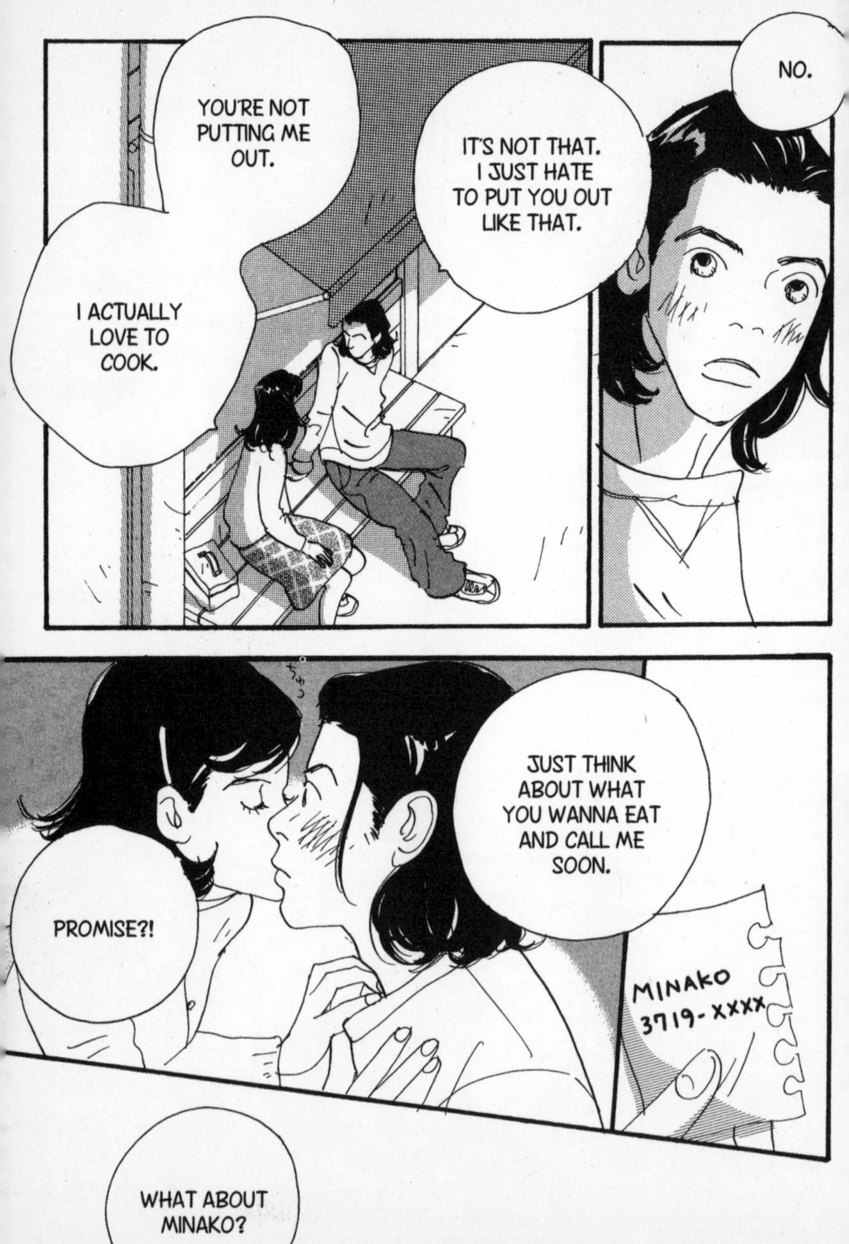
NO.
IT'S NOT THAT. I JUST HATE TO PUT YOU OUT LIKE THAT.
YOU'RE NOT PUTTING ME OUT.
I ACTUALLY LOVE TO COOK.
JUST THINK ABOUT WHAT YOU WANNA EAT AND CALL ME SOON.
MINAKO 3719-XXXX
PROMISE?!
WHAT ABOUT MINAKO?

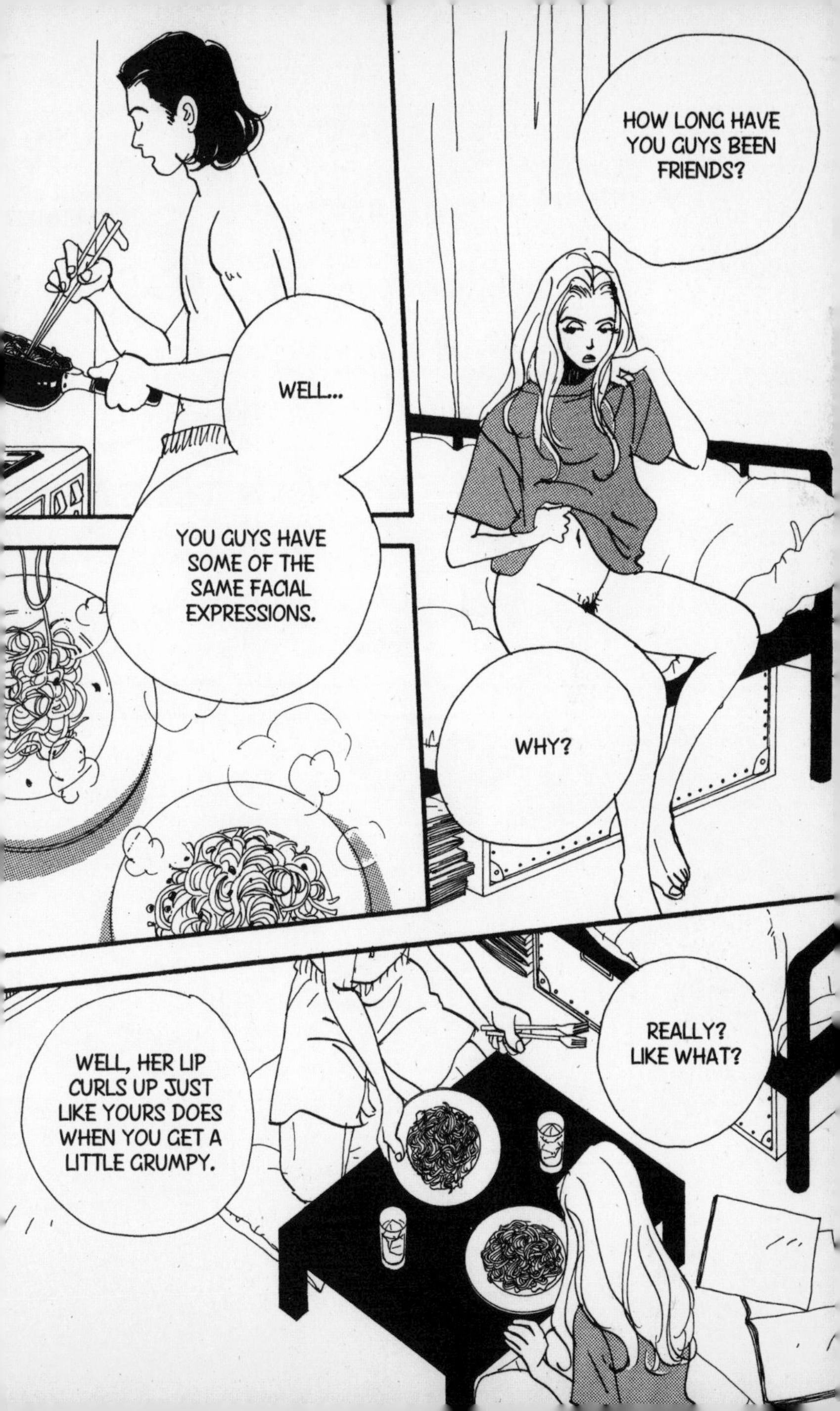
HOW LONG HAVE YOU GUYS BEEN FRIENDS?
WELL...
YOU GUYS HAVE SOME OF THE SAME FACIAL EXPRESSIONS.
WHY?
REALLY? LIKE WHAT?
WELL, HER LIP CURLS UP JUST LIKE YOURS DOES WHEN YOU GET A LITTLE GRUMPY.

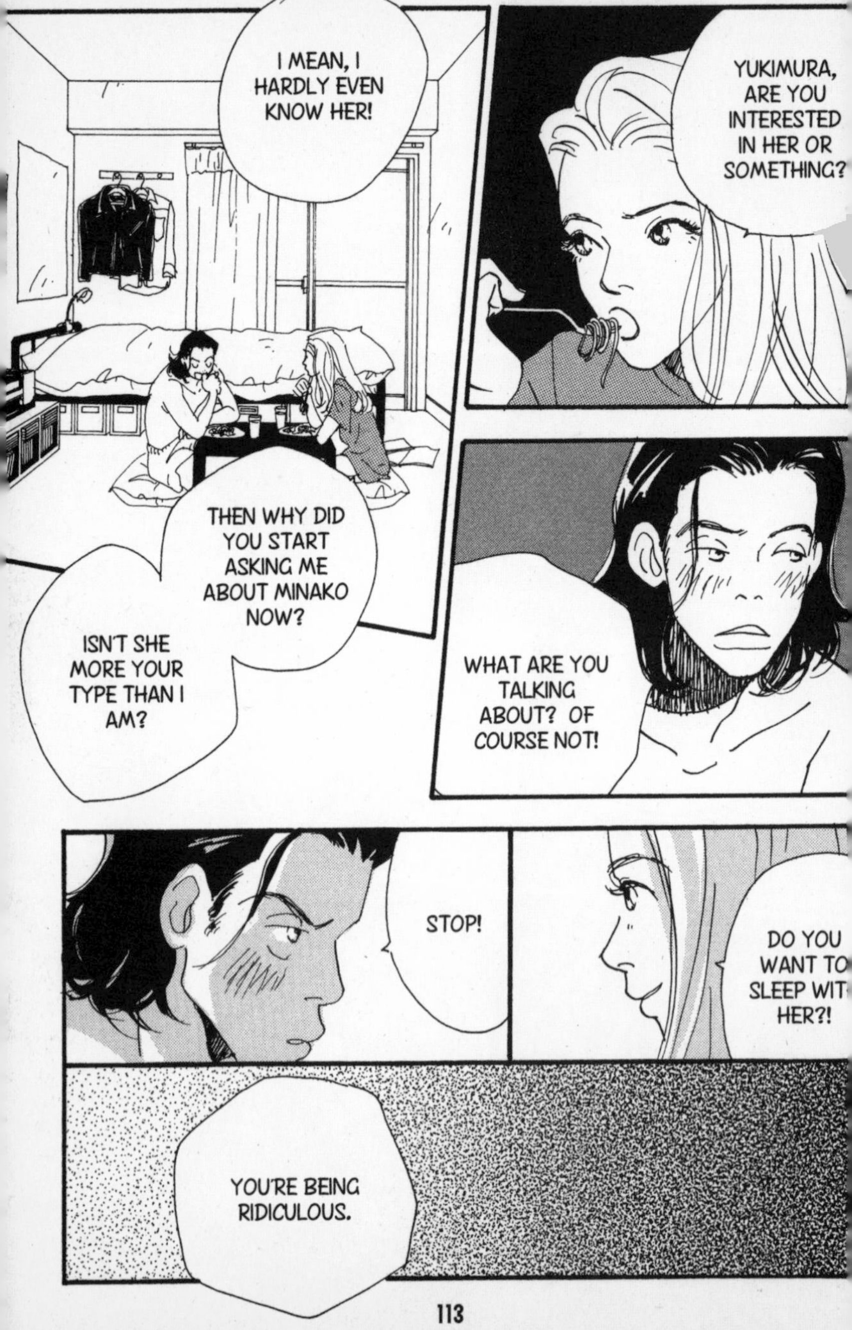
YUKIMURA, ARE YOU INTERESTED IN HER OR SOMETHING?
WHAT ARE YOU TALKING ABOUT? OF COURSE NOT!
I MEAN, I HARDLY EVEN KNOW HER!
THEN WHY DID YOU START ASKING ME ABOUT MINAKO NOW?
ISN'T SHE MORE YOUR TYPE THAN I AM?
DO YOU WANT TO SLEEP WIT HER?!
STOP!
YOU'RE BEING RIDICULOUS.

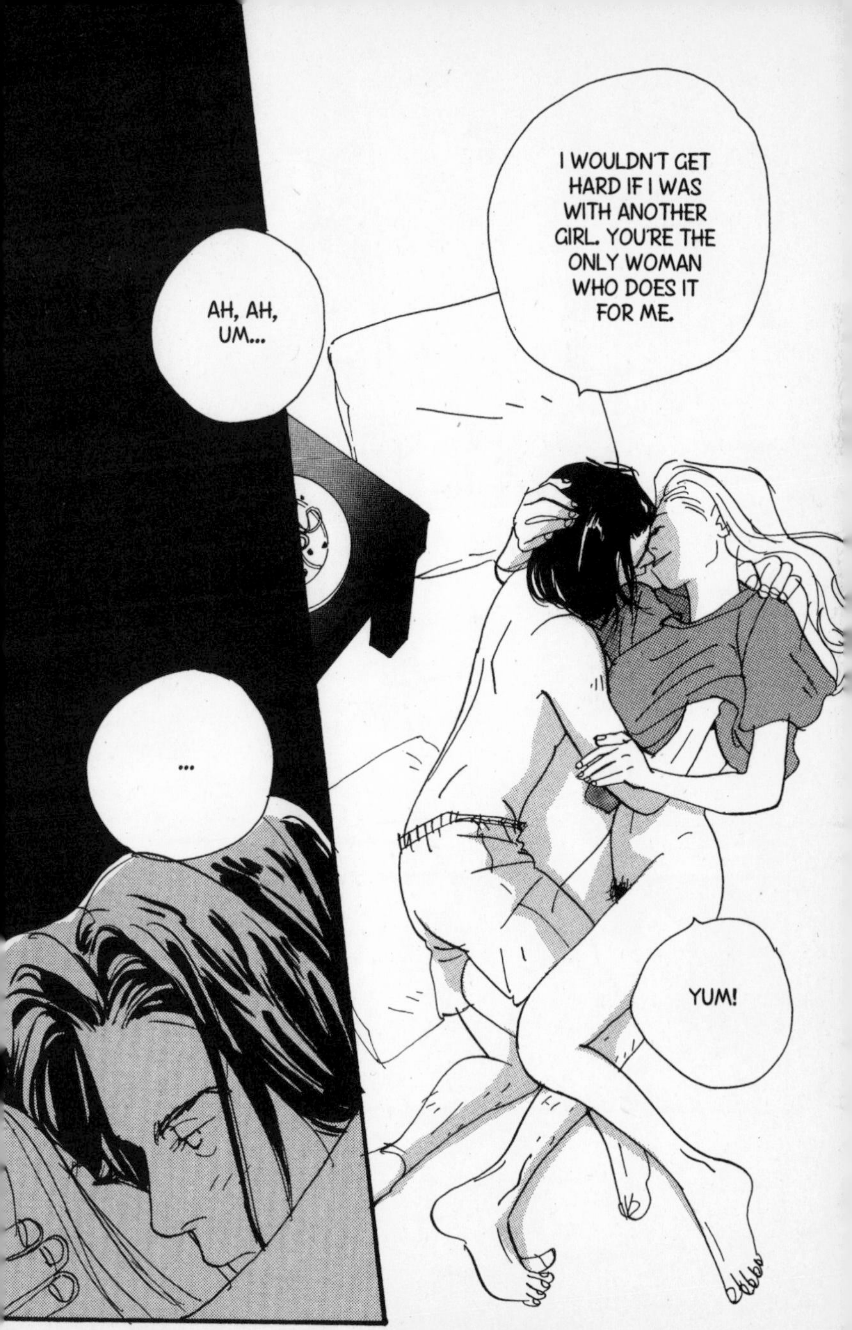
I WOULDN'T GET HARD IF I WAS WITH ANOTHER GIRL. YOU'RE THE ONLY WOMAN WHO DOES IT FOR ME.
YUM!
AH, AH, UM...
...

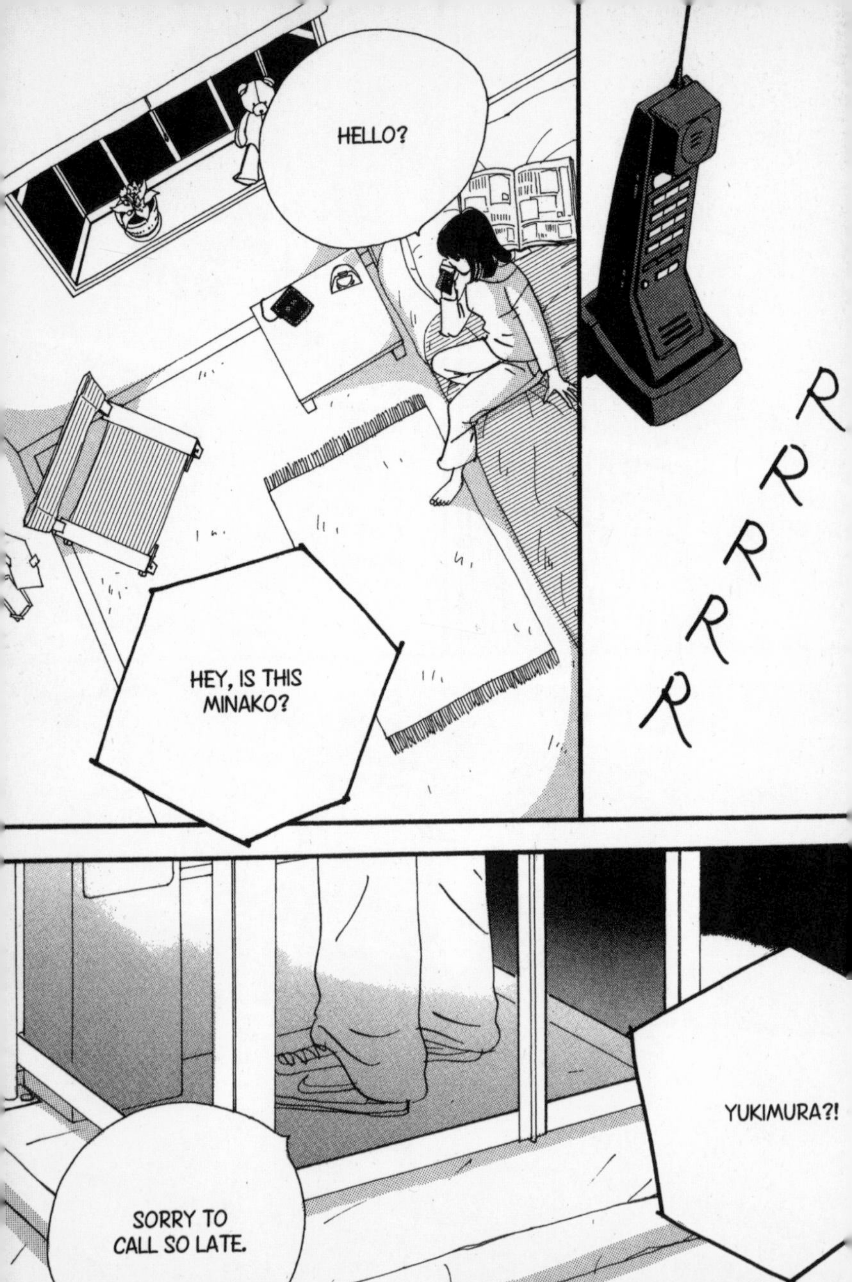
RRRRR
HELLO?
HEY, IS THIS MINAKO?
YUKIMURA?!
SORRY TO CALL SO LATE.

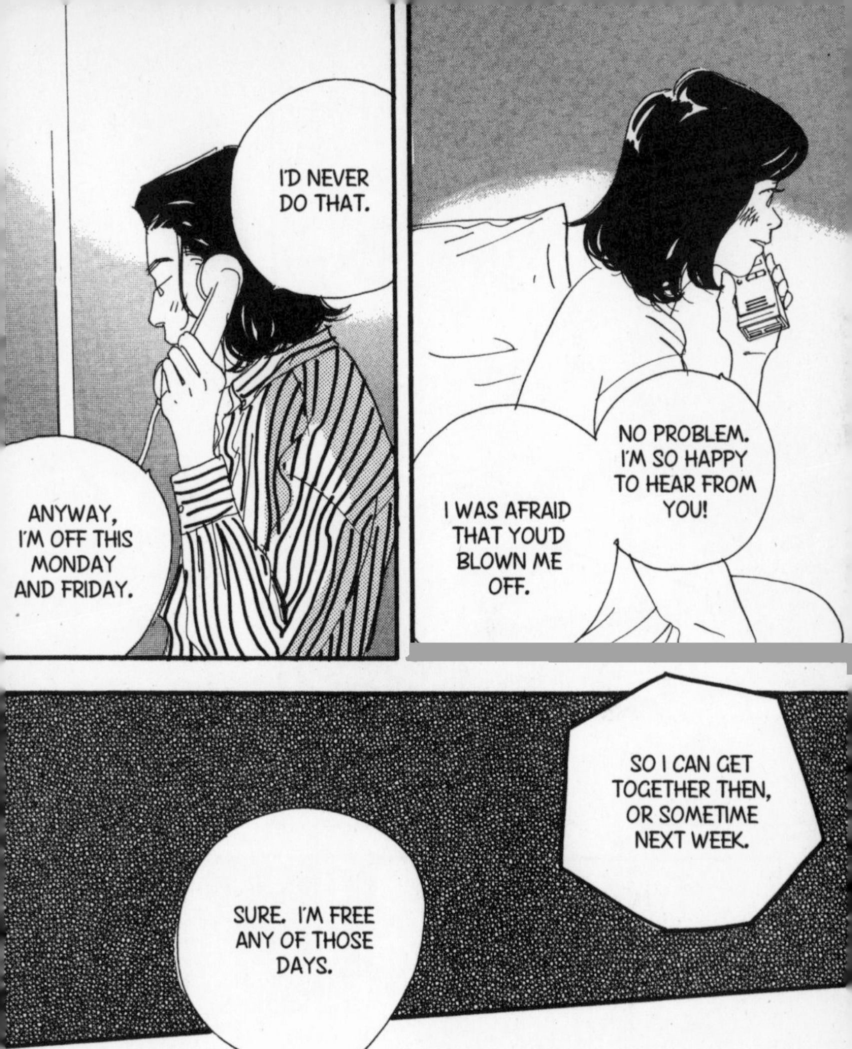
NO PROBLEM. I'M SO HAPPY TO HEAR FROM YOU!
I WAS AFRAID THAT YOU'D BLOWN ME OFF.
I'D NEVER DO THAT.
ANYWAY, I'M OFF THIS MONDAY AND FRIDAY.
SO I CAN GET TOGETHER THEN, OR SOMETIME NEXT WEEK.
SURE. I'M FREE ANY OF THOSE DAYS.
SEE, SAKI!

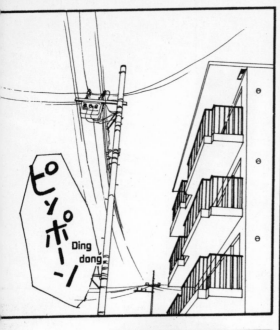

THIS IS ALL YOUR FAULT, SAKI.

ピッ
ポーン
Ding
dong

`CAUSE YOU DON'T CARE ABOUT HIM ENOUGH.

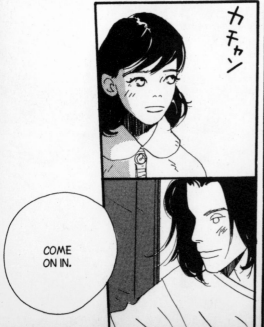

カチャン

COME ON IN.

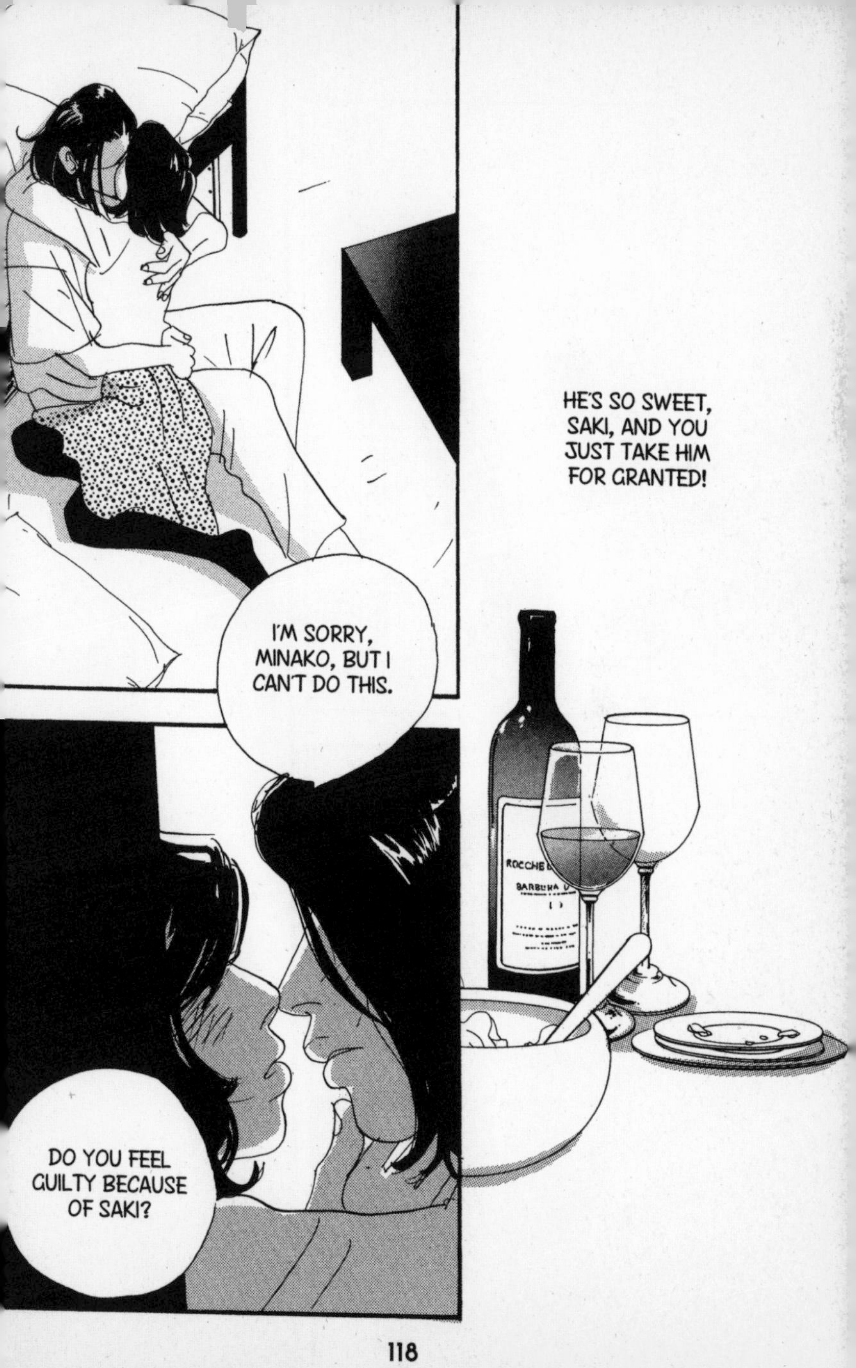
HE'S SO SWEET, SAKI, AND YOU JUST TAKE HIM FOR GRANTED!
I'M SORRY, MINAKO, BUT I CAN'T DO THIS.
DO YOU FEEL GUILTY BECAUSE OF SAKI?

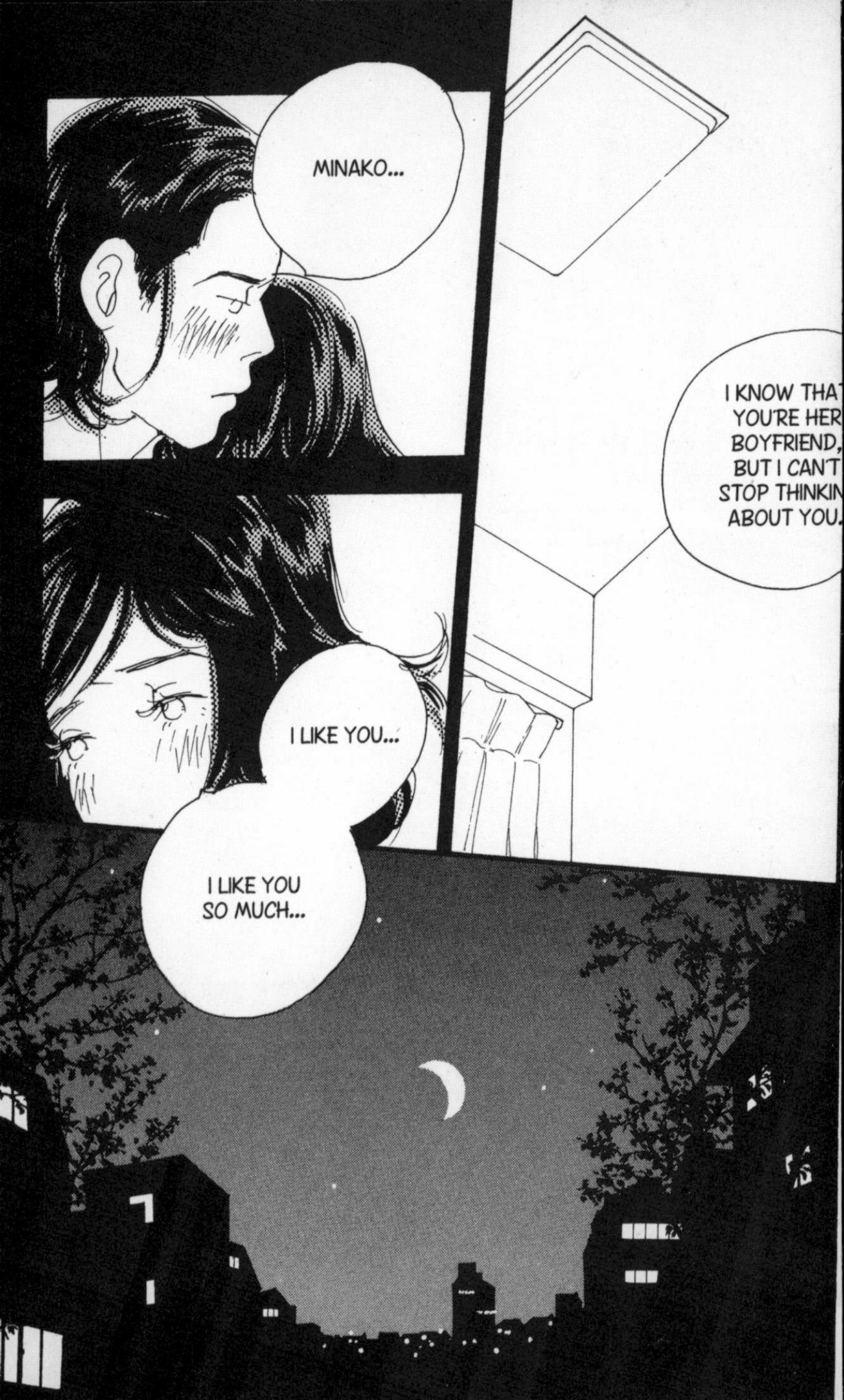
I KNOW THA YOU'RE HER BOYFRIEND, BUT I CAN'T STOP THINKIN ABOUT YOU.
MINAKO...
I LIKE YOU...
I LIKE YOU SO MUCH...

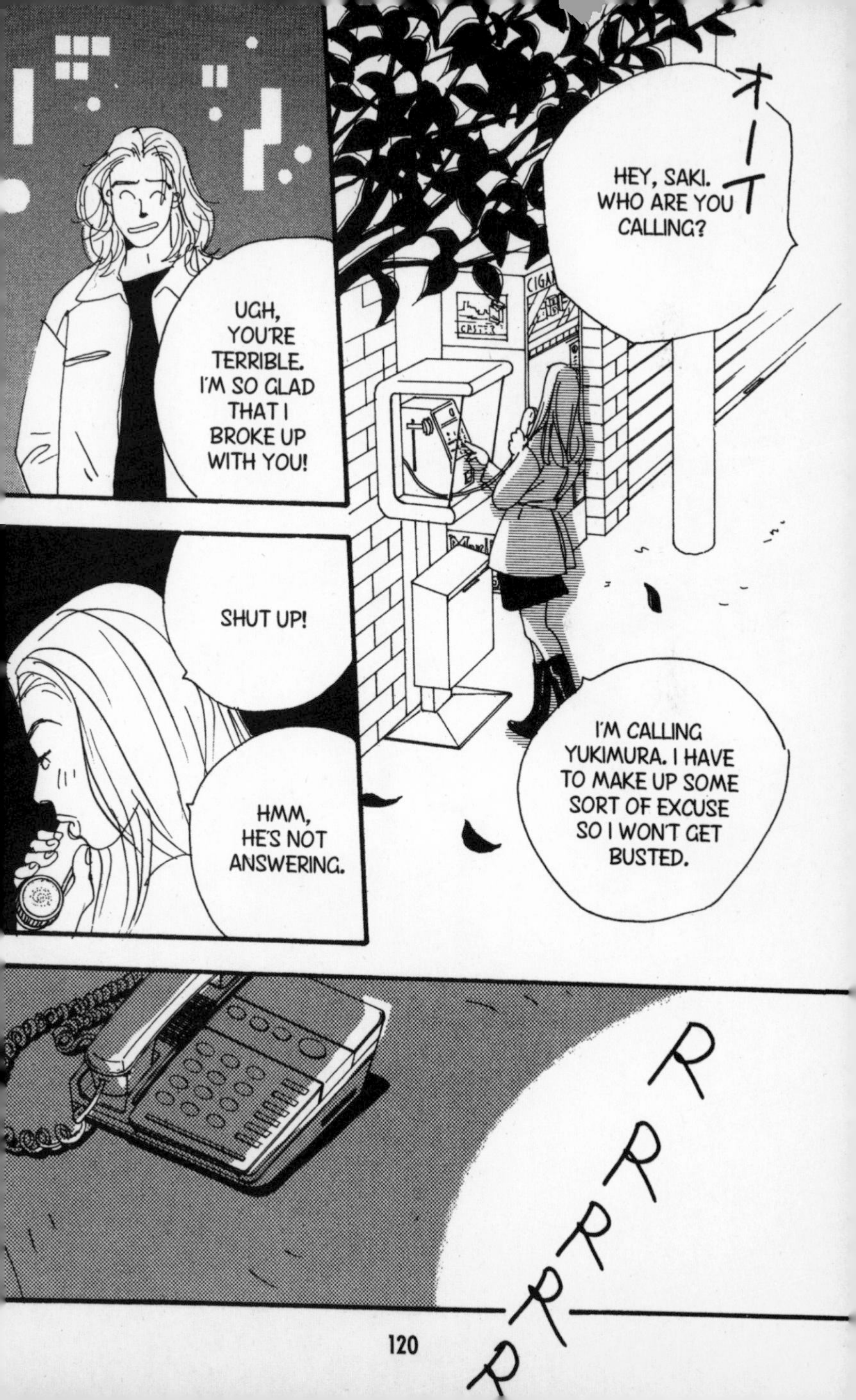
HEY, SAKI. WHO ARE YOU CALLING?
I'M CALLING YUKIMURA. I HAVE TO MAKE UP SOME SORT OF EXCUSE SO I WON'T GET BUSTED.
UGH, YOU'RE TERRIBLE. I'M SO GLAD THAT I BROKE UP WITH YOU!
SHUT UP!
HMM, HE'S NOT ANSWERING.
RRRRRR

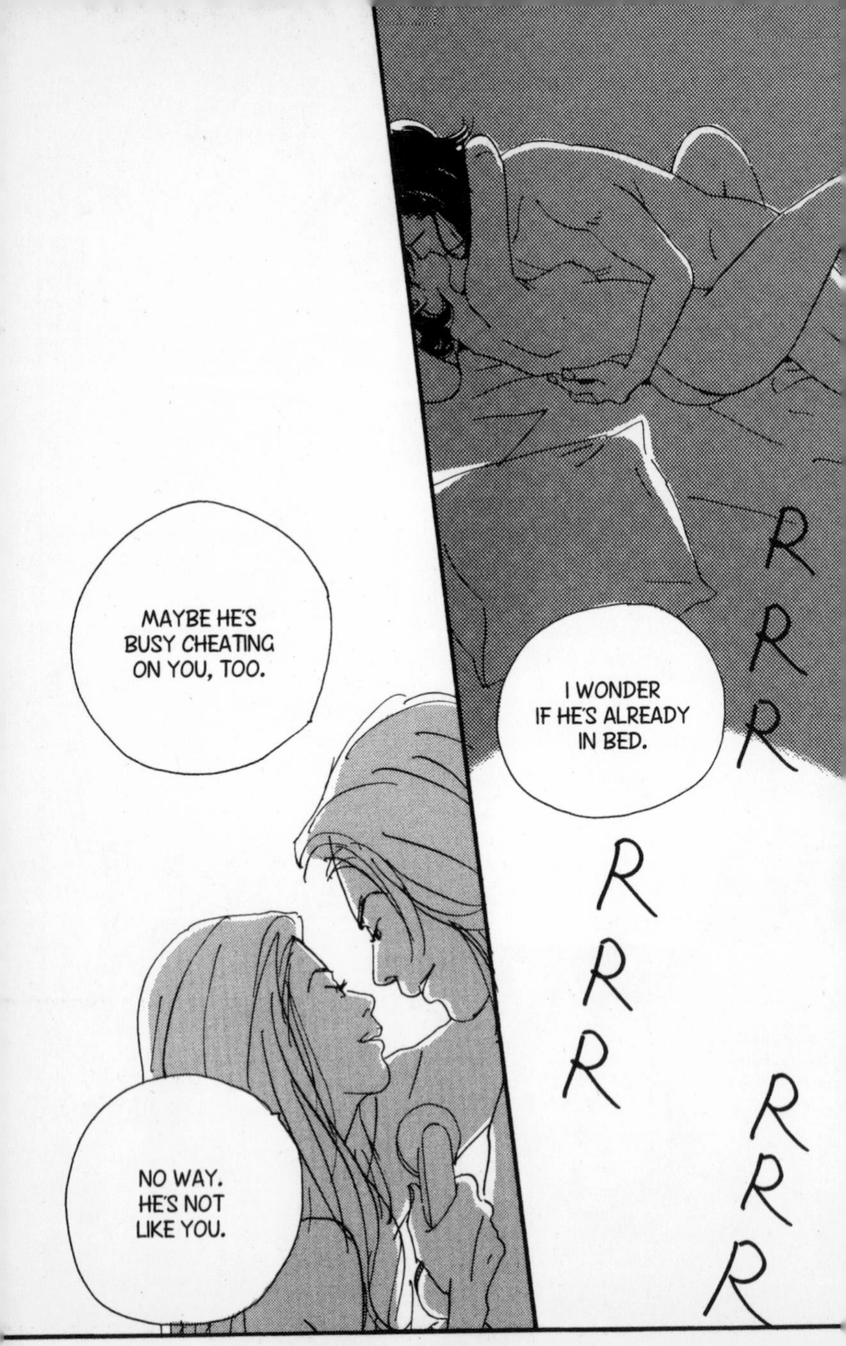
RRR
I WONDER IF HE'S ALREADY IN BED.
RRR
RRR
MAYBE HE'S BUSY CHEATING ON YOU, TOO.
NO WAY. HE'S NOT LIKE YOU.

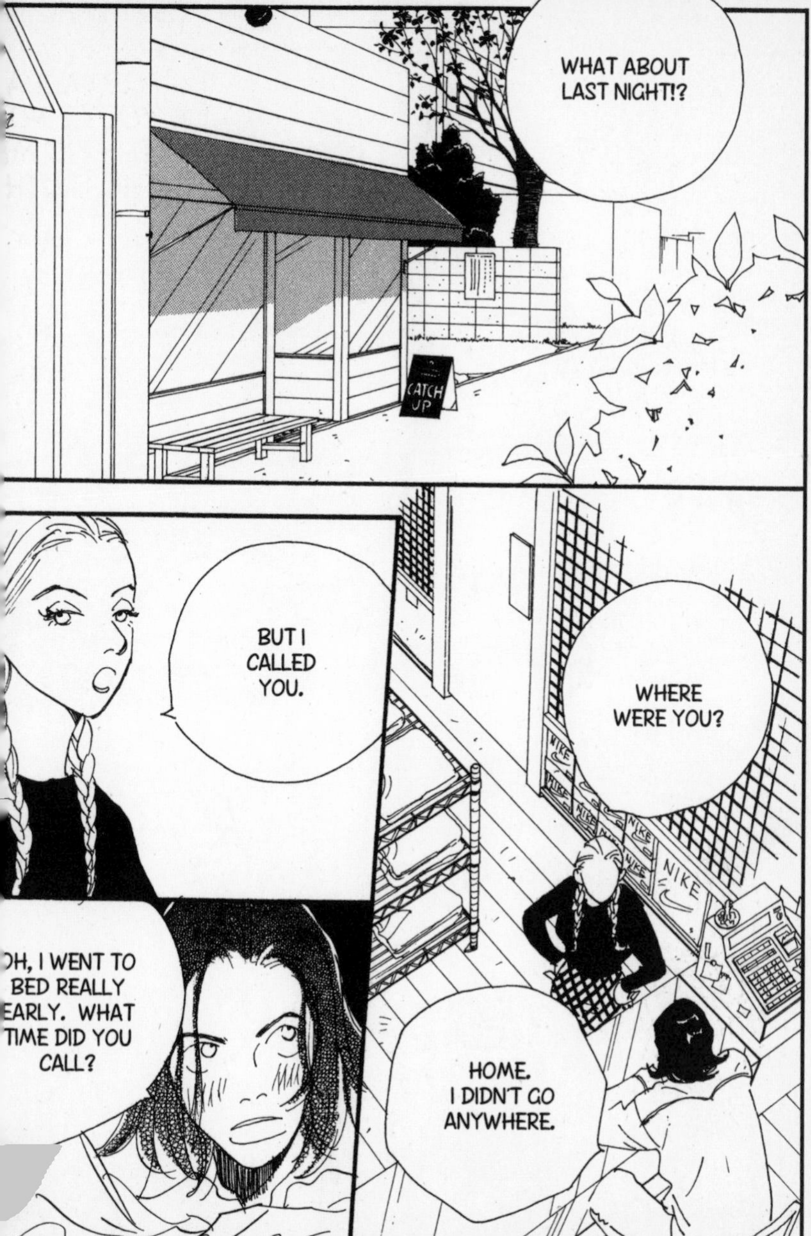
WHAT ABOUT LAST NIGHT!?
CATCH UP
WHERE WERE YOU?
HOME. I DIDN'T GO ANYWHERE.
BUT I CALLED YOU.
OH, I WENT TO BED REALLY EARLY. WHAT TIME DID YOU CALL?

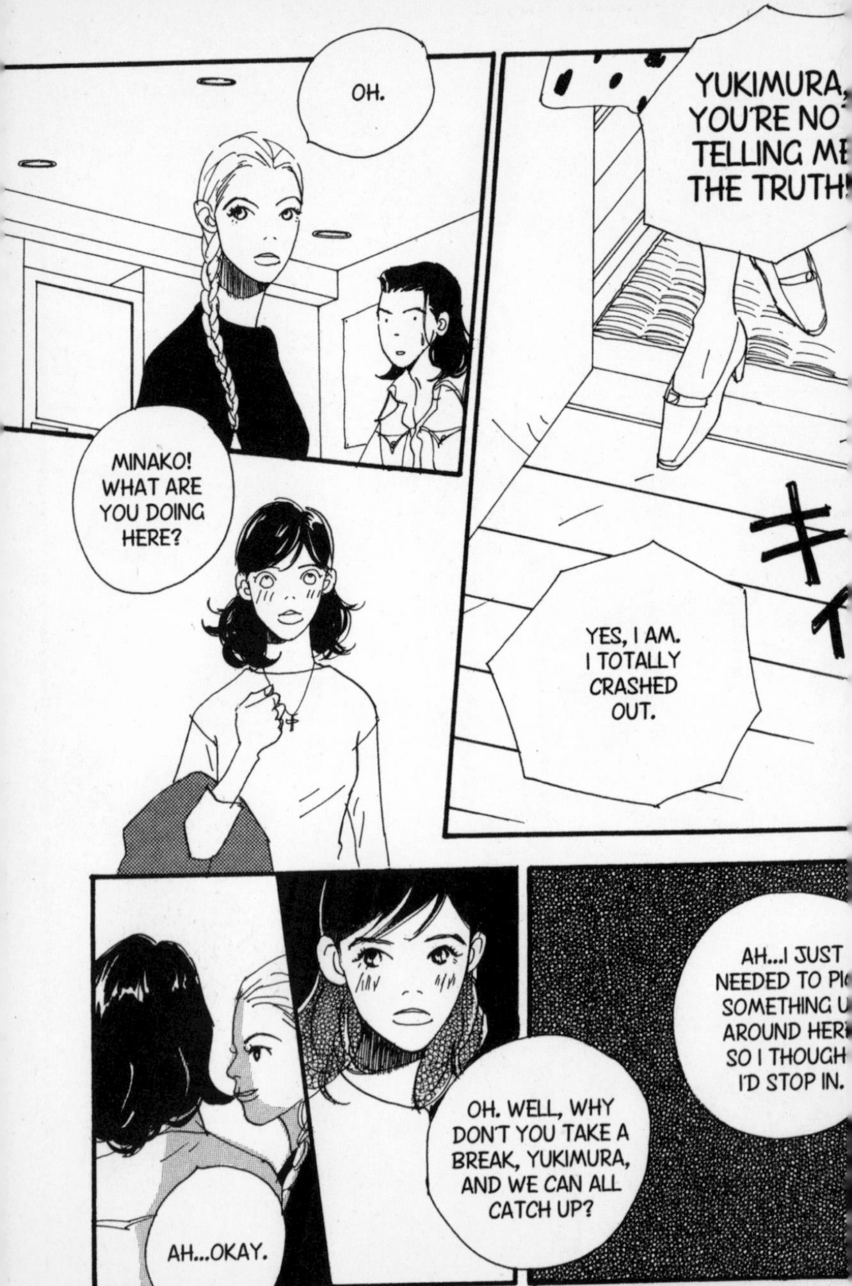
YUKIMURA, YOU'RE NOT TELLING ME THE TRUTH!
キイ
YES, I AM. I TOTALLY CRASHED OUT.
OH.
MINAKO! WHAT ARE YOU DOING HERE?
AH...I JUST NEEDED TO PIC SOMETHING U AROUND HER SO I THOUGH I'D STOP IN.
OH. WELL, WHY DON'T YOU TAKE A BREAK, YUKIMURA, AND WE CAN ALL CATCH UP?
AH...OKAY.

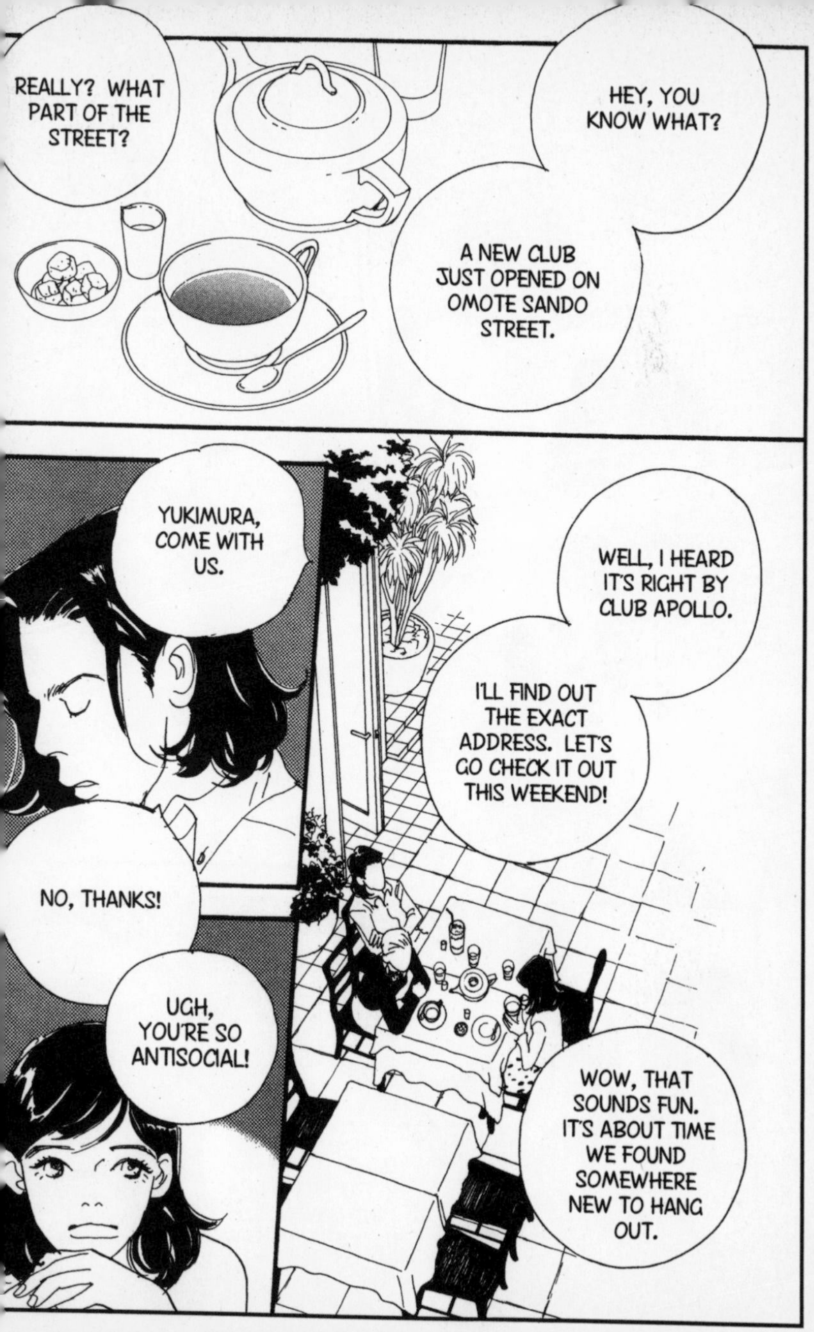
HEY, YOU KNOW WHAT?
A NEW CLUB JUST OPENED ON OMOTE SANDO STREET.
REALLY? WHAT PART OF THE STREET?
WELL, I HEARD IT'S RIGHT BY CLUB APOLLO.
I'LL FIND OUT THE EXACT ADDRESS. LET'S GO CHECK IT OUT THIS WEEKEND!
WOW, THAT SOUNDS FUN. IT'S ABOUT TIME WE FOUND SOMEWHERE NEW TO HANG OUT.
YUKIMURA, COME WITH US.
NO, THANKS!
UGH, YOU'RE SO ANTISOCIAL!

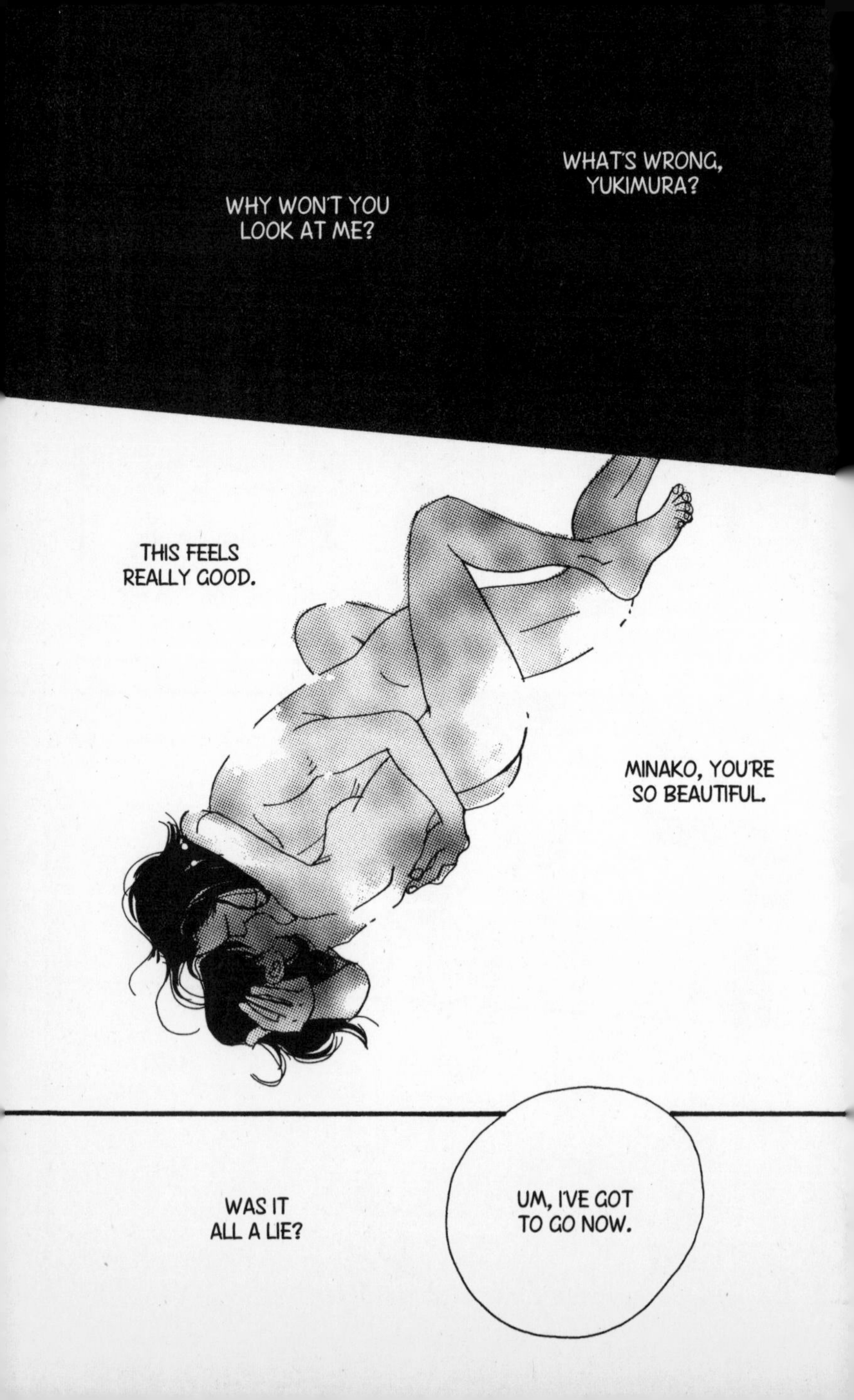
WHAT'S WRONG, YUKIMURA?
WHY WON'T YOU LOOK AT ME?
MINAKO, YOU'RE SO BEAUTIFUL.
THIS FEELS REALLY GOOD.
UM, I'VE GOT TO GO NOW.
WAS IT ALL A LIE?

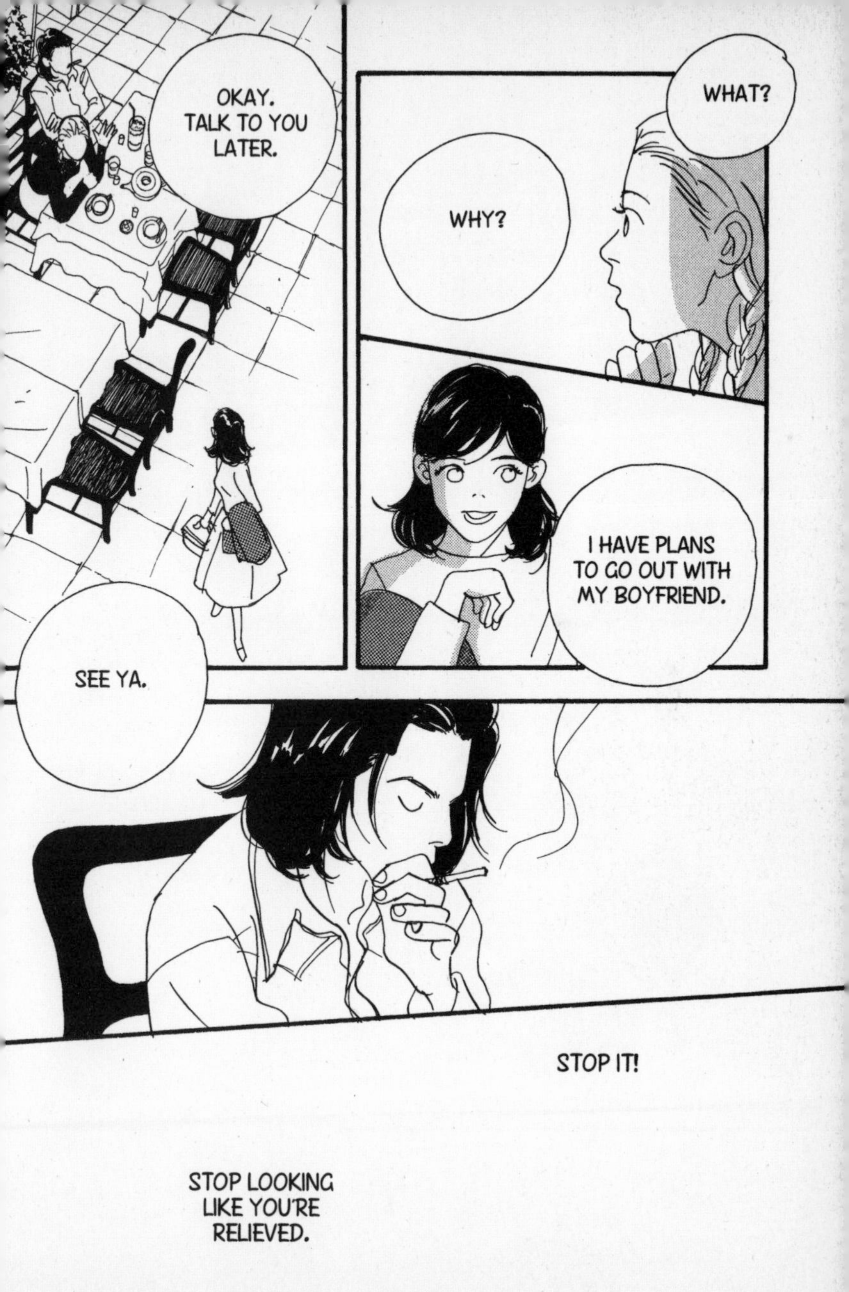
WHAT?
WHY?
I HAVE PLANS TO GO OUT WITH MY BOYFRIEND.
OKAY. TALK TO YOU LATER.
SEE YA.
STOP IT!
STOP LOOKING LIKE YOU'RE RELIEVED.

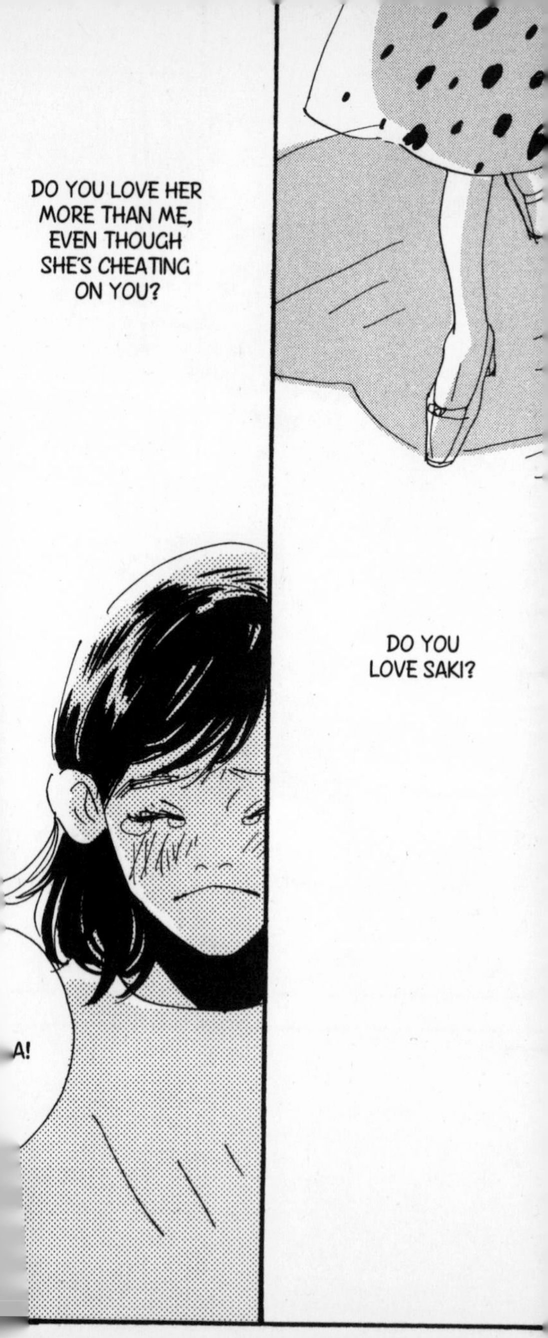
DO YOU LOVE SAKI?
DO YOU LOVE HER MORE THAN ME, EVEN THOUGH SHE'S CHEATING ON YOU?
A!

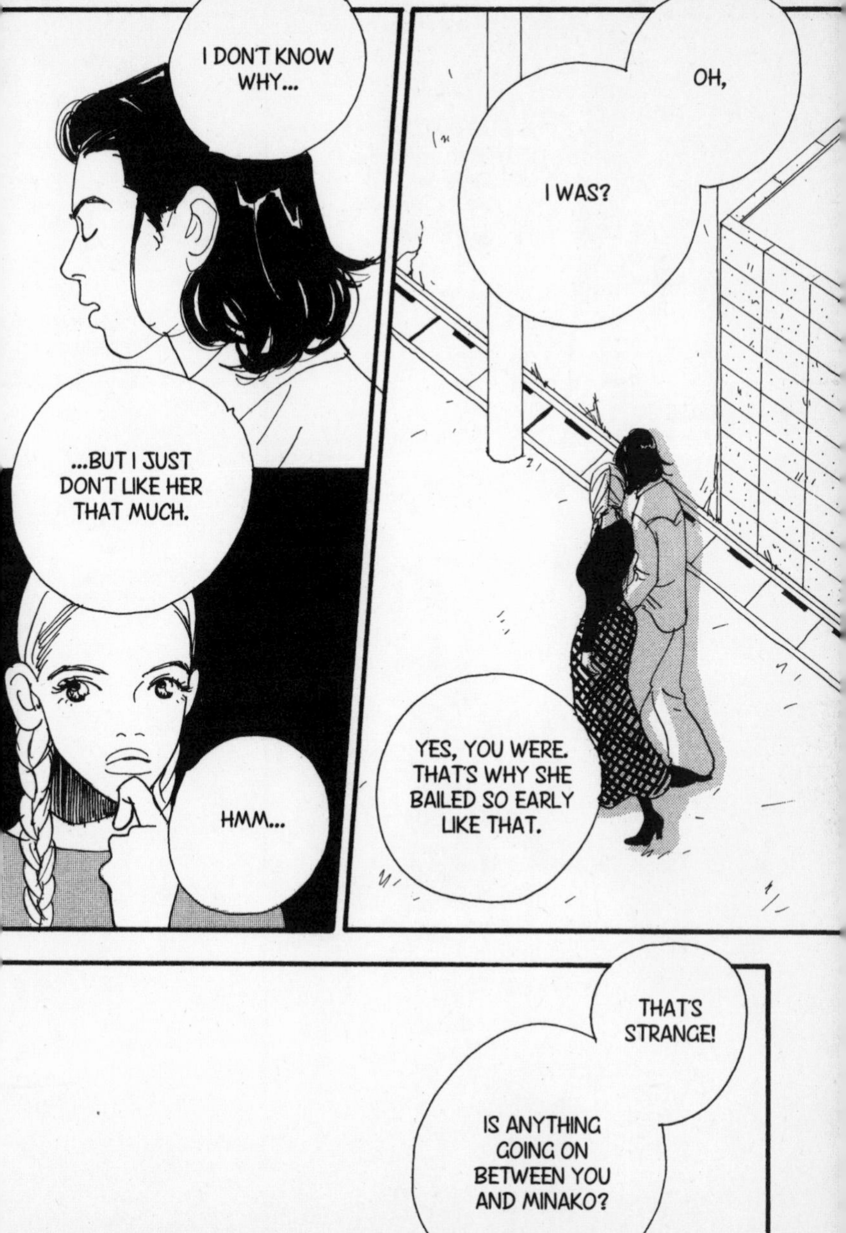
OH,
I WAS?
YES, YOU WERE. THAT'S WHY SHE BAILED SO EARLY LIKE THAT.
I DON'T KNOW WHY...
...BUT I JUST DON'T LIKE HER THAT MUCH.
HMM...
THAT'S STRANGE!
IS ANYTHING GOING ON BETWEEN YOU AND MINAKO?

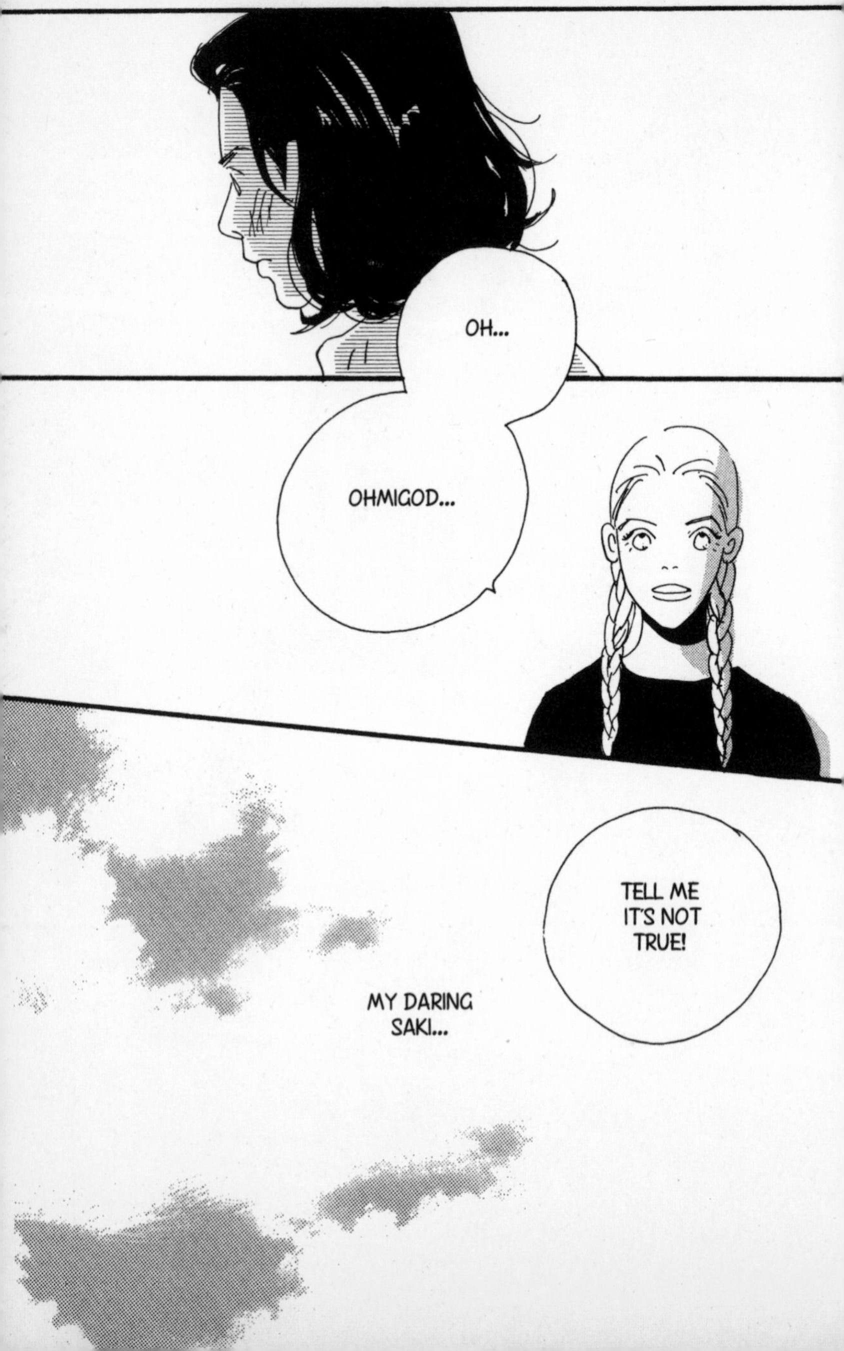
OH...
OHMIGOD...
TELL ME IT'S NOT TRUE!
MY DARING SAKI...

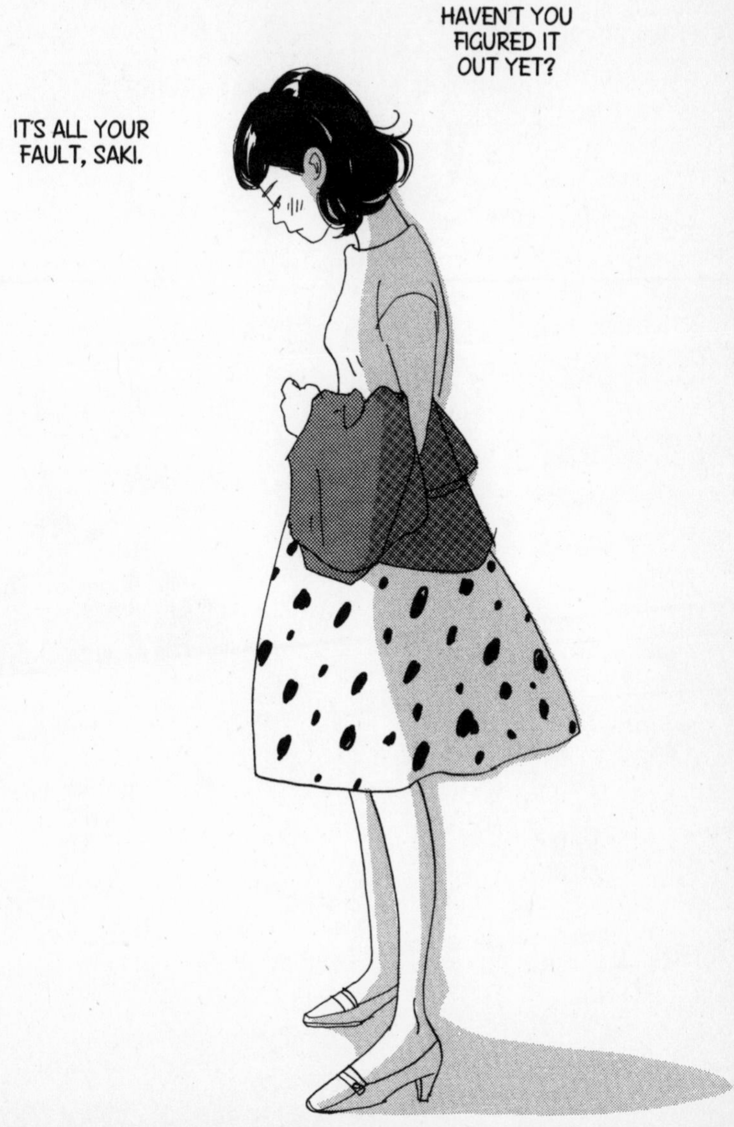
HAVEN'T YOU FIGURED IT OUT YET?
IT'S ALL YOUR FAULT, SAKI.

between the sheets

chapter 5

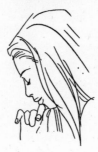

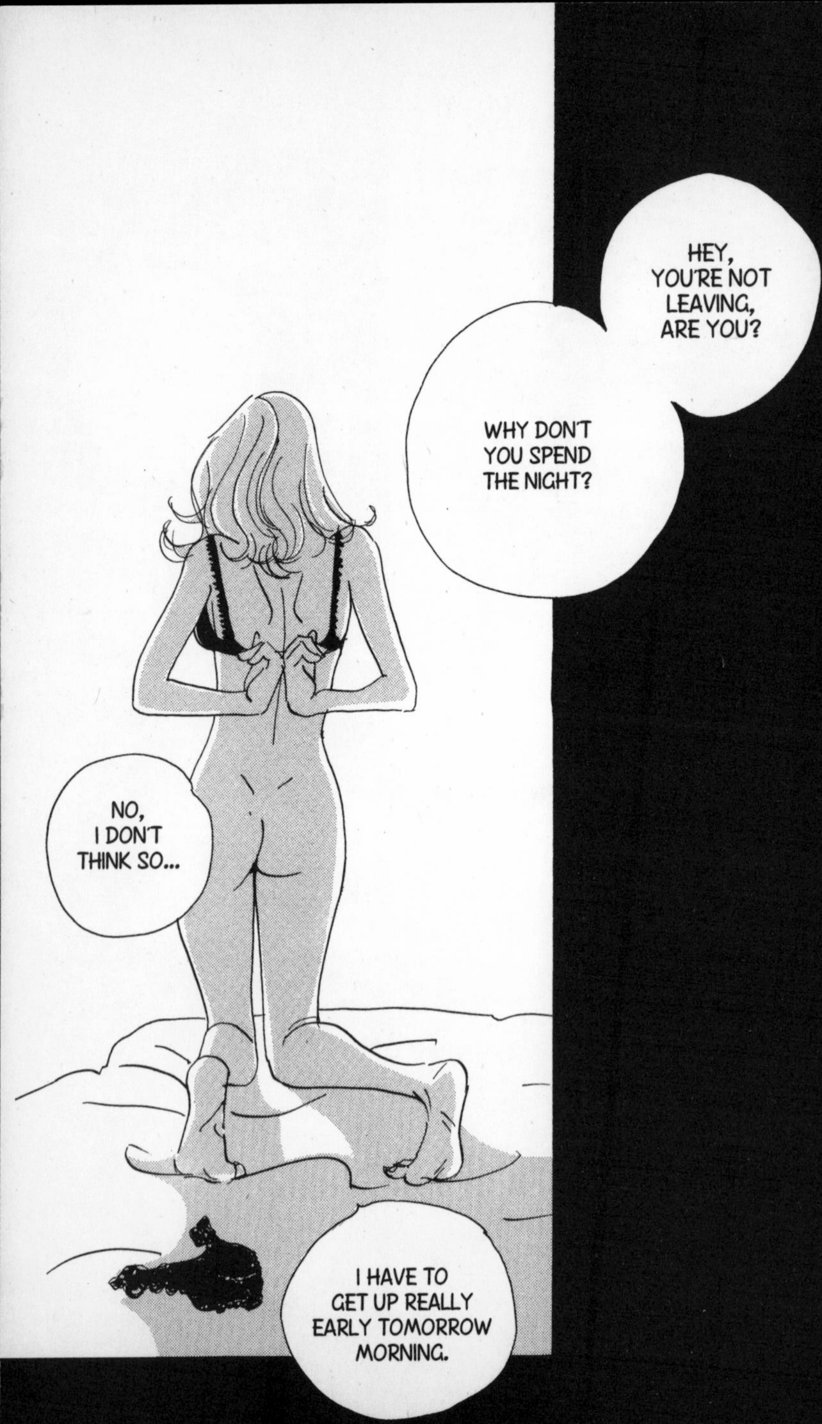
HEY, YOU'RE NOT LEAVING, ARE YOU?
WHY DON'T YOU SPEND THE NIGHT?
NO, I DON'T THINK SO...
I HAVE TO GET UP REALLY EARLY TOMORROW MORNING.

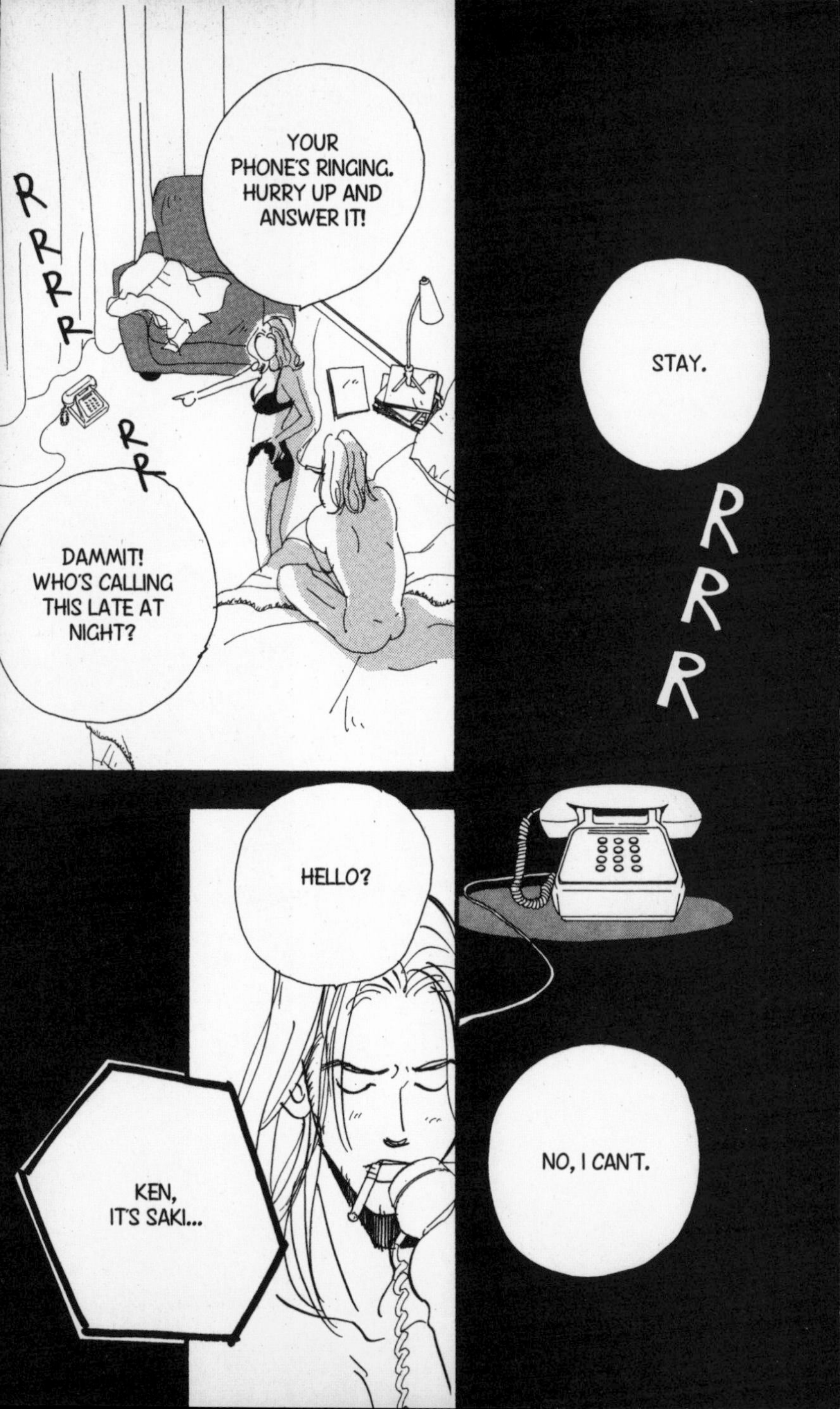
STAY.
RRR
YOUR PHONE'S RINGING. HURRY UP AND ANSWER IT!
RRRR
RR
DAMMIT! WHO'S CALLING THIS LATE AT NIGHT?
NO, I CAN'T.
HELLO?
KEN, IT'S SAKI...

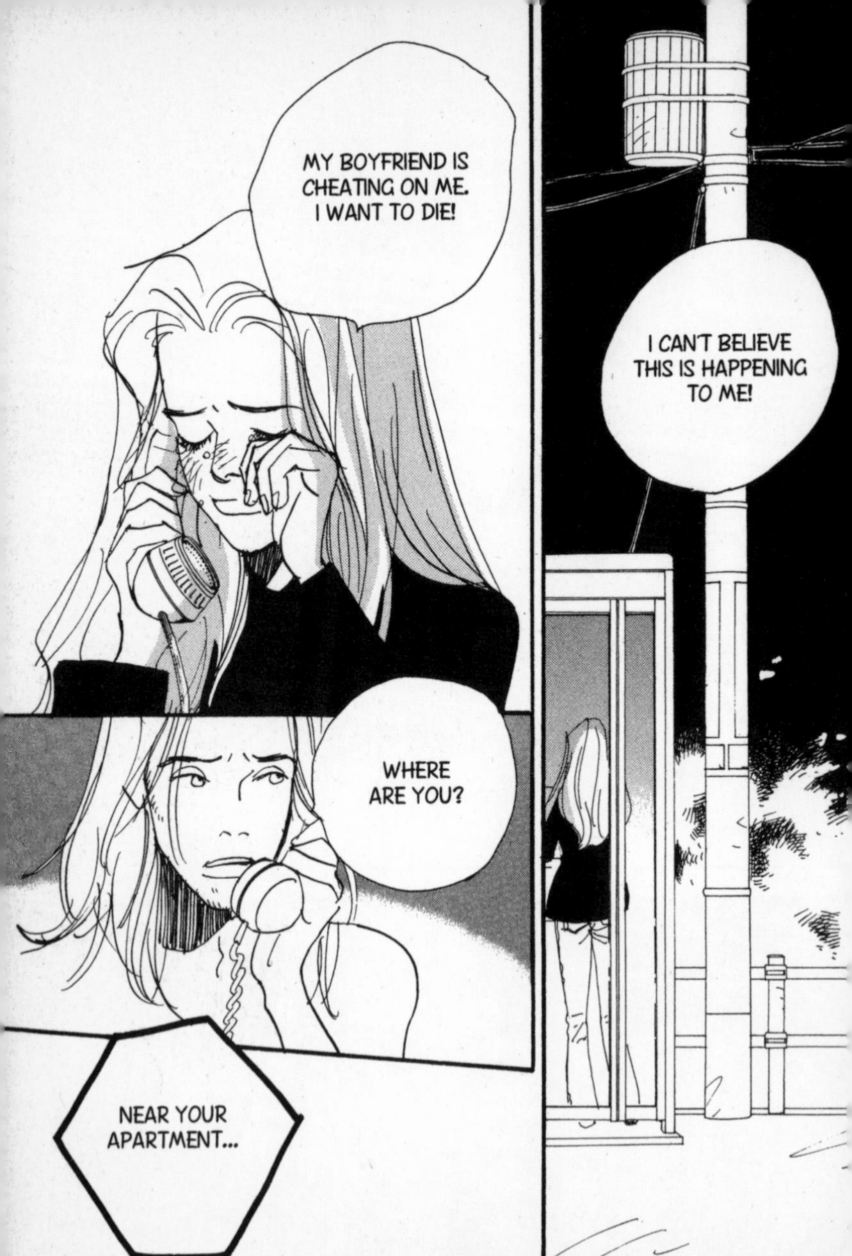
I CAN'T BELIEVE THIS IS HAPPENING TO ME!
MY BOYFRIEND IS CHEATING ON ME. I WANT TO DIE!
WHERE ARE YOU?
NEAR YOUR APARTMENT...

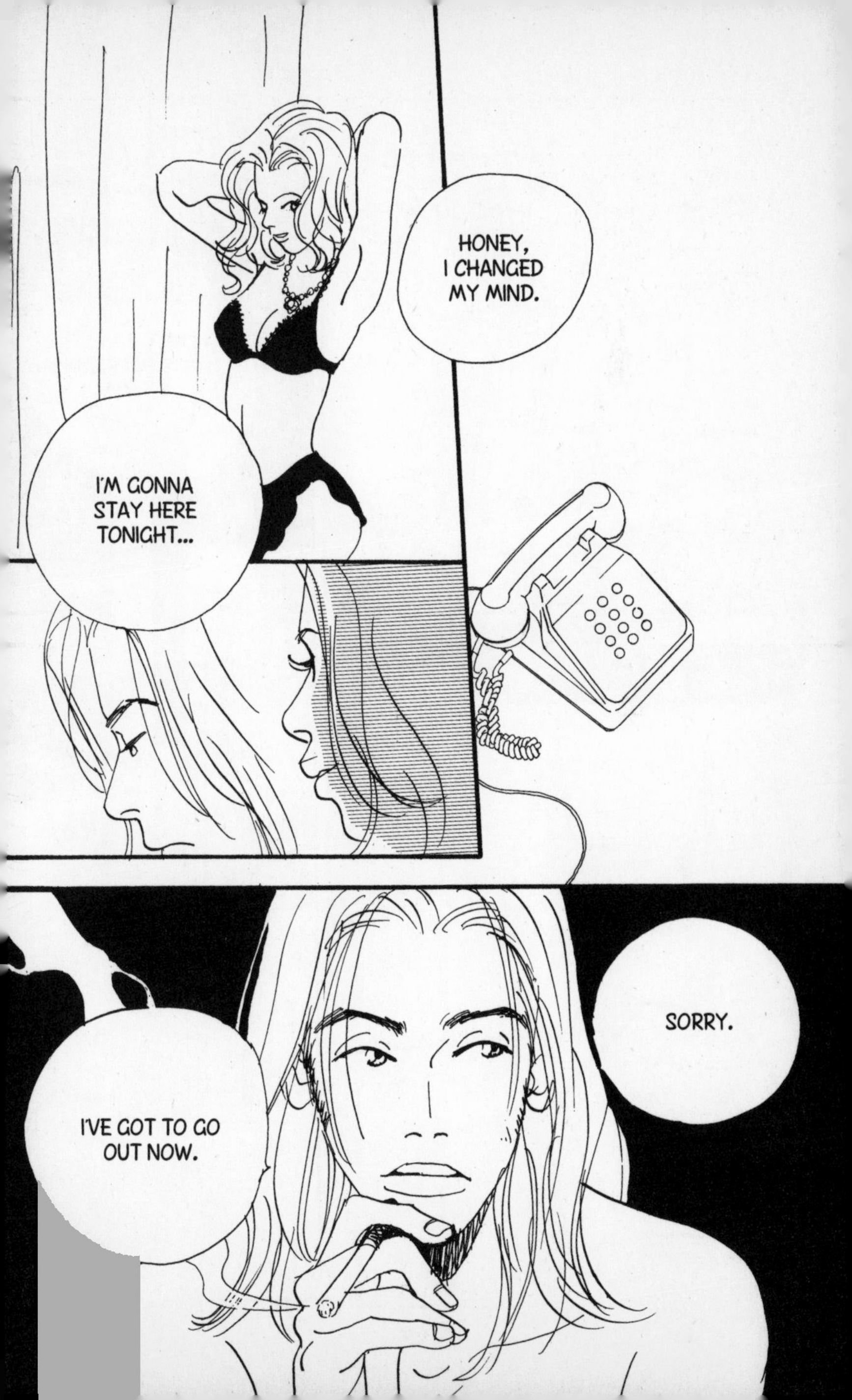
HONEY, I CHANGED MY MIND.
I'M GONNA STAY HERE TONIGHT...
SORRY.
I'VE GOT TO GO OUT NOW.

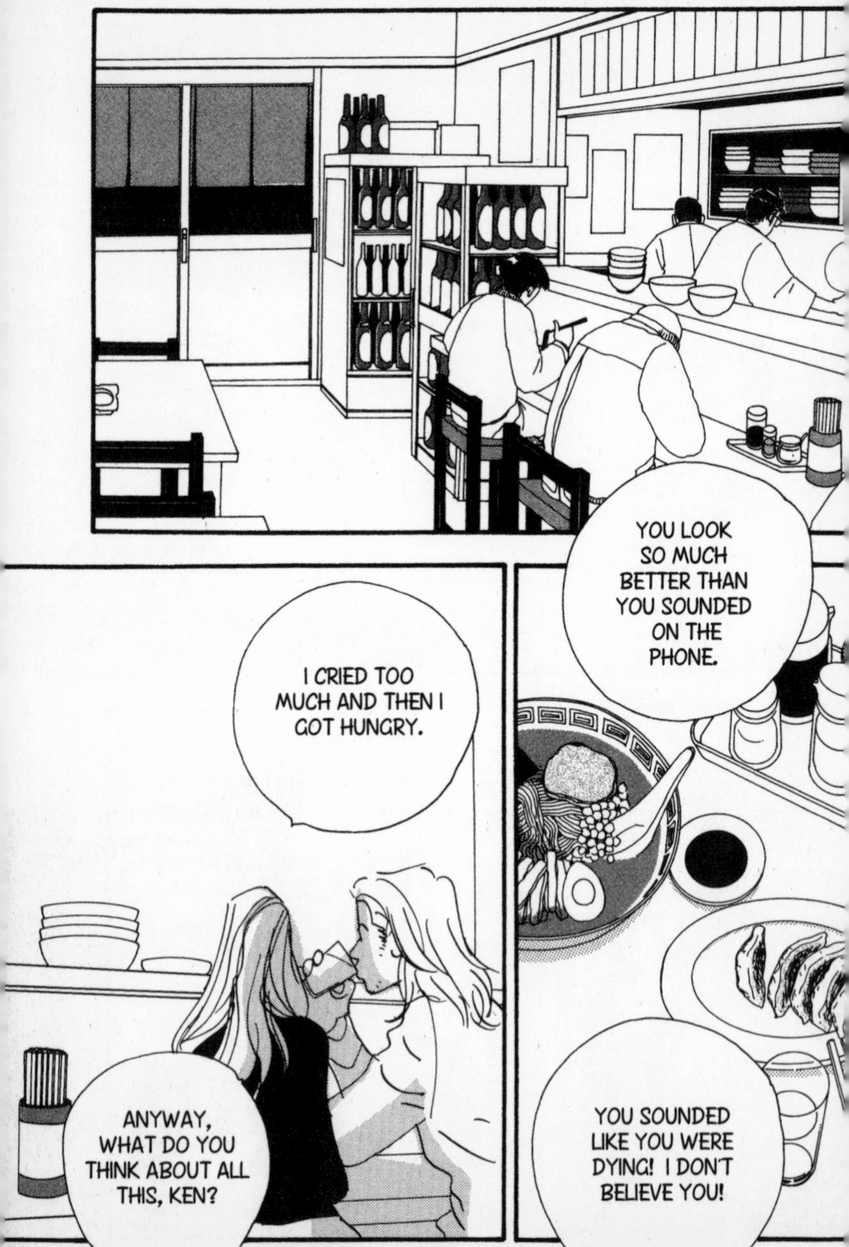
YOU LOOK SO MUCH BETTER THAN YOU SOUNDED ON THE PHONE.
YOU SOUNDED LIKE YOU WERE DYING! I DON'T BELIEVE YOU!
I CRIED TOO MUCH AND THEN I GOT HUNGRY.
ANYWAY, WHAT DO YOU THINK ABOUT ALL THIS, KEN?

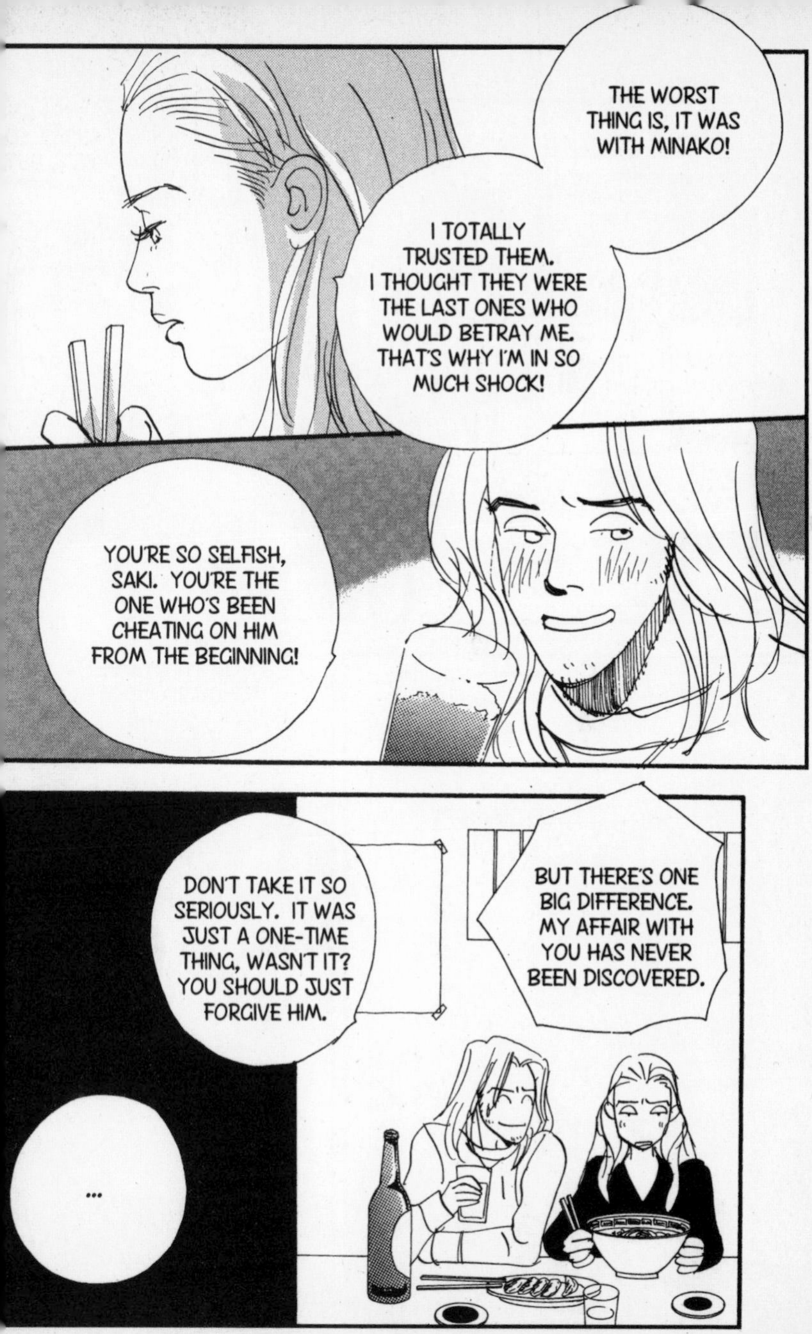
THE WORST THING IS, IT WAS WITH MINAKO!
I TOTALLY TRUSTED THEM. I THOUGHT THEY WERE THE LAST ONES WHO WOULD BETRAY ME. THAT'S WHY I'M IN SO MUCH SHOCK!
YOU'RE SO SELFISH, SAKI. YOU'RE THE ONE WHO'S BEEN CHEATING ON HIM FROM THE BEGINNING!
BUT THERE'S ONE BIG DIFFERENCE. MY AFFAIR WITH YOU HAS NEVER BEEN DISCOVERED.
DON'T TAKE IT SO SERIOUSLY. IT WAS JUST A ONE-TIME THING, WASN'T IT? YOU SHOULD JUST FORGIVE HIM.
...

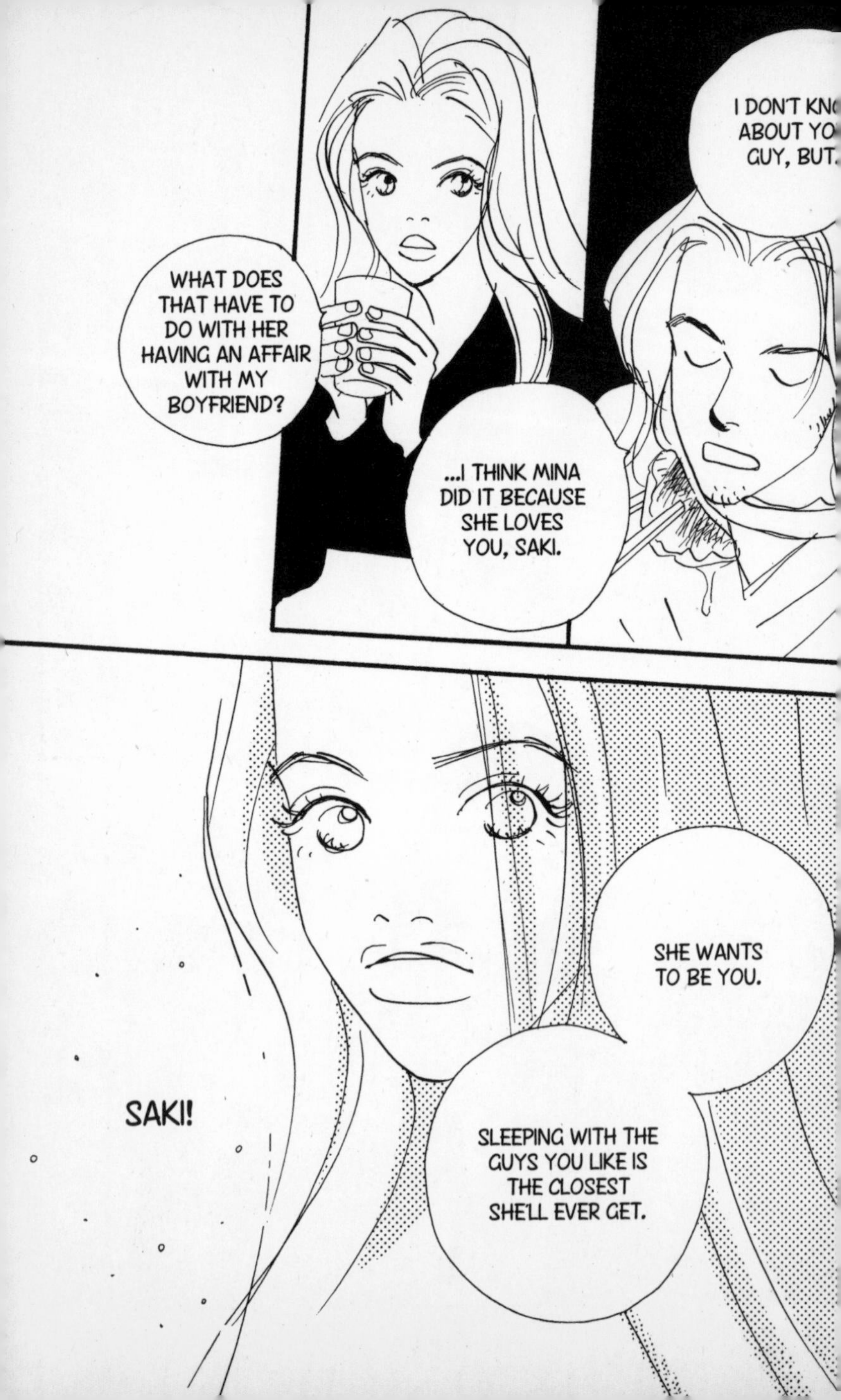

I DON'T KN
ABOUT YO
GUY, BUT.
...I THINK MINA DID IT BECAUSE SHE LOVES YOU, SAKI.
WHAT DOES THAT HAVE TO DO WITH HER HAVING AN AFFAIR WITH MY BOYFRIEND?
SHE WANTS TO BE YOU.
SLEEPING WITH THE GUYS YOU LIKE IS THE CLOSEST SHE'LL EVER GET.
SAKI!

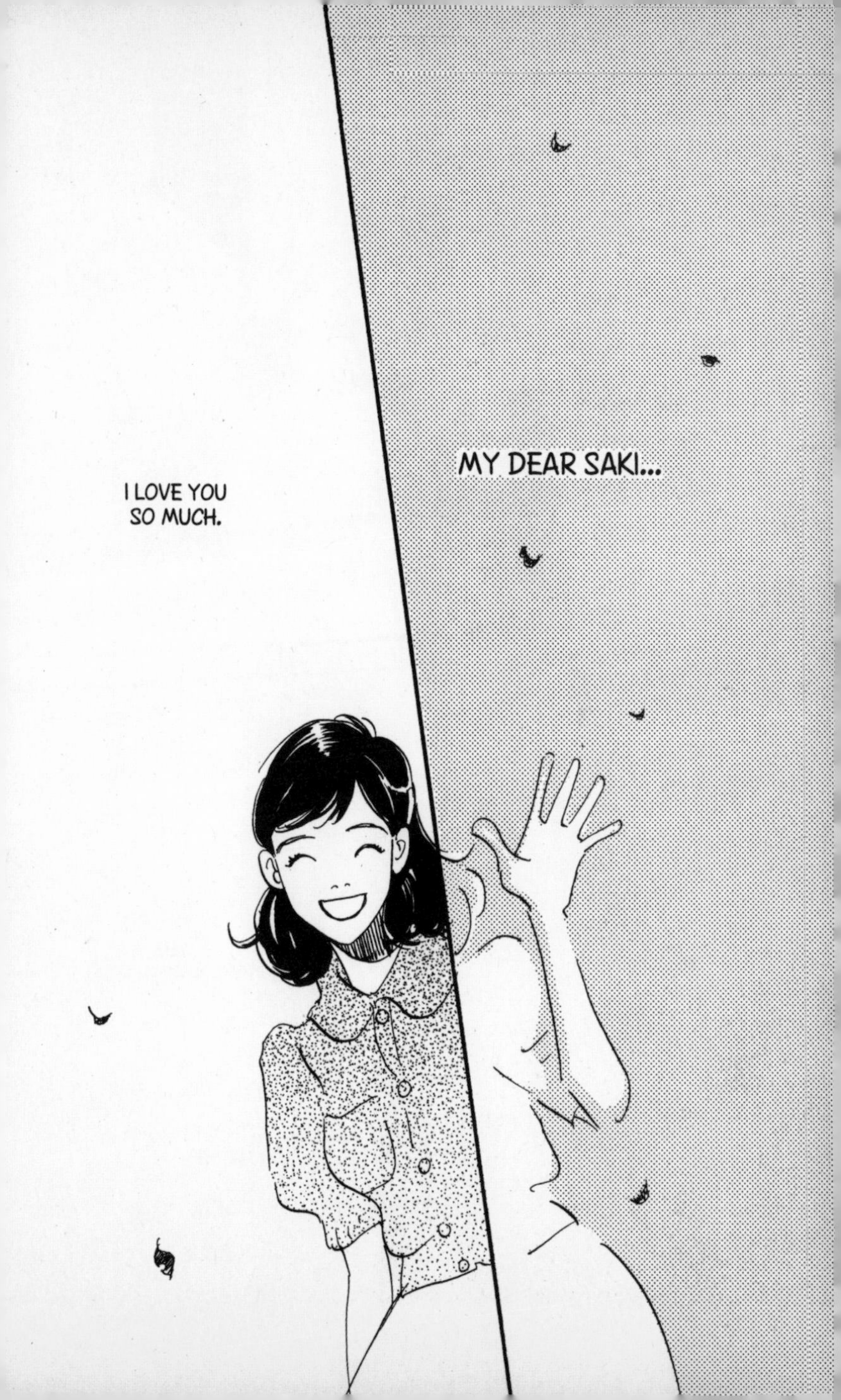
MY DEAR SAKI...
I LOVE YOU SO MUCH.

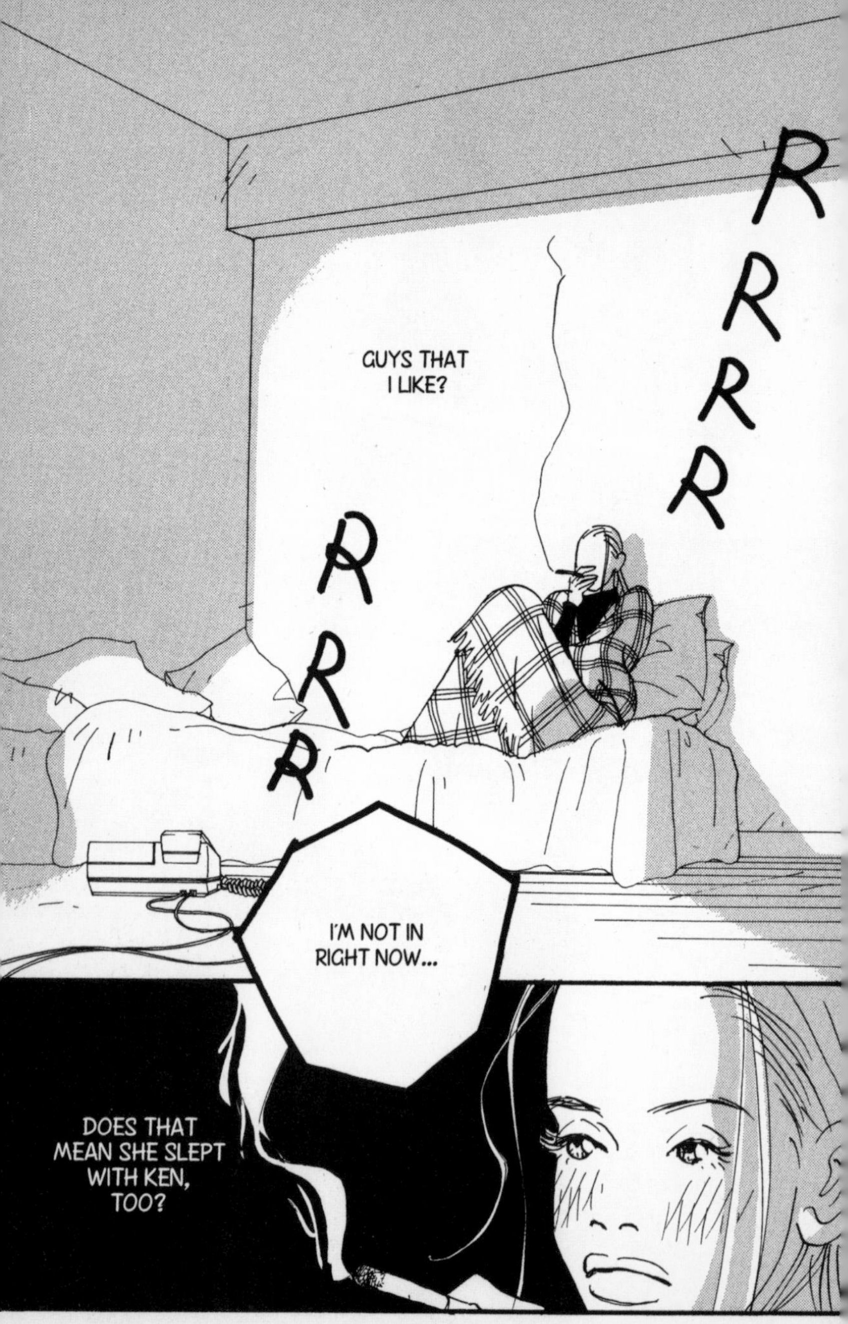
RRRR
GUYS THAT I LIKE?
RRR
I'M NOT IN RIGHT NOW...
DOES THAT MEAN SHE SLEPT WITH KEN, TOO?

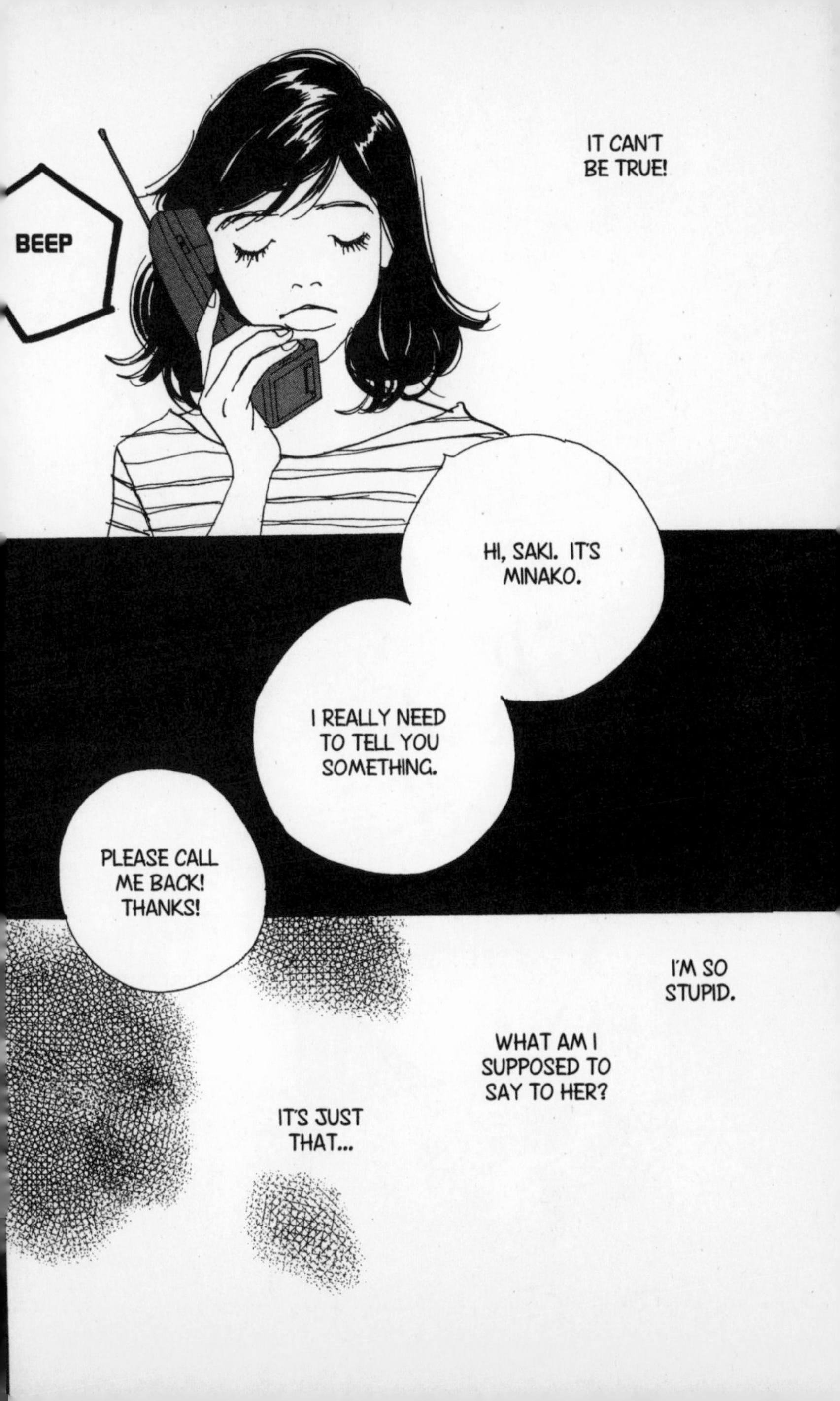
IT CAN'T BE TRUE!
BEEP
HI, SAKI. IT'S MINAKO.
I REALLY NEED TO TELL YOU SOMETHING.
PLEASE CALL ME BACK! THANKS!
I'M SO STUPID.
WHAT AM I SUPPOSED TO SAY TO HER?
IT'S JUST THAT...

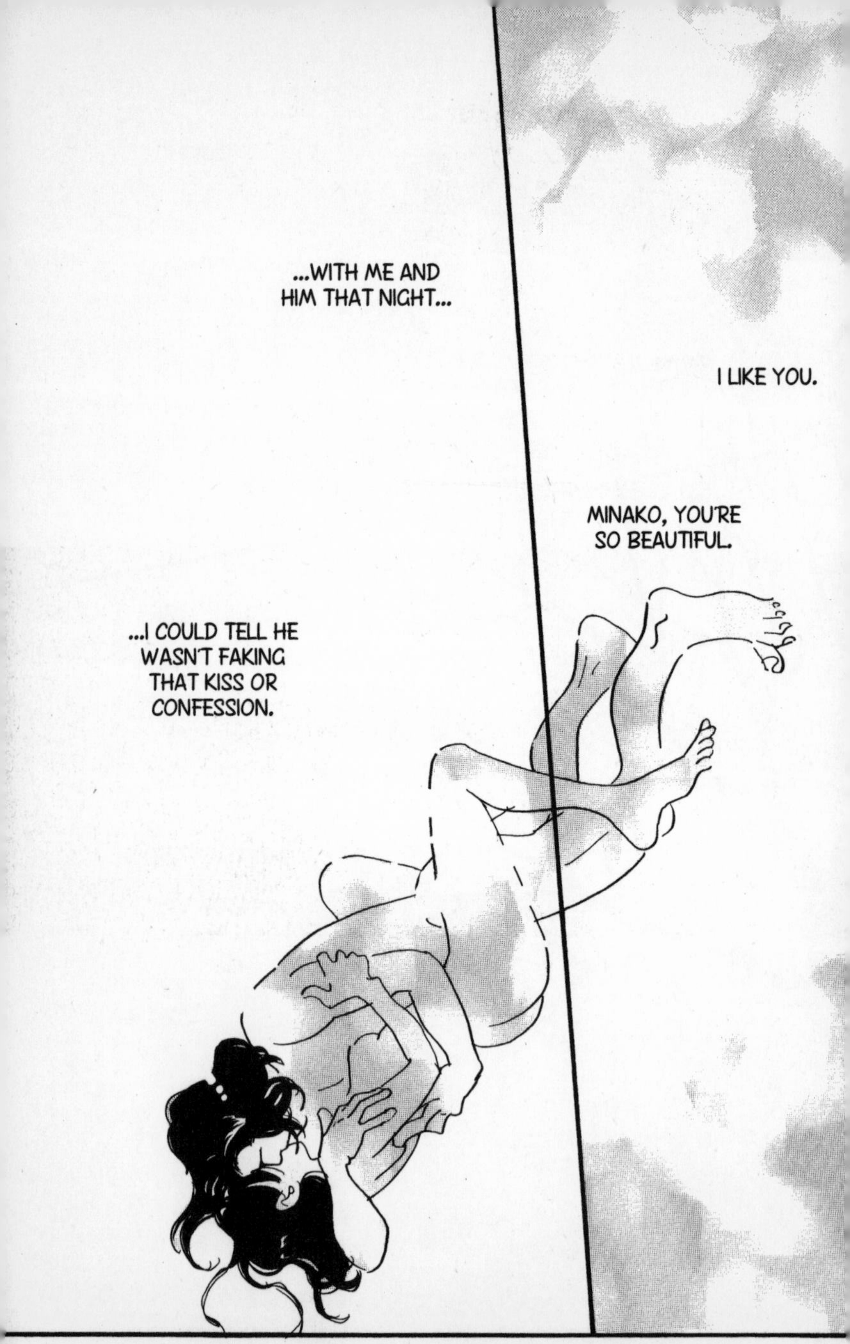
I LIKE YOU.
MINAKO, YOU'RE SO BEAUTIFUL.
...WITH ME AND HIM THAT NIGHT...
...I COULD TELL HE WASN'T FAKING THAT KISS OR CONFESSION.

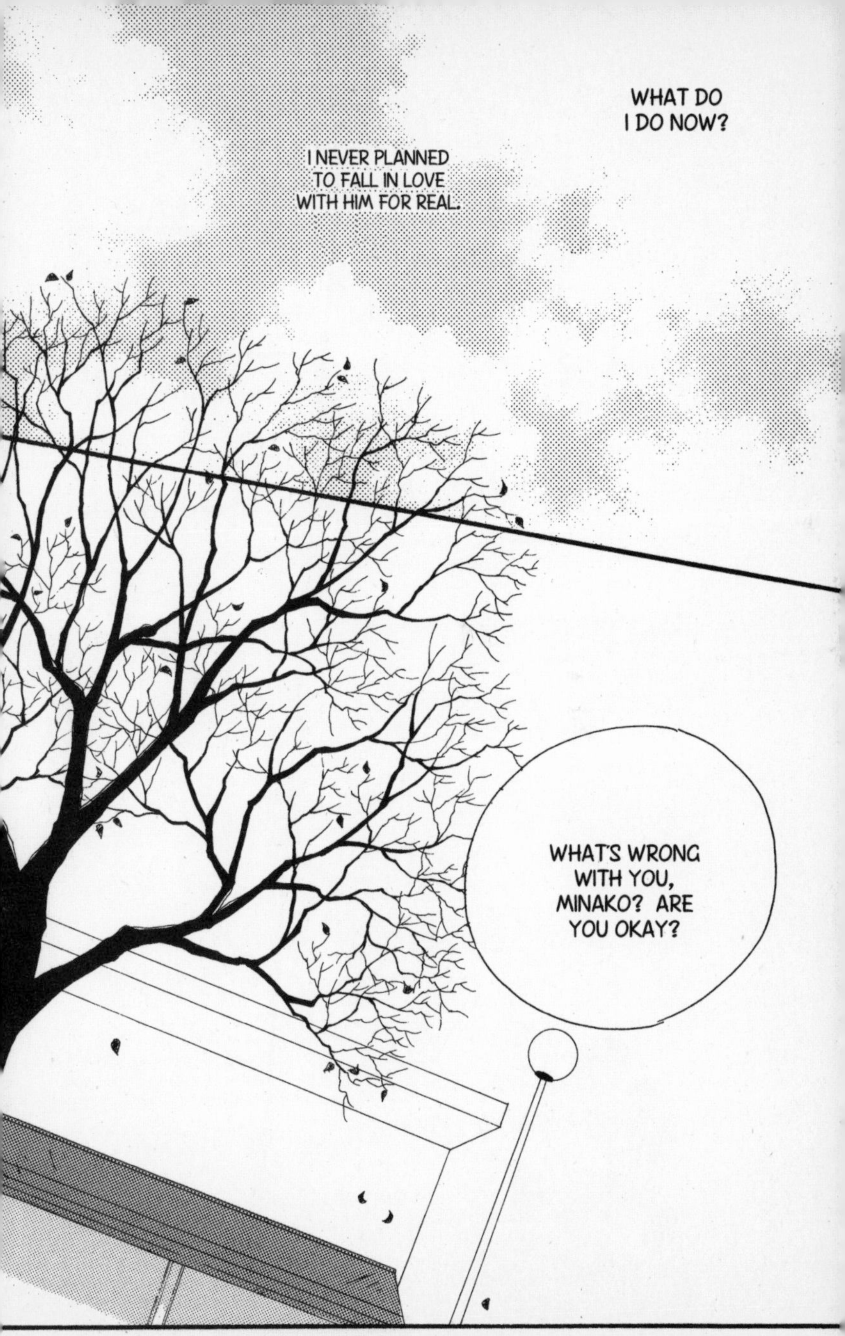
WHAT DO I DO NOW?
I NEVER PLANNED TO FALL IN LOVE WITH HIM FOR REAL.
WHAT'S WRONG WITH YOU, MINAKO? ARE YOU OKAY?

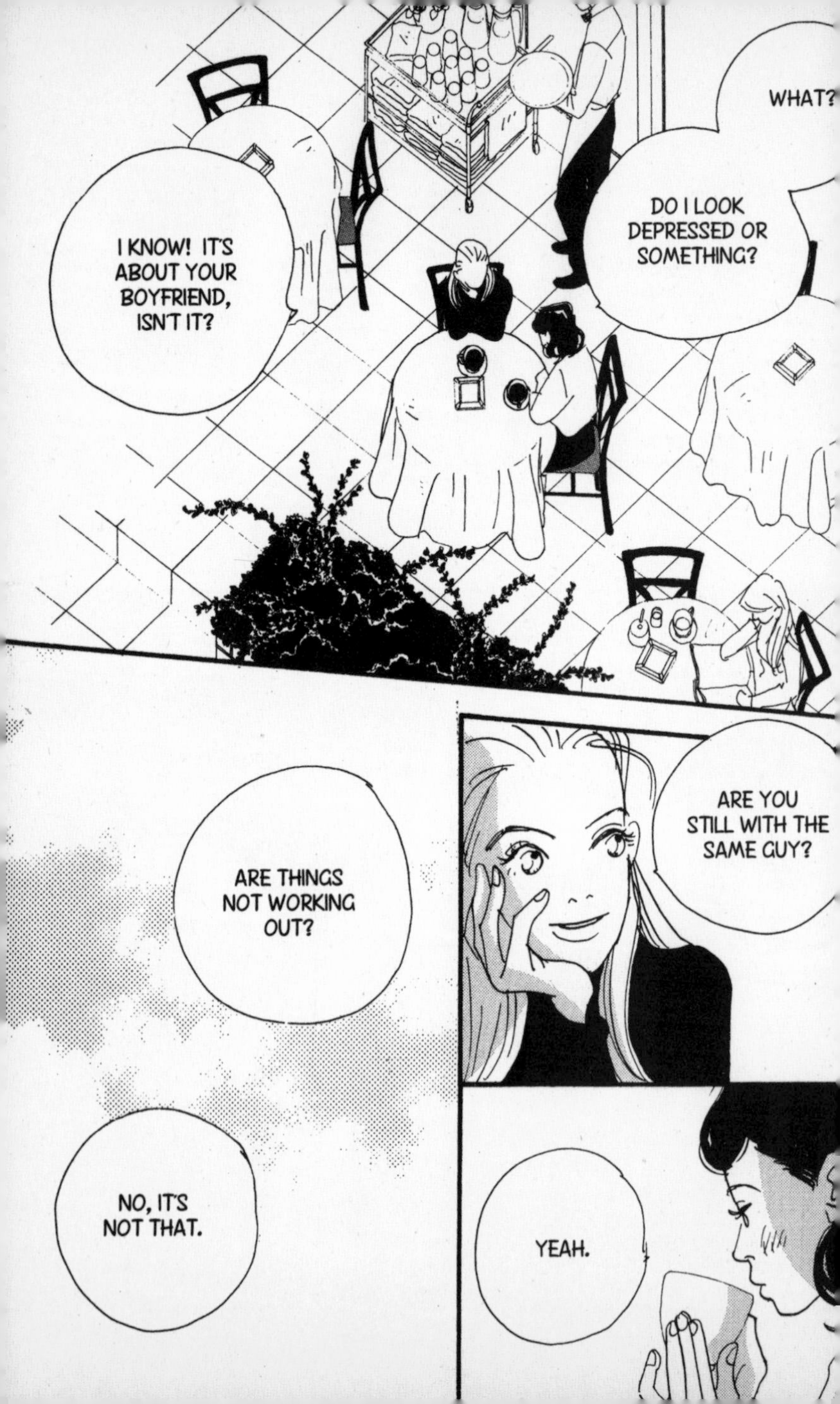
WHAT?
DO I LOOK DEPRESSED OR SOMETHING?
I KNOW! IT'S ABOUT YOUR BOYFRIEND, ISN'T IT?
ARE YOU STILL WITH THE SAME GUY?
YEAH.
ARE THINGS NOT WORKING OUT?
NO, IT'S NOT THAT.

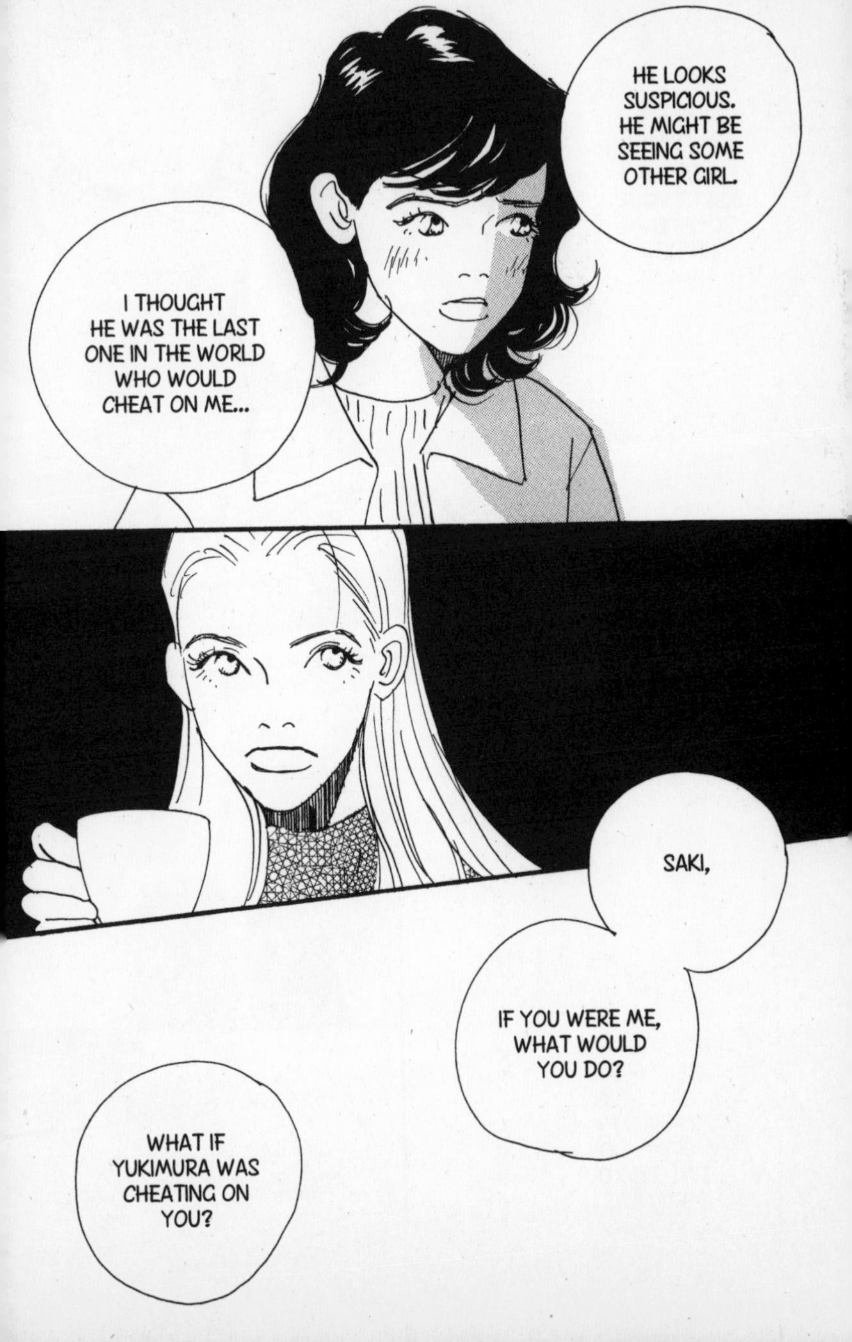

HE LOOKS SUSPICIOUS. HE MIGHT BE SEEING SOME OTHER GIRL.
I THOUGHT HE WAS THE LAST ONE IN THE WORLD WHO WOULD CHEAT ON ME...
SAKI,
IF YOU WERE ME, WHAT WOULD YOU DO?
WHAT IF YUKIMURA WAS CHEATING ON YOU?

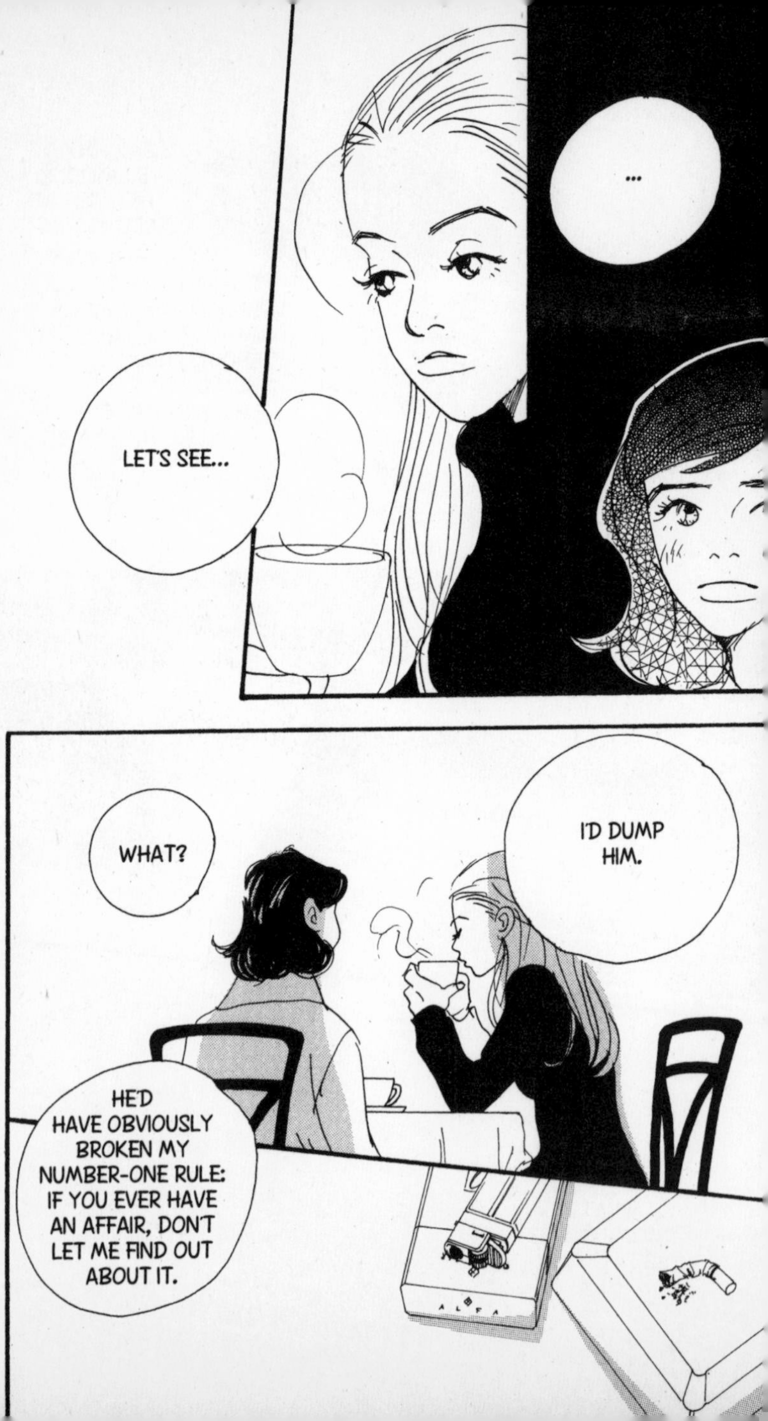
...
LET'S SEE...
I'D DUMP HIM.
WHAT?
HE'D HAVE OBVIOUSLY BROKEN MY NUMBER-ONE RULE: IF YOU EVER HAVE AN AFFAIR, DON'T LET ME FIND OUT ABOUT IT.
ALFA

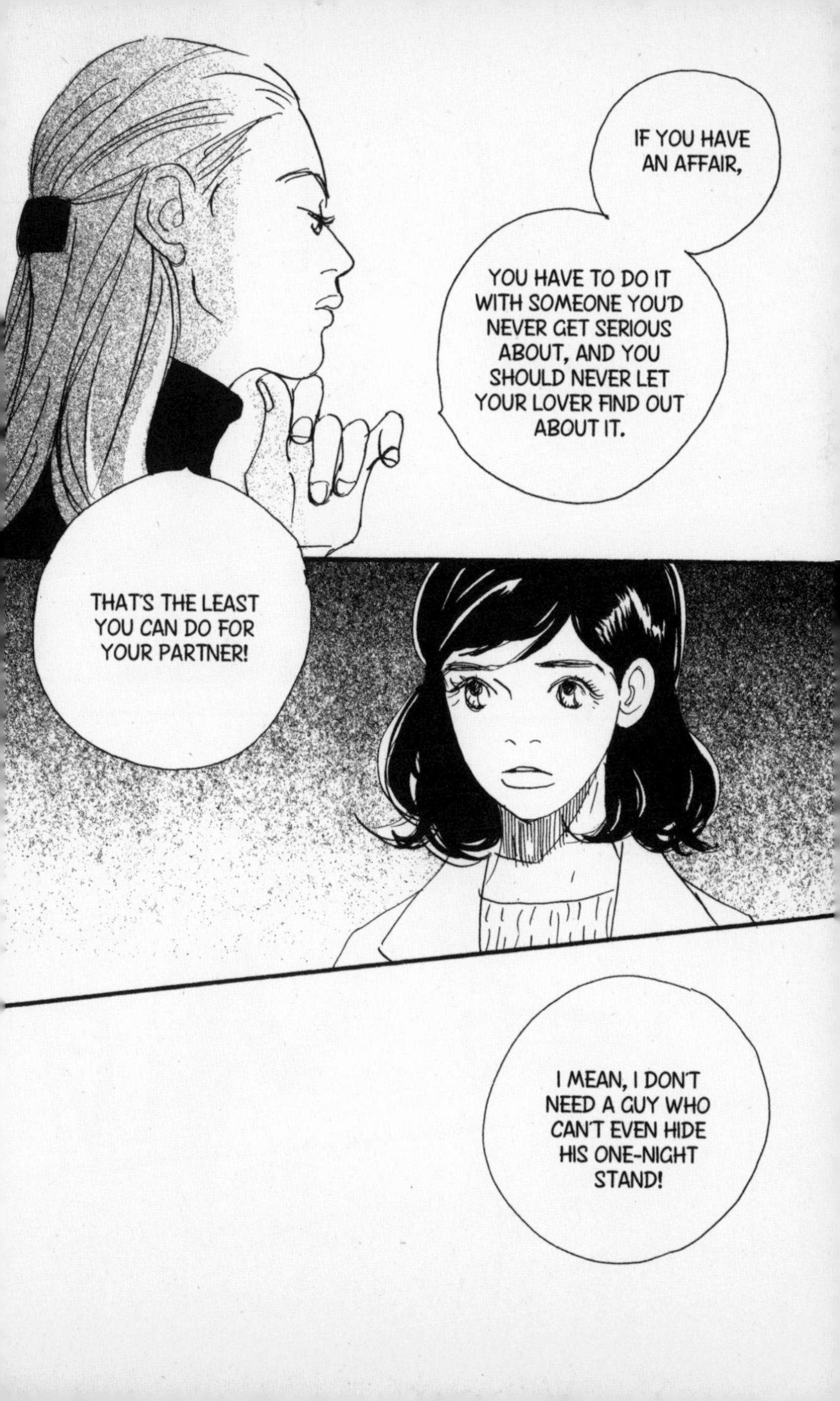
IF YOU HAVE AN AFFAIR,
YOU HAVE TO DO IT WITH SOMEONE YOU'D NEVER GET SERIOUS ABOUT, AND YOU SHOULD NEVER LET YOUR LOVER FIND OUT ABOUT IT.
THAT'S THE LEAST YOU CAN DO FOR YOUR PARTNER!
I MEAN, I DON'T NEED A GUY WHO CAN'T EVEN HIDE HIS ONE-NIGHT STAND!

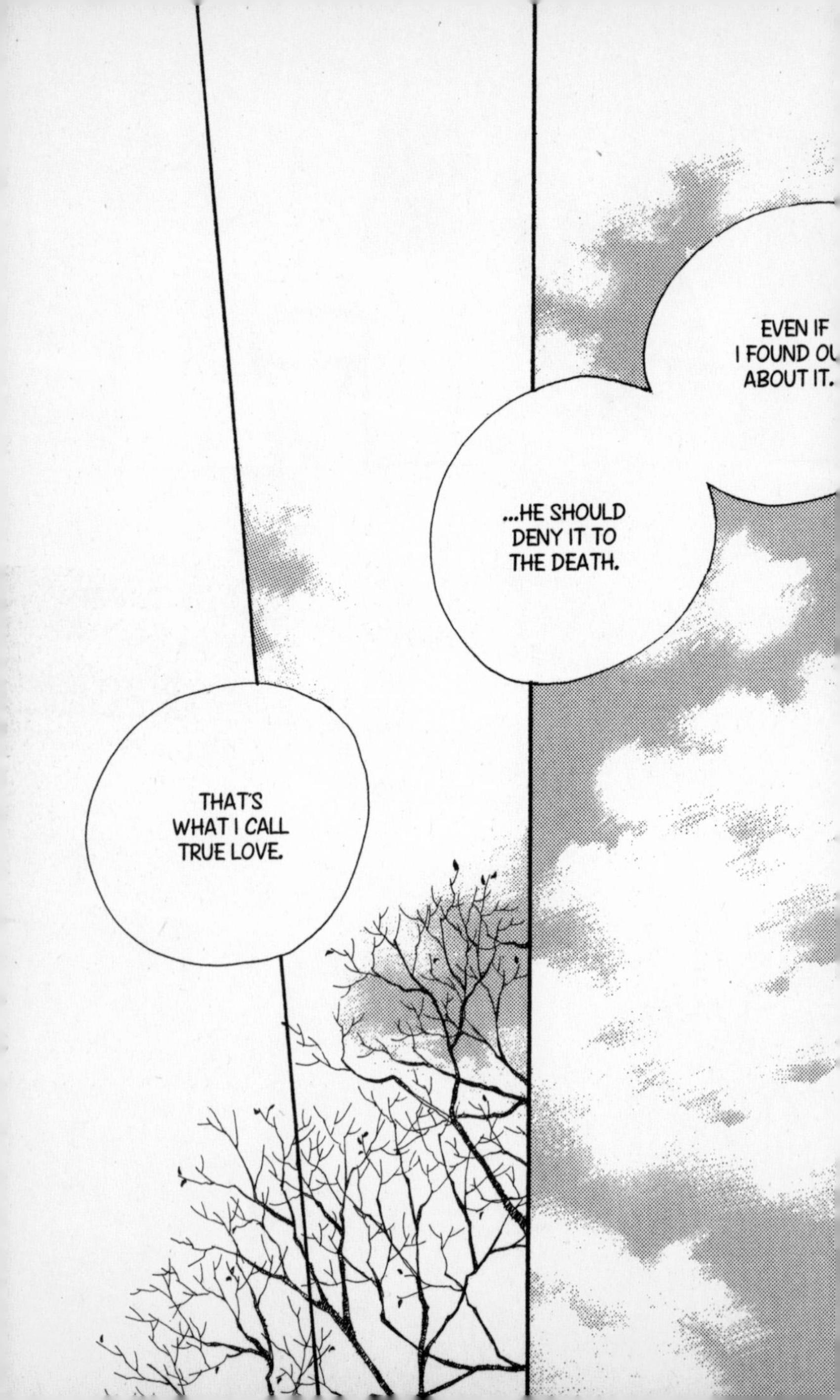
EVEN IF I FOUND OU ABOUT IT.
...HE SHOULD DENY IT TO THE DEATH.
THAT'S WHAT I CALL TRUE LOVE.

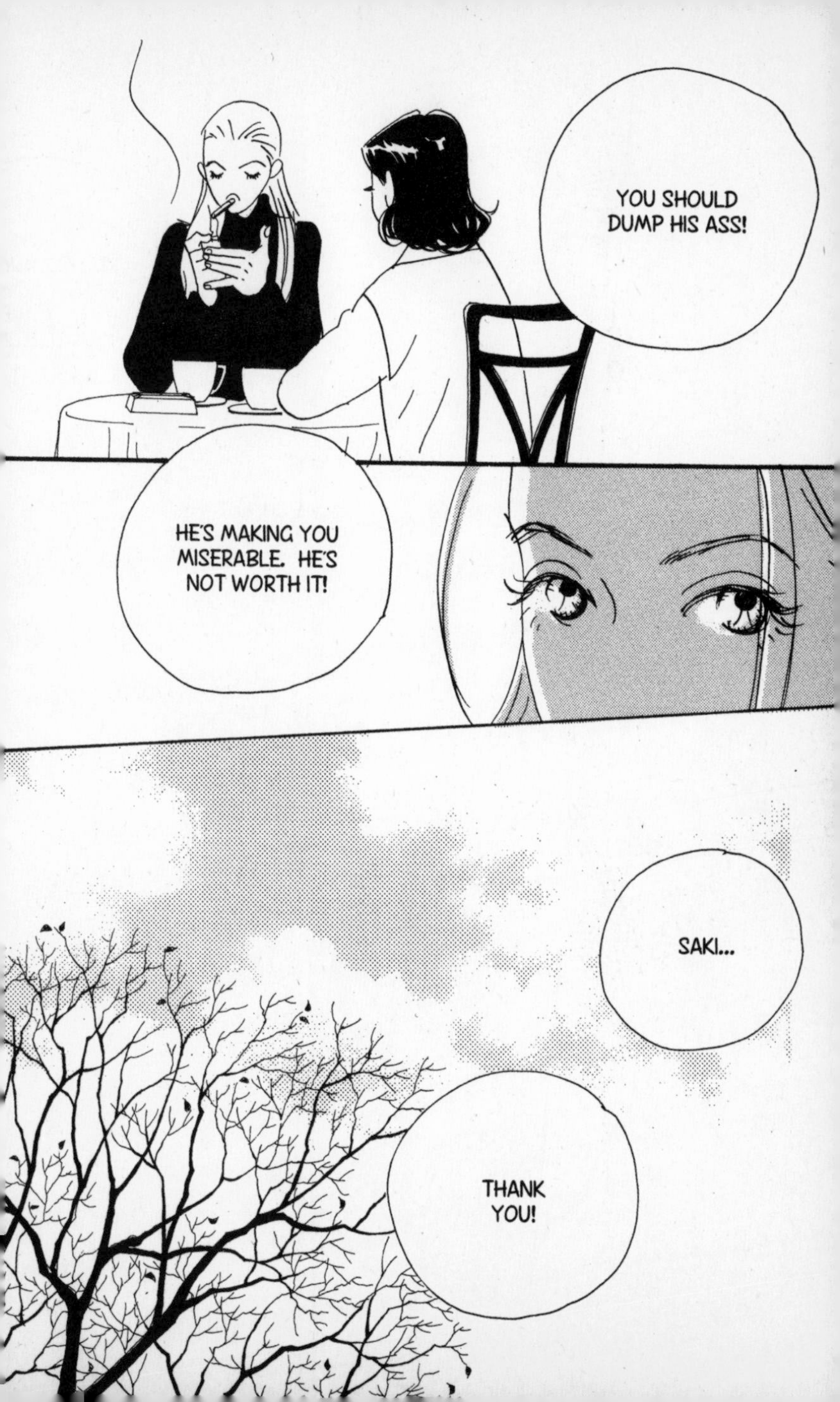
YOU SHOULD DUMP HIS ASS!
HE'S MAKING YOU MISERABLE. HE'S NOT WORTH IT!
SAKI...
THANK YOU!

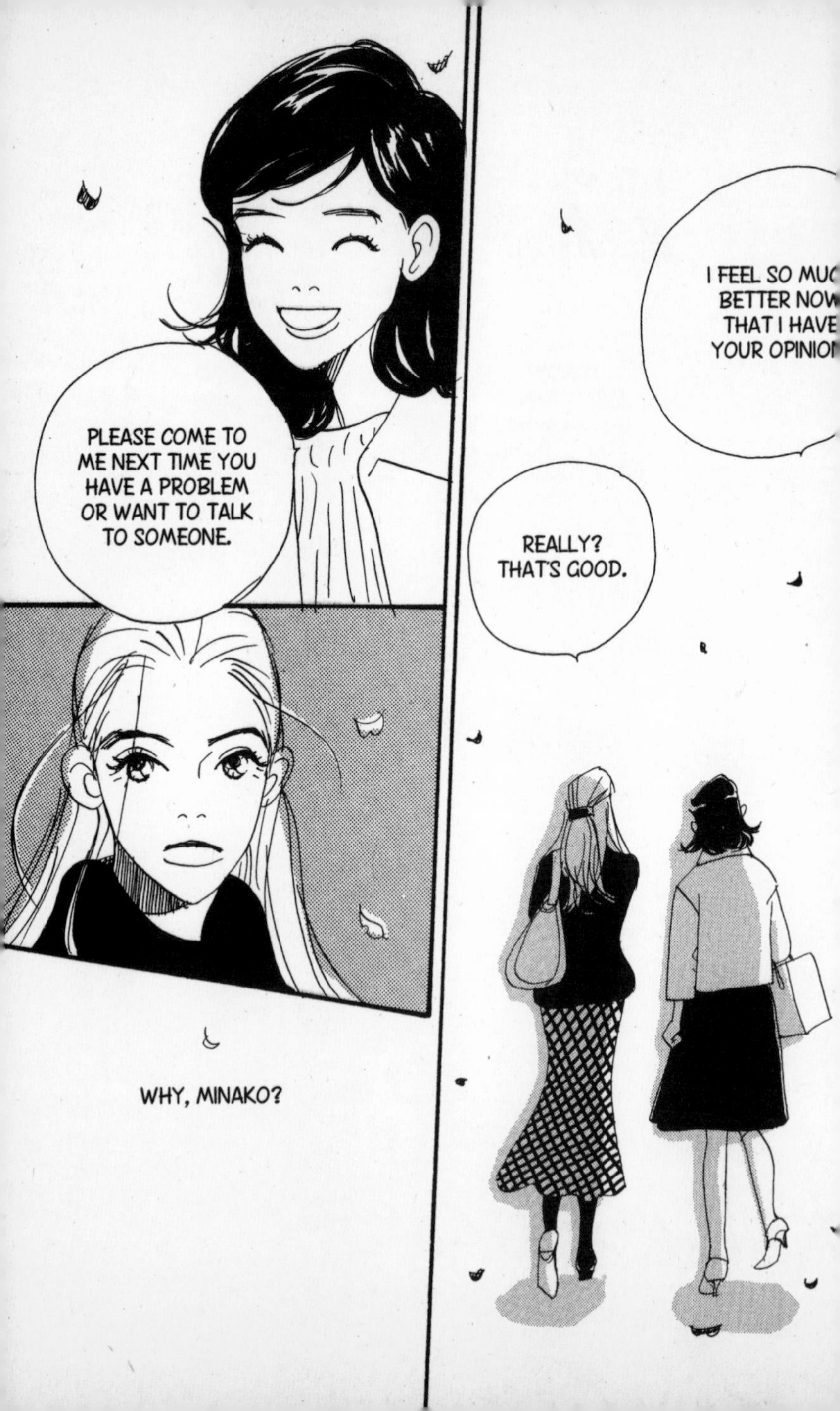
I FEEL SO MUC BETTER NOW THAT I HAVE YOUR OPINIO
REALLY? THAT'S GOOD.
PLEASE COME TO ME NEXT TIME YOU HAVE A PROBLEM OR WANT TO TALK TO SOMEONE.
WHY, MINAKO?

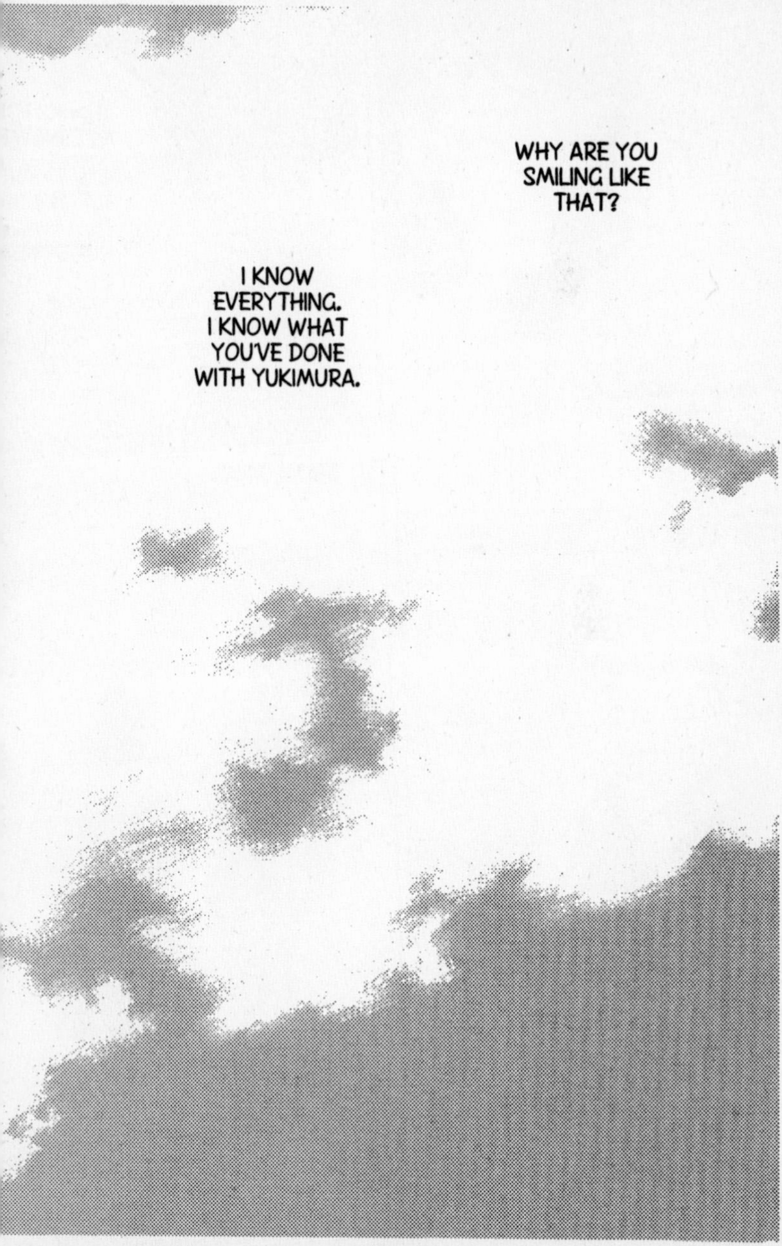
WHY ARE YOU SMILING LIKE THAT?
I KNOW EVERYTHING. I KNOW WHAT YOU'VE DONE WITH YUKIMURA.

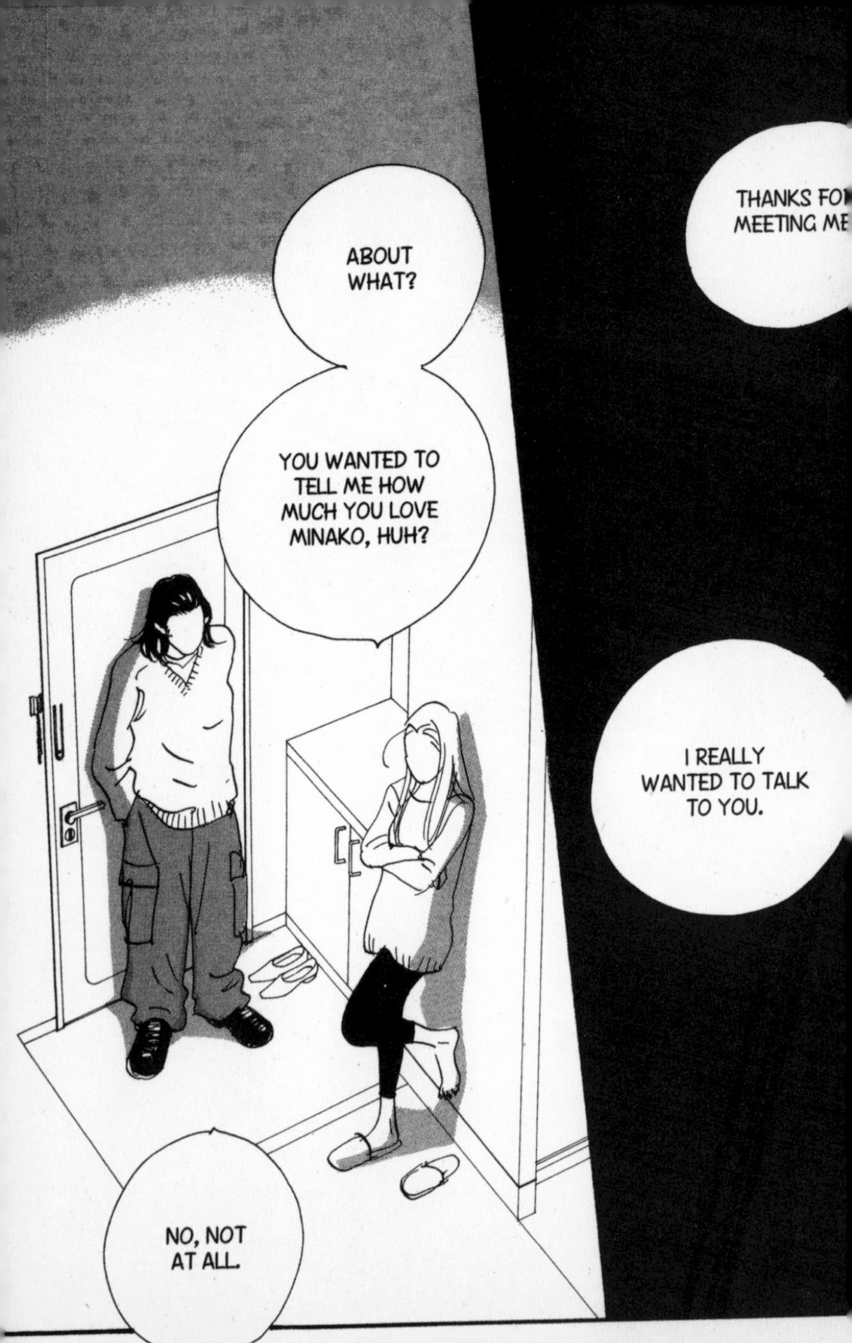
THANKS FO
MEETING ME
I REALLY WANTED TO TALK TO YOU.
ABOUT WHAT?
YOU WANTED TO TELL ME HOW MUCH YOU LOVE MINAKO, HUH?
NO, NOT AT ALL.

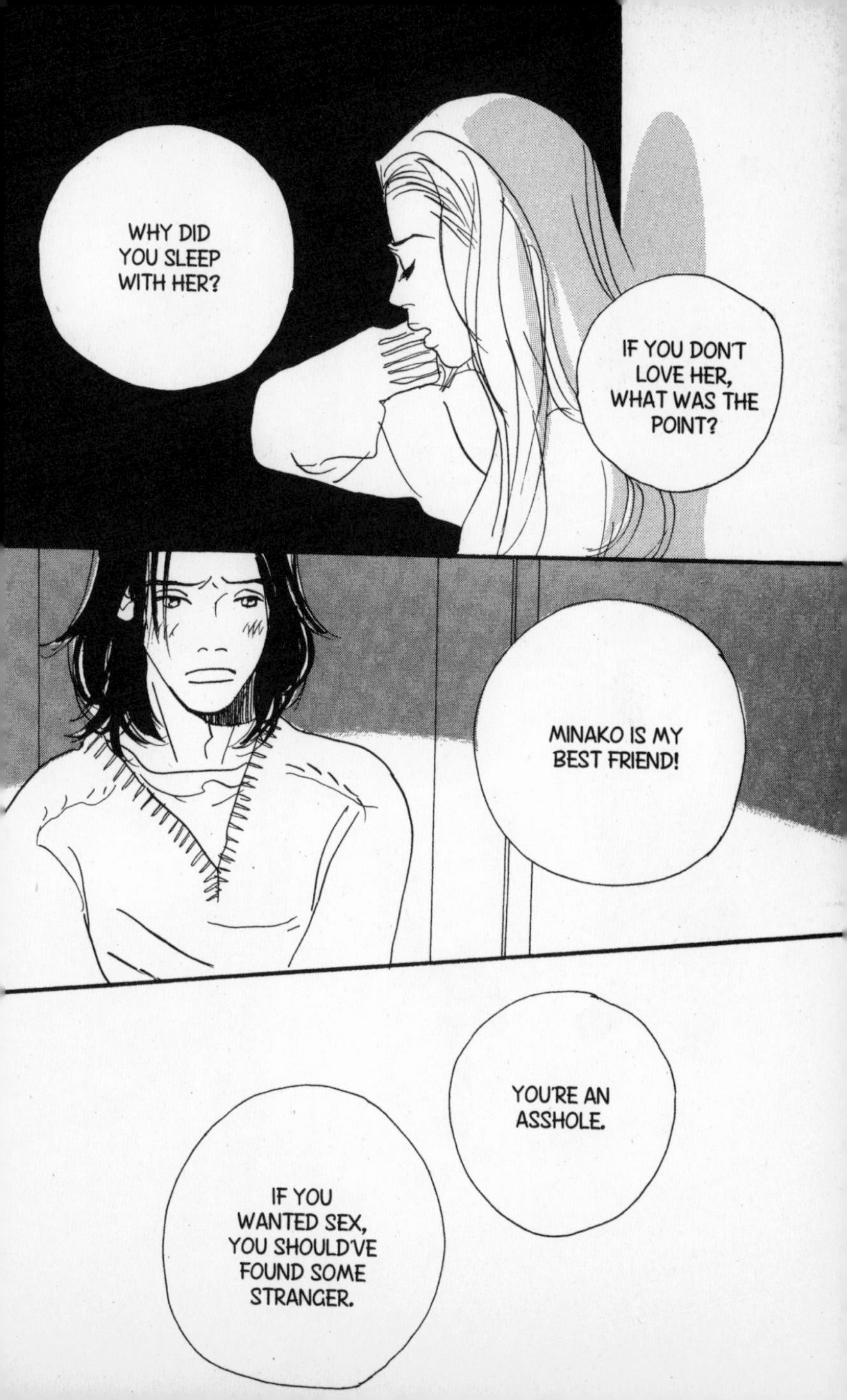
IF YOU DON'T LOVE HER, WHAT WAS THE POINT?
WHY DID YOU SLEEP WITH HER?
MINAKO IS MY BEST FRIEND!
YOU'RE AN ASSHOLE.
IF YOU WANTED SEX, YOU SHOULD'VE FOUND SOME STRANGER.

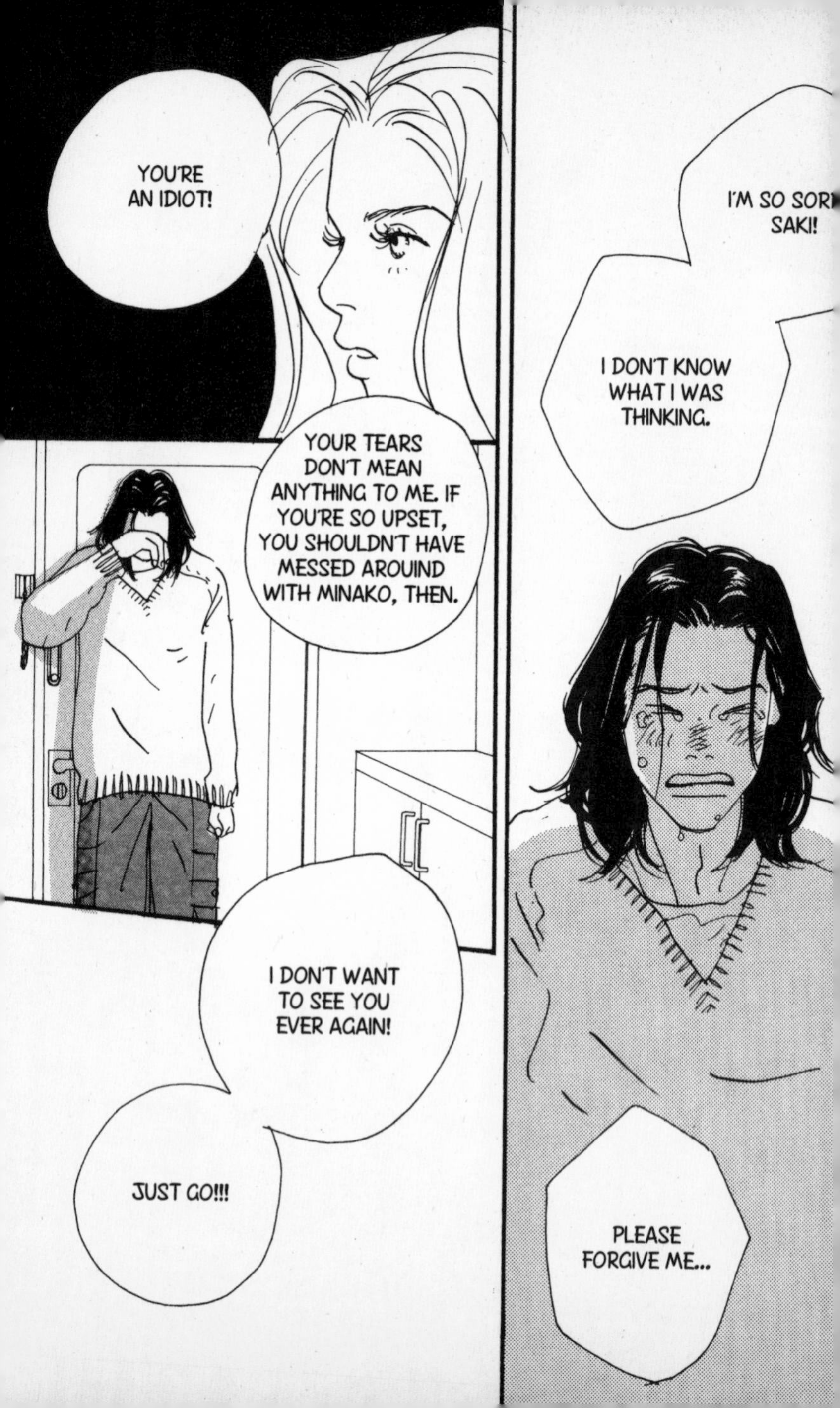
I'M SO SOR SAKI!
I DON'T KNOW WHAT I WAS THINKING.
PLEASE FORGIVE ME...
YOU'RE AN IDIOT!
YOUR TEARS DON'T MEAN ANYTHING TO ME. IF YOU'RE SO UPSET, YOU SHOULDN'T HAVE MESSED AROUIND WITH MINAKO, THEN.
I DON'T WANT TO SEE YOU EVER AGAIN!
JUST GO!!!

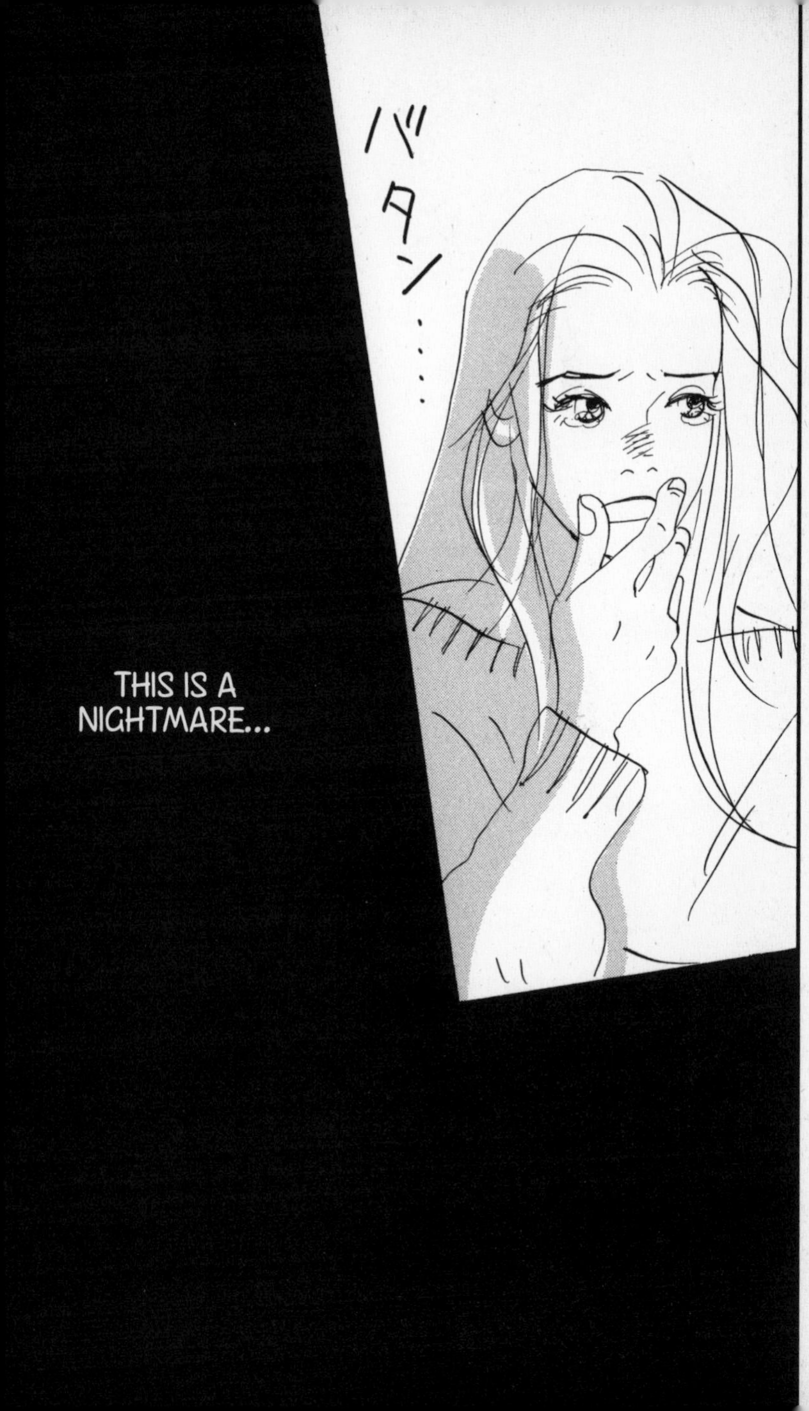
バタン…
THIS IS A NIGHTMARE...

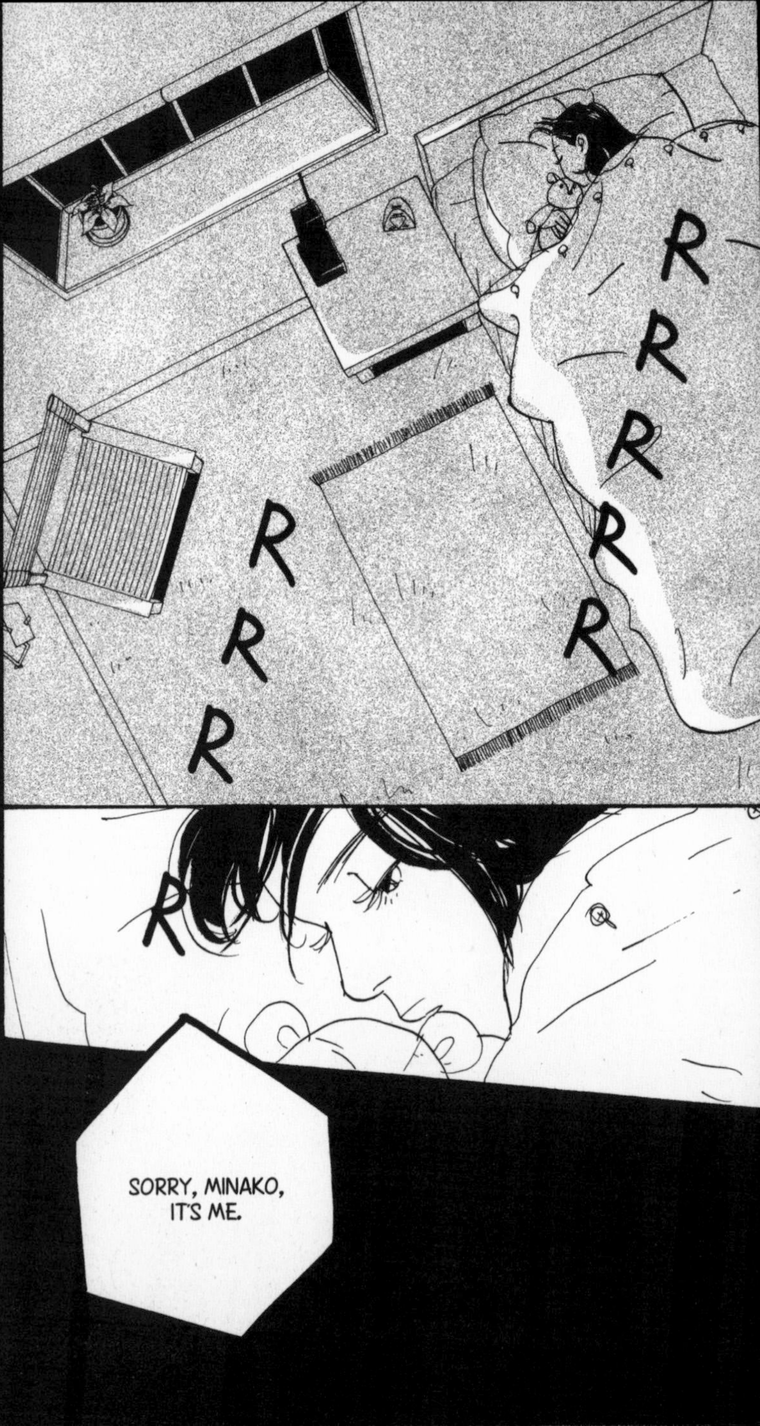
RRRRR
RRR
R
SORRY, MINAKO, IT'S ME.

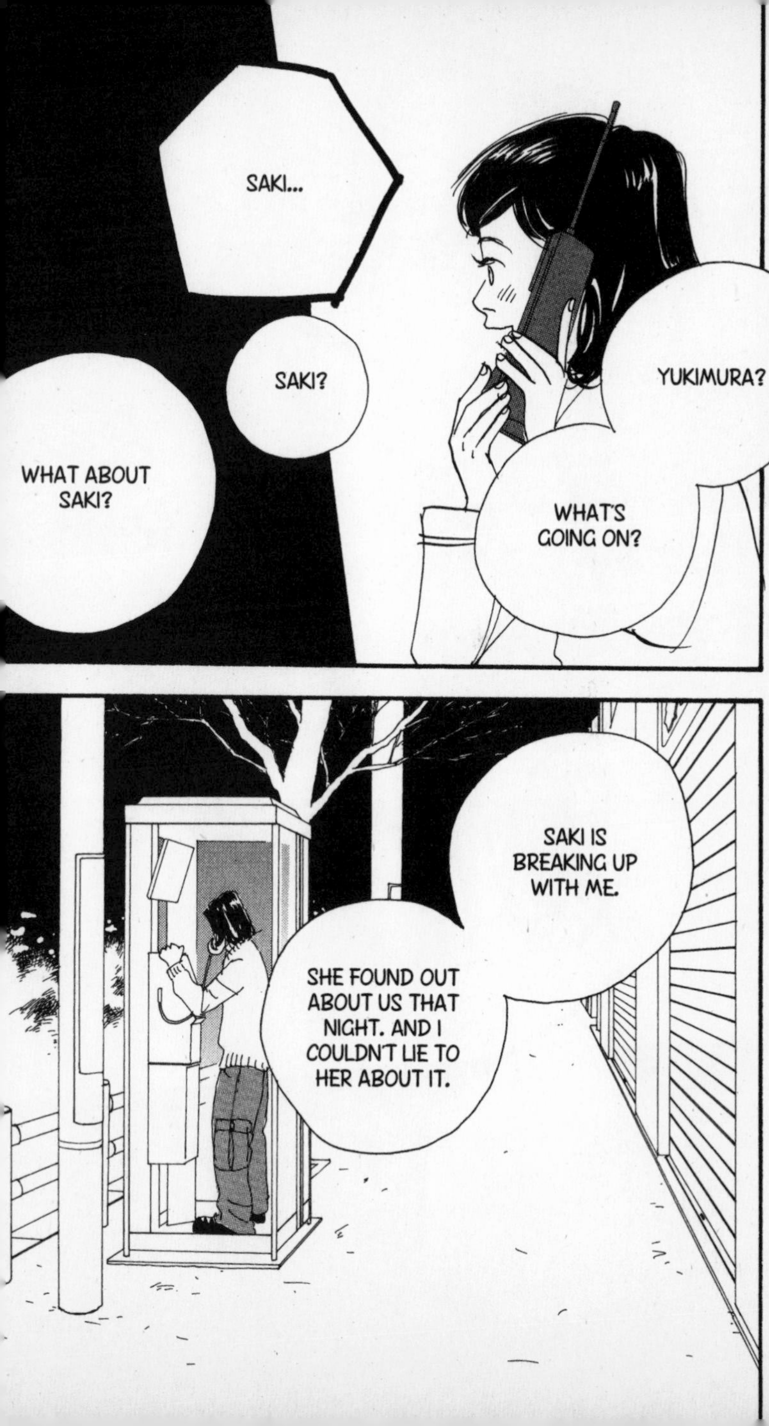
YUKIMURA?
WHAT'S GOING ON?
SAKI...
SAKI?
WHAT ABOUT SAKI?
SAKI IS BREAKING UP WITH ME.
SHE FOUND OUT ABOUT US THAT NIGHT. AND I COULDN'T LIE TO HER ABOUT IT.

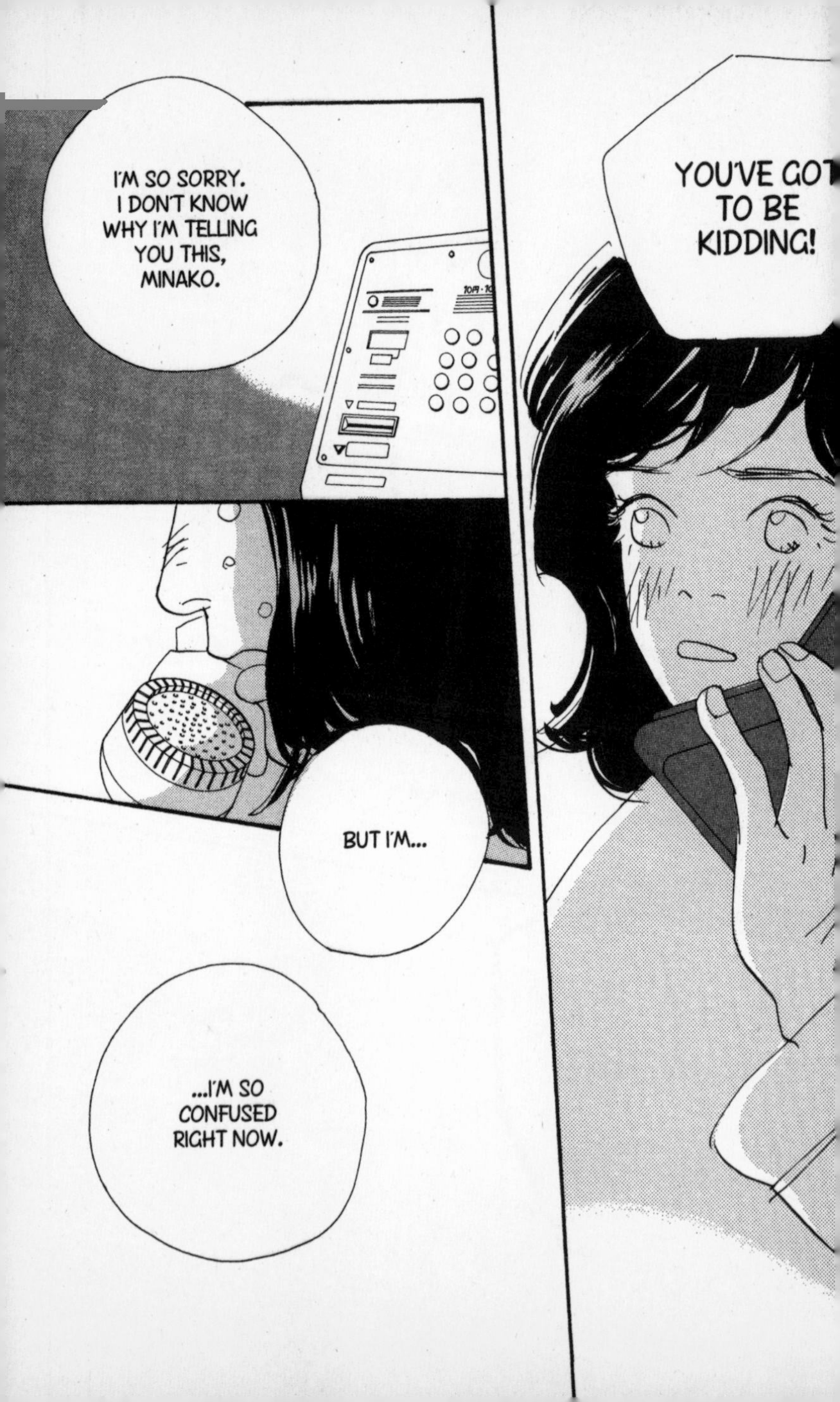
YOU'VE GOT TO BE KIDDING!
I'M SO SORRY. I DON'T KNOW WHY I'M TELLING YOU THIS, MINAKO.
BUT I'M...
...I'M SO CONFUSED RIGHT NOW.

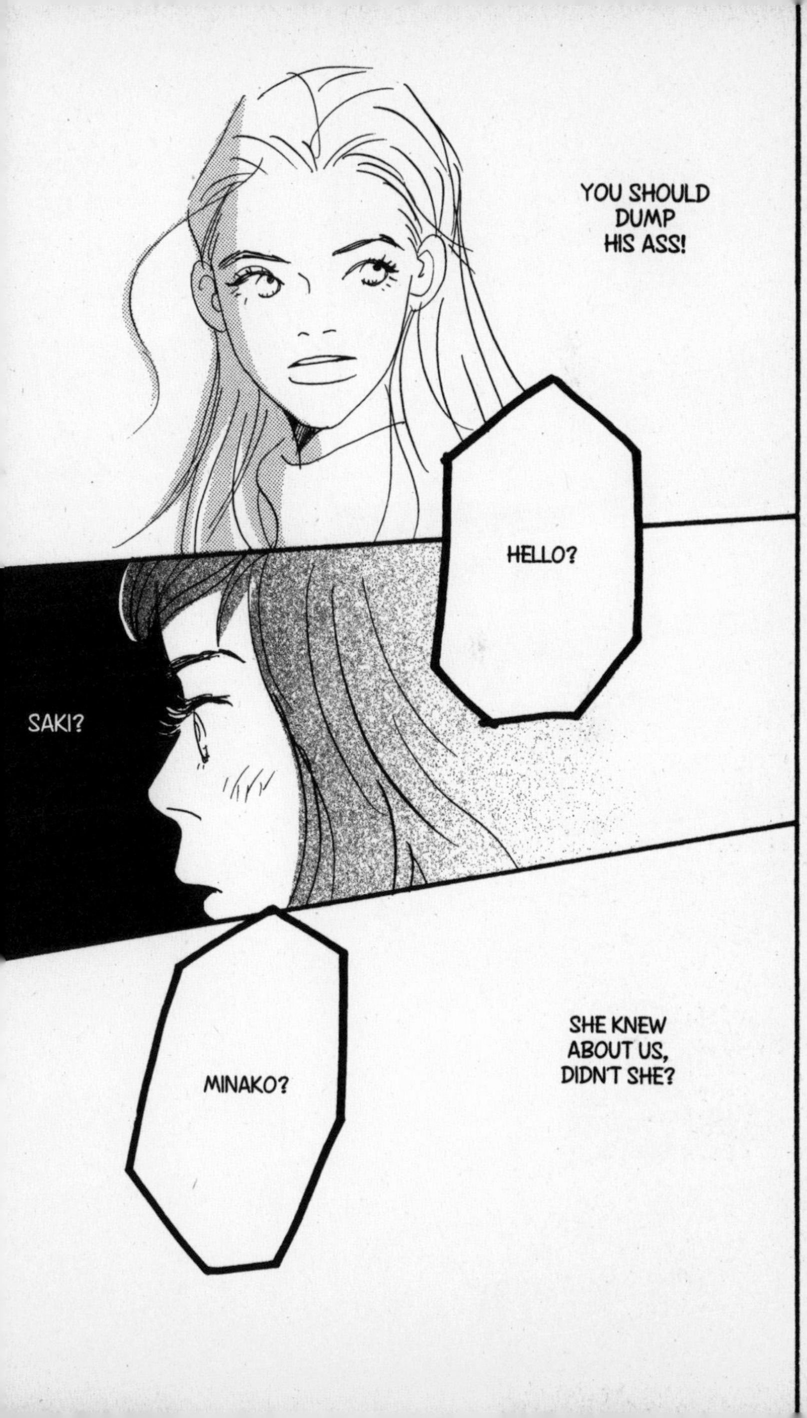
YOU SHOULD DUMP HIS ASS!
HELLO?
SAKI?
SHE KNEW ABOUT US, DIDN'T SHE?
MINAKO?

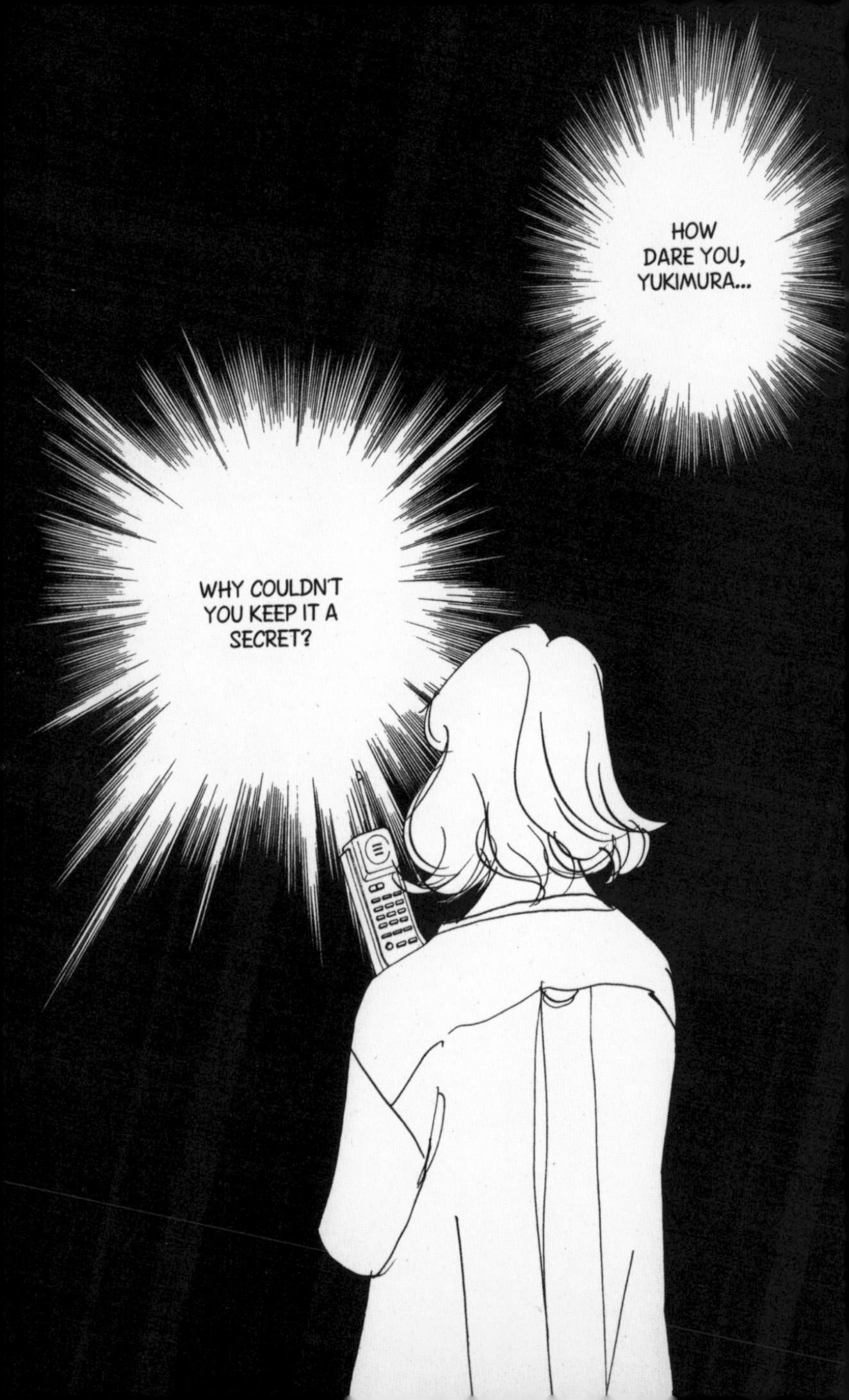
HOW DARE YOU, YUKIMURA...
WHY COULDN'T YOU KEEP IT A SECRET?

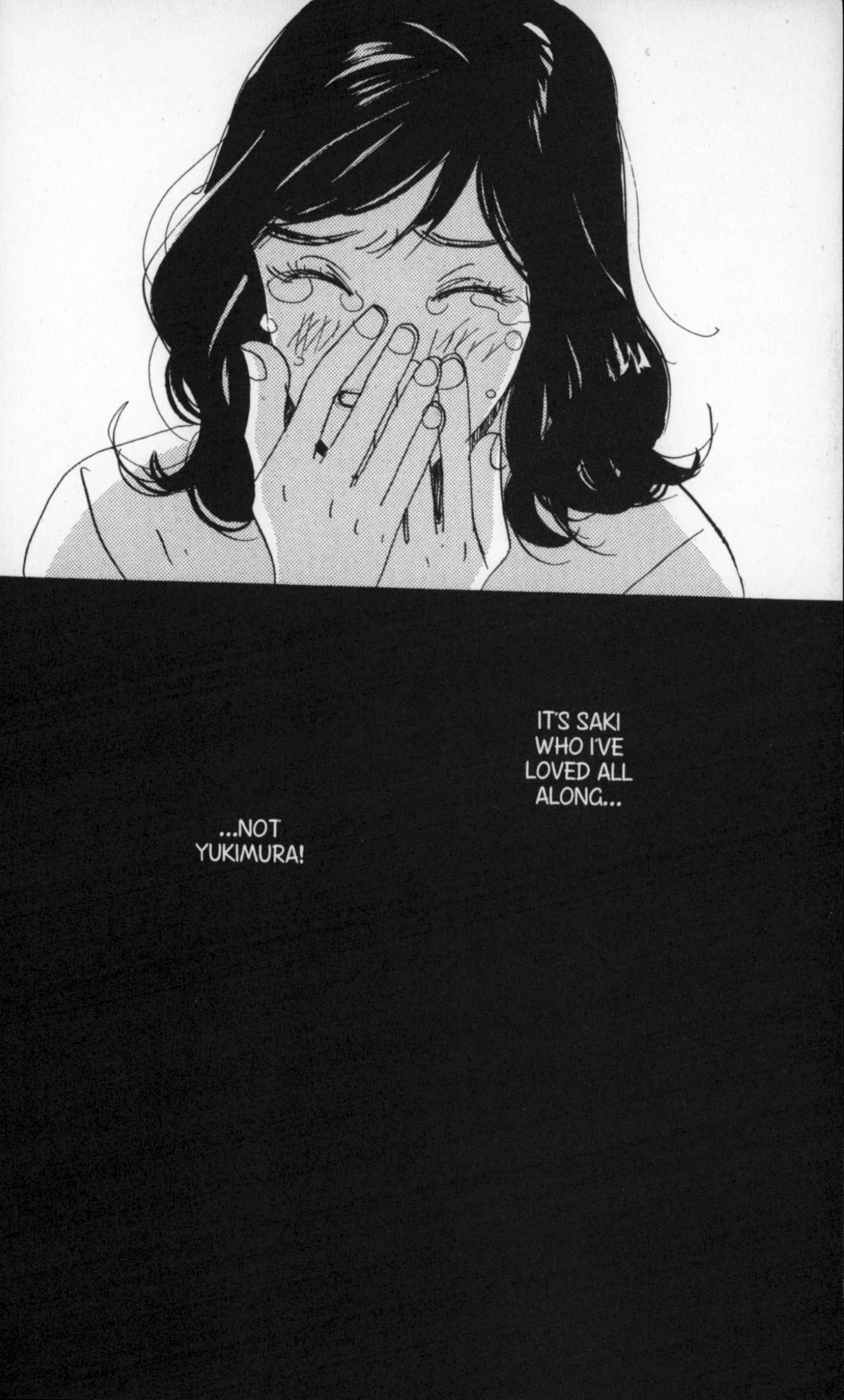
IT'S SAKI WHO I'VE LOVED ALL ALONG...
...NOT YUKIMURA!

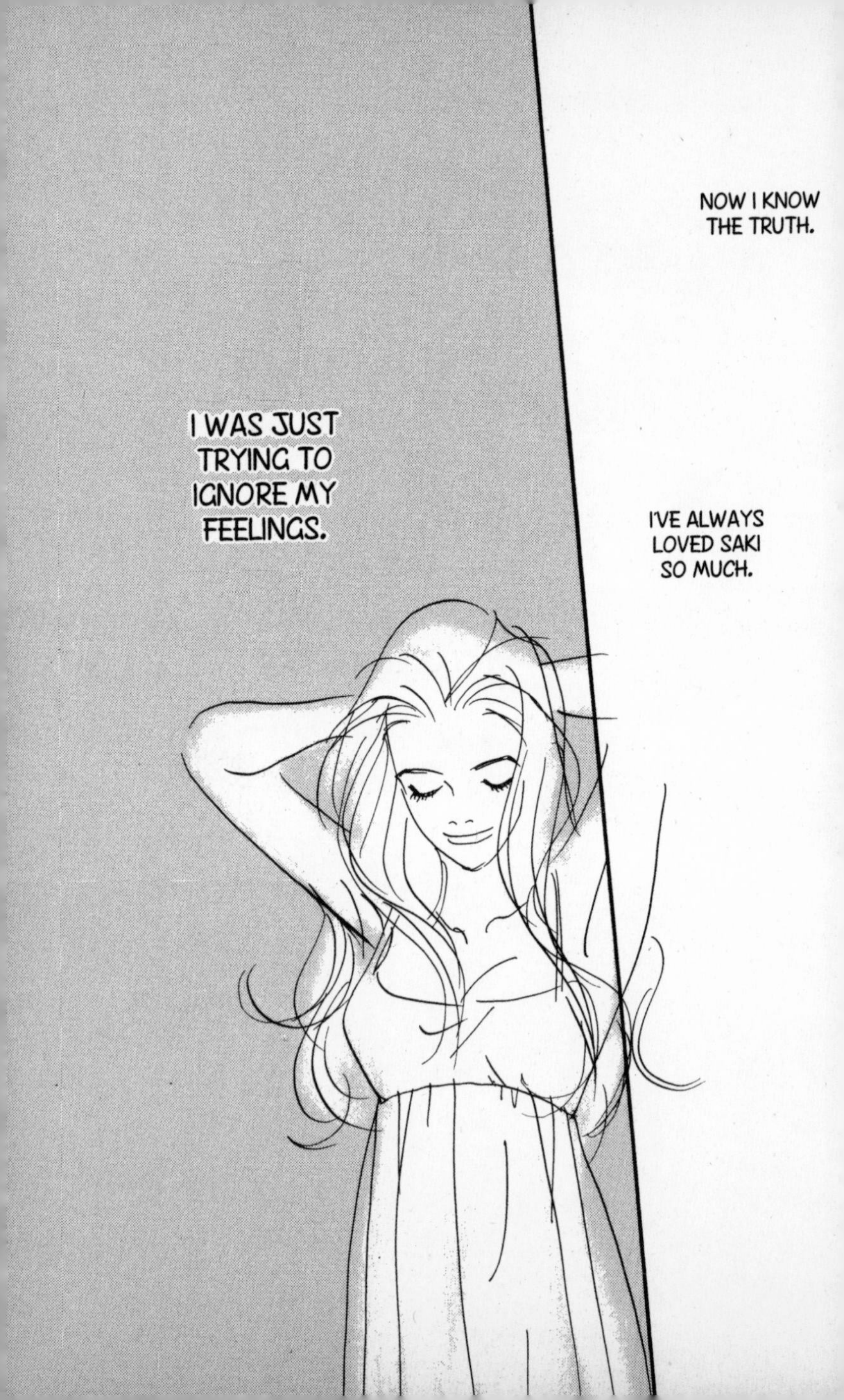
NOW I KNOW THE TRUTH.
I'VE ALWAYS LOVED SAKI SO MUCH.
I WAS JUST TRYING TO IGNORE MY FEELINGS.

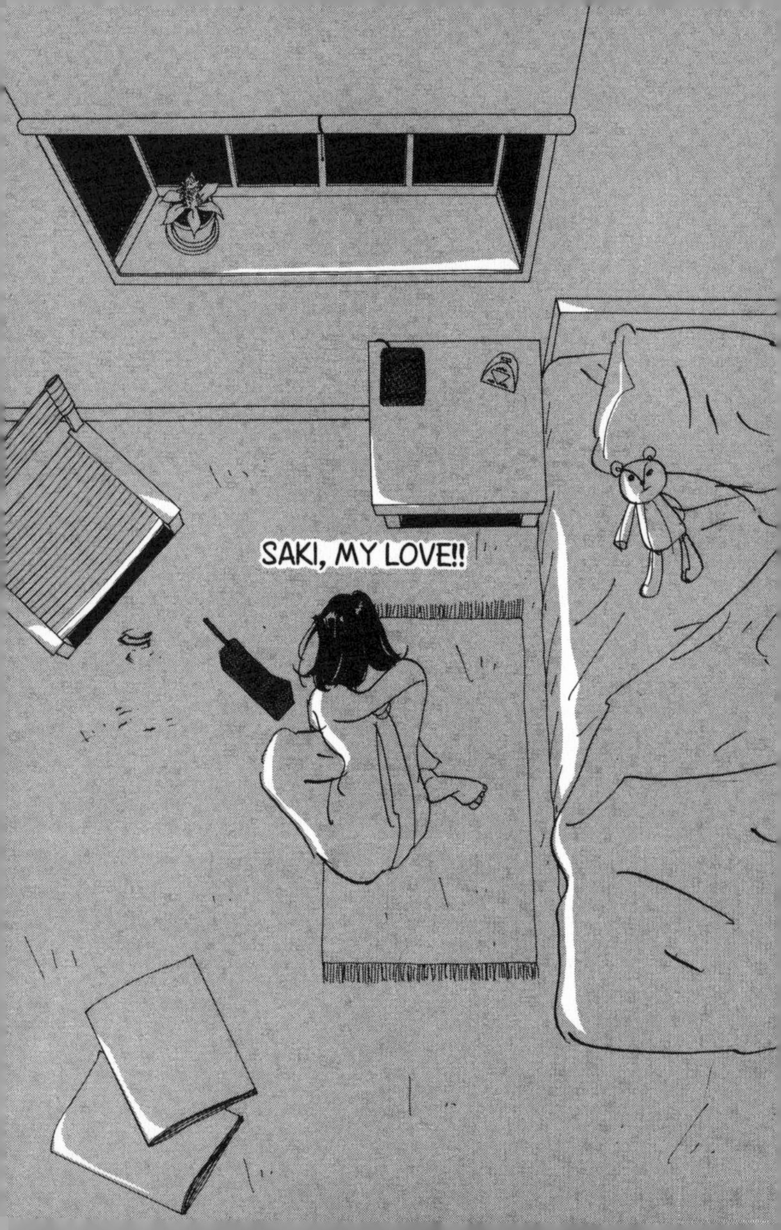
SAKI, MY LOVE!!

between the sheets

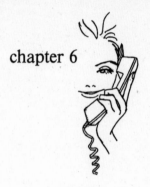

chapter 6

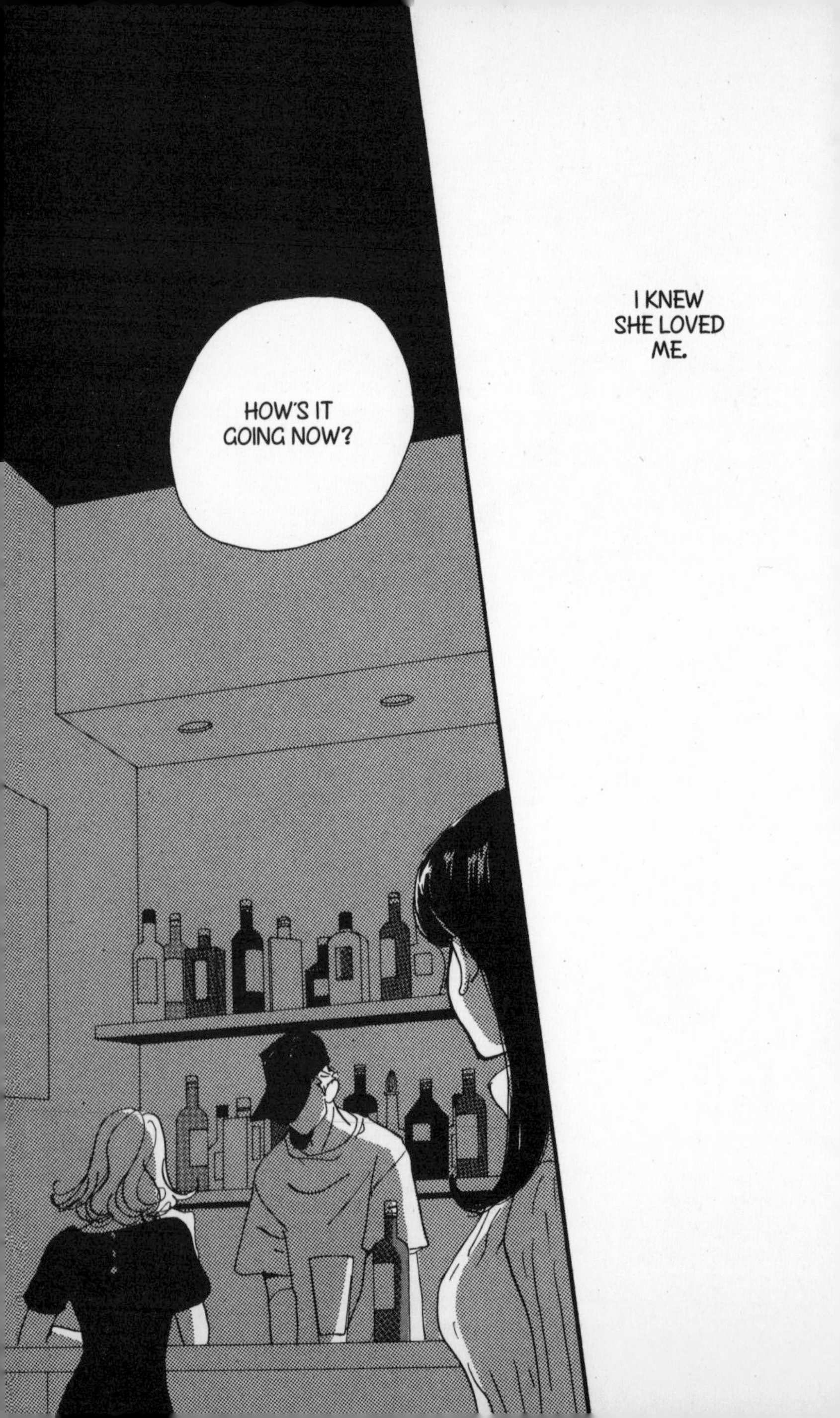
I KNEW SHE LOVED ME.
HOW'S IT GOING NOW?

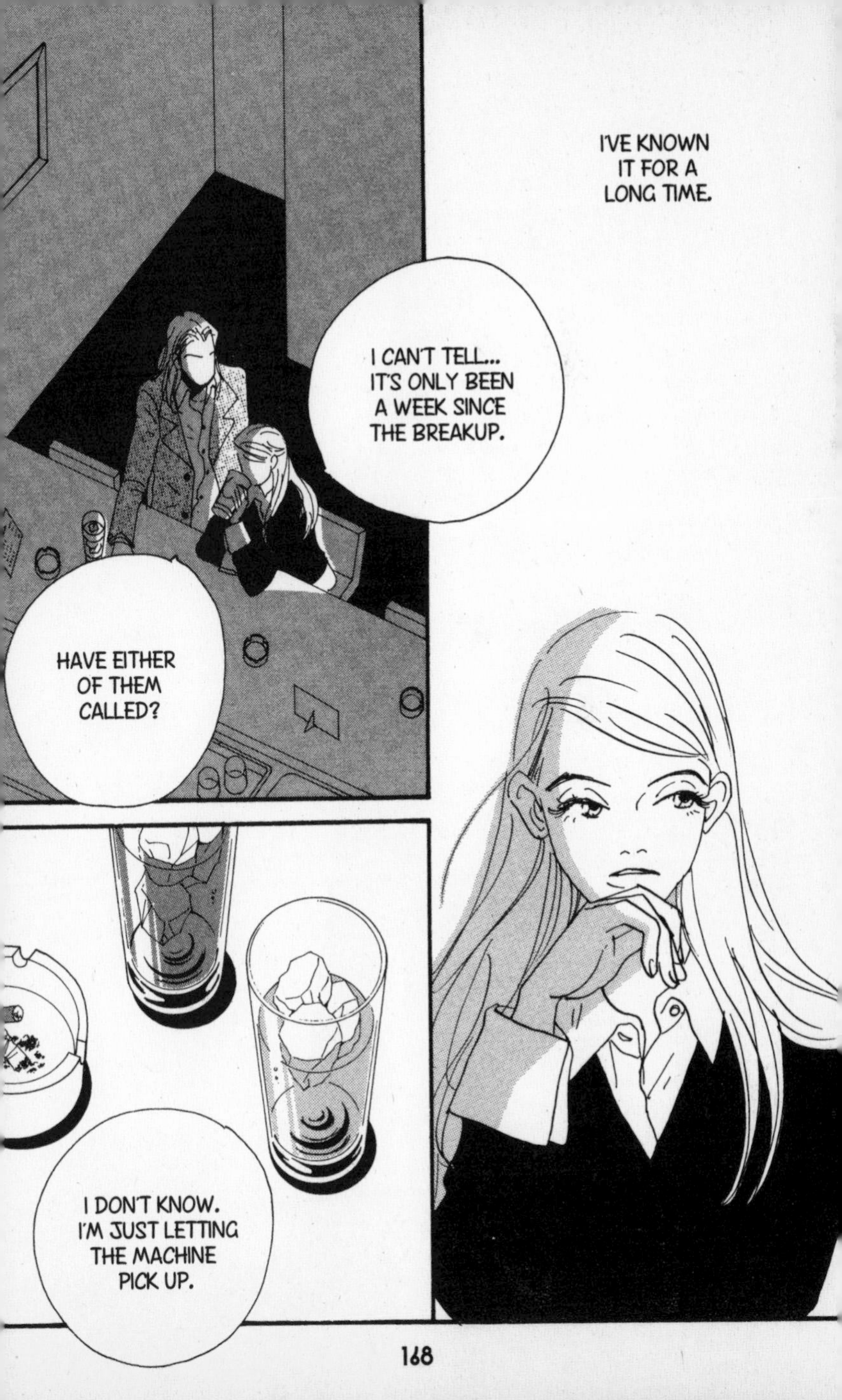
I'VE KNOWN IT FOR A LONG TIME.
I CAN'T TELL... IT'S ONLY BEEN A WEEK SINCE THE BREAKUP.
HAVE EITHER OF THEM CALLED?
I DON'T KNOW. I'M JUST LETTING THE MACHINE PICK UP.

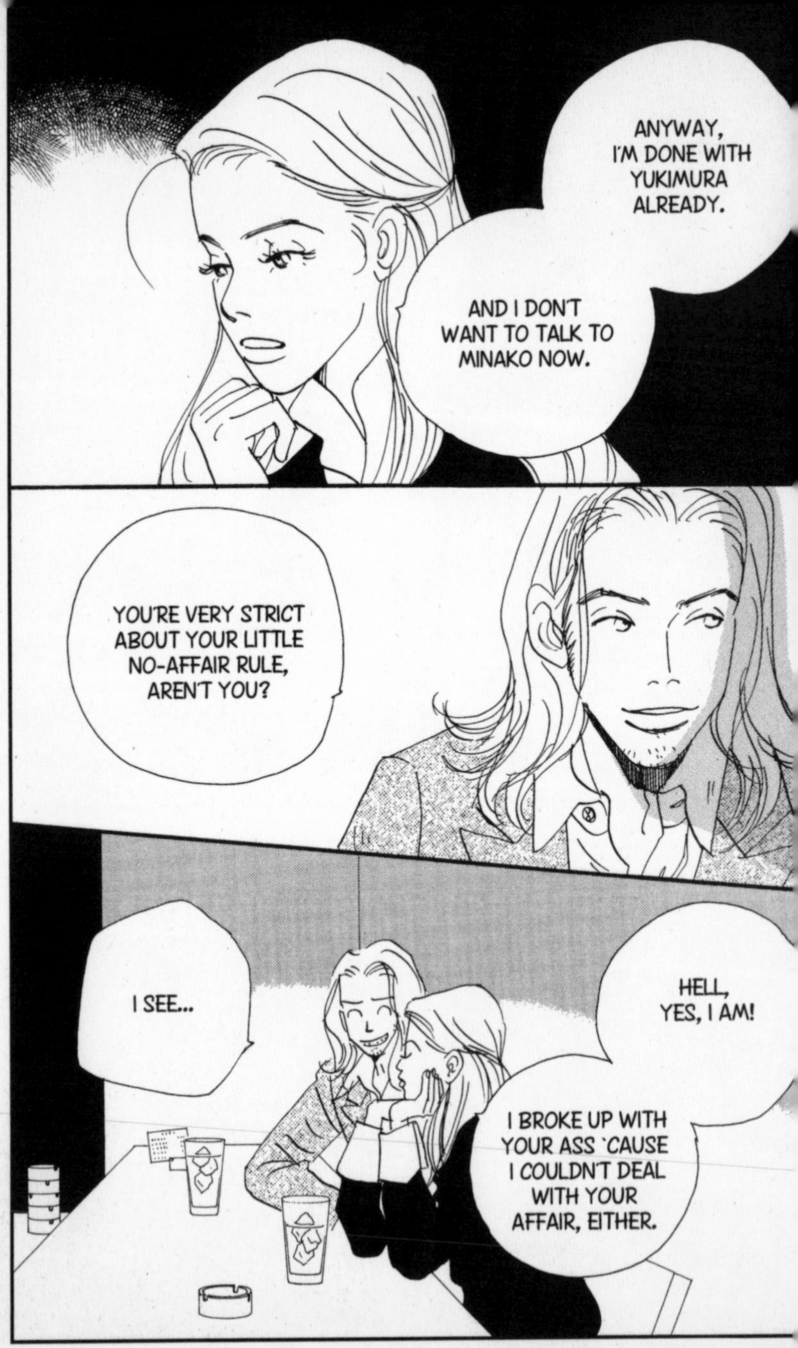
ANYWAY, I'M DONE WITH YUKIMURA ALREADY.
AND I DON'T WANT TO TALK TO MINAKO NOW.
YOU'RE VERY STRICT ABOUT YOUR LITTLE NO-AFFAIR RULE, AREN'T YOU?
HELL, YES, I AM!
I BROKE UP WITH YOUR ASS 'CAUSE I COULDN'T DEAL WITH YOUR AFFAIR, EITHER.
I SEE...

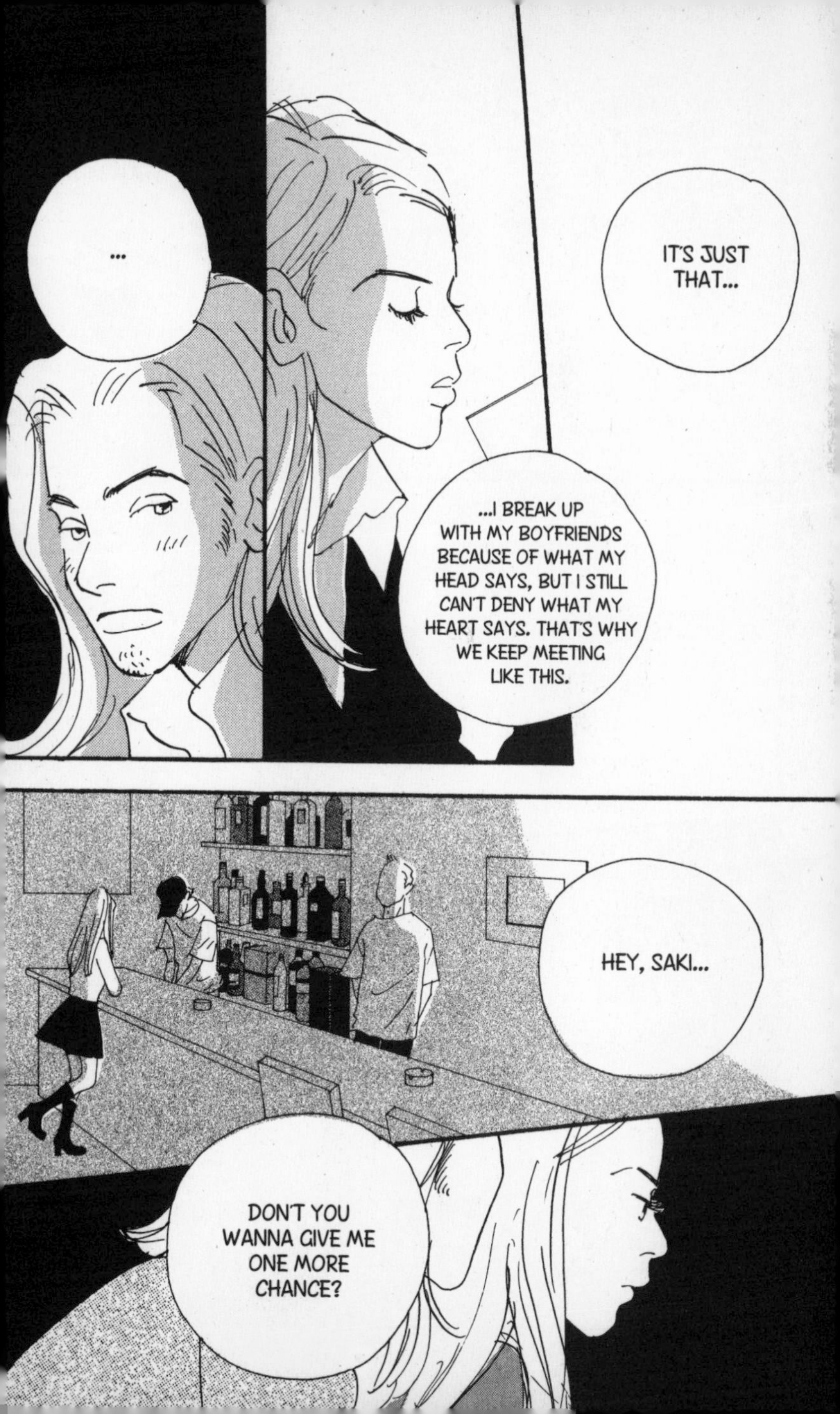
IT'S JUST THAT...
...I BREAK UP WITH MY BOYFRIENDS BECAUSE OF WHAT MY HEAD SAYS, BUT I STILL CAN'T DENY WHAT MY HEART SAYS. THAT'S WHY WE KEEP MEETING LIKE THIS.
...
HEY, SAKI...
DON'T YOU WANNA GIVE ME ONE MORE CHANCE?

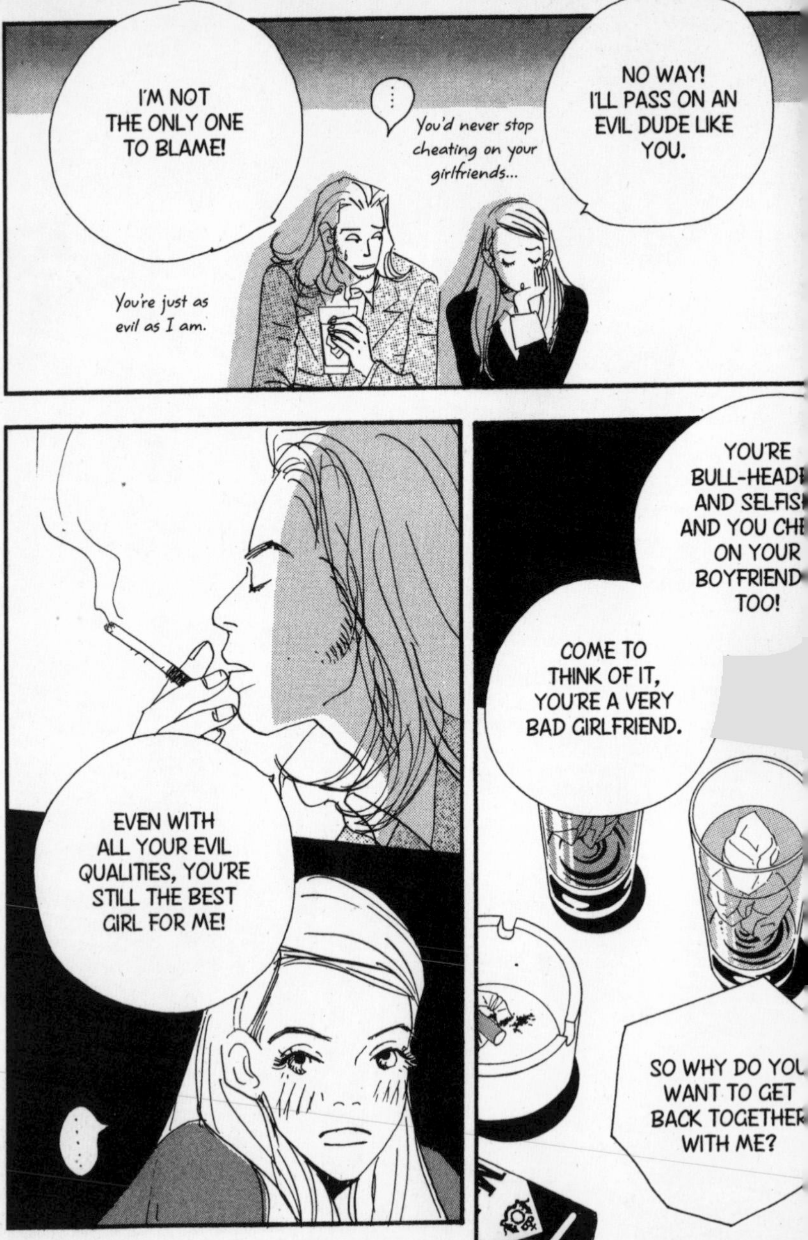
NO WAY! I'LL PASS ON AN EVIL DUDE LIKE YOU.
...
You'd never stop cheating on your girlfriends...
I'M NOT THE ONLY ONE TO BLAME!
You're just as evil as I am.
YOU'RE BULL-HEAD AND SELFIS AND YOU CH ON YOUR BOYFRIEND TOO!
COME TO THINK OF IT, YOU'RE A VERY BAD GIRLFRIEND.
SO WHY DO YOU WANT TO GET BACK TOGETHER WITH ME?
EVEN WITH ALL YOUR EVIL QUALITIES, YOU'RE STILL THE BEST GIRL FOR ME!
...

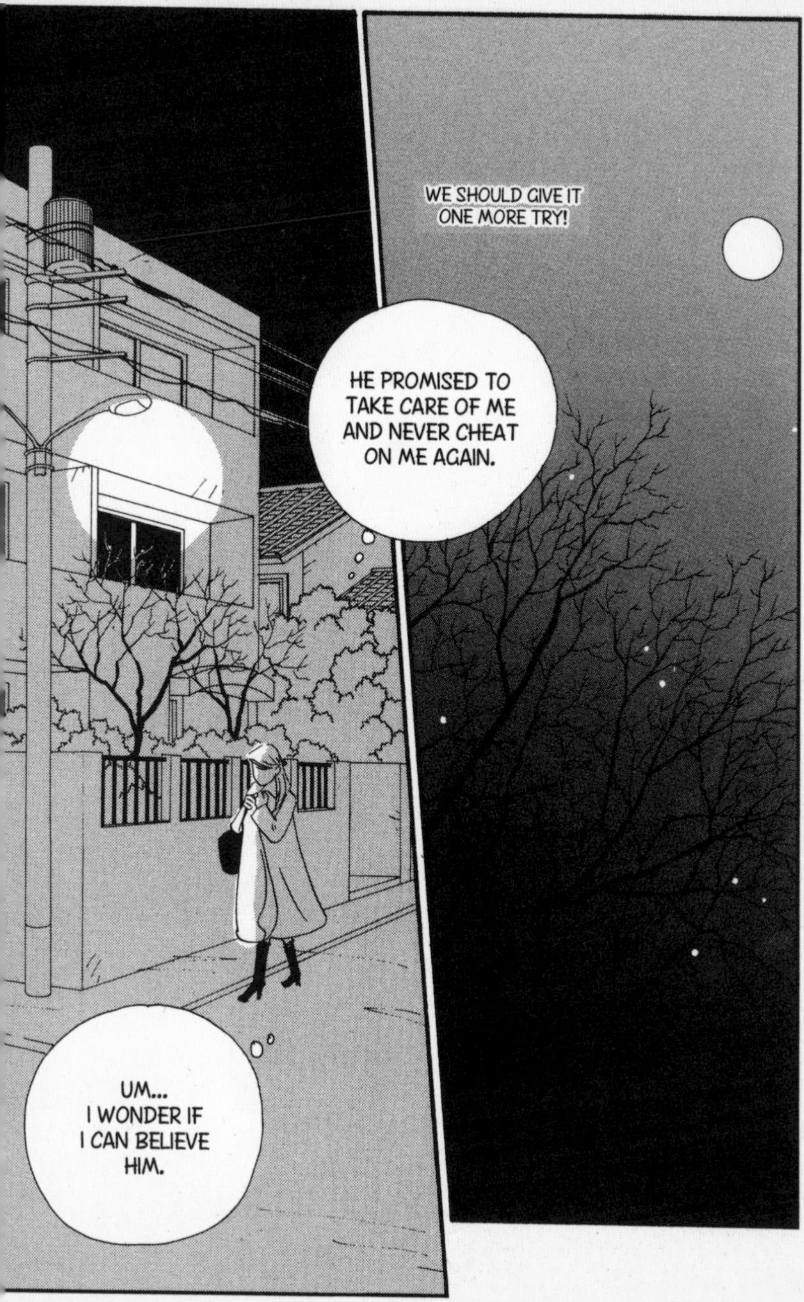
WE SHOULD GIVE IT ONE MORE TRY!
HE PROMISED TO TAKE CARE OF ME AND NEVER CHEAT ON ME AGAIN.
UM... I WONDER IF I CAN BELIEVE HIM.

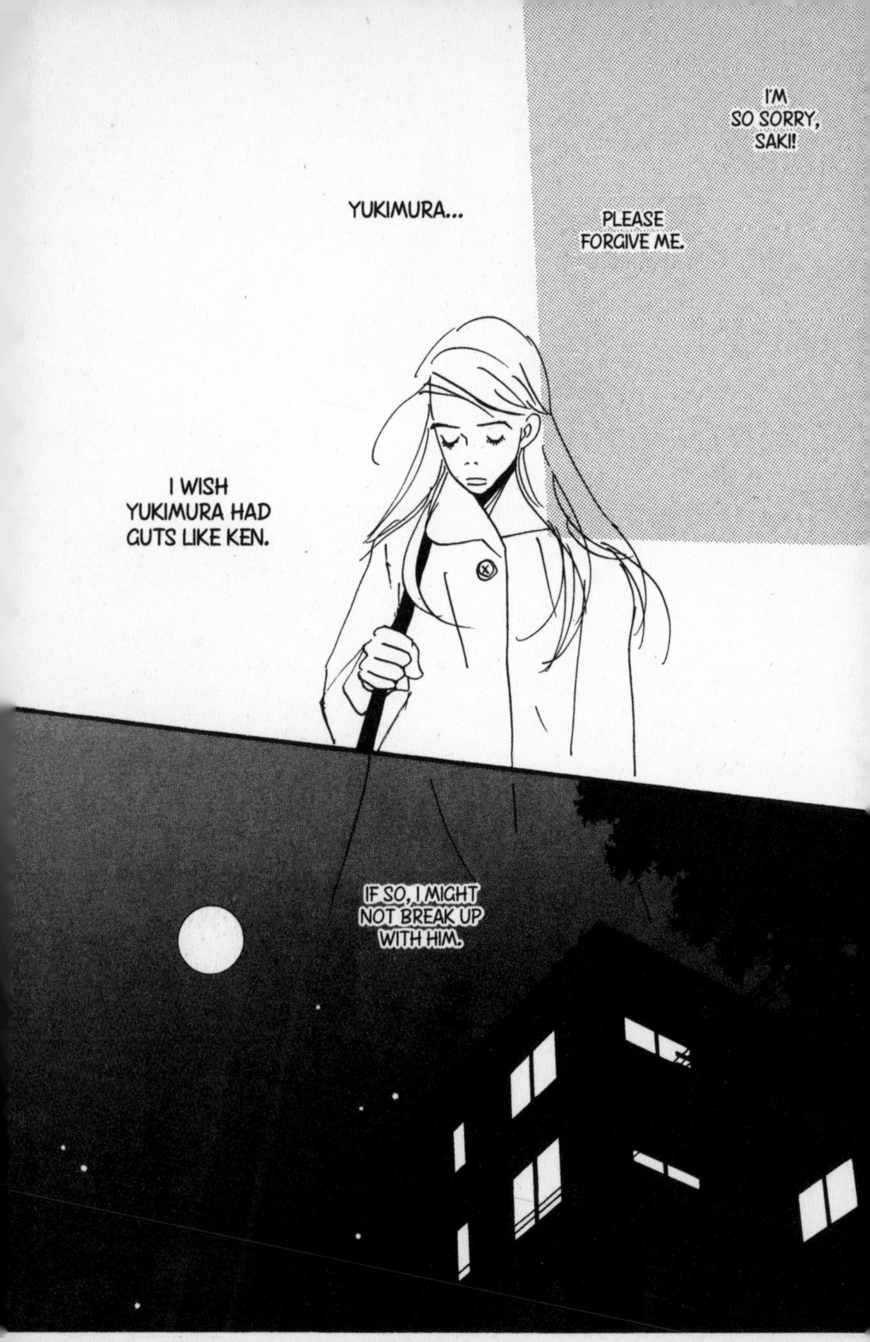
I'M SO SORRY, SAKI!
PLEASE FORGIVE ME.
YUKIMURA...
I WISH YUKIMURA HAD GUTS LIKE KEN.
IF SO, I MIGHT NOT BREAK UP WITH HIM.

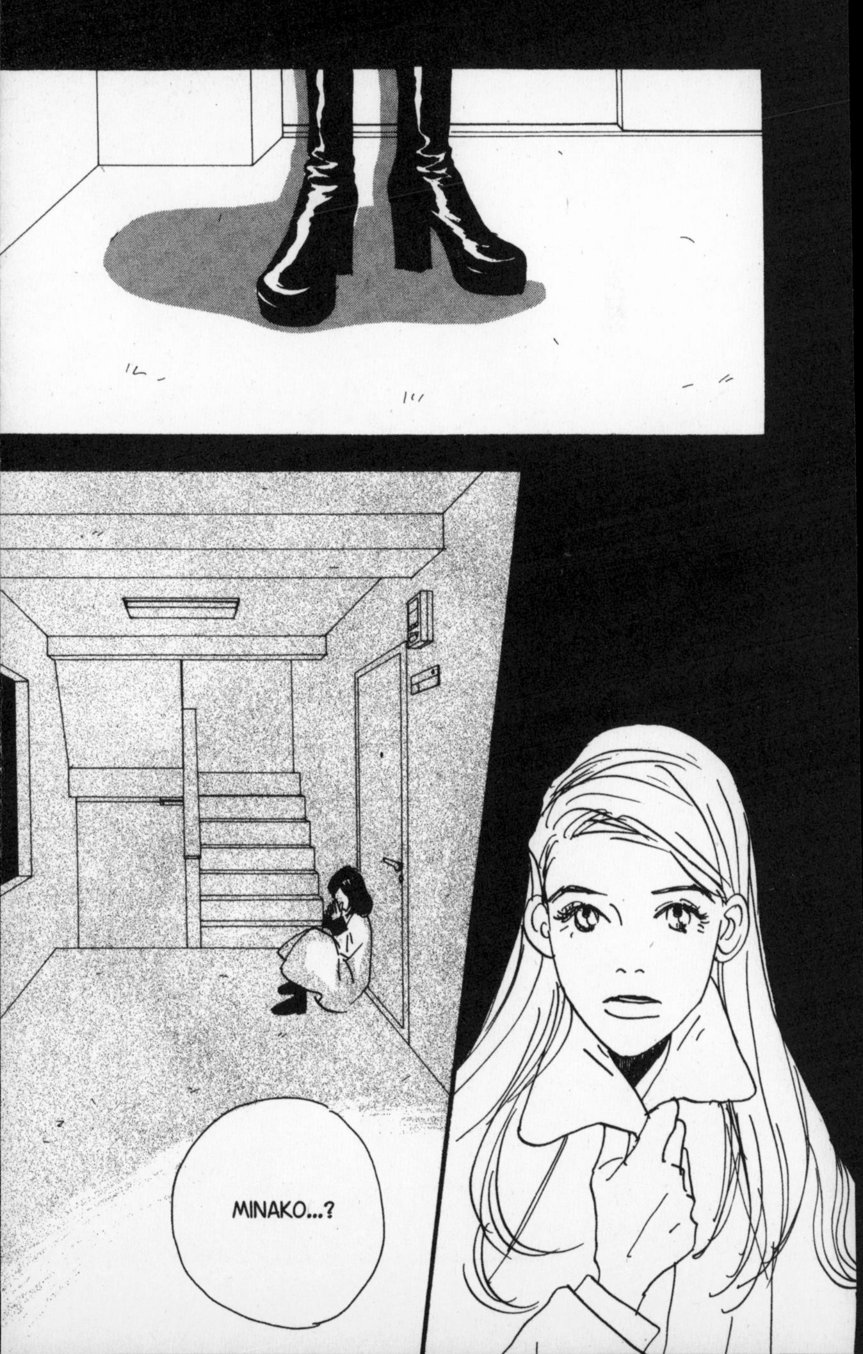
MINAKO...?

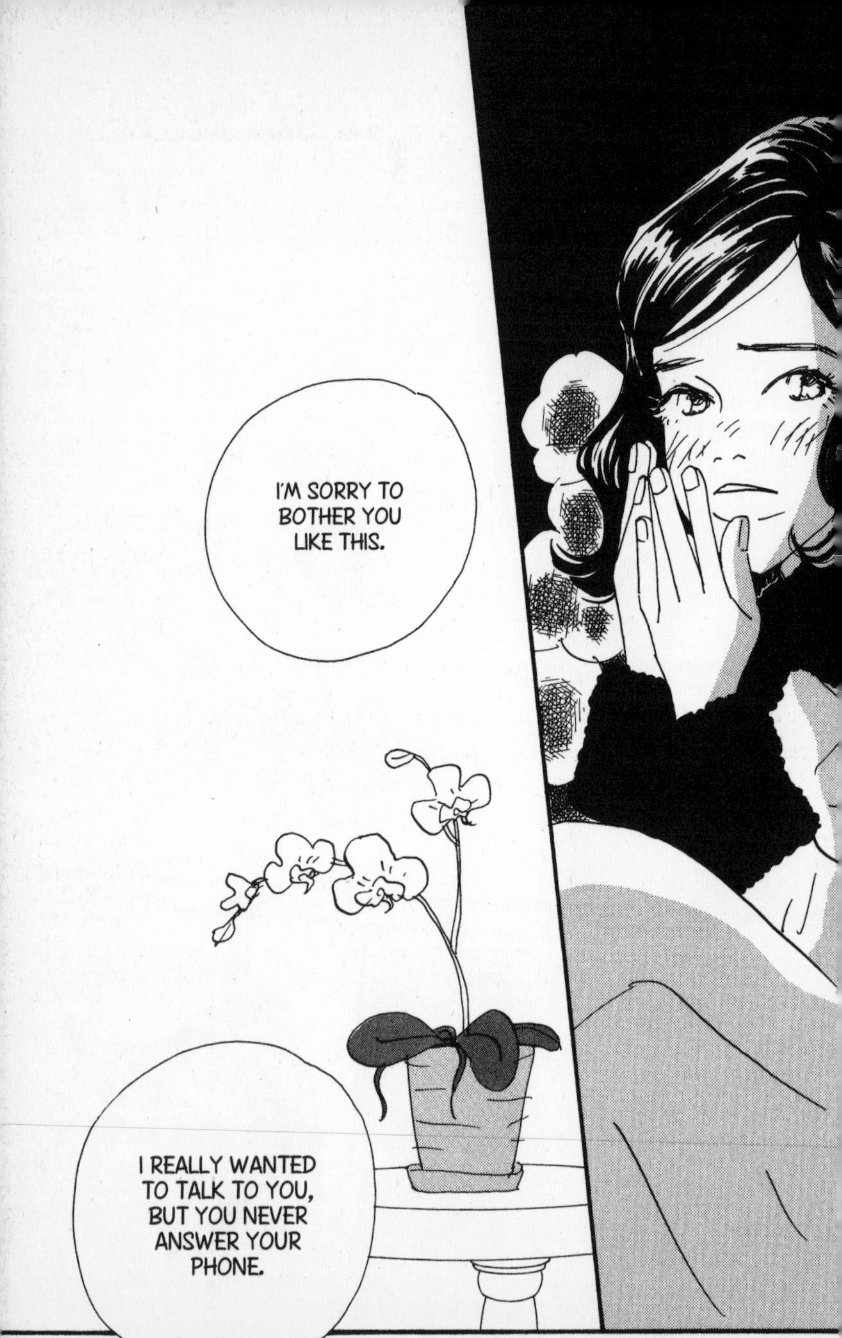
I'M SORRY TO BOTHER YOU LIKE THIS.
I REALLY WANTED TO TALK TO YOU, BUT YOU NEVER ANSWER YOUR PHONE.

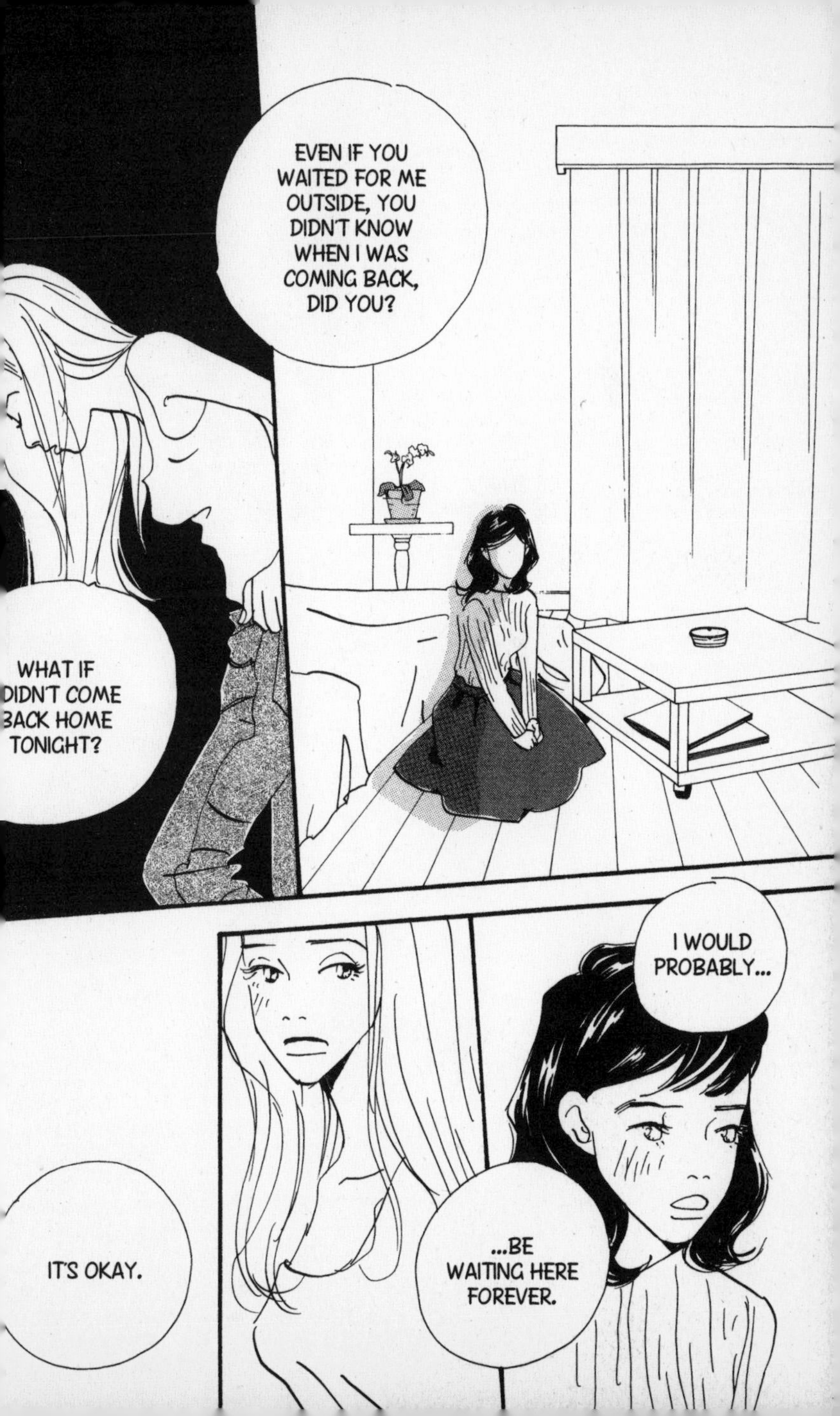
EVEN IF YOU WAITED FOR ME OUTSIDE, YOU DIDN'T KNOW WHEN I WAS COMING BACK, DID YOU?
WHAT IF DIDN'T COME BACK HOME TONIGHT?
I WOULD PROBABLY...
...BE WAITING HERE FOREVER.
IT'S OKAY.

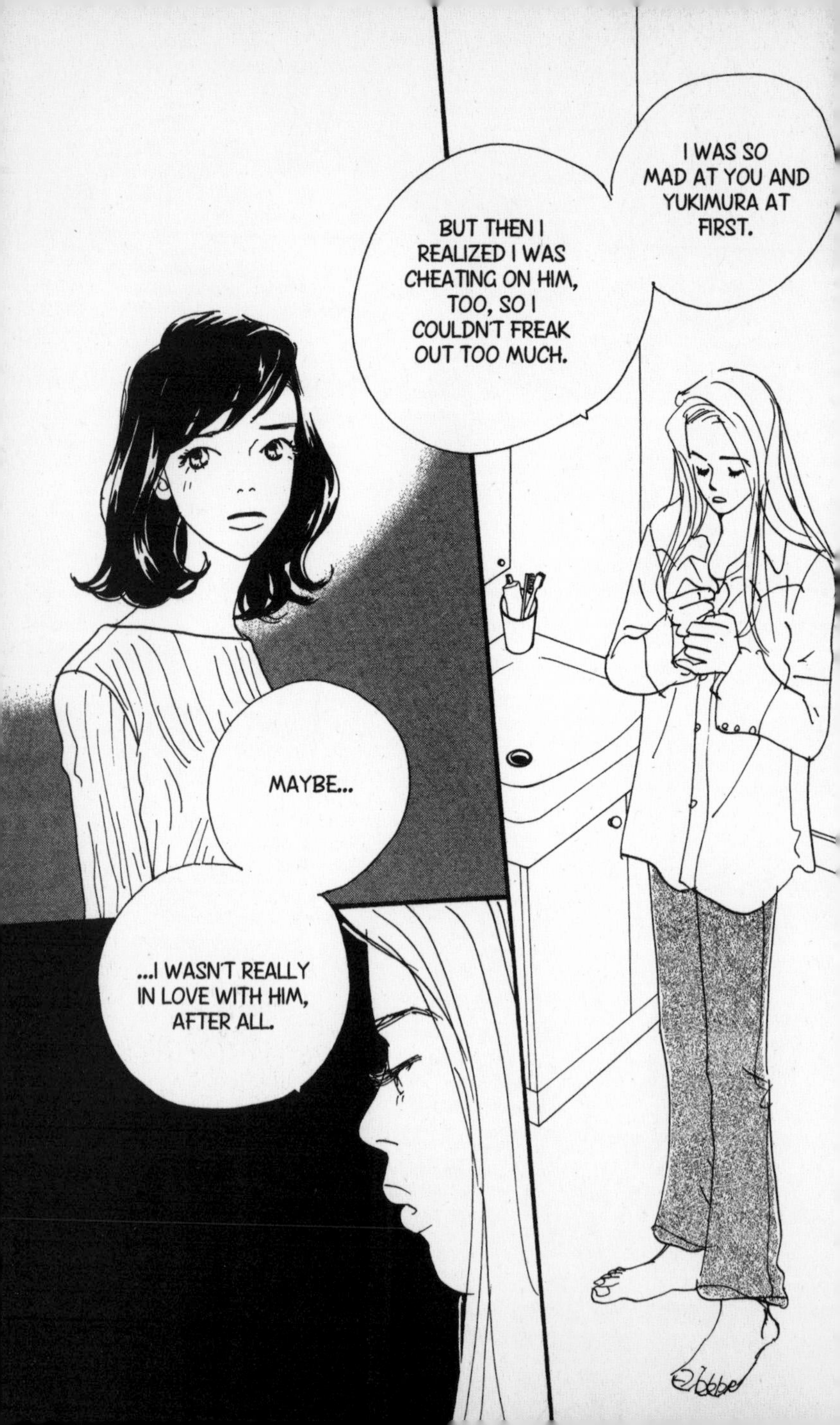
I WAS SO MAD AT YOU AND YUKIMURA AT FIRST.
BUT THEN I REALIZED I WAS CHEATING ON HIM, TOO, SO I COULDN'T FREAK OUT TOO MUCH.
MAYBE...
...I WASN'T REALLY IN LOVE WITH HIM, AFTER ALL.

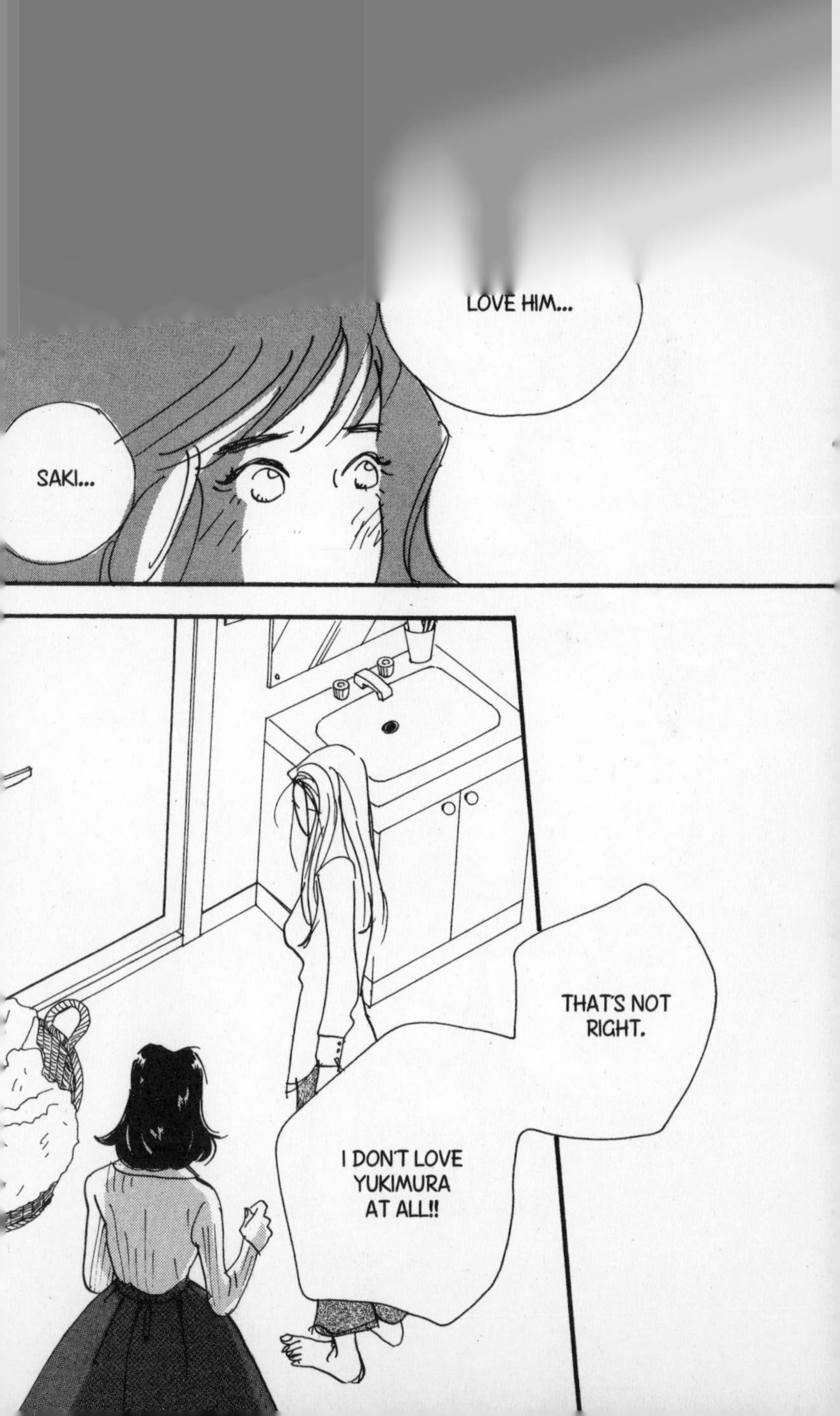
LOVE HIM...
SAKI...
THAT'S NOT RIGHT.
I DON'T LOVE YUKIMURA AT ALL!!

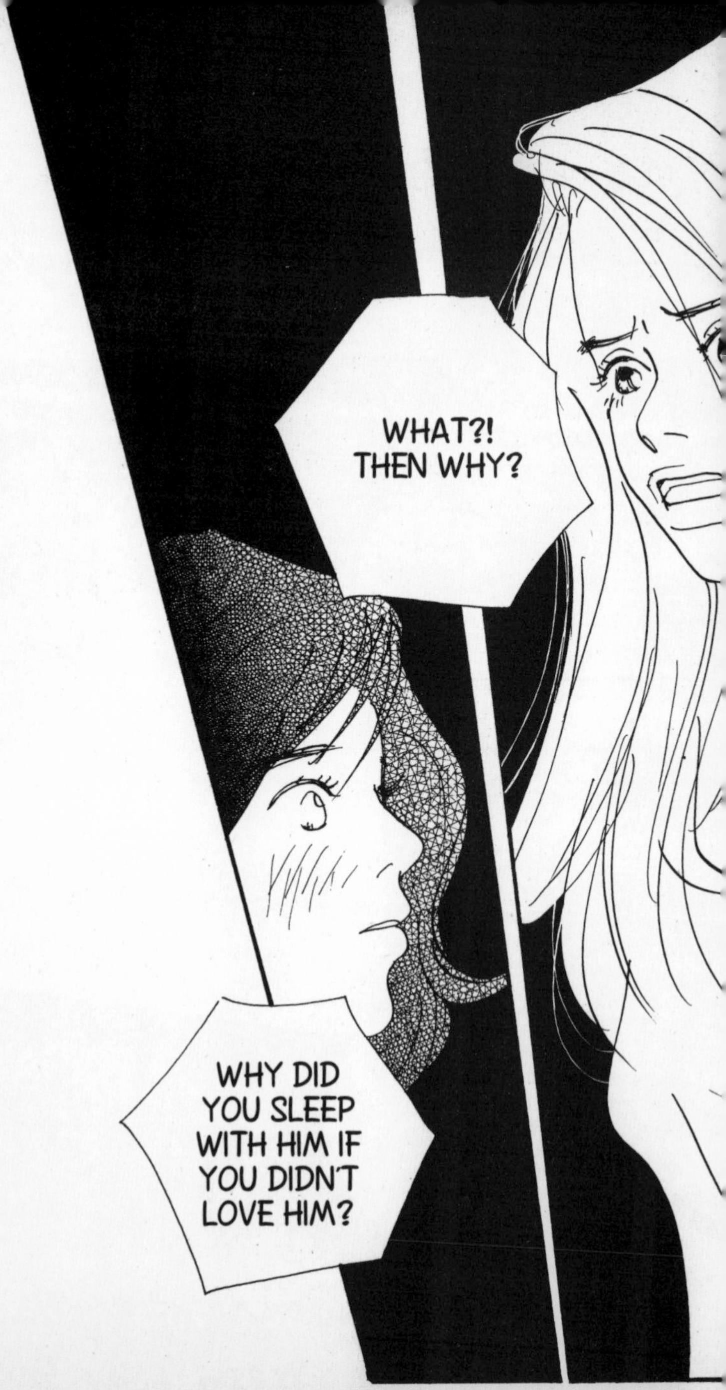
WHAT?! THEN WHY?
WHY DID YOU SLEEP WITH HIM IF YOU DIDN'T LOVE HIM?

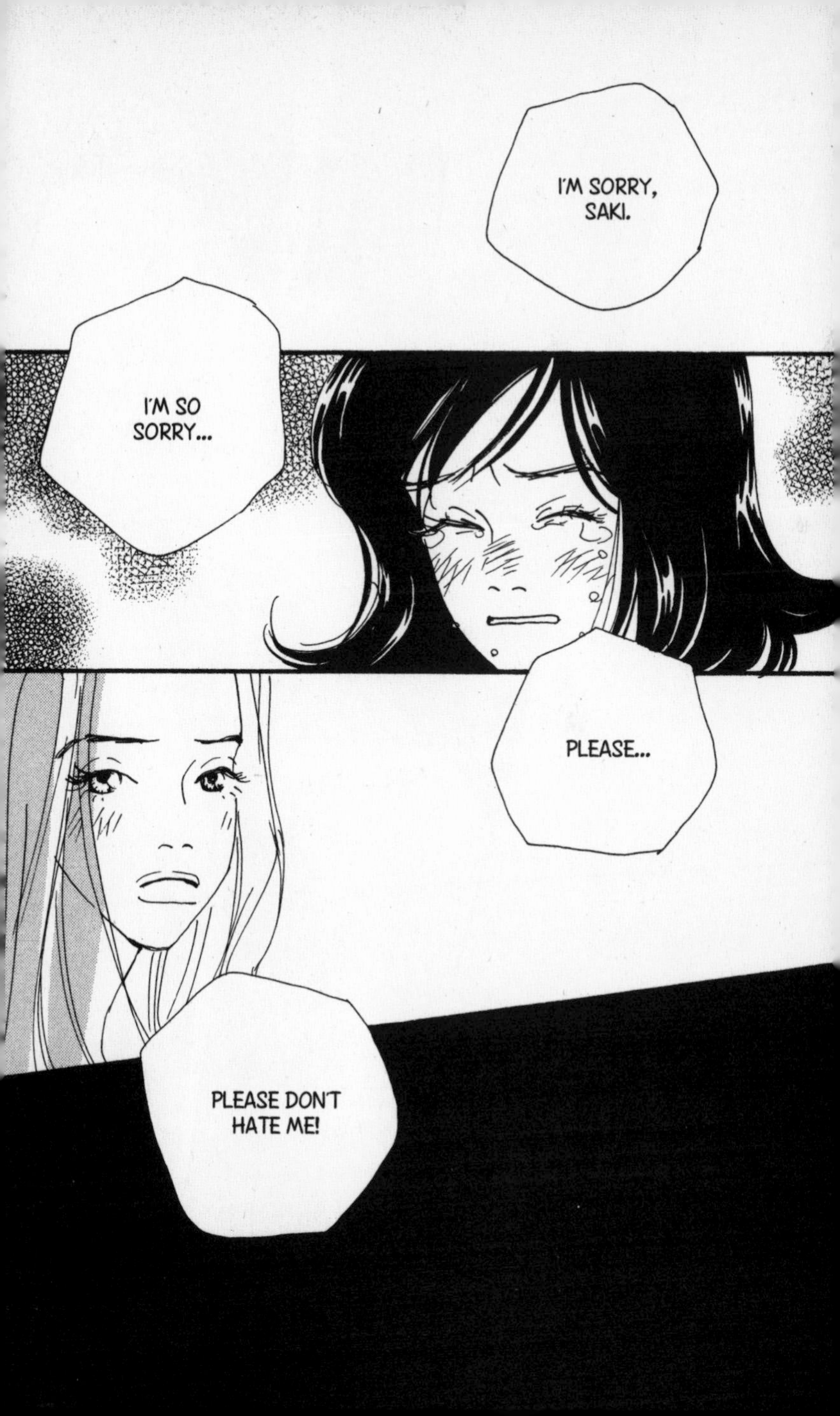
I'M SORRY, SAKI.
I'M SO SORRY...
PLEASE...
PLEASE DON'T HATE ME!

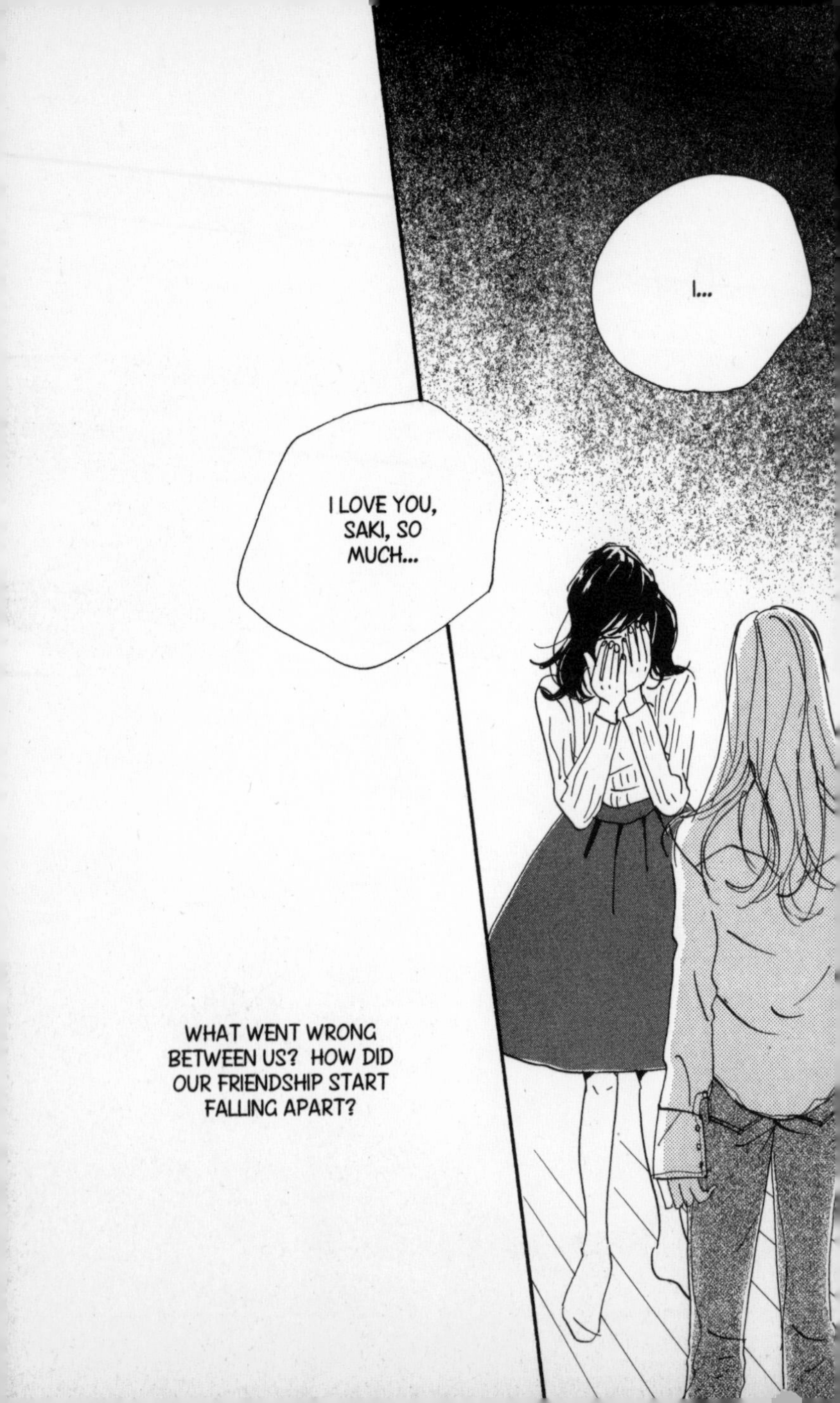
I...
I LOVE YOU, SAKI, SO MUCH...
WHAT WENT WRONG BETWEEN US? HOW DID OUR FRIENDSHIP START FALLING APART?

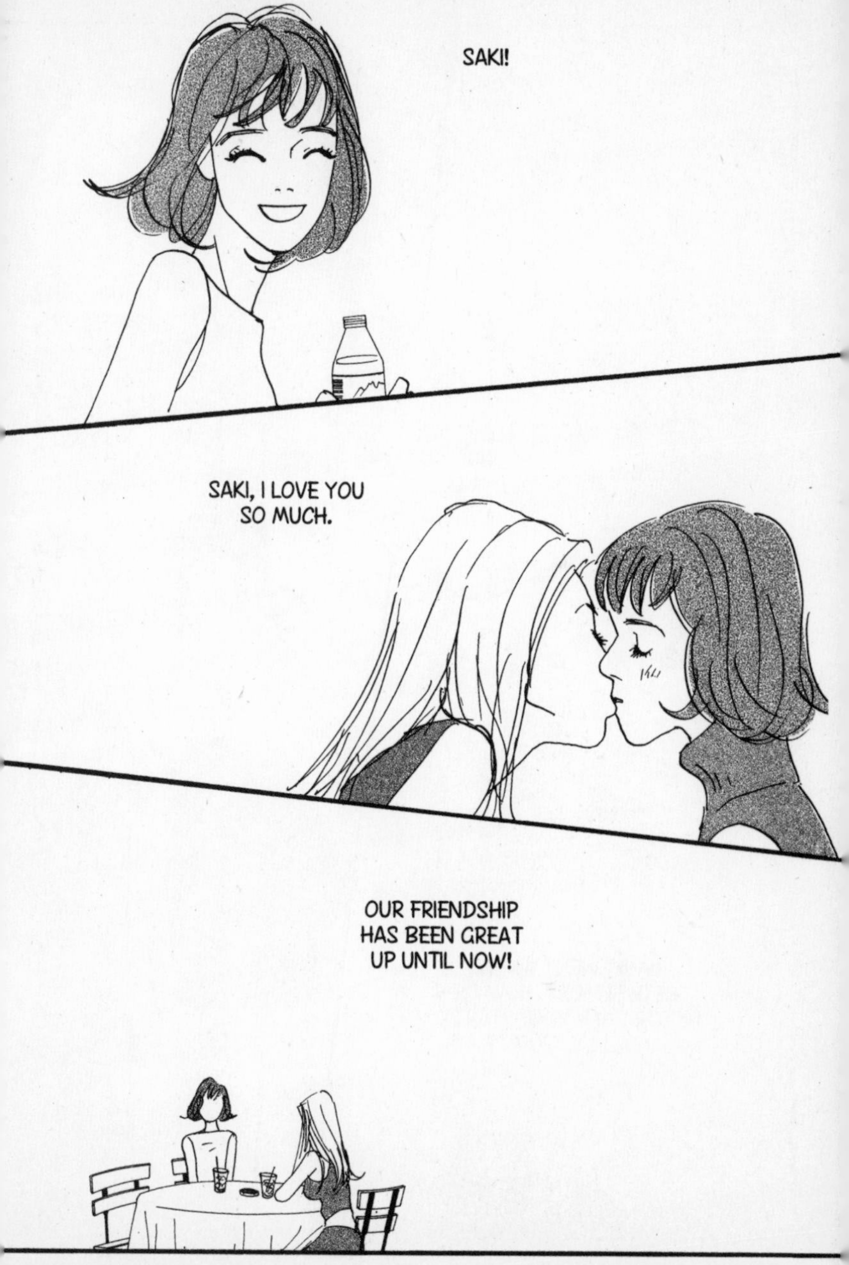
SAKI!
SAKI, I LOVE YOU SO MUCH.
OUR FRIENDSHIP HAS BEEN GREAT UP UNTIL NOW!

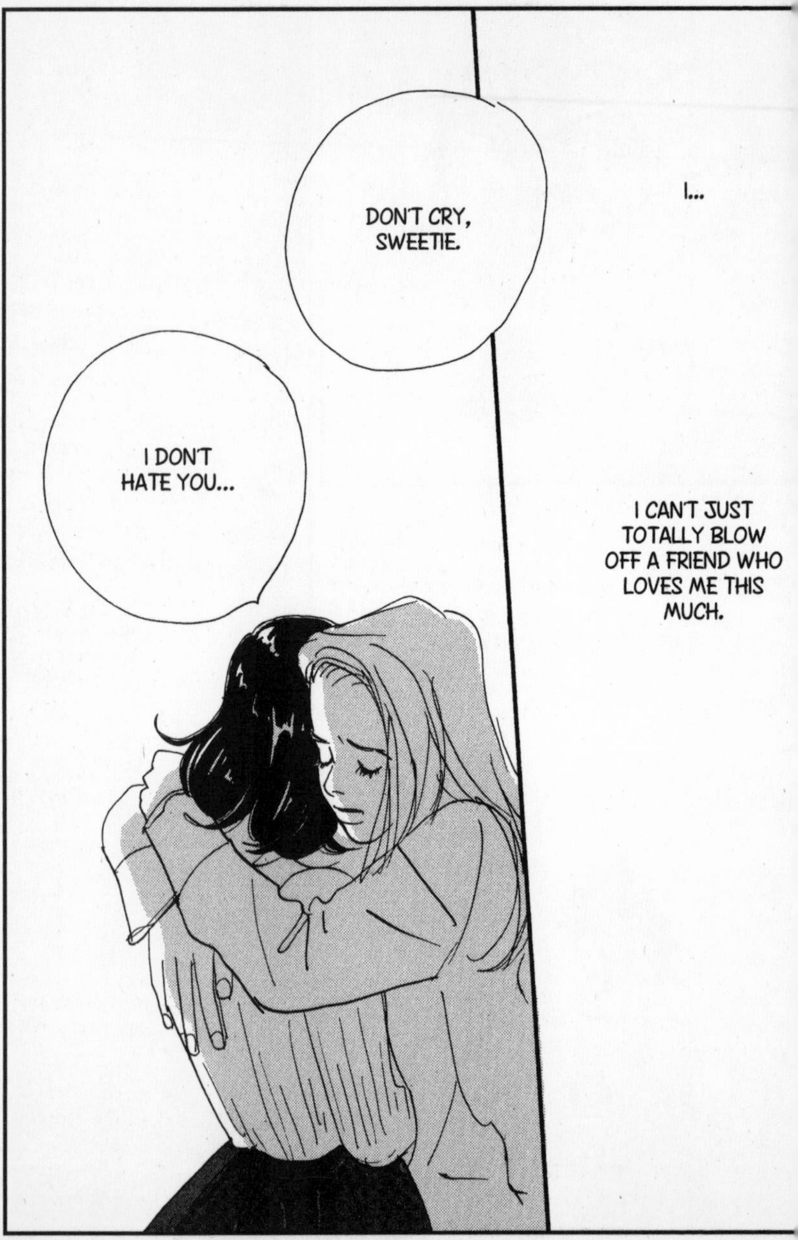
I...
I CAN'T JUST TOTALLY BLOW OFF A FRIEND WHO LOVES ME THIS MUCH.
DON'T CRY, SWEETIE.
I DON'T HATE YOU...

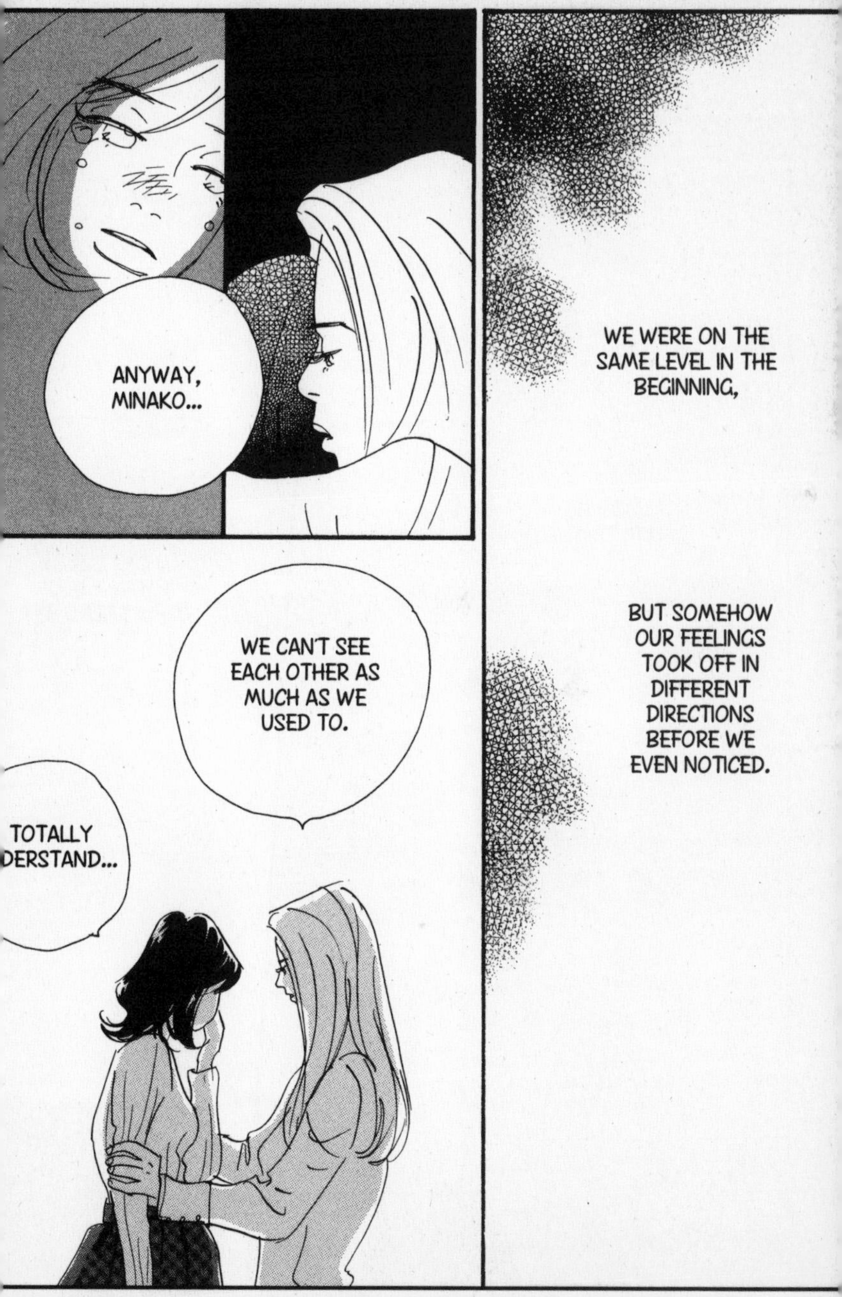
WE WERE ON THE SAME LEVEL IN THE BEGINNING,
BUT SOMEHOW OUR FEELINGS TOOK OFF IN DIFFERENT DIRECTIONS BEFORE WE EVEN NOTICED.
ANYWAY, MINAKO...
WE CAN'T SEE EACH OTHER AS MUCH AS WE USED TO.
TOTALLY DERSTAND...

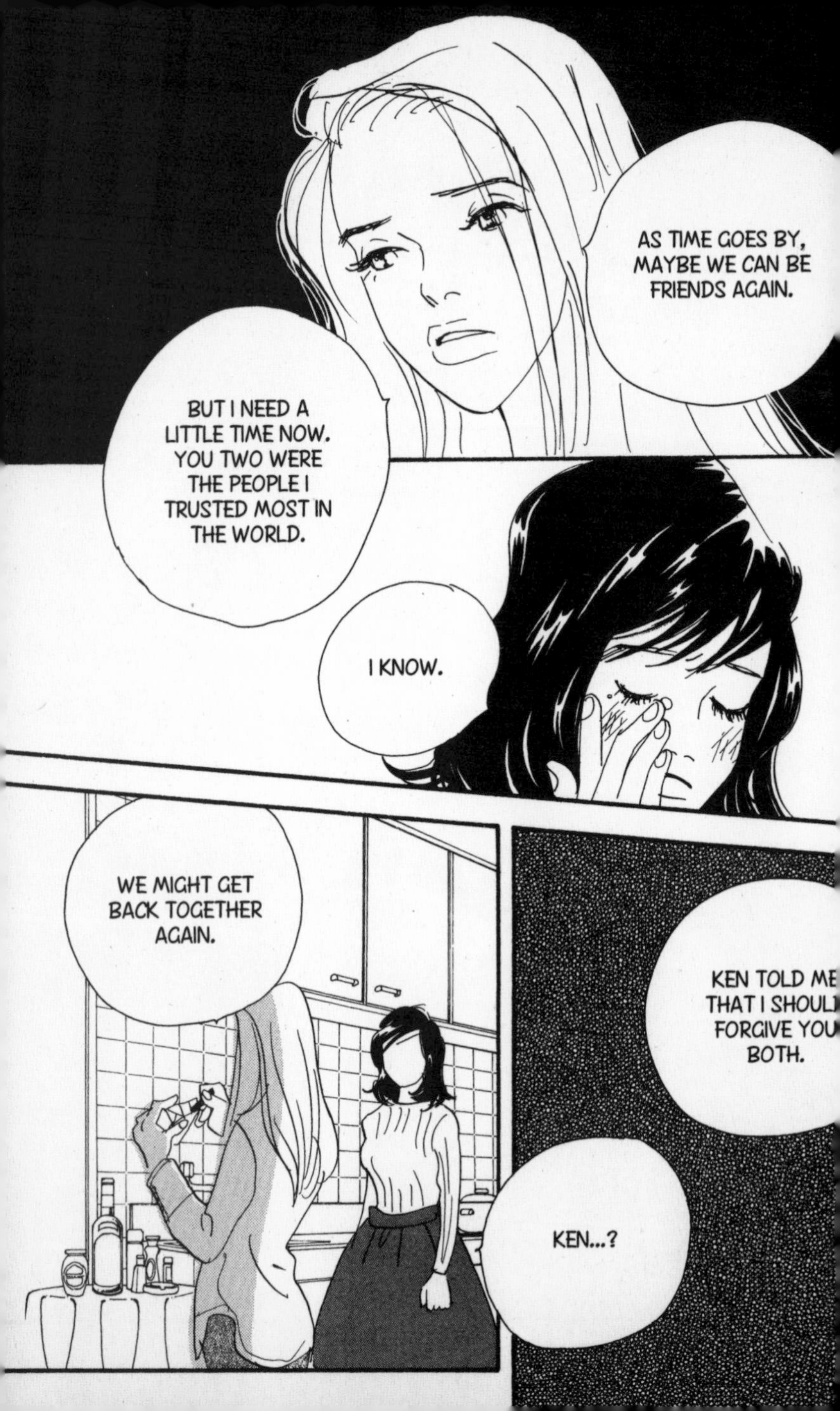
AS TIME GOES BY, MAYBE WE CAN BE FRIENDS AGAIN.
BUT I NEED A LITTLE TIME NOW. YOU TWO WERE THE PEOPLE I TRUSTED MOST IN THE WORLD.
I KNOW.
KEN TOLD ME THAT I SHOUL FORGIVE YOU BOTH.
KEN...?
WE MIGHT GET BACK TOGETHER AGAIN.

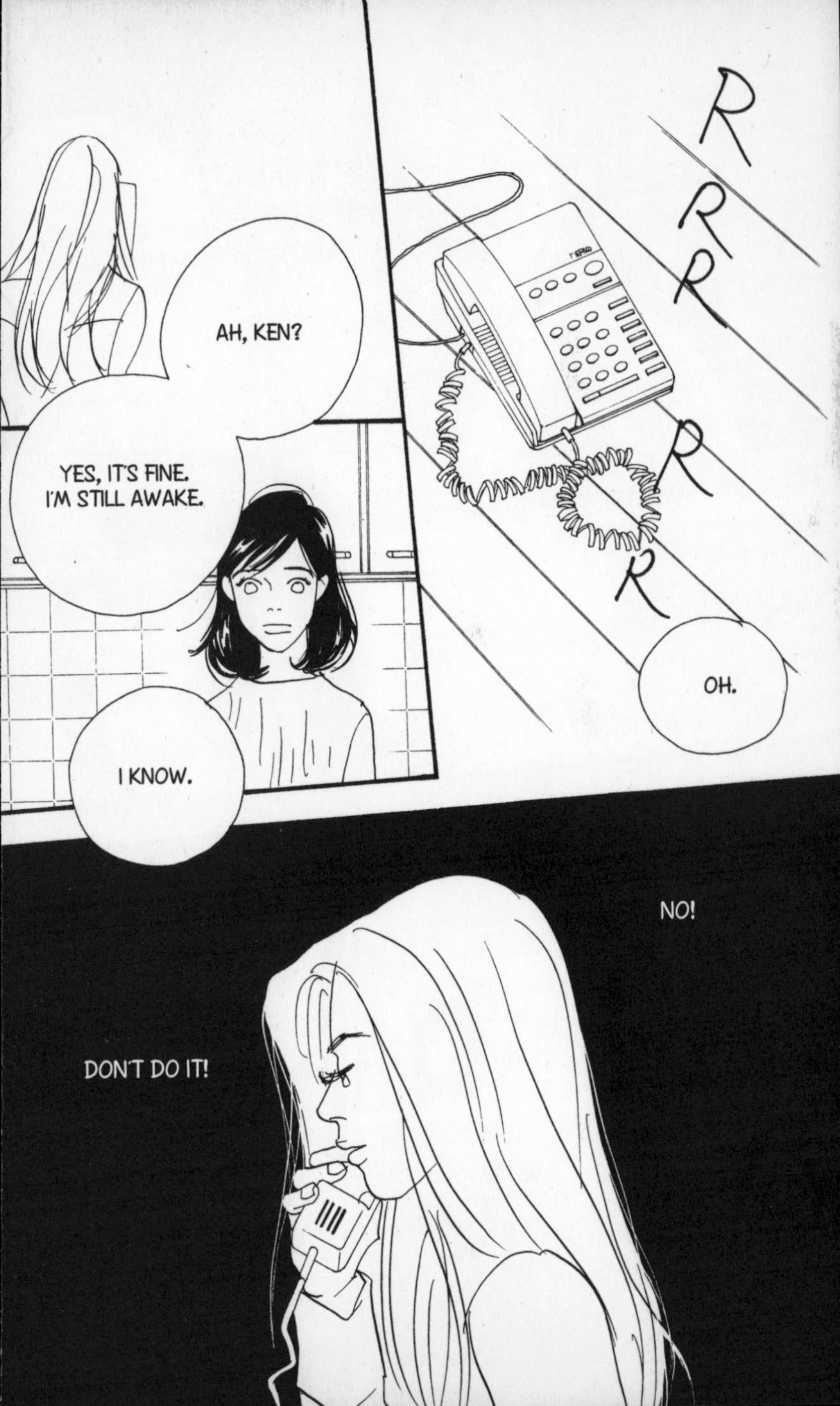

RRRRR
OH.
AH, KEN?
YES, IT'S FINE. I'M STILL AWAKE.
I KNOW.
NO!
DON'T DO IT!

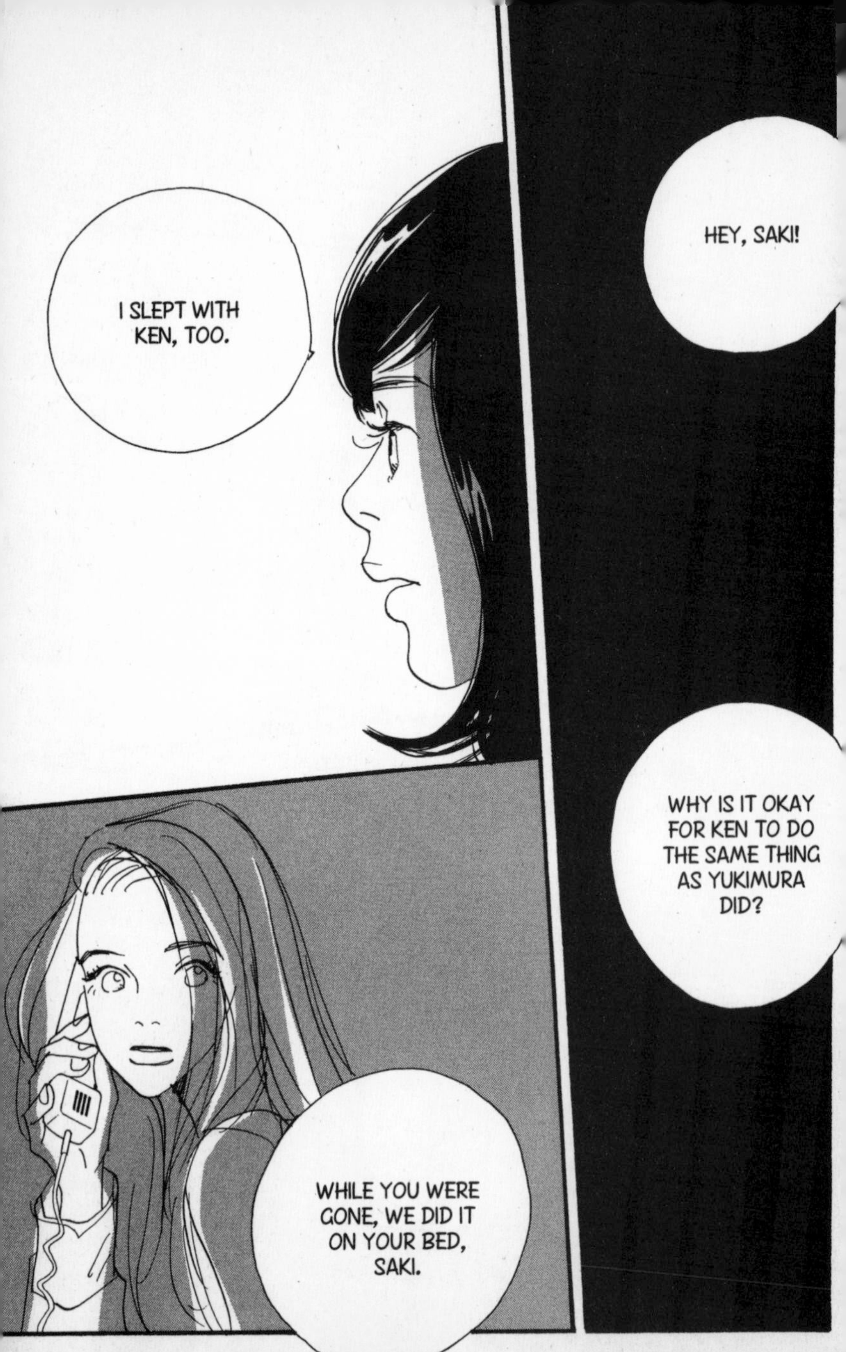
HEY, SAKI!
WHY IS IT OKAY FOR KEN TO DO THE SAME THING AS YUKIMURA DID?
I SLEPT WITH KEN, TOO.
WHILE YOU WERE GONE, WE DID IT ON YOUR BED, SAKI.

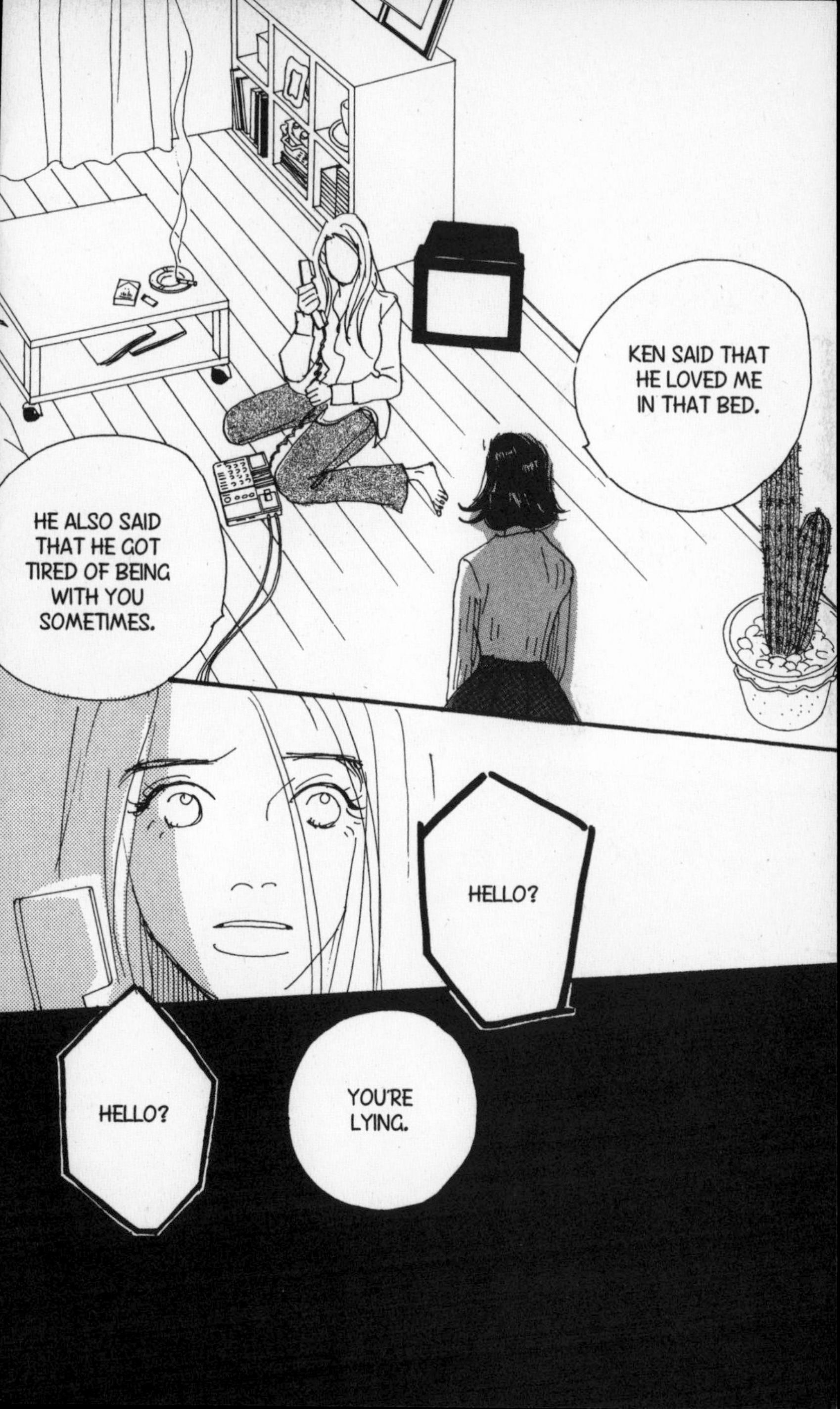
KEN SAID THAT HE LOVED ME IN THAT BED.
HE ALSO SAID THAT HE GOT TIRED OF BEING WITH YOU SOMETIMES.
HELLO?
YOU'RE LYING.
HELLO?

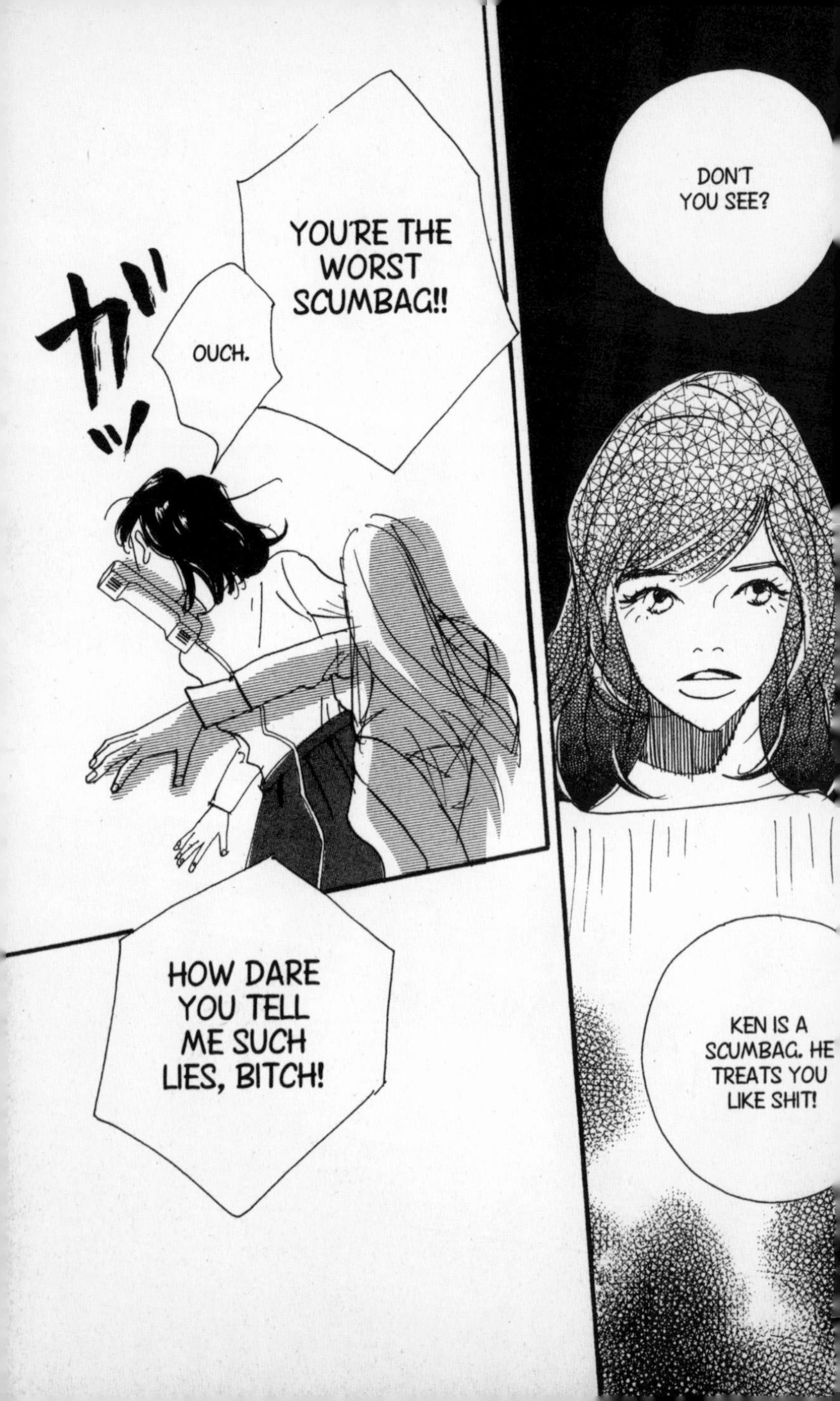
DON'T YOU SEE?
KEN IS A SCUMBAG. HE TREATS YOU LIKE SHIT!
YOU'RE THE WORST SCUMBAG!!
OUCH.
ガッ
HOW DARE YOU TELL ME SUCH LIES, BITCH!

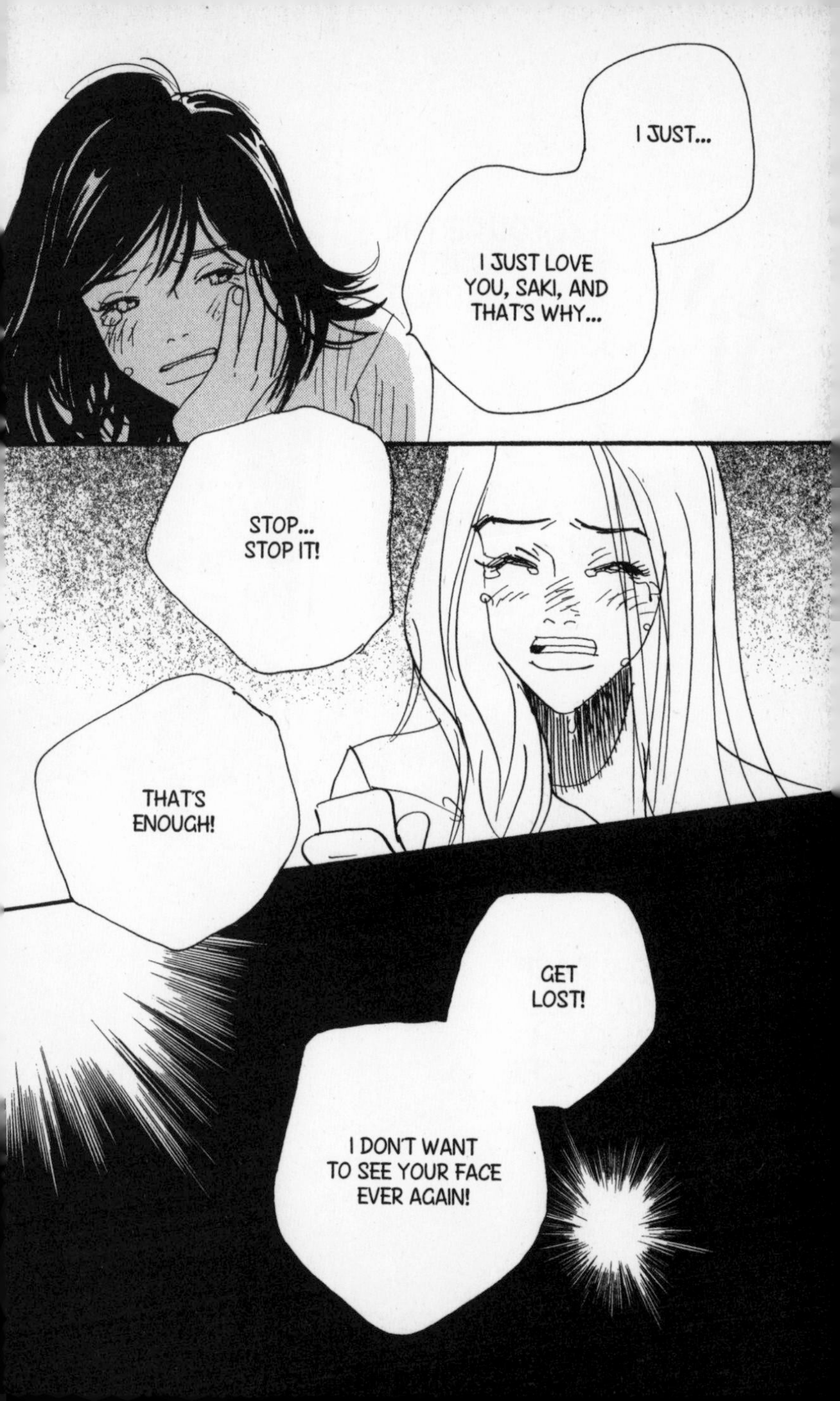
I JUST...
I JUST LOVE YOU, SAKI, AND THAT'S WHY...
STOP... STOP IT!
THAT'S ENOUGH!
GET LOST!
I DON'T WANT TO SEE YOUR FACE EVER AGAIN!

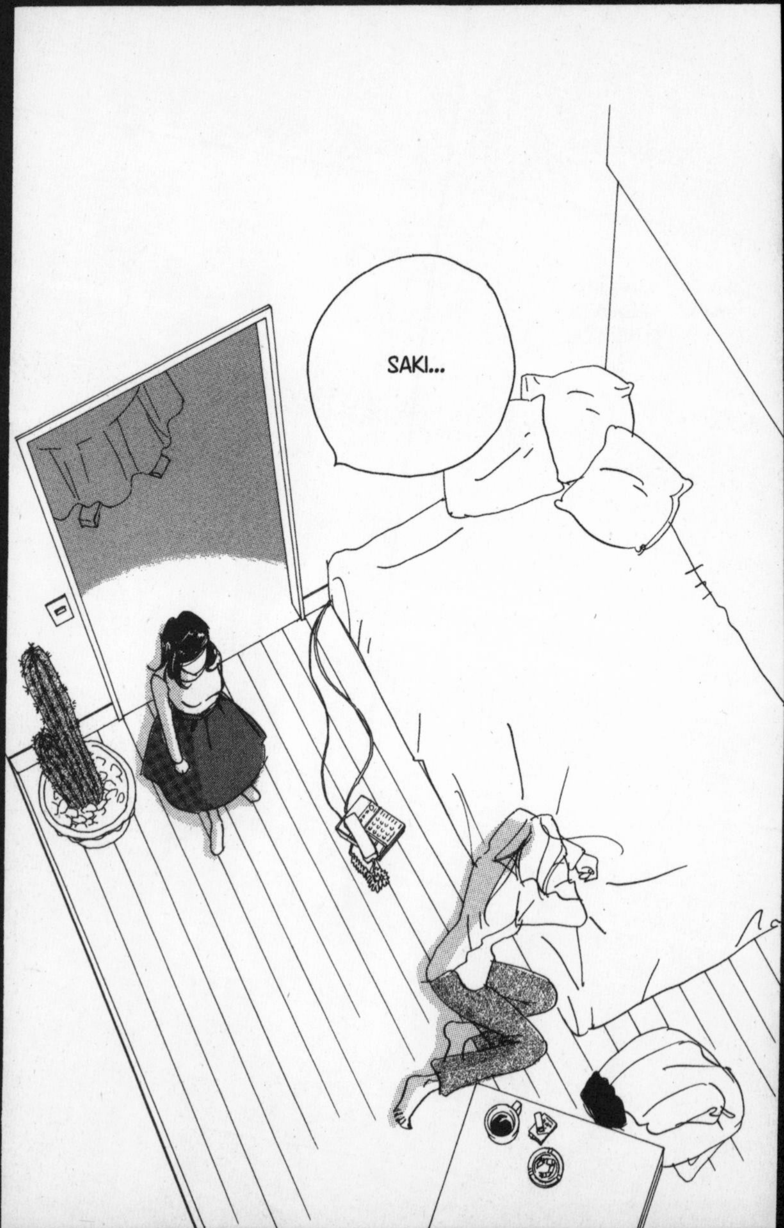
SAKI...

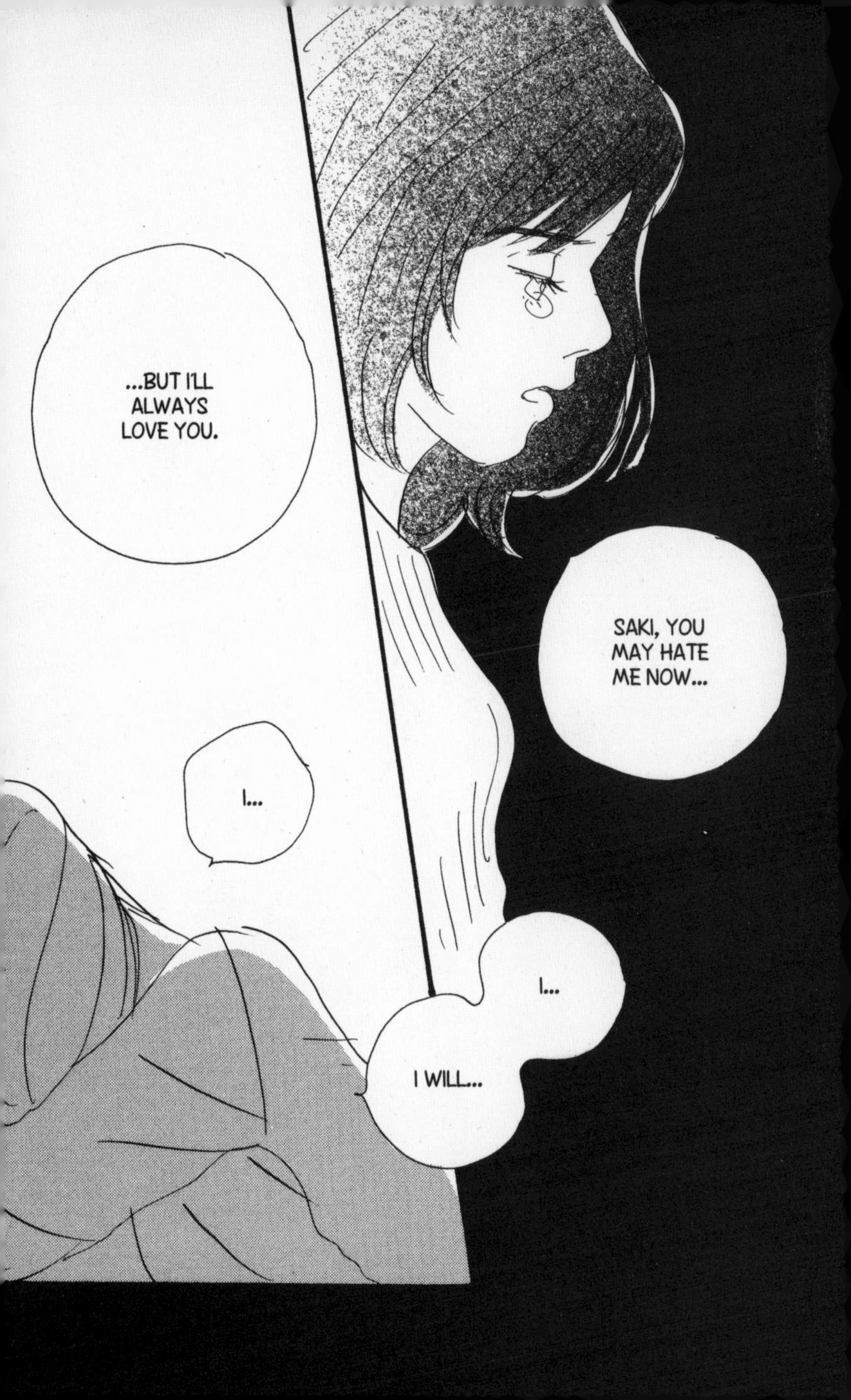
SAKI, YOU MAY HATE ME NOW...
...BUT I'LL ALWAYS LOVE YOU.
I...
I...
I WILL...

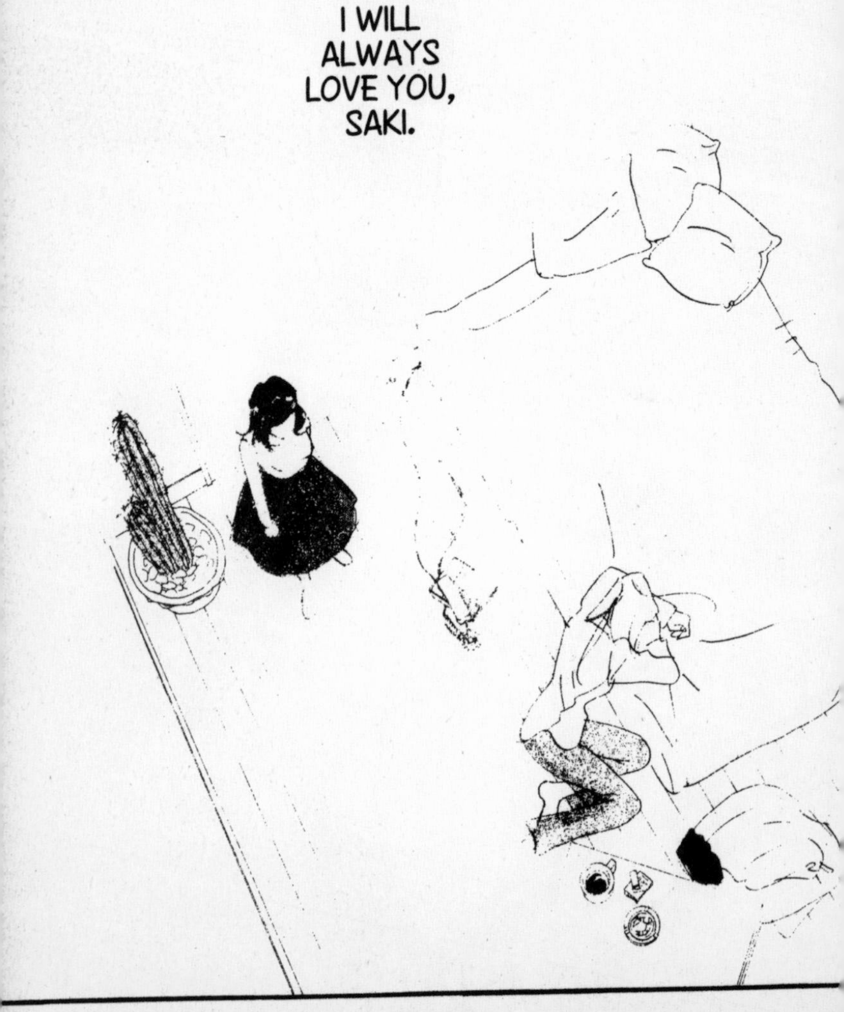
I WILL ALWAYS LOVE YOU, SAKI.

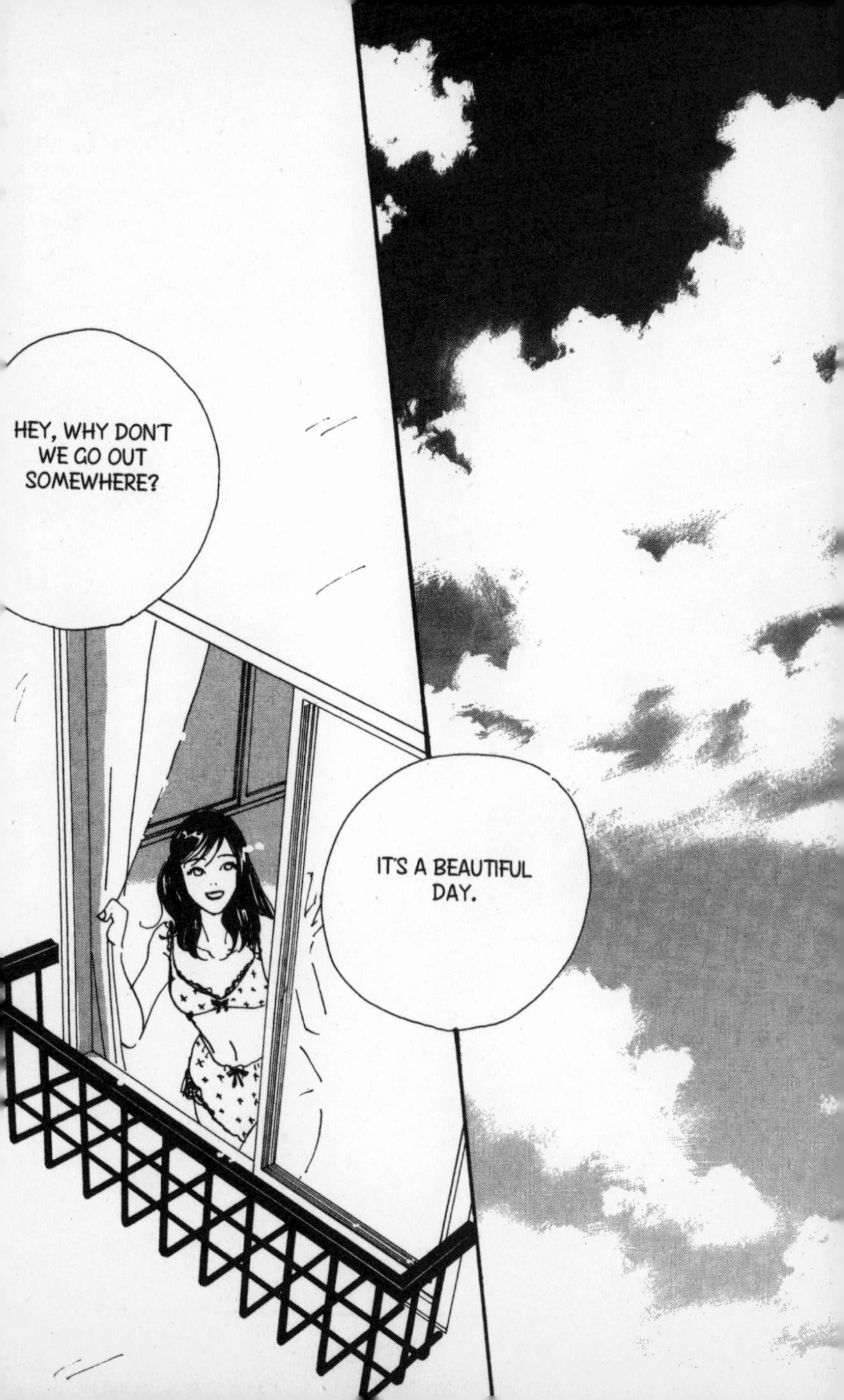
HEY, WHY DON'T WE GO OUT SOMEWHERE?
IT'S A BEAUTIFUL DAY.

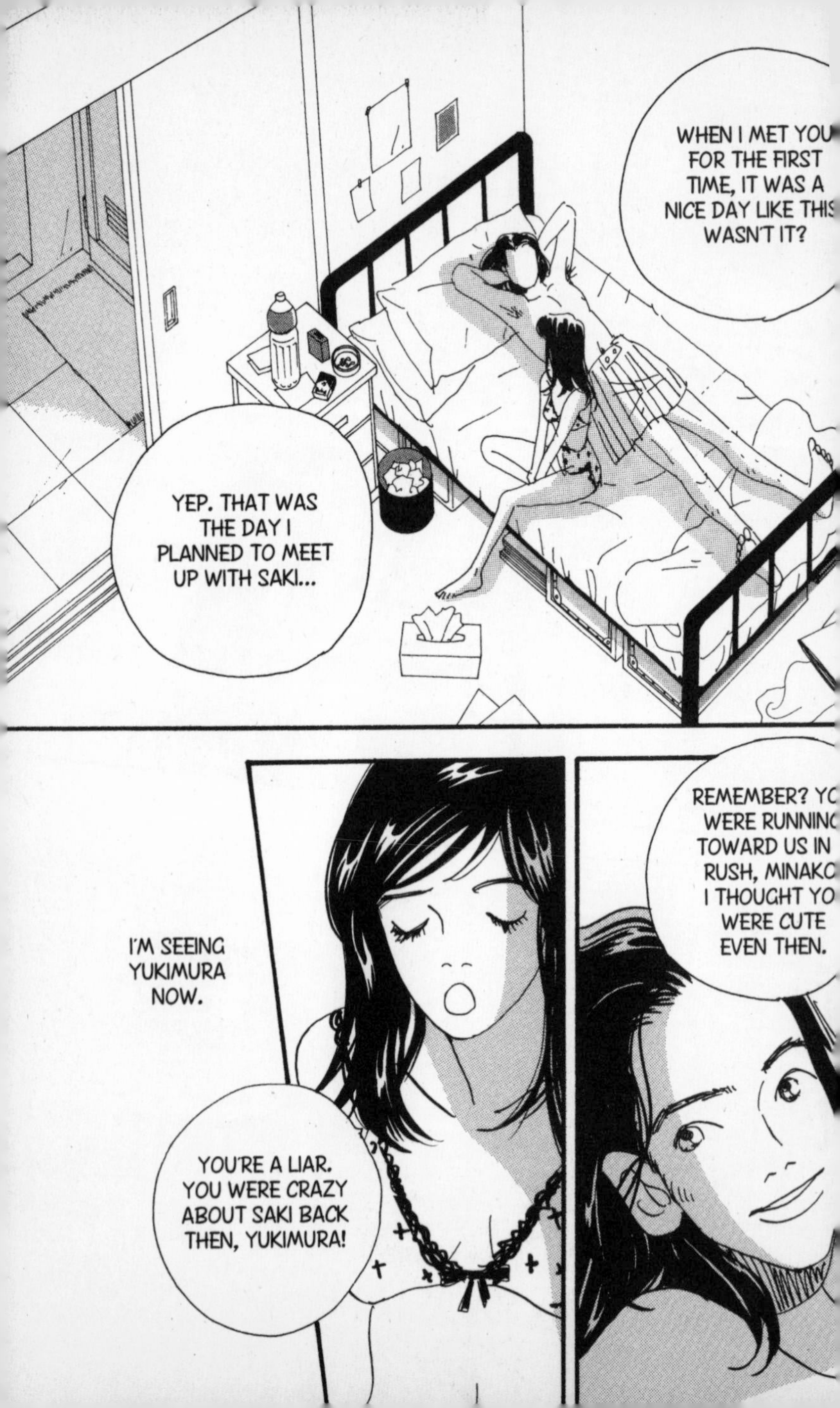
WHEN I MET YOU FOR THE FIRST TIME, IT WAS A NICE DAY LIKE THIS WASN'T IT?
YEP. THAT WAS THE DAY I PLANNED TO MEET UP WITH SAKI...
REMEMBER? YO WERE RUNNING TOWARD US IN RUSH, MINAKO I THOUGHT YO WERE CUTE EVEN THEN.
I'M SEEING YUKIMURA NOW.
YOU'RE A LIAR. YOU WERE CRAZY ABOUT SAKI BACK THEN, YUKIMURA!

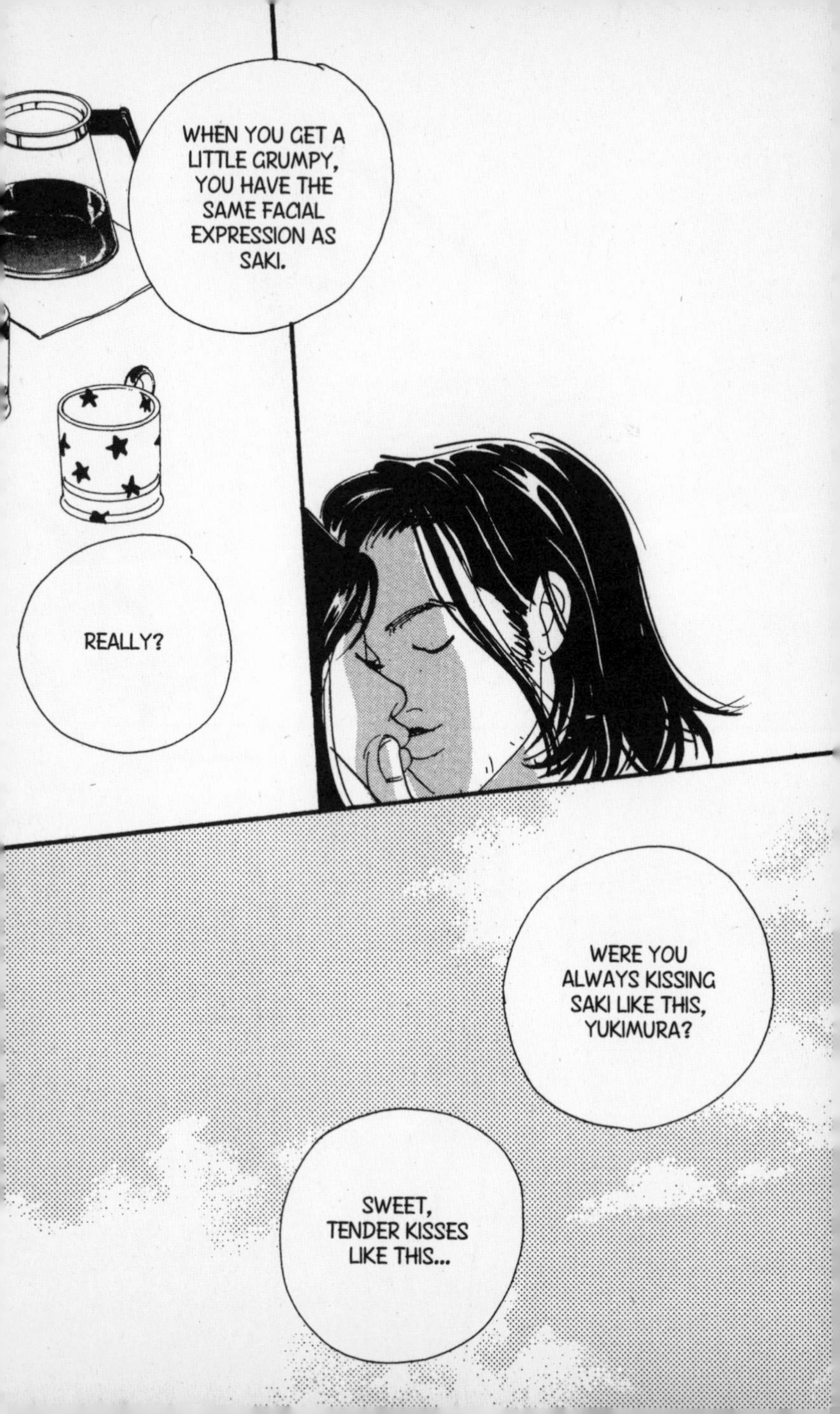
WHEN YOU GET A LITTLE GRUMPY, YOU HAVE THE SAME FACIAL EXPRESSION AS SAKI.
REALLY?
WERE YOU ALWAYS KISSING SAKI LIKE THIS, YUKIMURA?
SWEET, TENDER KISSES LIKE THIS...

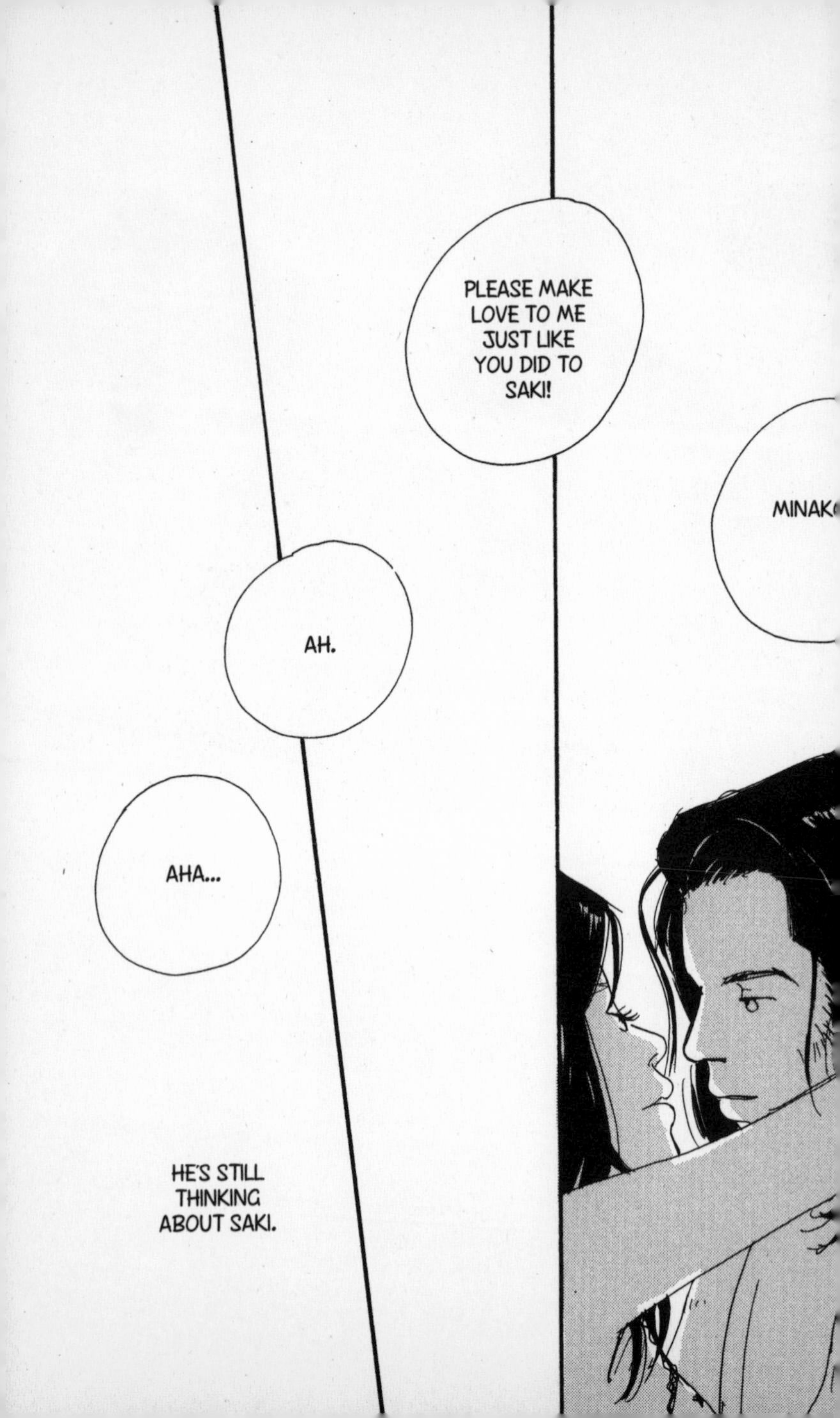
PLEASE MAKE LOVE TO ME JUST LIKE YOU DID TO SAKI!
MINAK
AH.
AHA...
HE'S STILL THINKING ABOUT SAKI.

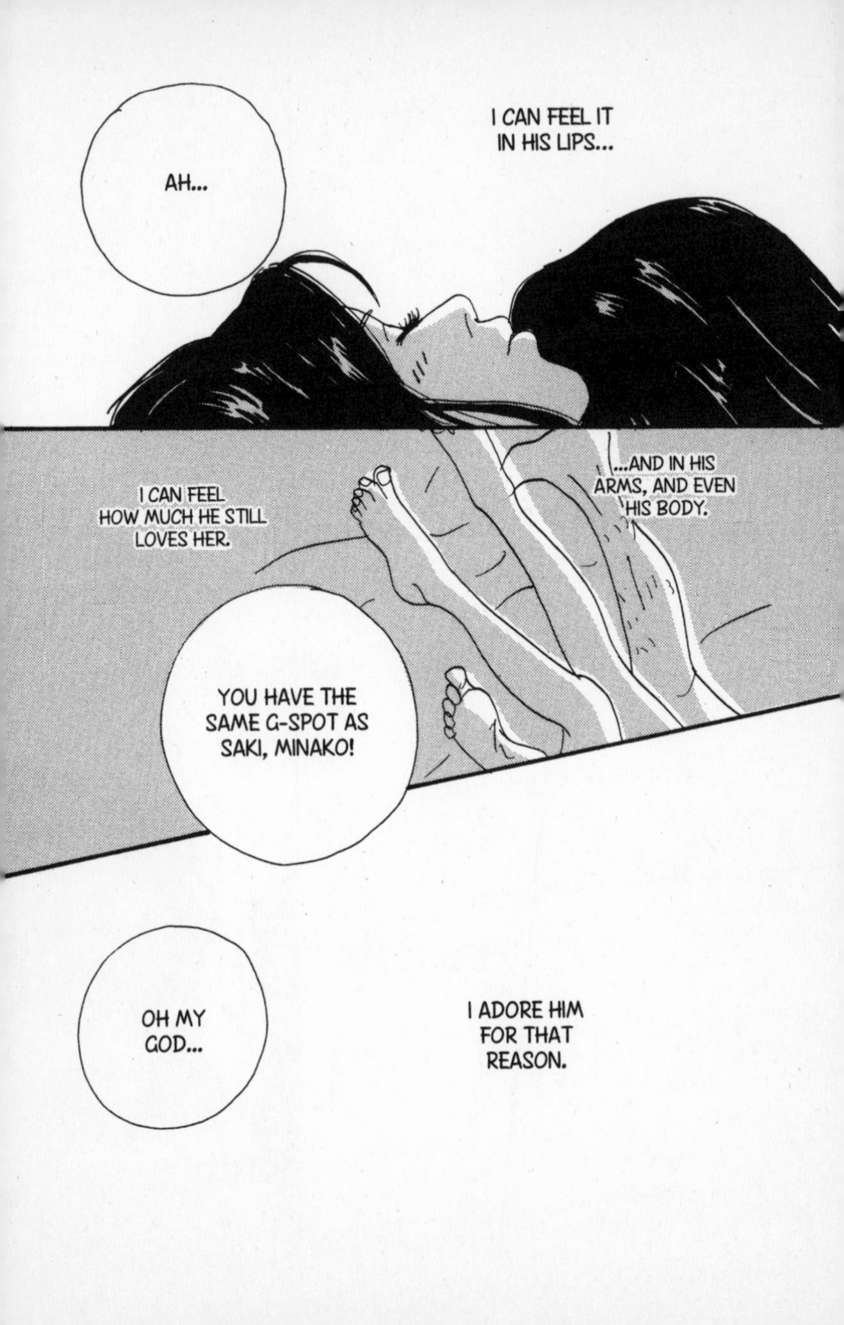
I CAN FEEL IT IN HIS LIPS...
AH...
...AND IN HIS ARMS, AND EVEN HIS BODY.
I CAN FEEL HOW MUCH HE STILL LOVES HER.
YOU HAVE THE SAME G-SPOT AS SAKI, MINAKO!
I ADORE HIM FOR THAT REASON.
OH MY GOD...

HEY, SAKI,

...BUT MY LOVE
FOR YOU HASN'T
CHANGED ONE BIT.

I MIGHT NOT
SEE YOU
ANYMORE...

AND IT WON'T.
FROM NOW ON.
FOREVER AND
EVER.

I LOVE YOU MORE
THAN LIFE ITSELF.
MY SWEETHEART,
SAKI...

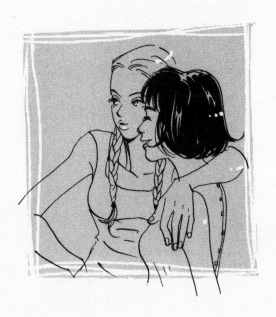

the end

COMING IN JULY...

angel

KATO IS JUST AN ORDINARY GUY WHO WORKS AT A CONVENIENCE STORE. THAT IS, UNTIL ONE FATEFUL NIGHT WHEN HE PICKS UP A BEAUTIFUL GIRL AT A BAR. IT TURNS OUT SHE IS AN ANGEL—LITERALLY! SHE'S MOVED INTO HIS BACHELOR PAD, AND HE FEELS LIKE HE'S IN HEAVEN. ALTHOUGH HE HAS NO IDEA WHERE SHE IS FROM OR WHY SHE IS LIVING WITH HIM, HE LETS HER STAY AS LONG AS SHE WANTS.

THIS ANGEL IS AN ABSOLUTE SAVIOR—AND THERE ARE A LOT OF PEOPLE WHO NEED SAVING! SHE LENDS HER CELESTIAL SUPPORT TO MIZUHO, A 14-YEAR-OLD GIRL ON THE BRINK OF SUICIDE, AND CHI-CHAN, AN ADORABLE FIVE-YEAR-OLD GIRL WHO IS BEING NEGLECTED BY HER MOTHER. NOTHING IS THE SAME AFTER THEY ARE "TOUCHED BY AN ANGEL."

WHEN KATO MEETS A HOTTIE NAMED MIHO, SHE CONFIDES SHE IS HUNG UP ON HER LOSER EX-BOYFRIEND. BUT AFTER SHE MEETS KATO'S GUARDIAN ANGEL, SHE HAS A REVELATION THAT CHANGES HER LIFE...AND KATO'S LIFE...FOREVER!

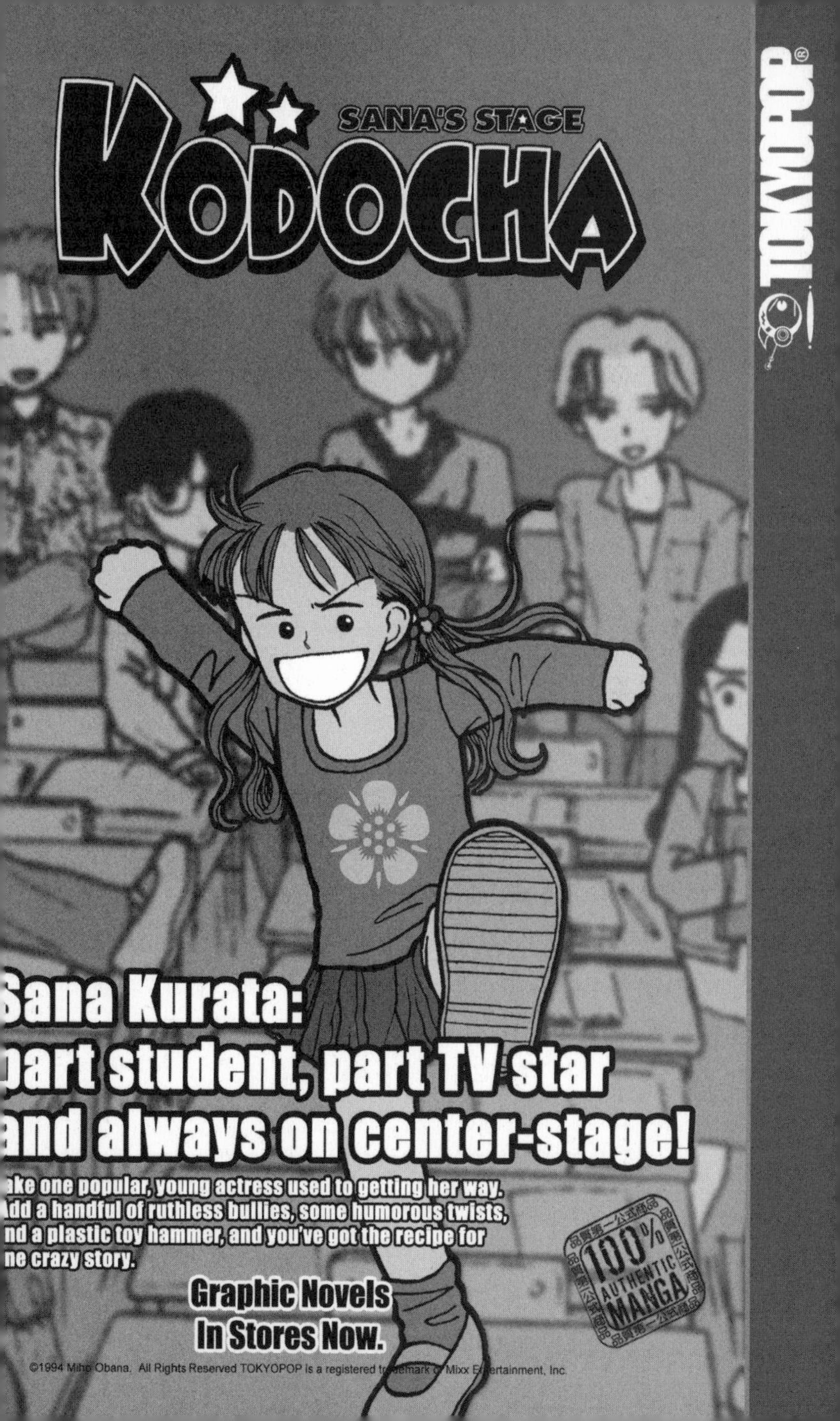

TOKYOPOP
KODOCHA
SANA'S STAGE
Sana Kurata:
part student, part TV star
and always on center-stage!
ake one popular, young actress used to getting her way.
Add a handful of ruthless bullies, some humorous twists,
nd a plastic toy hammer, and you've got the recipe for
ne crazy story.
Graphic Novels
In Stores Now.
100% AUTHENTIC MANGA
©1994 Miho Obana. All Rights Reserved TOKYOPOP is a registered trademark of Mixx Entertainment, Inc.

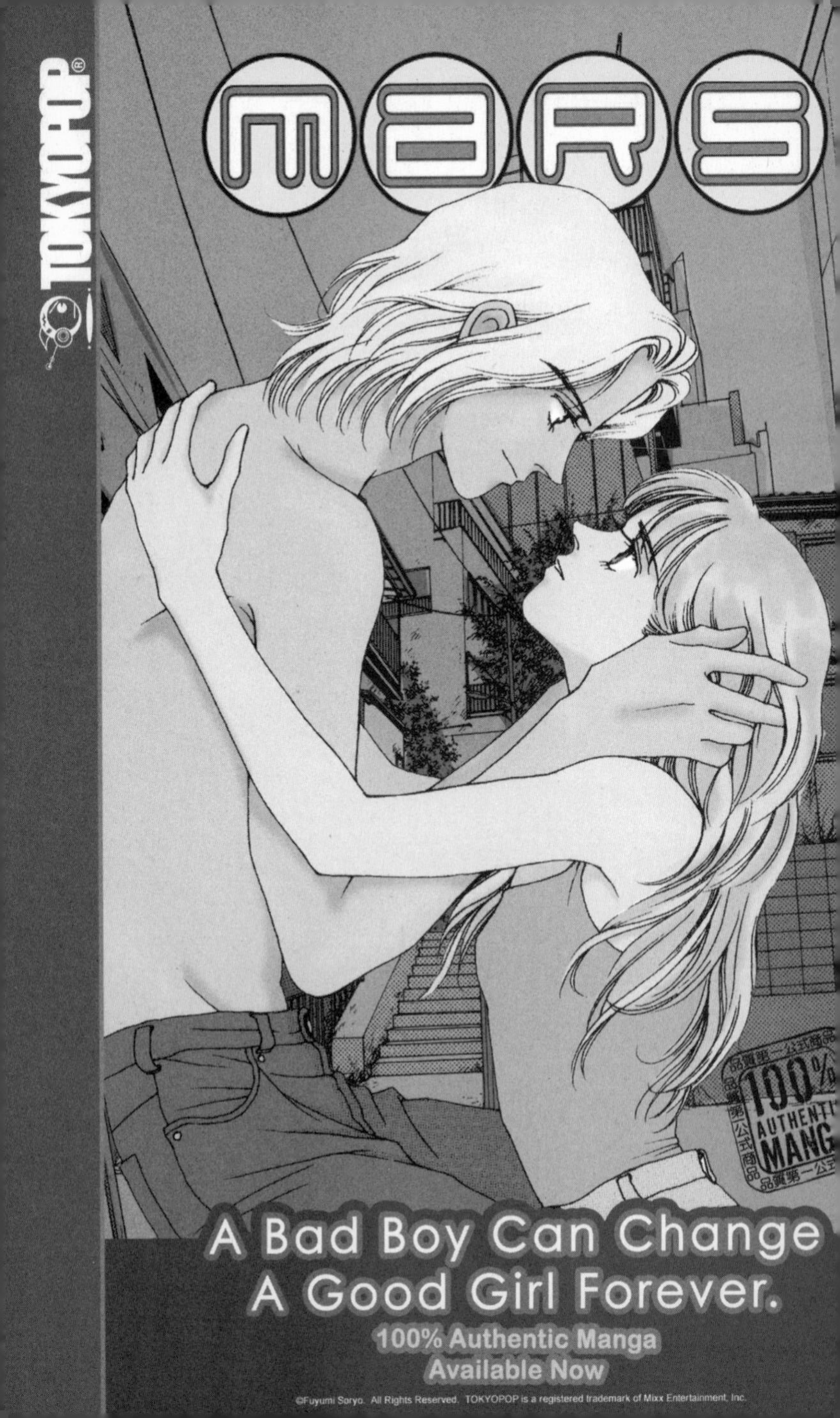
TOKYOPOP
MARS
100% AUTHENTIC MANGA
A Bad Boy Can Change
A Good Girl Forever.
100% Authentic Manga
Available Now
©Fuyumi Soryo. All Rights Reserved. TOKYOPOP is a registered trademark of Mixx Entertainment, Inc.

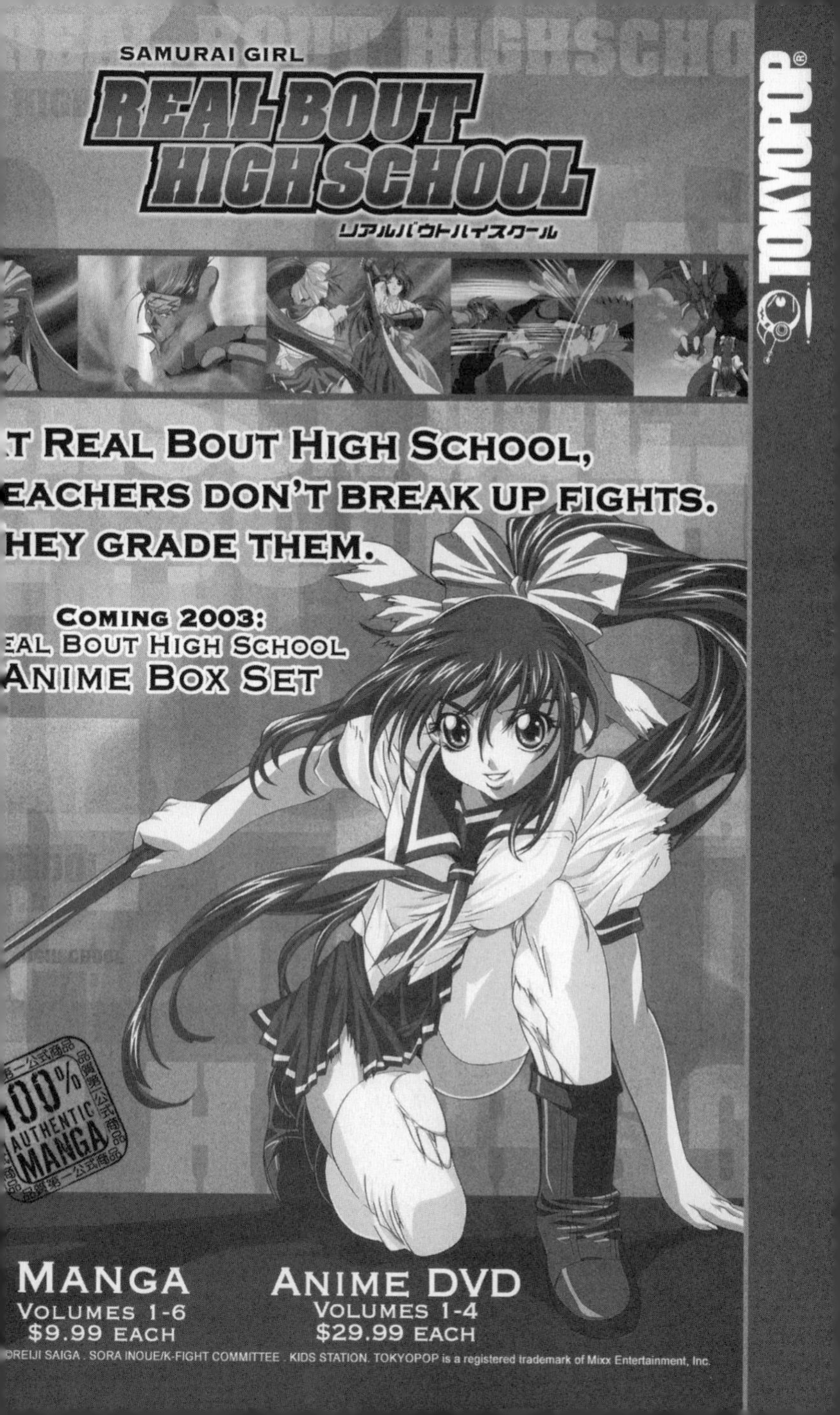
SAMURAI GIRL
REAL BOUT HIGH SCHOOL
リアルバウトハイスクール
T REAL BOUT HIGH SCHOOL,
EACHERS DON'T BREAK UP FIGHTS.
HEY GRADE THEM.
COMING 2003:
EAL BOUT HIGH SCHOOL
ANIME BOX SET
100% AUTHENTIC MANGA
MANGA
VOLUMES 1-6
$9.99 EACH
ANIME DVD
VOLUMES 1-4
$29.99 EACH
©REIJI SAIGA . SORA INOUE/K-FIGHT COMMITTEE . KIDS STATION. TOKYOPOP is a registered trademark of Mixx Entertainment, Inc.
TOKYOPOP®

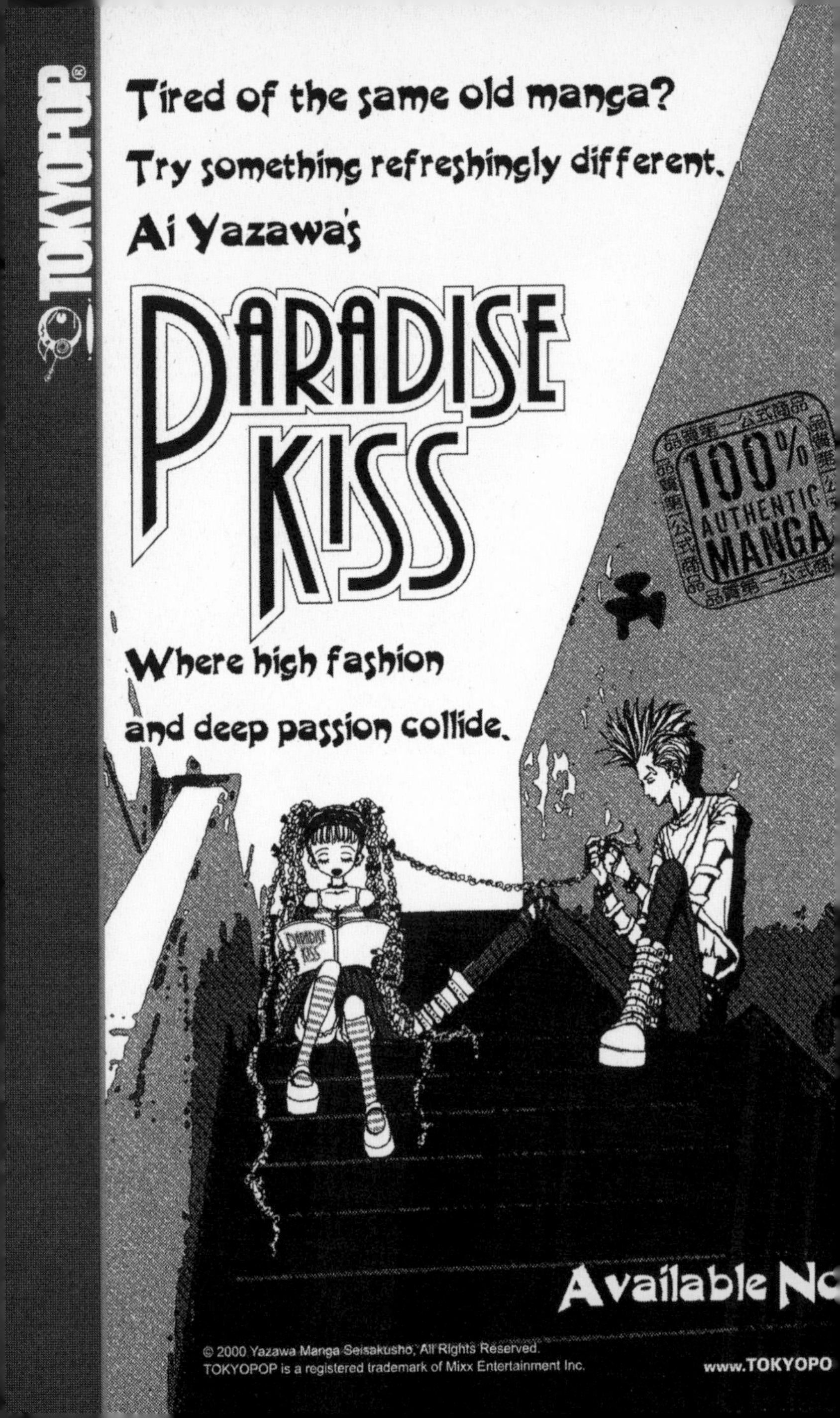
TOKYOPOP®
Tired of the same old manga?
Try something refreshingly different.
Ai Yazawa's
PARADISE KISS
Where high fashion
and deep passion collide.
100% AUTHENTIC MANGA
Available No
© 2000 Yazawa Manga Seisakusho, All Rights Reserved.
TOKYOPOP is a registered trademark of Mixx Entertainment Inc.
www.TOKYOPO

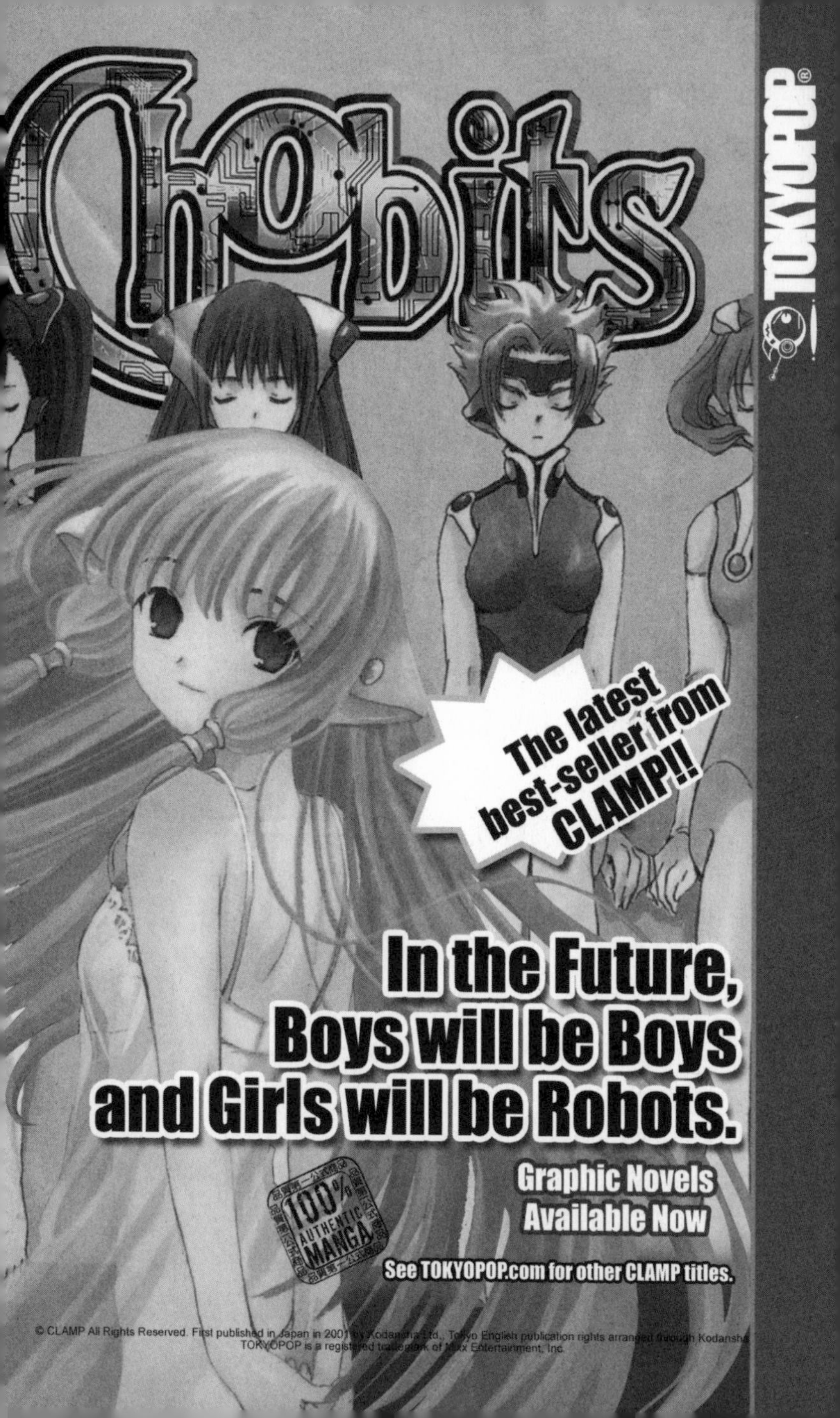
Chobits
TOKYOPOP®
The latest best-seller from CLAMP!!
In the Future, Boys will be Boys and Girls will be Robots.
100% AUTHENTIC MANGA
Graphic Novels Available Now
See TOKYOPOP.com for other CLAMP titles.
© CLAMP All Rights Reserved. First published in Japan in 2001 by Kodansha Ltd., Tokyo English publication rights arranged through Kodansha
TOKYOPOP is a registered trademark of Mixx Entertainment, Inc.

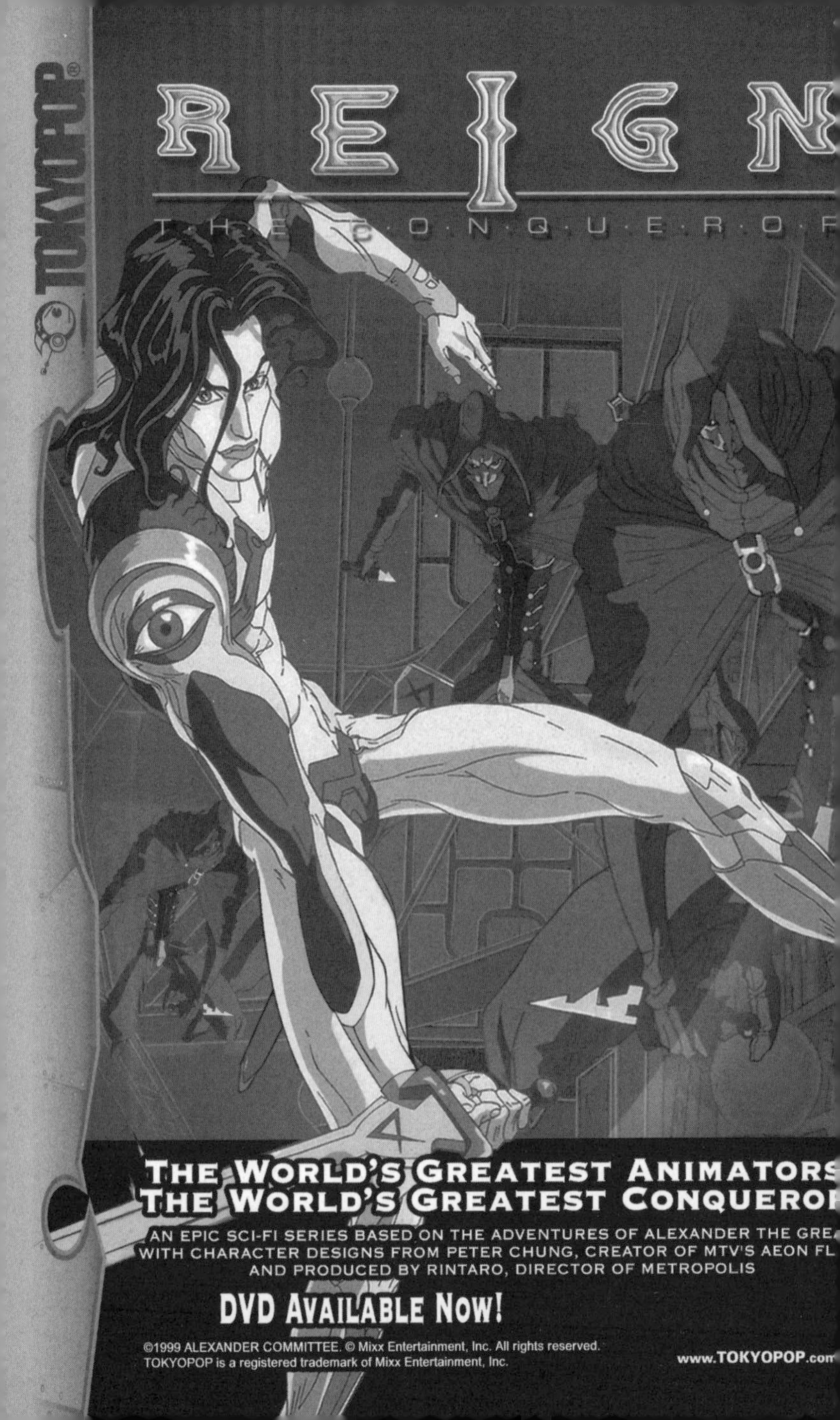
TOKYOPOP®
REIGN
THE CONQUEROR
THE WORLD'S GREATEST ANIMATORS
THE WORLD'S GREATEST CONQUEROR
AN EPIC SCI-FI SERIES BASED ON THE ADVENTURES OF ALEXANDER THE GREA
WITH CHARACTER DESIGNS FROM PETER CHUNG, CREATOR OF MTV'S AEON FL
AND PRODUCED BY RINTARO, DIRECTOR OF METROPOLIS
DVD AVAILABLE NOW!
©1999 ALEXANDER COMMITTEE. © Mixx Entertainment, Inc. All rights reserved.
TOKYOPOP is a registered trademark of Mixx Entertainment, Inc.
www.TOKYOPOP.com

STOP!

This is the back of the book.
You wouldn't want to spoil a great ending!

This book is printed "manga-style," in the authentic Japanese right-to-left format. Since none of the artwork has been flipped or altered, readers get to experience the story just as the creator intended. You've been asking for it, so TOKYOPOP® delivered: authentic, hot-off-the-press, and far more fun!

DIRECTIONS

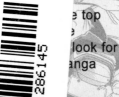

If this is your first time reading manga-style, here's a quick guide to help you understand

It's easy... e top right pane numbers. look for more 100 anga from TOK

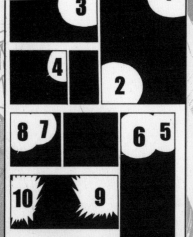

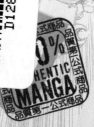